BACKSTOP

SEATTLE CASCADES
BOOK 3

C.M. KANE

COPYRIGHT

∼

Editing & book design by Maggie Kern @ Ms.K Edits

Cover art by Golden Czermak @ FuriousFotog

Photographer: Tonya Clark Photography

Model: Matthew Carothers

BOOK THREE

SEATTLE
CASCADES

DEDICATION

For AJ, Clint, Jimmy, and Luis, and an amazing weekend of love and acceptance.

PROLOGUE

*K*ylie...
     This waiting was going to kill me, I swear. Like, how hard was it to just give me what I wanted and not make me wait for hours and hours at this stupid courthouse? Thank the goddess it was spring break, and I could come to the courthouse without missing school.

"Miss Somerton," a man called from the front of the courtroom.

"I'm here," I said. "Although it won't be that for long," I mumbled under my breath.

I stepped to the front of the courtroom with my envelope of forms I had completed, as well as a cashier's check for the fee. Today would be the last time I would ever be called by my father's last name.

"Your paperwork, please," the man who had called my name said as he came to me, holding out his hand.

I opened the folder and pulled out the forms, handing them over to the man who walked them up to the judge. After taking them, the judge read them over, not giving anything away as to what she was thinking.

"Is this true?" she asked after her review.

"Which part?" I asked.

"That your father is—"

1

"Yes," I said, cutting her off. I didn't need the whole courtroom full of strangers knowing who my father was. "I kind of would like to put that behind me."

"I'm surprised this wasn't granted several years ago," she said.

"He refused to give me permission," I said. "Now that I'm eighteen, he has no further say over it, and I wish to remove him from my life permanently."

"I completely understand," the judge said. "I see no reason for this to not be granted, so I'm going to do so. Go forward, Miss..." she paused, looking back at the form, then continued, "Miss Harper. May you find happiness in your future."

"Thank you, Your Honor," I said.

She stamped the form with something, then handed it to the man who had taken it from me.

"Take this to the court clerk and they will accept your payment," he said. "Once that's done, you will receive the official authorization and can take it to the Department of Licensing and receive your new ID."

"Thank you," I said.

Walking out of the courtroom, I turned when I got into the hall, having already figured out where the court clerk was located. Once I was there, I pulled one of those ticket things and waited for the number to be called. It seemed like it took forever, but they finally did, and I walked to the window.

"What are you here for?" the clerk asked.

"Name change," I said. "Here's the paperwork from the judge."

"Perfect," the clerk said. "I need your ID as well."

I pulled that out of my wallet and handed it over.

"Do you have a cashier's check or money order?" she asked.

"I have a check," I said, pulling it out of the folder I had with everything I needed for today.

She took it from me and turned around to check something in her computer, clicking and moving the mouse with a speed I couldn't keep up with. I heard a printer running somewhere behind the glass and she slid her wheeled chair away from the computer screen and over to another area in her little space, pulling something out of what I assumed was her printer, then wheeled herself back over to me.

"All right," she said when she was back in front of the window. "First thing you will want to do is go to the Social Security Office. Sometimes they make you make an appointment, but stop in and see if you can get it started right away. It looks like they gave you the option to change your Social Security number if you want to. I would suggest going ahead and doing that, just to be safe. The closest one is at this address here. It's in Burien.

"This form right here will be what you want to take with you when you go to the DMV," she continued. "They'll take a copy of it and then give you a temporary ID to replace yours. If you want to get your license, you can do that with this form as well, then set up to take the tests. It will also allow you to register to vote, which you can do now that you're eighteen. Once you have the new ID, you should be able to make the changes everywhere else you need to. Do you have any more questions?"

"Umm…" I mumbled. "I'm not sure."

"Here's a pamphlet that will help you show what you need to do," she said, pulling one from behind the counter. "If you have any other questions, you can go to the website on the back of that booklet and you can probably find your answer there. If not, you can give a call to the number there. There is probably a way to contact them through the website."

"Wow," I said. "I didn't realize how many other things I was gonna have to do."

"But, from what I see, it will be really helpful for you," she said, and I looked at her, confused. "I know why you're changing it, and I don't blame you at all."

I didn't want to acknowledge the unsaid comment, so I just nodded and thanked her, then headed out to catch the bus back home. At least I had a few more days to get everything else done, but I was no longer tied to the monster that was my father.

CHAPTER ONE

*K*ylie…

"Girl, you have got to wear something that shows your curves," Remi said.

"It's just a baseball game," I replied. "Why do I have to dress up?"

"There's that meet and greet thing we're going to afterward," he said.

Remington Wilson was my absolute best friend. We'd known each other since we were teenagers, right after my world fell apart. He'd lived just down the street from my grandparents' house, and we became best friends almost immediately. Like me, he was an outcast. I can honestly say that without him, I probably wouldn't have made it out of middle school.

"I just don't understand why I have to dress up for this," I complained.

"Because baseball boys are sexy," he said. "And you should be at least half as sexy as them if you wanna catch their eye."

"Dude," I said, drawing the word out. "You're the one who is

5

bound and determined to get hitched to a baseball player. I don't want to outshine you."

"The players I wanna catch won't be swayed by your sexy," he replied, laughing. "They'll take one look at this fabulousness and ignore the rest of the world. Don't you worry about me. I got this. You, however, need to get out there and experience life."

"I experience life," I said, but it didn't sound convincing even to my own ears.

"In your little virtual world, sure," he said, and it was the truth.

My job was remote, even though I worked at the same company as Remi. He loved being in the office and around everyone, while I preferred to do my work without interruption. The office atmosphere was stifling to me, the absolute antisocial person that I was. It started as in-office, but they quickly saw the benefit of not having everyone in-office when they shifted their location. The ability for me to still do my job from home was one of the best things that happened to me. Don't get me wrong, I did go into the office when the need arose. I just didn't spend all day every day there.

"Okay, fine," I said and sat on the edge of my bed. "You pick the outfit, and as long as it isn't too risqué, I'll wear it. But I do get veto power."

"Yes," he said, clearly excited about the freedom I'd given him. "You won't be sorry about this. Trust me."

"I'm already doubting myself," I mumbled, watching him pull things from my little closet to find the perfect outfit.

"I FEEL COMPLETELY OVERDRESSED," I SAID AS WE STEPPED OFF THE train and started our walk toward the stadiums.

The crowd around us was definitely dressed for the game in their tee shirts and jerseys and such, while Remi and I looked like we were heading out to go clubbing. My dress was shorter than I really wanted to wear, but it looked good on me, so I went with it. My little boots had enough of a heel to give me a lift without making me feel like I would topple over in them. I had a tiny purse that had my EpiPen in it, along with my wallet, keys, and lip gloss. We'd read the team website to ensure we could bring it in, and since it had my emergency meds in the form of an injectable, they said it would be allowed. I didn't want to push anything, so I just went with the small bag.

Remi was decked out as well, rocking one of those utility kilts that had about a million pockets, along with some high socks and his Doc Martens. He paired it with a deep blue shirt that he left unbuttoned more than should be legal, but it looked good on him. He'd done both of our makeup, and he wore it better than me. I felt like a doll that had been dressed up as a prop, while he was confident with himself.

"Oh my God," someone shouted. "Is that a sighting of the elusive Kylie Harper? Out in public?"

We turned to see Carmen and Nadia, dressed much more for the game than we were, coming toward us.

"Hey, girls," Remi said.

"Have you ever been to a game?" Carmen asked when she looked at us.

"Of course I have," Remi replied. "Can't catch the boys' eye if you don't stand out."

He made a quick turn, his kilt floating out a bit, before coming to a stop, facing our friends.

"Besides," he added. "Little Miss Kylie needs to show herself off. Don't you think?"

I stood there, a blush running up my cheeks, waiting for them to say something. Finally, after entirely too long, Nadia said, "You look good."

"Thanks," I said. "How do we get into this building?"

"This way," Remi said, as if he was our own personal tour guide.

We walked around a long ramp that went up and over the train tracks that ran next to both the football and baseball stadiums. The crowd grew the closer to the top we got. Once there, I looked and could see a set of stairs leading down to the street level we'd just come from. Our group got caught up in the rush to get down the stairs, and people separated me from the rest of them. I was going down the stairs as quickly as I could, but felt something against my back. I shifted to the side where the handrails were and the feeling went away, but I noticed a kid who had to be less than twenty smirking next to me, holding his phone, the camera app open.

"Did you just…"

Before I could finish, he rushed between some people and got away from me.

"What was that?" Remi asked.

"I think that kid just took a picture up my skirt," I said, unable to keep the horror out of my voice. "This is why I stay home."

While Remi was basically a teddy bear, he was scary when he got angry. Being over six feet tall helped to give him an advantage over my shorter stature, and he obviously saw who I was talking about. He shoved his way through the throng of people and disappeared from my view.

"Where's he going?" Carmen asked.

"He's on a mission to save my ass, literally," I said.

We heard a scuffle, some shouting, then Remi's booming voice.

"You let me see your pictures or you lose your phone," he said.

"Oh, God," I muttered, trying to catch up to him.

The crowd seemed to open up, and I saw he had the guy by the shirt, shoved up against a pillar from the ramp above. The kid looked terrified. I mean, here he was, this little boy, being held against the wall by a giant of a man in a kilt with makeup, booming at him to open his phone.

"Fine, here," the guy said, handing the phone over.

"Unlock it," Remi demanded.

The kid did as he was told, swiping his finger in a pattern across the screen. Remi took the phone in his free hand and opened up what I assume was the photo collection.

"You are one sick little fucker," he said, and when Remi swore, you knew it was bad. "Deleting all of these and removing them from your cloud. Next time you do this, you might lose more than just your collection of crotch shots. You get me?"

He shook the kid pretty hard, enough for the sentiment to be clear, then let him go.

"I see you do this again, you're gonna wish you hadn't," Remi said in parting, then turned and beamed at us, winking in my direction.

That was the thing about him. He could be pissed the fuck off and terrifying one second, and the next, he was your best friend once again, just a happy-go-lucky guy.

"Let's go see the boys," he said, linking arms with me and guiding us toward the gate.

I turned around to see if I could see the kid, but he wasn't there. Either he'd walked away to find another victim, or he was smart enough to know that being anywhere in the vicinity of my protector was not a wise decision. Either way, I was glad I couldn't see him.

CHAPTER TWO

$\mathcal{C}$ole...

"All right guys," Coach said. "We've given a few of you the get-out-of-it card, but the rest of the team will need to stick around after the game for this great and meet thing or whatever."

"Meet and greet," Regina said. She worked in the same section at Panacea that Remi worked, but we kind of connected when we met. "We've been asked to stay around and help with the bonus party for Pinaceae Tech, who bought out a very large section of seats. Their employees will be meeting with you as a reward for all their hard work. I know this isn't the most fun thing for you guys, but we really appreciate it."

"So," Coach said. "Win or lose, we're happy they're here and more than happy to take some pictures with them."

"Go win for us," Regina added, then turned and walked out the door toward the stadium.

"Like she said," Coach added once she was gone. "Let's go win this one."

"Let's go," I said, and was chorused by others with similar sentiments.

We'd already done batting practice and had come back to the clubhouse to get changed for the game. It was still early enough that I had a few minutes before I had to head out to the bullpen and get our Aussie warmed up. With it still being early in the season, we were still working on routine and what each pitcher needed. I'd been Tanner's catcher throughout spring training, and he was comfortable with me. We worked well together.

After the cheating scandal of the previous year, they had decided to implement the new pitch calling system, which had taken some time to get used to. It was originally supposed to start in the minors, but because of what the Dragons had done, it was pushed through to all levels starting this year. Some of the pitchers really didn't like having that voice in their ear when I pressed the buttons for the pitch call, but others, like Tanner, had taken to it right away.

"You ready to warm up?" I asked him as we stepped into the dugout.

"Let's do it," he said, an Australian tint to his words.

We walked up the steps and onto the field, making our way out toward the outfield to start our warm-up. I already had my shin guards on, but was carrying the rest of my gear. With it being early in the year, it was still on the cool side, so I was wearing a long-sleeved shirt under my jersey. When we made it to the grass near the bullpen, I dropped my helmet and chest protector and set up to catch the first throw from Tanner. He stepped several feet away and tossed the ball to me. I tossed it back, and we continued the game of catch, extending our throws each time until we were about thirty feet apart. He was throwing hot and hitting the mark with each toss. I knew he liked to do this for longer than a few of the other pitchers, so I waited for him to indicate he was ready to step into the bullpen itself and continue the warm-up process.

Game days were an unusual time, and each pitcher had their own idiosyncrasies when it came to their warm-up routine. Most of them were so focused that they didn't even notice that there were hundreds of thousands of fans right there, within reach of us as we warmed up. Others, like Tanner, would smile and nod at someone if they called his name. Once he was on the bump, though, everything else went away and it was just him and I throwing the ball back and forth, him getting his heater up to speed and me trying my best to not drop or get hit by something that was pushing one hundred miles an hour.

Tanner gave me a nod after he threw the last ball and started walking to the gate that would lead us to the small space where we would get his arm ready for the game. The crowd was wild tonight, especially since we'd been on a pretty good winning streak to start the year. I pulled my chest protector over my head and strapped it on, then pulled my helmet, which resembled a hockey mask more than the old-fashioned ones they wore in the past, over my head. I stood behind the painted-on plate and waited for him to throw. He got a few more tosses in before he gave me the hand wave of his mitt, indicating I should go ahead and squat behind the base.

Getting down into my position, I waited for him to start throwing. He had this rhythm he always did. Starting with fastballs, throwing those about a dozen times, then switching to his curveball, which he was throwing with great control in his last couple of starts, before again switching to the cutter. I had to be on my toes when he started throwing those because they had a tendency to drop faster than he wanted when he first started, which meant they could bounce before they even got to the plate. The ricochet of that ball had nearly knocked me on my ass a few times when I wasn't paying attention. Today, though, he had control, and it dropped just enough to be out of reach of any hitter without actually bouncing on the ground.

Coach Roof, the pitching coach, watched as the Aussie warmed up, just to be sure he wasn't messing up his mechanics. Roof was a good guy, and I respected the attention he paid to each pitcher, ensuring that the team got the best effort out of each one, pushing them to do what was needed without overextending their abilities. If the pitcher was "on," like Tanner was today, he'd just stand and watch as he got ready for the game. It didn't take long for the starter to get warmed up, and once he felt he had control of his pitches, he changed back to the fast-ball to get more heat on it. The guy threw hard, but it was his location that made him nearly unhittable. Of course, there were the odd times when he left a curveball hanging, or a slider didn't drop as much as he'd like, but he was a great pitcher with a good head on his shoulders and a knowledge of the game unlike many I had worked with in the past.

He gave me a nod, then threw the last pitch of his warm-up session, stepping off the mound in the small space we were working in. Coach Roof said something to him, but it was clear that he was impressed with how on task and focused Tanner was. We usually didn't pay much attention to the fans, and it was a good thing, too. Seemed that since we acquired him during the off season, everyone still remembered where he came from. Houston's cheating scandal from last season was still on everyone's mind, even now, after several months. It was crazy the first time he pitched. Even *our* fans were booing him.

The rest of the players had talked to him about it and he had genuinely not known about what was going on. When he was starting, his focus was on his warm-up, game performance, and what was going on while he was on the mound. When he wasn't pitching, he kind of kept to himself. He'd seen things happening but hadn't put it together because he never was up to bat, so he never benefited from the cheating that was done. It took a while for us to believe him, but finally we understood that he was just so out of touch with the hitting side of the game that it never even crossed his mind.

"Let's do this," he said as we walked toward the dugout from the bullpen out in left field.

"You got it," I replied.

CHAPTER THREE

*K*ylie...

"There are so many people here," I complained. "How did I let you talk me into this?"

"Because baseball guys are hot," Remi said. "Besides, I couldn't go stag to this event. I need someone to keep me in check."

"'Cause I'm so good at that," I said, laughing.

The last time we went out on the town, Remi had ended up finding a really cute guy he wanted to hook up with, but the dude thought he was being a wingman for me and wanted me to go home with him, not Remi. When we straightened it out, the dude was completely offended and made a huge scene at the bar. Needless to say, neither of us went home with him.

"At least it's a more controlled environment," he said. "Now, let's go gaze at the splendor that is a major league baseball team."

"You're ridiculous," I said, but followed him down the stairs toward the field.

He'd told me we had good seats, but when he kept walking down further and further, I assumed it was because he wanted to get close to the field for a better vantage point. He stopped at the second from the front row, right behind the place where the players stayed when they weren't on the field. I was completely out of my element when it came to baseball, and knew nothing of the game, let alone the terms used for anything inside the stadium.

"Here we are," he said, pointing to the seats.

I could see a few people I recognized from the office, but because we were such a large company, and everyone was allowed to bring their family, there were many faces I wasn't familiar with. The people sitting in the row we were in were all the guys who had their pictures up in the office because of their position in the company. These were not the people I regularly saw any time I went into the building.

"You're sure these are the seats?" I asked.

"Girl," he said, drawing the word out. "I asked for the best seats in the stack, and because upper management loves me, they obliged. I told them I had to have you sitting next to me, so that's why we got these seats."

The way he explained it made it clear this was a logical thing, but I still didn't know how we got such good seats. I mean, we were far from upper management material, so they should have probably gotten the better seats. I did know that Remi was a well-loved person in the office, so it made sense that they would give him something special. Whatever the case was, I was happy that we were close. At least then I could actually see the players and not just see them as little blips on the field.

There were players on the field, hitting the ball from inside a cage, and catching the balls out near the fence, then throwing them into the inner part of the field where the dirt ring for the bases was. I was confused because everyone around us was wearing blue and gray and black colors, but the players on the field were wearing purple and orange.

"Hey, Remi," I said, tapping his arm. "Why are the players wearing a different color than the jerseys I see in the stands?"

"That's the Houston team on the field," he replied. "We hate them."

"Why?"

"They cheated," he said, as if that was the end of the conversation.

"How did they cheat?" I asked.

"Sweetheart," a man sitting next to us said in such a condescending voice, I almost threw up. "Baseball is a complicated sport. If you don't get it, that's fine. Your brain probably isn't smart enough to understand it."

"Did you just call my best friend in the entire world stupid?" Remi asked, clearly pissed off.

"I just said she wouldn't understand it," he said, then looked Remi up and down. "You probably don't understand it, either, though. Don't worry, you won't be bored."

"Okay, first of all," Remi said, holding his finely manicured index finger up. "I know more about baseball than your ordinary dude. I have played it for years, learned everything there was to it, and probably know more than even you do. Second, if you ain't got nothing nice to say, don't say nothing at all. Just a little reminder from Bambi, in case your mother didn't teach you right."

The dude looked stunned, like he'd never been talked to like that before. He fumbled around to find some words before finally saying, "You're in the wrong area. This is a private section."

"Oh, I know," Remi said. "I have seats that are the best because everyone at Pinaceae Tech loves me, especially Garrett Roberts."

The way he dropped the big boss's name was like pure gold. The guy looked like he'd sucked on a lemon the way he puckered his mouth, then turned away from both of us as if we weren't important at all. I was worried that he may come down to see the guy near us and Remi would be called out on, saying he was loved by our CEO, but figured we'd cross that bridge when we got to it.

"Anyway," Remi said, clearly dismissing the other man's comments. "They had some video equipment placed in such a way that they were able to steal the signs the catcher was putting out for the pitcher. By doing this, they knew what was coming, and that increased their hitting at home. It took a couple of years before it was found, and our guys were the ones who figured it out. Rumor is our short stop, the very sexy Beckett Hennings, was the one to find it and point it out, getting things rolling on the league catching them in the act."

"I don't know what all of those terms are, but it sounds like something that could definitely help them," I said. "I mean, I'm sure it's hard to hit the ball anyway, but knowing what to expect would make it easier, I would think."

"It sure would," Remi said. "There are a bunch of pitches they throw. Fastball, curveball, slider, knuckleball. The list is almost endless. The thing about it is, if you're looking for something that is going to come fast, you want to swing earlier. If they throw something that is going slower, you swing too soon. If you're looking for the slower ball and get a fastball, then you're late. Either way, you miss the ball. By knowing what kind of pitch is coming, it helped them time their swing. Really sketchy shit if you ask me."

"Sounds like it," I said.

Turning to look at the field, I was surprised to see that the players were going into the bench seating place on the other side. That must have meant that the Seattle players were sitting on this side, although I could have been totally wrong. There were a couple of little golf cart type things that they were stacking the fences out on the inner part of the field on the back of them, then they hooked up the big cage thing to the back of it and drove it around the field out to the middle of the fence way on the outside of the field.

There were other people wearing the same thing as the guys who were moving the fences and stuff, bringing out what looked like a really big fire hose or something. They sprayed down the dirt areas of the field in the big part of the space, then brought the hose all the way up to where the dirt ring and hump in the middle of that space were and sprayed that down as well. They pulled the little cushion things up on posts while they sprayed, then put other ones down instead that were a bright white. I was just taking it all in, enjoying the time I was given to not have to think about anything but what was in front of my eyes.

"Oh, hey," Remi said, patting my arm. "Here comes our pitcher."

He was pointing out toward the fence, along the line next to where the big cage was taken. It was right under a board that had a bunch of spaces that I assumed were where they kept the score for the game. I couldn't really see any of the three guys that were walking toward us, other than to tell they were players. Who they were, or which one Remi was pointing out specifically, I wasn't sure. They just looked like three guys walking in from the fence area.

"Who is who?" I asked.

"The guy who is wearing all the gear," he said. "Like the chest protector and shin guards and stuff. He's the catcher. The guy that doesn't have anything is the pitching coach. The one with the mitt is the pitcher. He's from Australia and every time they interview him after the game, I swoon. That man's voice is so damn sexy."

"Oh my God, Remi," I said, completely blown away by his sheer audacity. "There are people around us. Someone might hear you."

"Every girl in here is lusting after one of these guys," he said nonchalantly. "Like, every single one. And the guys are either wishing they were one of them, or wishing they could be with them. Nothing new in that."

"You're horrible," I said, but couldn't help but laugh.

As the players that were coming in got closer, I noticed that Remi was right. They were pretty good looking. The one he said was a coach or whatever seemed older than the players, but I suppose that should be expected. The one with all the extra stuff on was talking to the one who would be pitching. I think that's what Remi said. When he looked up into the stands, my heart did a little flip. He was just so cute. Like, I wouldn't say he was sexy or anything like that, but he was absolutely adorable.

I'm not sure why or how or what stars aligned to make it happen, but he looked right at me and smiled this absolutely adorable smile, with dimples and everything. I damn near swooned in my seat. Then he winked at me and I could have died.

"Girl, look at you," Remi said. "You already caught one. Good for you."

"Shut up," I said, but my blush was running up into my cheeks and I couldn't help but smile this stupid big grin that probably made me look desperate or something.

"Hope he's one of the guys we get to meet at the thing after the game," Remi said, and I turned to him, my eyes wide.

"Oh no," I said. "I can't meet him. That would be horrible."

"What are you talking about?" he asked. "This is the best thing ever to happen, and I am all in for this. Don't worry, I'll be right by your side, making sure you don't get taken advantage of."

"No, Remi, I can't," I said, pleading with him to understand why it was a really bad idea for me to meet with someone famous.

"Because of..." he broke off, not wanting to say anything out loud.

"Yeah," I said, confirming his assumption. "It's a bad idea all around."

We both knew that if anyone dug up my past, my world could come crashing down around both myself and anyone who was connected to me. That wasn't something I really wanted to do to even my worst enemy, let alone someone I liked. It was the reason I changed my name at eighteen and made sure that my diploma and every subsequent degree had my new name on it.

CHAPTER FOUR

*C*ole...

"You think we'll have to stick around after the game?" Tanner asked.

"I know I have to," I said. "But you should check with the coach to see if you're stuck with it."

"You don't like these things?"

"It's the first time we've done it," I said. "They'll probably let you off since you're new, and the starter, so I wouldn't be too worried about it. But, to answer your unasked question, I don't mind meeting the fans. Gives me a chance to practice my mad skills as a flirt."

"I reckon you do enough of that during the game," he said, that accent coming through loud and clear.

"That I do," I agreed. "Speaking of which…"

I let the words trail off as I looked up into the stands. I always wanted to see who was sitting near the dugout. Most of the folks who sat there were on the more mature side, as my momma would call it. Sometimes we'd be lucky and get some pretty good-looking young women sitting near us. With the big showing from that company that basically bought us for the night, I was hopeful I'd find some sexy computer type gal to keep my eye on.

Scanning the crowd around the dugout, I zoned in on a woman who was definitely not dressed for the game. She wore a thin-strapped dress that showed enough cleavage to be interesting but covered enough to still be modest. I couldn't tell if it was blue or purple, because it looked like both whenever she shifted. She wasn't in the front row, but the one right behind it, and she was damn cute. I couldn't help but smile when she saw me looking at her. Watching her blush and try to act like she didn't notice just made her even more sweet looking.

The guy sitting next to her was really big, especially compared to her. He had makeup on that was actually really well done, and his deep blue shirt made him look like he just stepped off the cover of one of those magazines that were right by the checkout in the grocery stores. He saw her looking, then looked at me and smiled really big and started talking to her. From the looks of it, they were just friends, and he was encouraging her along. I didn't mind that at all.

We dropped into the dugout and I grabbed a cup from the water dispenser after the Aussie got his, swallowing down the cool liquid. It was still early in the year, just barely into May, and we were experiencing some unexpected heat, which I was fine with. Growing up in Southern California made it so that the heat didn't bother me too much. No, the thing that bothered me on road trips was when we went to the Midwest while it was still winter there and had to deal with snow. Or the trips to Texas, Atlanta, or Florida where they had humidity that nearly choked you in the summer.

A nice, balmy, seventy-degree day in Seattle was something I lived for. Sure, we had some humidity with the water being so close, but it wasn't like down south. It was just enough to keep you warm all night, which was a good thing for us. We always played better in the warm weather. The fact that tank tops were more prevalent when the sun was out was just a bonus.

"You ready for this?" Hennings asked as he came over to me.

"Always," I said. "I live for the life between the lines."

"You and me both," he said.

"Unless you're with your little woman," I said, laughing.

"Don't knock it 'til you try it," he said, slapping my back.

Never in my life would I have thought that Beckett Hennings would settle down with just one woman. He was the life of the party, the one who was always with all the ladies. I mean, that would be fine and all if I was interested in that sort of thing. Nah, I wanted a woman I could spend the rest of my life with. Eventually I'd find her.

~

"WHO'S THAT?" HUFFMAN ASKED AS HE CAME PAST ME AT THE TOP step of the dugout.

He'd just hit a home run. I was set to go up to bat after Hennings and Matsui, so was waiting near the top step of the dugout steps. I turned around and saw the lady with the blue-and-purple dress simply staring at me, like she couldn't get enough. I did a head nod to her and gave her my best smile. She blushed and ducked her head down.

"Hoping to find out at the after party," I said, turning back to him.

"You sure she's coming?" Matsui asked, obviously overhearing our conversation.

"Assuming she is," I said. "Otherwise, she's very overdressed for a simple baseball game."

The crowd was loud enough that I was sure she couldn't hear us over their noise, but she could see me looking back at her every chance I got. Yeah, she definitely was coming to the party, and I looked forward to meeting her in person as soon as possible.

Hennings struck out, and that ended the inning. I trudged back down the steps and put my gear back on, knowing Phil was out there catching for Tanner until I was ready to head out. Before putting my helmet on, I stepped up to the top step and turned to look at my mystery girl right in the eye. She looked at me, seeming to be surprised that I was checking her out.

"See you tonight," I shouted over the crowd, and her eyes went wide with surprise. Instead of sticking around to see what she might say or do, I turned and headed out to home plate to get back to work.

"Here you go," Phil said, stepping out of my way.

Squatting behind the plate, I waited for Tanner to throw his remaining warm-up tosses before I made the toss out to Cote at second for him to do the throw around the horn and back to Tanner. After the cheating scandal from last season, the fans were relentless with the players who were portrayed as the main players in the issue, booing them as they each came up to the plate. It was kind of fun to hear the booing, but honestly, most of them probably just shut it all out.

One of the good things that came from the cheating was the rapid implementation of the use of the electronic system catchers were now using for calling the pitch. Catcher, pitcher, second baseman, shortstop, and center fielder all had receivers, so everyone up the middle knew what we were throwing. It took a bit to get used to it, but that was what spring training was for. We'd come to the point where it made the game go much faster.

"Let's go," the ump said, urging Houston's third baseman to get into the box.

He stepped in and I looked to the dugout to get the sign from the coach, then turned and covered the sending device with my glove, punching in the sequence of buttons that told the pitcher what he should throw. He nodded, turned, kicked, and threw a slider that dropped at the very last minute, their batter swinging and missing it wildly.

"Damn," he said, setting himself back up into the box.

"Strike one," the ump called over him.

Another look to the bench, punch of the numbers, set up, and wait. Tanner was killing it tonight, and he was honestly one of the best pickups we got in the off season. He threw a fastball just outside the box, but the guy thought it was gonna come back in. He reached out while his ass went the other direction. It was a helpless feeling when you were the one swinging like that, but comical when you were on defense.

"That's two," the ump said, calling the second strike on the guy.

"Shit," the guy said, shaking his head and stepping back into the box.

Look to the bench, send the signal, this time calling for another fastball, this one even further outside the zone, and then set to wait.

Tanner came set and did his rock and throw and the pitch took its own course well outside the zone and I reached way out to catch it, barely making the snag.

"That's a ball," the ump said, and I really wanted to say, "no shit," but refrained, tossing the ball back to Tanner from my standing position.

"It's all good," I shouted to him, giving a nod of my head. "Here we go," I said after squatting. "You'll never catch it," I said to the batter, a guy I didn't know that I'd met before.

The call was for a slow curve, and the way it came out of Tanner's hand made it look just like the slider that was much faster. He did the set, rock, and throw, and the guy swung before the ball even came close to the plate, where I caught it without a problem.

"Three," the ump shouted behind me and I popped up and made the throw down to Cammy at third, who tossed to Hennings and on to Cote before being sent back to Cammy, who then threw it to Tanner.

"That's one," I said, punching my mitt.

The rest of the inning went pretty much the same, with a pop out to Hennings at short and a fly out to Huffman in center. As we made our way back to the dugout, I looked behind it to see the woman was gone.

"Shit," I said, looking back and forth to see if she was just moving up the stairs or something.

"What's up?" Tanner asked as we went down the steps.

"She's gone," I said, dropping my helmet onto the ledge behind the bench.

"Sorry, mate," he said, walking past me and further down the bench.

I proceeded to take the rest of my gear off, setting it with my mask before pulling my batting helmet out of its cubby, along with my batting gloves. Snagging my bat, I headed into the on-deck circle to begin my warm-up swings. Watching their pitcher, I timed his throws, watching the way the ball came out of his hands as he tossed the different pitches he had. Matsui was in the circle next to me, getting himself timed up as well.

CHAPTER FIVE

*K*ylie...

"I gotta go pee," I said, nudging Remi.

"I shall escort you to the loo," he replied in his worst British accent, holding an arm out to me as I stood.

"You are ridiculous," I said, emphasizing the first word. "You know that, right?"

"Whatever do you mean?" he asked, continuing with his horrible accent.

I just shook my head, took his arm, and walked with him up the steps to the main walkway. It was during a break in the play, where one team was leaving the field and the other was going out onto it.

While the game was interesting to watch, I really had no idea what was going on at any time. It was exciting to see them hit the ball, and I had figured out sort of how things were supposed to happen. Like, when our team was on the field, we wanted the other team to not hit the ball, and if they did, we had to catch it. If we didn't catch it, then we had to try to throw the ball at another player to step on the bases or to touch them with the glove they wore with the ball inside it. Honestly, it was super confusing on that side.

On the other hand, when the other team was on the field, we had to try to hit the ball and not let them catch it. One of the players, a really big guy, hit it so hard that it went over the fence at the back of the field. Everyone was jumping up and down and cheering, so I did too, assuming it was a good thing. After everyone sat down, I looked over at where they were keeping score and saw that they moved the zero from the spot under the number at the top, which was a five, and replaced it with a yellow two. After everything was done and they switched spots again, they changed the number to a white two.

Remi did his best to try to explain what was going on, and why things were done the way they were, but it was honestly so much that I couldn't keep track of it all. I just took my cues from the crowd around me and cheered when they did. It was the best I was probably going to be able to do at this point.

We got to the top of the stairs and I looked around, trying to find the bathroom. I didn't have to go so bad that it was urgent, but I knew at events like this, lines tended to be longer than in normal circumstances. I didn't want to wait if I didn't have to.

"Over there," Remi said, pointing to my right. Sure enough, above the people walking around up here, I could see the sign for the restroom. "I'll grab us a beer," he said as we split up.

He knew I wasn't really a drinker, so he was just being polite in saying that he'd share one with me. I would probably only drink three or four sips while he had the rest. We did that all the time, though. It was like we were siblings because we shared almost everything. As I got closer to the restroom, I could see that it was pretty open, which I was thankful for. I went in, did my thing, washed my hands, and headed back out to the walkway.

It was getting a bit chilly, so I wandered over to where they were selling souvenirs to look at sweatshirts and stuff.

"Can I help you find anything?" one of the salespeople asked.

"Just deciding whether I want to get a sweatshirt," I said.

"If you need any help, give a holler," he said.

"Thanks," I replied, continuing my perusal of the rack where they had them.

I was filtering through the options, trying to find something that might fit me and not look ridiculous with my dress when I felt someone close behind me. I shifted to the side, assuming they wanted to look as well, but they moved with me. Feeling their presence there pushed my instincts to that fight, flight, freeze feeling, and of fucking course, my body decided to use the last one and just not move, not continue looking for a shirt, not even hardly breathe.

"I can keep you warm," a deep voice said from behind me, one I definitely didn't recognize. I shuddered involuntarily. "Let me just wrap you up so you don't get cold," he continued, and I couldn't move.

"Hey," I heard Remi shout, but it was too far away. "Move your fucking funky ass away from my girl, you beast. No, not the Beast, you're more of a Gaston. Now git."

The presence moved away from me and I could feel the chill in the air as it rushed around me, which only served to make me shudder again.

"You okay?" Remi asked near my ear.

He'd seen me have panic attacks before, but usually it was in relation to my family. He knew I didn't do well in crowds, knew I needed someone to hold my hand and keep an eye on me in case I just shut down, and he hadn't been there until it was already too late for me. I broke down, just let the tears fall, without sound, as I stood there.

"Hey, now," he said, setting his beer on the top of the rack I'd been looking through. "Come on, girl. You're gonna ruin my fabulous makeup job."

He wrapped me up in his arms, pulling my face to his chest as I just let it all out. I didn't sob or choke on the tears, just let them fall and breathed through it. When I'd done enough and gotten over the hard part of it, he released me a little, letting me away from his chest. I looked up at him and he smiled.

"You do look pretty when you cry," he said. "But let's fix you up a bit before we have our big shindig with your new beau."

"You are *incorrigible*," I said, but there was a smile on my face.

Picking up his beer, he threw his arm out and I grasped his elbow again as we made our way toward the bathrooms and found a family one that was unoccupied. We stepped in and in just a very few minutes, he'd redone my makeup from the stash he had in his multitude of pockets. That man was always prepared, even though he'd never been a scout.

By the time we got back to our seats, we'd missed a good portion of the game, but I was fine with that. It looked like we were winning, which meant that the meet and greet we were doing after the game would probably be more fun than if we'd lost, so at least there was that.

CHAPTER SIX

*C*ole...

It was the top of the ninth, and Strawberry had come in to close the game out and get the save. While he spoke some English and I spoke a little Japanese, we had our own communication system worked out. I'd say things like pineapple, which meant nothing to anyone other than the two of us. He'd know that I wanted him to throw the ball inside and high. Another one we'd use was puppy, which was a slow curve ball. We didn't do it often, especially with the new system in place, but it was fun to call that out and have him know exactly what to throw without anyone else knowing.

Why we came up with these particular words was a mystery, but he'd come to me in spring training last season to discuss what we wanted to do, with the interpreter, of course. It was one of those, "How are we gonna talk to each other?" kind of things. That lasted all of about five minutes until we just kind of figured our own thing out, and it had worked ever since.

We mostly relied on the pitch com, but every now and then, we would throw things out. Eventually, our team, as well as our opponents, figured things out, so we had to switch our words around. After a while, though, I would just give ridiculous hand signals that meant nothing at all, and I'd let him pitch whatever he wanted. I could tell what he wanted to pitch, which was almost always a fastball, so I was always ready for it. The only time we got into trouble was if we had runners on and he wanted to throw a slider. I had to be prepared for that pitch because it could get away from me really quick and lead to bad things happening on the basepaths.

With the heart of the Houston lineup coming up, we knew he had to be on the whole time, which was a good thing. That pressure seemed to just push him to the next level. I mean, he had always been one of the best pitchers, and he seemed to just keep getting better and better.

He'd told me early on that his ultimate goal was to be able to get through the ninth inning on three pitches—one to each of the three players he wanted to get out. It had been close a few times, with him throwing just six and eight. More often than not, he'd be in with some really good players and have to pitch either around them, or try to get them to strike out, neither of which he shied away from.

"Today," he said when I handed the ball back to him.

I nodded, knowing exactly what he meant when he said it. Today was the day he was going to make his ultimate goal come to life. The announcers always talked about the immaculate inning being three pitches to three players, all strikes, and striking each one out. From where I stood, though, the tougher thing was one pitch each to three players, each resulting in an out. In order to master that feat, you had to know your opponent, trust your defense, and be vigilant in throwing exactly the right pitch each and every time. If anyone could do it, Strawberry was the one, and he wanted to do it tonight.

I walked back to the plate and stepped behind it, their first baseman coming up to bat, swinging just outside the batter's box. I waited, watched him closely, and decided not to say anything. I didn't want to jinx the chance that my guy would get his dream inning. Instead, I ducked down behind the plate and just sat there waiting.

"You gonna call a pitch?" the batter asked.

"Nope," I said, not even looking up at him.

"You guys are nuts," he said. "The video thing isn't even out there anymore."

"Doesn't matter," I said.

"Whatever," he said, grinding his right foot into the back of the box before stepping in.

I set myself up, crouched down behind the plate and waited for my guy to hurl the ball. His smirk told me he understood what I was doing, just letting him pitch. It was never done, like ever, because the guys behind you had to know what was coming. They moved a bit on the infield, positioning themselves into the best locations where the ball should come and waited. The set by Strawberry, the wind up, and the pitch, a fastball that was damn near down the middle, just inside enough to keep their guy from getting good wood on it. Instead, he was a little late and pushed the ball on the ground to our first baseman, Matsui, who picked it up and beat the guy to the bag, then threw the ball over to Cote who completed the circuit around the infield.

"That's one," I shouted, holding one finger up.

The next guy up was their new shortstop. The guy who Hennings had so many issues with last season had been traded to Sacramento, so at least we didn't have that issue this series. Once again, I squatted behind the base and waited for him to dig in and get ready. This guy didn't say anything, just looked at our guy like he was gonna pummel the cover off the ball.

"Call the pitch," he said as I squatted there.

"No need," I said, without elaborating further.

He stepped out, taking another practice swing. He glared at me like he was daring me to refuse what he'd said again, but I just stayed there, down on the pads strapped to my shins, waiting for him to get back into the box.

"Let's go," the ump said, indicating that he was growing just as impatient as I was.

"Tell him to call the pitch," he said to the ump.

"You do know it's not required, right?" I asked him.

He looked at me again, then watched as the infielders scooted slightly more toward left field, just enough that it was clear they were positioned for him to pull the ball. I just bobbed my head to the music

31

in my mind, waiting for my guy to throw. Finally, the batter stepped into the box and swung through the zone a few times.

Set, wind up, pitch. This time it was a little further out over the plate, and the batter caught it on the heart of the bat, but it was high enough that he got under it a bit and sent it sky high on the infield toward Hennings. I could hear him shouting and saw him waving his arms to indicate that he was good to catch the ball, which he did.

"That's two," I said, holding my pinky and pointer up to indicate the two outs.

Just one more and we'd be done. I was looking forward to being done, especially if that pretty lady from the stands was coming to the after party.

"Let's go," I said, punching my mitt a couple of times, then taking my position once again behind home plate.

Their batter this time was a left hander, and he seemed to be angry. Not like angry in the sense that he'd been struggling, but like something was really bothering him.

"Time," I called, standing up from behind the plate.

Strawberry stepped off the rubber and the batter stepped out of the box.

"What's up your butt?" I asked him.

"Shut the fuck up," he barked back.

"Just trying to help," I said, then squatted back down and waited for my guy to do his thing.

The batter stepped in and took a couple of swings, then got set and waited. Strawberry set, wound up, then tossed in a slow breaking curveball which crossed the plate just as the batter's bat went through the zone. It connected, and I was worried that he got enough of it, but then saw that it was gonna be a lazy fly out toward our left fielder, Adams, who came in a few steps and caught the ball.

Strawberry had done it. I couldn't believe it, but he'd actually fucking done it. The smile on his face was the biggest one I'd ever seen, and I'd seen him smile a lot in the last couple of seasons.

"Yatta," Strawberry shouted, punching his fists in the air.

I headed to the mound to give him a hug, and the rest of the infielders came in as well. The outfielders were doing whatever it was they did after games, then headed in too. High fives were handed all around, with some of the guys doing their silly handshakes and shit. I was a keep it simple kind of guy, just doing the traditional high five.

We headed off the field toward the dugout, and the reporter from the station that aired our games locally called out to me, asking for an interview. I dropped my helmet on the ground at my feet and stepped next to her.

"Cole," she began. "Tell me, what was going on out there in the ninth? Seemed like there was something going on with calling the pitches."

"Didn't call any of them," I said. "Ichigo knew what he wanted to pitch, and so did everyone else on the field. It was just him against each batter, heat on heat, and he was on fire tonight."

"For sure he was," she said. "It looked like you had some words with Robinson that last at bat. What was that all about?"

"He just seemed like something was bothering him," I said. "Wanted to give him a minute to clear his head. Good sportsmanship and all that."

"Didn't seem to help him any," she said.

"No," I replied. "He didn't seem to want the help, so I dropped back down and let our Guardian take him out."

"It seemed to be a good inning all around," she said.

"One of the best," I replied.

"Thanks for the chat," she said, then turned to the camera. "Let's throw it back up to the booth, guys."

The light on the camera shut off, and I knew we were clear.

"Seriously," Jenn said. "What was really going on with Robinson?"

"I honestly don't know," I said. "He was pissed about something, but just told me to shut up, so I did."

"Yikes," she said. "I'll let you head in."

"Thanks," I said and reached down to pick up my helmet. "We've got that after party tonight with Pinaceae Tech, so I've got to get showered and to it."

"That's right," she said. "Have fun."

"Always do," I replied, then headed to the clubhouse.

CHAPTER SEVEN

*K*ylie...
　　I was on my feet with the rest of the crowd when they started this crazy music going all around the stadium. I saw the big video screen showing helicopters, and that's when I could hear them mixed in with the music. It was like they were showing several different ones coming to the rescue of people, and then there was this smoke going across the screen. Not like real smoke in the stadium, but like those fog machines that throw it out and people walk through it to make a grand entrance.

At first the camera was low, just showing feet walking, then it panned up and showed this superhero kind of figure walking in, all in shadow. There was lightning flashing on the screen and the image changed to a player, his mitt on his one hand and a ball in the other. He was tossing the ball up into the air and catching it, over and over again. His hat covered his face as he was looking down, then he looked up and his face was revealed and the whole crowd pitched to another level.

The player was Japanese, at least I thought so, and he gave this kind of menacing look into the camera. When the image shifted, which was pretty cool visually on the big screen, I could tell that they were showing live footage of the guy walking in from where they got them-selves ready out past the fence. He was walking in slowly, like it was all a big production or something. The rest of the players seemed to have stopped what they were doing and just watched as he made his way to the inner part of the field. The catcher, who I had seen at the beginning of the game, was standing on the bump of dirt in the middle of the field, waiting.

When the guy who would be throwing the ball got to the bump, the catcher handed him a ball and then walked to the place where the batters stood. He got low to the ground and the pitcher guy threw the ball to him. Even with how loud the crowd was, I heard a loud pop when the ball got to the catcher. It was very clear that he was throwing really hard.

It was all very exciting and I could feel the crowd building to a fever pitch with what was going on. The score was two to nothing, so we were ahead. That much I had figured out with the little bit of knowledge I had about the sport. I saw the referee, no, the umpire, motion to the pitcher, and then the guy threw one more ball to the catcher, who threw it out to the people in the inner part of the field. They threw the ball around to each other and back to the catcher who was standing on the bump.

The pitcher must have said something to the catcher because he nodded his head and handed him the baseball. He walked back to the place where the batters were and got into his place behind the plate. I'd picked up a few of the terms but was woefully unknowledgeable about almost all things baseball. Their player came up to try to hit the ball and everyone in the stadium sort of held their breath in anticipation.

The pitcher threw the ball, and the batter swung and hit the ball down the line on our side of the field that showed what was in play and what wasn't. It stayed on the other side of the line and the guy at the base there picked it up and touched the base. The umpire pulled his fist up to say that he was out. Everyone around us started jumping and cheering, so I followed suit.

After they had thrown the ball all around the guys on the inner part of the field and back to the pitcher, the catcher shouted something and held up his hand with his pointer finger up. My guess was that it was because they had one out for the other team. The way Remi had explained it, each team got three outs for their section of the inning to try to get some runs. If they got three outs before anyone came in to score, then they were done for that part of the game.

The next player came up and did what they had all done to get ready to swing their bats by grinding his foot at the back part of the place where they had to stand. It looked like he was waiting for something, then stepped back out of the box area. I think he said something to the catcher or the umpire or something, but then went back to standing inside the chalk box by the plate. The pitcher threw the ball and there was a loud pop when the batter swung and connected to the baseball and it went way up in the air. The short guy on the field was waving his hands around, clearly saying he was going to catch the ball, and he did.

Once again, they threw the ball around the guys until it went back to the pitcher. The catcher came out with his hand out, his pinky and pointer were out. My assumption was that he was saying there were two outs, but it was weird that he did it that way. I didn't know why he didn't just put two fingers up like normal people did. He went back behind the plate, punched his mitt a couple of times, then squatted down again. All that up and down must have been hard on his knees and stuff because I wouldn't want to be doing all those things. Good thing I never planned to play the game.

When the next guy came up to the plate, he looked like he was mumbling under his breath or something, but I couldn't hear anything over the cheering of the crowd, which had grown steadily with each out that our team got. I saw him step into the box area and swing a couple of times. After a few seconds, the catcher stood up with his hands out and the umpire then did the same gesture. I think the catcher was saying something to the batter, but again, it was too noisy to hear any of it. By the time he was done talking, he squatted back down and waited for the pitcher to throw the ball.

In that split second, the entire crowd went nearly silent, like everyone was holding their breath, just waiting to see what would happen. The pitcher threw the ball, and the batter swung and hit it really far out to the outer part of the field. I was sure that it was going to go all the way over the fence like what happened when our guy did it, but it didn't. Instead, it came down close to the fence and the guy out on the other side caught it easily.

It was like a bomb went off. The entire crowd cheered all at the same time, and it was nearly deafening. Everyone was jumping up and down and cheering, giving high fives to strangers around them, and the guys in the inner part of the field ran to the pitcher and hugged him. Someone even picked him up. The beauty of all these grown men getting so excited about a game was really fun to see. Of course, the crowd was also excited, and most of the people around us stayed standing in their space as the team came off the field.

"We won?" I asked Remi, shouting to be heard over the crowd.

"We sure did," he said, scooping me up a bit to pick me up in a bear hug. "That means the guys are gonna be super excited at the after party. We are gonna have so much fun."

"I just don't know about this," I said as he set me down.

"What's there to know?" he asked. "They won, we get to meet them, and maybe, just maybe, you'll get a chance to meet the catcher. You know, the guy you were flirting with before the game started?"

"Don't remind me," I said, but I was smiling.

We knew that it was going to take some time for everyone to clear out of the stadium, as well as for the players to get cleaned up after the game. I assumed they would all shower and change, then come back out onto the field, which was where we were doing the meet and greet. Oof, this waiting was not something my anxiety needed, but I had Remi with me, so I was sure everything would be just fine.

CHAPTER EIGHT

*C*ole...

Why they thought an after-game event was a good idea, I couldn't tell you. All I knew was this company paid a pretty penny to keep us late, simply to schmooze with people who didn't matter. The only potential light was the fact that the woman I saw in the stands might be there, be available, and be willing to chat me up. It was the only thing that helped me get through my post-game routine fast enough to show up on time.

The party was technically going to be in the outfield, and they were setting up a handful of tall bistro-type tables for folks to hang around while they got to rub elbows with professional athletes. They had a bar, but we'd been instructed not to partake of that particular option so as not to sully the team's name as a bunch of drunk and belligerent jocks. Not that it mattered to most of us, though. We knew how to be belligerent without alcohol. Either way, we finished our post-game clean up and headed out through the dugout to the outfield grass.

"This is fucking bullshit," Huffman said as he trudged out of the dugout.

"Exactly," Hennings echoed. "Why do we have to play nice with a bunch of suits?"

"All about the image of the team," I replied. "Besides, it looks like there are at least a few ladies out there."

"Fine for the two of you," Hennings said. "But I've got someone waiting for me at home, and the sooner I can split, the sooner I can get her under me."

"You think of sex more than anyone I know," I said.

"Bullshit," he said. "Adams and Swift think about sex more than anyone."

"There is that," I agreed.

Those two had a freaky relationship that none of us really under-stood. It wasn't that they were gay, not that it would matter. Just that they were always hanging around each other, plotting world domina-tion or some such thing, and we never saw them with more than one girl. They probably did that sharing thing which, don't get me wrong, I have no issue with. I just couldn't do it. No, if I met the right girl, I'd need her to be mine, and mine alone.

When I was in high school, I thought that girl was Mindy. What I didn't know was that she was just using me to make the guy she really wanted to be with jealous. I'd heard the rumors but was sure that she wouldn't do something like what she'd done to me. Boy had I been wrong. It took a while for me to trust anyone again after that. Who goes out of their way to sleep with you, get pictures of you two sleeping together, then plasters them all around school to pretend that I was the jerk who was sharing? It ended up screwing some things up for me, but in the end, she'd gotten what she wanted, which was not a baseball player but the quarterback of the football team. I had the last laugh though, because he blew his ACL in the Homecoming game our senior year and lost his scholarship and potential NFL career.

Mindy tried to say she didn't mean to make me the bad guy and tried to reconcile with me, but I shut that shit down before she even got started. No, I was not about to be someone's side dude, the safety net. None of that for me. If she didn't want to be with me, she should have just left me the fuck alone.

"You're deep in thought," Hennings said.

"Just making sure my brain remembers all the shit it's been

through," I said. "I will flirt with everyone at this party, but not a damn one of them will get past my lovely exterior."

"Gotta do what I did," he replied. "Fuck 'em and leave 'em."

"I'm not you, though," I replied. "If I'm gonna be with someone, then I'm all in. I don't need that in my life right now, though."

"Never say never," he said, then laughed.

Huffman was laughing a bit, too, which was odd because that dude never even smiled.

"IT'S BEEN NICE TALKING WITH YOU," I SAID TO A WOMAN WHO WAS easily my mom's age. "I should really circulate some more, though. Coach and the brass want to ensure that everyone gets a chance to talk to each of us."

"You don't have to—"

"I really do," I said, turning my back on the woman who, wow, was she a lot of work.

It had been about half an hour since we made it out to the outfield, and this woman had damn near cornered me, keeping me near her the entire time. She was a nice-looking woman, but not in my age bracket, and not someone I was even remotely interested in. I'd been looking at the crowd of people, hoping I could see that blue-and-purple dress, or at least the guy who she was with. Finally, after I'd gotten away from Mrs. Moneybags, I spotted him. Making a beeline, I headed in their direction, hoping that she was still here.

"Hey there," the guy said to me when he saw me coming.

"Hey, yourself," I said, being polite, but also looking for the woman.

"She's getting a glass of wine," he said, low and near my ear.

He was a little close, and I wondered if they were together. That would definitely not be what I was looking for. I didn't really do that sharing thing that Adams and Swift did.

"You two together?" I asked.

"Kylie and me?" he asked. Realization must have dawned on him because he added, "God, no. I don't do girls, and she's practically my sister, so, that would be awkward as fuck. Oh, sorry. Guess I should watch my mouth, huh?"

I sighed in relief, thankful they weren't looking for someone to join their group thing.

"My name's Remington Wilson," he said, sticking his hand out. "My best friend in the entire world is Kylie Harper. She's super shy, but an amazing woman, and I don't say that just because I've known her forever and love her. It's the truth. But," he added, pointing his finger at me, "you hurt her, I will find you and end you. Are we clear?"

While the tone was genial and kind, the words caught me off guard.

"Wouldn't dream of hurting her," I said.

"That means, if you flirt, then walk away, I'm gonna be upset," he said. "She doesn't date, is anxious as fuck being here, and didn't even want to come. Please, whatever you do, if you aren't really interested in her, walk away now."

That last thing caught me by surprise and I wasn't sure how to respond.

"I don't even know her," I said. "How do I know we won't get along? Or how do I know we even will?"

"She gets along with everyone," he said. "She's the kindest person in the world. I, on the other hand, am not, so watch yourself."

Just then I saw her. She was coming out of the bullpen and I couldn't help but stare. Never in my life had I been this starstruck, and I'd met a ton of famous people. They all paled in comparison to her.

"She has that effect on everyone," her friend said when he caught me staring.

The whole way over, she'd had her head somewhat down, just looking up enough to keep from running into people. It wasn't until she was almost next to us that she looked up enough to see that I was there. Stopping in her tracks, her eyes getting big, she just stared at me.

"Hi," I said, taking a step to close the space between us. "My name's Cole. What's yours?"

I knew that her friend had told me, but I wanted to hear her say it. She stuttered a bit before she actually spoke.

"I'm Kylie," she finally said and her voice was sweet, like the taste of honey in the springtime.

"It's a pleasure to meet you," I said, holding my hand out to her.

She looked down at it, back at me, then over my shoulder to her friend. Whatever she saw with him gave her the courage to reach her own hand out to mine. I took it and noticed that it was so soft, like she cared very much for her hands, took care of them to ensure that they were nearly perfect. I held her hand longer than was probably necessary, but I didn't want to let go. Her friend cleared his throat behind me and I finally let her go, but it was like I lost everything I wanted. She kept looking between me and him, her eyes wide, and I just wanted to make her feel comfortable.

"Would you like me to sign a baseball for you?" I asked, hoping that a safe topic would be enough to get her to relax.

"Umm, sure, I guess," she said, but at least she looked like she was a little more at ease.

The team had put buckets of balls all around the area for players to sign and give to the people from Pinaceae Tech as souvenirs from the event. I grabbed one of the balls in the bucket and picked up a pen from the table that her friend was standing next to. I signed the ball, then printed my name and put my phone number on it.

"In case you want to connect," I said, although it sounded dumb, even to me. "You can totally just ignore it or throw it away, too."

Good God, where was the cool, smooth, suave, and sophisticated Cole that I always was, because he certainly wasn't anywhere around here.

"Thanks," she said, taking the ball.

She looked at it and a small smile crossed her lips before she tried to shove it into her purse. The thing was tiny, though, so I wasn't sure if she could make it fit, but she did. It was still sticking out of the small bag but seemed to be secure.

"So, you're the catcher, right?" she asked. "That's the right name for that position, right?"

"I am, and yeah, that's the name of the position," I said with a smile. "I take it you aren't very familiar with baseball and it's terms and such."

"Remi's been helping me," she said, pointing to her friend who was surprisingly silent at the moment. "He's the all-knowing of any of my friends when it comes to anything sports."

"He's a good friend to have around," I said, smiling at the man.

"I'm good for a lot of things," he said. The innuendo was there, but I kind of doubted he was more than just a friend to her. Something about the way they stood next to each other made it seem like more of a sibling situation than anything else.

"I don't doubt it," I said. "Love the makeup, by the way. It's really well done."

"Thanks," he said, and it appeared that he relaxed just the tiniest of bits.

"So, you guys work for Pinaceae Tech," I said. "What kind of things do you do?"

"I work in the office," Remi said. "Lots of meetings with lots of people who know very little but pretend they know a lot. Mostly, I just make the big bosses look good."

"And I bet you're a pro at it, too," I said.

"He is," Kylie said. "Like, he's the best at his job, and management knows it. They're always happy when he's assigned one of their projects."

"Don't sell yourself short," Remi said. "You're beyond amazing when it comes to the backend designing and coding shit. Like, don't ask me how, but it's like you were born with a computer for a brain. It's freaky how quickly she can code out something."

"Sounds like you're more than just a little bit smart," I said. "It actually sounds like you're a genius. I know nothing about computers other than how to turn them on and use the internet and my emails. Watching film is the only thing that's slightly more advanced, and honestly, it's just point and click to get them going because the coaches send them in links for us to get to."

"You must at least know something," she said, as if it was clearly simple.

"I'm more of a jock than a nerd," I said. "Not that nerds are bad, it's just that I am totally not knowledgeable about any of that sort of stuff."

"Do you have a smartphone?" she asked. "Because that's basically a minicomputer. It's easier with the apps and such, but there does take some skill to even work one of those."

"I use social media and stuff on it," I said. "Play a few games, but mostly I like to just hang out on the field. It's where I'm happiest."

"Yeah, no, I'm not the outdoors kind of person," she said.

"You liked going camping with us when we were kids," Remi said. "I mean, you went with us and we always had fun."

"Sure," she said. "But that was more of a way to get out of the house and away from other people."

"People are dicks," he said, and the way he said it made it sound like there was a reason for it. As if she'd been bullied or something, but that didn't make sense to me.

"I'm assuming there's a story there," I said, leaving the question in the air and not asking it outright.

"There is," he said, and that was it. No elaboration whatsoever.

"Maybe we'll get to a point where you trust me enough to share," I said, and meant every word of it. "I would really like to get to know you better. And no," I continued, looking at Remi. "I'm not just saying that. You're beautiful, obviously smart, and your sense of humor is definitely my kind of amusement."

"There you are," the woman I had been talking to earlier said as she came to us. "I've been looking all over for you."

"Sorry," I said, hoping it sounded more sincere than it felt. "As I told you before, I've got to meet several people tonight."

"You should come with me, then," she said. "I can introduce you to the really important people at Pinaceae Tech."

"I'm sure you could," I replied. "But I've been instructed to mingle with the crowd. If I were to go with you, I wouldn't be following my instructions. I'm sure you can understand how it goes when the folks above you give you instructions. You kind of have to follow them."

The woman blinked, like she'd never heard anyone say something so preposterous to her in all her life. It felt like both Remi and Kylie were holding their breath, waiting for some rampage to happen from this woman. But she was just stuck, not quite sputtering, but definitely had that look of a fish out of water, trying to find some way to express her discomfort.

"Well, I never," she began, but didn't finish whatever it was she was going to say. She just sort of stomped off away from us.

Once she was aways away, both Remi and Kylie kind of let out explosive breaths.

"I take it that was someone important," I said, turning back to them.

"Only the wife of one of the highest-ranking managers in the company," Kylie said with a laugh. "I've never seen her speechless before."

"Nice job," Remi said, and I think I'd just proven something to him.

"No problem," I replied. "Sometimes people need to be reminded that just because they have a big paycheck, doesn't mean they're more important than anyone else. Some positions are crucial, for sure, but honestly, you two probably do way more work than the managers."

"I like you," Remi said.

"Thanks," I replied. "Unfortunately, I do have to do a little more mingling, but I'd love to have lunch or dinner or something with you if you wouldn't mind."

"I might do that," she said, patting the ball that was still sticking out of her bag.

"If you want tickets or anything, too, just let me know," I added. "Hope to hear from you soon."

I was walking backward away from them because I couldn't keep my eyes off her. Finally, though, I needed to turn around and try to pretend to not want to rush back and spend the entire night with her. I just hoped she'd call or text me, because this onetime meeting was not nearly enough for me.

CHAPTER NINE

*K*ylie...

"If you want tickets or anything, too, just let me know," he said. "Hope to hear from you soon."

He backed away from us, then turned around and disappeared into the crowd. Just like that, it was just me and Remi once again.

"I'm serious," Remi said, and I looked at him, completely confused. "I like him," he added.

"Oh, yeah," I said. "He seems really nice."

"But..." he said, drawing the word out.

"I can't," I said. "It's too much of a risk."

"It's been over a decade," he said. "I doubt anyone even remembers."

"They remember," I said. "Besides, I wouldn't want to screw his life up like that monster did mine. It wouldn't be fair."

"You became a new person when you changed your name," he said. "That new you is the person he likes. He doesn't know anything about your past, and probably won't make the connection, so I say go for it. Give him a call or send him a text and let him know you want to meet. Worst-case scenario, he finds out and ghosts you. You gotta try to live, baby. I want you to have everything you want, and from what I saw, you kinda liked him, too."

"I mean…" I couldn't say it out loud. Like, if I spoke the words, the universe that had fucked me so royally with my genes would pull it away, just because it could.

"If you don't," he said. "Well, let's just say, I'll see if I can convert him to my way of playing. Maybe he's a switch hitter and plays for both teams."

I laughed. I couldn't help it. Remi was one of the few people who could bring out an honest to goodness full-on laugh out of me. It took a while before I could even breathe right to say anything.

"You're horrible," I said.

"Am not," he replied, then stuck his tongue out at me.

"Real mature," I said.

"Never claimed to be mature," he said. "That would just be awful and absolutely no fun at all."

I just shook my head, still feeling the giggles coming up. We stood there, my best friend and me, and sipped our drinks and waited until it was time enough that we could head out.

"Text him," Remi said as we were getting ready to leave the stadium.

"Not now," I replied. "It will seem desperate."

"If you don't think he's hoping he gets a text from you before he leaves tonight, then you know absolutely nothing about guys," he said. "Text him. Trust me."

We had stopped before going into the place behind the fence where the pitchers got ready. I think Remi had called it a cow pen or something like that. Didn't matter. I pulled out my phone and opened it up, getting to the texting app. I started a new thread and pulled the ball from my bag, typing in the number into the recipient's section.

> Hey. It's Kylie. Wanted to thank you for the
> baseball. Have a good night.

I showed the text to Remi, and he grabbed my phone, backspacing to erase what I had written, then quickly typed something in before hitting send. He didn't even let me look at it before he sent it off. He had this smug look on his face when he handed the phone back to me. I read what he wrote and nearly died.

> Hey. It's Kylie. Wanted to thank you for the baseball. It was really nice to meet you. I would love to meet up for coffee some time, maybe lunch, or a drink after a game some night. I'm available tomorrow if you're interested.

"Why would you do this to me?" I whined.

"Because he is hot and into you," he replied, as if that was all that mattered.

"I can't believe you just did that," I said, still staring at my phone. "What if he wants to meet?"

I could feel my chest starting to get tight, my breathing coming in shallow breaths, and thought this is it, this is how I die.

"Breathe, Kylie," Remi said, putting his arm around my shoulders. "Just breathe. Everything will be just fine, I promise."

My phone buzzed, and I jumped. I didn't want to look, didn't want to see the rejection that I knew was there. Instead, I handed the phone to Remi for him to tell me how bad it was.

"You have a date," he said. "Tomorrow at noon. He wants to know where you want to go."

"Wait, what?" I asked. "He does?"

"Let's pick something close," he replied. "How about Kau Kau Barbecue in the International District?"

"Maybe," I hedged.

"Come on," he said. "You can get there on the train, they have good food, and if you need to get away quick, you know your way around and can get lost in the crowd."

I looked at him. He was sincere, like he really wanted me to go on this date with this guy I just met.

"What if he's a—"

"He's not," Remi said, cutting me off mid-question. "There is no way that could happen. Trust me, he's not."

I sighed, still unsure about whether this was a good idea or not.

"Let's head to the train," he said, guiding me out of the small space we'd been standing in. "You think better when you're moving. Besides, we don't want to miss the last one."

"Okay," I said, letting him steer me out of the stadium and toward the light-rail and the stop we got off at when we came to the game.

The crowd was much smaller at this late hour. It was a bit spooky walking on the street that was so empty, but Remi had this air about him that made us look like we shouldn't be messed with. Not really sure how he managed it, but he did, and I was grateful he was with me. We made it to the platform, tapped our card to pay for the fare, and walked to one of the handful of benches that were there for waiting riders. It didn't take long before the train came to take us north toward our place on Capitol Hill.

"What am I going to wear?" I asked once on the train.

"I got you," he said. "I know the perfect outfit for a Saturday lunch date."

"Will you go with me?" I asked.

"I'll be around," he said. "But you're a big girl and you can do this."

I sighed. He was right in that I could do this. I just hadn't really done anything quite like this before. Even in college I was pretty much a homebody, going with groups, but never doing anything one-on-one before. I'd always had Remi around to protect me, but I knew I needed to grow up a little and figure out what I wanted in life. Eventually, Remi would find someone to settle down with, and I would have to fend for myself at that point, I was sure.

During high school, I never dated. I didn't trust anyone at that point, as it was still too close to the chaos that had been my life since everything went to shit. Graduating and going to college had helped a bit with my anonymity, but it wasn't until I started working that things really felt like I was not my father's daughter any longer, no longer living in the shadow of who and what he was. Some people made the connection, but I usually wasn't asked too many details about what happened.

When someone did ask something that was completely inappropriate, I had learned the art of the silent stare. If you didn't answer someone's question and simply stared at them, they would get uncomfortable and change the subject or just walk away. It took a while to get there, though, so I would sometimes just say that I didn't want to talk about it, or I didn't know the answer to what they were asking. Thankfully, my work spoke for itself, and if people were curious; about my past, my father, the crimes, and the aftermath, they just lived with their curiosity, because I didn't entertain anything of that sort.

CHAPTER TEN

*C*ole...

"Who's the chick?" Hennings asked.

"None of your business," I replied.

He was that player, the one who everyone knew would bang anything in a skirt. Once he met his girlfriend, though, it was like he was a different person.

"Didn't mean anything by it," he said, taking a sip of his drink. "Just making small talk. Don't let J see you chatting up the fans, though. He's kind of a hard-ass about that sort of thing."

"Pretty sure it was just you he had an issue with," I said, but laughed. "Don't need to worry about that anymore, though, do we?"

"Fi is very good at keeping my mind off anyone but her," he said, and the smile on his face made me realize that he was well and truly head over heels for that girl.

"Hey," Huffman said as he stepped up to where we were standing. "When do we get to bail?"

That man was not one who liked to hang out. He'd come to the stadium, get his work in, and even sometimes go to the bar with us, but he was always very serious. About everything. It was weird, but he was good in center and had bailed the team out more than once with his bat and glove.

"Not sure," I said. "There's Coach. Want me to ask?"

"Yeah," he said, so I did just that.

On the walk over, though, my phone buzzed, so I pulled it out and took a look. It was a text from a number I didn't recognize but did have the Seattle area code on it.

> Hey. It's Kylie. Wanted to thank you for the baseball. It was really nice to meet you. I would love to meet up for coffee some time, maybe lunch, or a drink after a game some night. I'm available tomorrow if you're interested.

I blinked a couple of times at the words. She didn't seem like the kind of person who would be so forward, so I had a sneaking suspicion that her friend had been the author of the text and not her.

> Was great to meet you, too. Lunch tomorrow? Say noon?

I was glad that she had reached out, and I saved her number to my phone. I also did the extra thing of emailing it to myself. Hennings had told me how he'd lost his girl's number, so I decided to go ahead and do this, just in case. By the time I looked up, Coach Johnson was alone, so I approached him with our question.

"What's the exit plan?" I asked.

"Regina said we needed to stay until she gave the all clear to head out," he said. "Let me ask her right now."

He walked away to find the woman who spoke to us before the game today, and I was left alone. Unfortunately, the woman who cornered me at the beginning of the event found me there and came up to me. I knew it wasn't gonna be a good conversation, but I decided that I would be polite and let her down easy.

"We meet again," she said, and I could tell she'd had at least one too many drinks. "Seems like fate is pushing us together, wouldn't you say?"

"Small event, ma'am," I said. "We're bound to run into each other more than once."

"But it seems like you're always busy with someone else when I come by," she complained. "You should just come with me to my place and we can have a grand time, just the two of us."

"I'm sorry, ma'am," I said. "We're not allowed to leave the event right now."

"I know the owner of Pinaceae Tech," she said. "He won't mind if I steal you away."

She'd gotten closer to me with each statement she'd made, and I was backed up to the outfield wall when Huffman came by.

"'Scuse me, ma'am," he said, then grabbed my arm and pulled me with him away from her.

"Thanks," I said under my breath, only loud enough for him to hear me.

"No prob," he replied.

"There you are," Coach said. "You're good to go any time. Regina said they're wrapping things up."

"Thank God." I sighed and Huffman chuckled next to me.

"Troubles?" Coach asked.

"Just one woman," I said. "She doesn't understand that we aren't her playthings. I think she's either a very high-ranking person in this company, or she's married to one."

"Then scoot out quietly," he said. "No need to cause a scene if you can help it."

"No argument here," I said.

Huffman and I headed toward the bullpen, which was where they had a bar of sorts set up. Thankfully, the woman who had been dogging me the entire party wasn't in there, so we were able to sneak out the back and hightail it to the parking garage.

"See ya tomorrow," Huffman said with a wave.

I waved back and climbed into my car, closing and locking my doors. I didn't bother to do much else until I was out of the parking structure and on the streets heading to my place in West Seattle. It wasn't too far to get home, thankfully, and by the time I got there, I was ready for bed. I parked, walked up to my condo, and let myself in, locking the door behind me.

Flipping on the light by the front door, I headed into my laundry room to flip my laundry from that morning. Once the dryer was going, I went to the kitchen and grabbed a bottle of water from the fridge and then headed to my bedroom.

Undressing, I pulled my phone out of my pocket and realized I had a text. I opened it up and saw that Kylie had suggested we go to Kau Kau Barbecue in the International District, which sounded really good. I hadn't eaten there but was pretty open to most foods. I should be good to go when I got there. I climbed into bed, sent a text confirming I'd meet her there, plugged my phone in, and set an alarm to make sure I was up and ready to go in time to get there.

THE INTERNATIONAL DISTRICT WAS SUPER BUSY ON A SATURDAY UNDER normal circumstances, but the fact that it was the first real good-weather weekend made it extra busy. I'd found the restaurant Kylie mentioned on my phone and had figured out the fastest way to get there. Driving and parking downtown was never an easy task, so I opted to park at the stadium. We were fortunate to be able to get into that parking garage very early in the day when we had games, so it wasn't a problem. It was just a quick walk over the train tracks and across Fourth to get to the light-rail, which went directly to the district.

It had been forever since I'd used public transportation, but it was easy to figure out. I got my ticket for the round trip and waited for the northbound train. With it being late morning, I'd missed the bulk of the early riders, but since it was coming up on the lunch rush, there were still several people on the train. Luckily, there were plenty of empty seats, and we were fairly close to the bigger stops where most travelers would exit. There was one stop before it pulled up to the one I wanted. While it wasn't too crowded, it did take a bit to get off the train since most of the travelers were intending to spend their Saturday afternoon in the same place I was.

The map app on my phone said it would be a short walk, and I was listening to the directions in my AirPods, but the amount of people that were going from shop to shop was way more than I expected. I think I said "excuse me" about fifty times before I saw the bright pink awning and the green walls of the restaurant. Thankfully, there didn't seem to be a line to get in, so I stepped through the door and smelled the wonderful flavors they used in their food.

"Just one?" the woman who was next to the door at the cash register asked.

"I'm meeting someone," I said. "I don't know if she's here, yet though."

"Take a peek," she replied, and I did just that.

Since the space was pretty small, I didn't need to look much, and realized that Kylie wasn't here. I went back to the front and said as much to the woman.

"You want to wait for her or get a table?" she asked.

"I think I'll wait," I said. "If you don't mind."

"No problem," she replied.

"Thanks," I said, and sat in one of the two chairs by the front.

I'd barely sat down when she walked in. She was dressed much more casually than the night before, with tight jeans and a tee shirt. Her hair was pulled up in a ponytail on the top of her head, and she had that same small purse slung across her chest. I stood up when she walked in and she smiled, but also blushed, then looked out the door over her shoulder. I followed her gaze and noticed that her friend was out there.

"He should join us," I suggested.

"Oh, no," she said, clearly caught off guard. "He just came with me because he has some other things to do here."

The words were rushed, and I wasn't sure I believed her, but I let it go. No need to make her uncomfortable right off the bat.

"Ready?" the woman at the cash register asked.

"Yeah," I replied.

"Right this way," she said, then headed into the building.

We followed her through the few tables that were full to one that was against a side wall. It was one of those small ones that was really only big enough for two people at most.

"I'll bring you some tea and water," the woman who seated us said.

"Thank you," Kylie replied.

I pulled out the chair on one side of the table and she looked at me a bit sheepishly.

"Do you mind if I sit on this side?" she asked.

"No problem," I replied, crossing behind her to pull the other chair out.

She sat and picked up one of the menus. I sat in the first chair I'd pulled out and did the same.

"You come here often?" I asked.

"Sometimes," she replied.

"What do you recommend?"

"Everything is really good," she said. "I like the barbecue pork, but I haven't tried anything I didn't like."

"Good to know," I said.

I looked down the menu and found their barbecue section, which had several meats to offer. I wasn't sure whether I would like some of them, but you honestly couldn't go wrong with barbecue pork or ribs, so I figured I'd get the pork. Didn't want to make a mess of myself if I could help it.

When the woman came back with the tea and water, she asked if we were ready to order.

"I am," I said, then looked at Kylie.

"Me too," she replied.

"Ladies first," I said, letting the waitress know she should take her order first.

She ordered the pork, so I said I'd take the same, and the waitress went away to put the order in. Kylie poured two cups of tea, leaving plenty of room for any additions either of us wanted to make. She pulled one of the little packets of sugar and opened it, pouring the contents into the cup, then set the paper aside. When she finally looked up at me, she was blushing. I didn't know if it was that she hadn't stopped, or if she started again. Either way, she was absolutely adorable.

"So," I said, taking my cup of tea. "How long have you worked for that company?"

I couldn't remember the name of it, but knew it was one of those weird names that probably meant something interesting.

"I actually interned there before I graduated from college," she said, and her eyes lit up. "When I was in school, they had someone come to talk to the students who were studying computer sciences. I guess I must have impressed them, because they were practically falling all over themselves to offer me a position."

The way she spoke about the job made me realize that it was her passion, something she loved and was good at. Kinda like what baseball was for me.

"Sounds like it was a good fit, then," I said.

"Absolutely," she replied.

The waitress brought our food out, setting the plates on the table in front of us. It looked absolutely amazing.

"Enjoy," she said, then went back to whatever it was she was doing.

Kylie sat and watched me, and I wasn't sure what she was waiting for.

"What?" I asked after she just stared.

"I wanna know what you think," she replied.

"Smells good," I said, and she just kept looking at me.

I picked up my fork and took a bite and my God it was divine. I must have moaned or something because she gave a little giggle, then covered her mouth.

"Don't let me stop you," I said, talking around what was left of my first bite. "You need to enjoy yours as well."

CHAPTER ELEVEN

*K*ylie...

"What?" he asked.

"I wanna know what you think," I replied.

"Smells good," he said.

I waited, hoping he'd just take a bite, so I'd know whether he was happy about my choice of restaurant. He sat there waiting, but I didn't know what for. Finally, he picked up his fork and took a bite. The moan he let out sounded like something I'd hear from Remi's room when he was hooking up, so it got me giggling. I put my hand over my mouth, trying not to look like a fool, but I couldn't stop.

"Don't let me stop you," he said. "You need to enjoy yours as well."

That just sent another set of giggles through me, and I almost couldn't stop. Finally, I got myself under control and took a bite, and he was right. It was really good. Remi had introduced me to all the fun little places here in the International District. I loved trying new things, but this was my all-time favorite place to eat, and any chance I got, I'd pick it up. Didn't hurt that it was priced low and was affordable.

I continued to eat, enjoying the delicious pork and all its flavors, taking sips of my tea throughout the meal.

"So," he said, once he'd finished his food. "You grew up in the area?"

I nodded, finishing my last bite of rice, then took another sip of tea.

"I did," I said, without elaborating more.

"I'm a Southern California boy, myself," he said. "I do love it up here, though. It's just so green and everything. With the mountains so close, it's like the perfect place to be."

"It really is," I said.

"Have you traveled much?" he asked.

"Not really," I replied. I knew I was being vague, and that this was supposed to be a "get to know you" kind of thing, but I wasn't really ready to open up about much.

"I've been lucky enough to be able to travel with the club to several places," he said. "I think the coolest thing we did was go to Japan to open the season a few years ago. That was a total culture shock."

"That would be really cool," I said. "I do love me some anime, so I bet there was a lot of that stuff over there."

"There definitely was," he said. "There was a guy on our team, he's not with us anymore, who was an absolute maniac when it came to that kind of stuff. He picked up so many souvenirs that he almost had to ship things back to the US. We were kind and helped him out by letting him put some of his things into our bags."

"You guys were nice," I said. "I'm sure I would have to pack a whole shipping container if I ever ended up over there."

"We were only there a couple of days," he said. "Otherwise, I think he would've had to do the same."

I laughed, honestly laughed, which I didn't do.

"I like that sound," he said, and I stopped almost immediately. "I'm sorry," he said, clearly concerned.

"No," I said. "It's just…" I couldn't finish.

"I didn't mean to upset you," he said, and he was obviously sincere.

I could feel it coming on. My chest was getting tight, my eyesight was narrowing down, and I couldn't breathe. I tried to get up, but my body didn't want to cooperate. I could hear him talking but couldn't make out what he was saying. Oh God, not now.

Suddenly, without any warning, I was swirling in the air, the lights and lanterns on the ceiling of the restaurant were spinning and I didn't know what was happening. Then, I was outside, in the open, and even with the crowd, I was able to find a way to breathe.

"That's it," I could hear him say, his voice breaking through to me.

It was a rumble underneath my ear, and I realized that I was standing up, my head against his chest.

"Breathe in slow," he continued. "One, two, three." The words were slow, even, and spaced out, like he was reminding me what I had to do. "Now let it out slow," he added after a moment, and I followed his directions. "In again," he said, and I took a slow deep breath, held it, then let it out. "That's right," he said when I had found my own rhythm. "You got this."

He loosened his grip on me, allowing me to put some space between us, but I didn't move much. When he looked down at me, I could see the concern on his face, that he was worried about me. No one worried about me but Remi.

"I'm fine," I said, trying to push away from him.

He let me go, but kept his hands on my arms, loose, but there.

"I'm really fine," I said, trying to convince myself as much as him.

"I know," he said, and I could see that this wasn't his first rodeo with a panic attack. "I just want to make sure you're steady before I let you go completely."

Remi was suddenly there, at my elbow. I knew it was him, could smell his cologne that he always wore, and it was a comfort.

"Hey," he said. "You good?"

Cole looked at me and waited for me to answer. I took another deep breath and let it out slowly before answering.

"Yeah," I said, though it wasn't nearly as in control as I wanted it to be. No, the one word was warbly and very much not okay.

"Panic attack, I think," Cole said. "My sister used to get them."

"Thanks, man," Remi said, and I was surprised he said that.

Normally, Remi is the only one who can get me to find my center, find the space I need to be in to come back from the darkness that invades me. It's one of the reasons I didn't do crowds or anything, especially not without a backup plan. Today, though, this man I'd just met had figured out what was going on and helped me. He didn't even know me, and yet he was being more than just kind to me.

"Oh no," I said, looking at him. "I didn't pay."

"I got it," he said. "Dropped a fifty and picked you up. I knew you needed space, at least I hoped that's what you needed. It's what worked for my sister. Get her out in the open, away from people, and remind her how to breathe."

"Damn," Remi said, slow and drawn out. "Dude knows all the things and is sexy as fuck. He's a keeper."

Cole laughed, and I was glad, because if Remi approved, then this was seriously a good thing. My best friend could get a read on people with just one meeting, and the party the night before was the first. The fact that he was saying my lunch date was a keeper was definitely nice.

"You good?" Cole asked, squeezing my upper arms a little.

I took stock of myself, then nodded. He let go, and I missed his hands on me. It was a strange sensation to say the least, and I wasn't sure whether I liked it. Taking a shuddering breath in, I tried to compose myself.

"Think we can go for a walk?" he asked, looking at me and not Remi.

I turned to see Remi just waiting for me to answer. His face was neutral, like he didn't want to influence me, but his eyes had a little sparkle in them that was definitely saying I should say yes. Instead of answering, I just nodded and smiled. Cole stuck his arm out and waited for me to grip his elbow. Once my hand was there, he tucked it in a little further, just to be sure I had a good hold on him, I guess, and then he looked to Remi.

"Want to join us?" he asked.

"I think I'll leave her in your capable hands," he said, then smiled down at me.

Oh boy, this was going to be a test. While I trusted Cole to some extent, not having Remi close by might prove to be disastrous. The smile Remi gave me though, told me that he'd be close enough to watch over me and still give me the illusion of being alone with my new friend.

CHAPTER TWELVE

*C*ole...

Walking through the International District with Kylie was a delight. We took it slow, always making sure that she didn't lose her grip on my arm when we got surrounded by people, and eventually, I felt her loosen up a bit and relax. Each store held something wonderful to look at, and while I wasn't in the habit of coming here, it was fun to explore it with her.

"Where to, next?" I asked after we'd walked for about an hour or so.

"I think we've seen everything," she replied, still looking around.

We'd stopped in front of a small shop that served boba tea. It wasn't anything I'd tried before, so I asked if she wanted to get some.

"Oh, yeah," she said, her smile brightening. "This will be nice after all the walking."

I opened the door for her, allowing her to enter before me, then stepped into the small space. There was a menu of sorts on the wall, but it was all in characters from one of the languages in Asia. I didn't know which one and had no idea what I should get.

"What do you like?" she asked me.

"I have no idea," I replied. "This will be my first time."

"Ooh," she said, drawing the word out. "I get to take your boba virginity."

I don't know whether she knew what she was going to say, or if it just kind of came out, because as soon as she'd said it, she blushed about as bright a red as I'd ever seen on someone and looked at her shoes.

"No one I'd rather lose it to than you," I said, hoping to take the embarrassment from her.

"I can't believe I said that," she mumbled, and if I hadn't been right next to her, I would have missed it.

"Hey," I said, and waited for her to look up at me. "It's all good. You're good."

I waited, hoping she'd figure it out, and finally she did, looking up at me. I winked at her, giving my best smile to show I wasn't upset or embarrassed or anything.

"Do you trust me?" she asked.

"Absolutely," I replied.

She walked up to the counter and said something to the young woman behind it. It was rapid and definitely not in English, and I was impressed all over again. The woman looked at me, gave me a smile, then got to work on what I assumed was the tea that Kylie had requested. She grabbed two thick plastic cups and dumped some ice into them. Then she added a dark liquid, then pulled out milk from the fridge and poured that in as well.

Sliding the cups down the counter, she scooped some small balls of something and dropped a scoop into each cup, then added a powder. Finally, she went to this contraption that took the cups and sort of shook them to mix everything up. While that was working, she pulled out a couple of thinner plastic cups that were fairly large and set them up on the counter. When the machine was done, she took the big mixing cups and poured the liquid into the thinner ones that I assumed were what she would hand to us.

Next was a machine that had this sort of film stuff in it which sealed each of the cups with a covering. Once she'd done that, she sort of tipped the cups sideways to blend whatever was inside up a little more, then handed the cups to us with these big straws that had a pointy end on them. Kylie handed her a twenty, then handed me one of the cups.

"Try it," she insisted, an impish smile on her face.

I kind of looked at her, because I had no idea how I was supposed to do that. She took her straw and stabbed it through the film on the top, showing me what I was supposed to do. I followed suit, stabbing my drink. Her smile grew as I took a small sip of the liquid, being careful not to suck up any of the little balls that were in the drink.

It was sweet, not overly so, but definitely had some type of sweetener in it. I wouldn't say that I liked it, but then again, I wouldn't say I didn't.

"What are the little balls?" I asked.

"Tapioca," she said. "You have to chew them if you suck them up."

I laughed. I couldn't help it. The way she said it was just so innocent, but the words could be taken in such a dirty way.

"What?" she asked.

"Just my gutter mind going places it shouldn't," I replied.

We'd stepped out of the shop and started back the way we'd come, but she stopped, just full-on halted in the middle of the street. It took me a couple of steps before I realized she wasn't beside me and turned around. She was staring at me with a look I couldn't quite make out. It wasn't bad, but it wasn't exactly good, either.

"You okay?" I asked.

"I'm trying to figure out if I should laugh or ask you what you meant," she said.

"Definitely laugh," I replied with a smile.

Her lips curled up at the edges, but it was like she wasn't quite sure what the joke was. I had to wonder how innocent this girl was because she seemed so shy and skittish.

"Need an explanation?" I asked after a bit.

"I do," she said. "But I'm also not sure I want one. You know what I mean?"

"Tell you what," I said. "Why don't we table it for now and you can ask Remi when you guys are alone. That way you can get his opinion and decide if it was funny or if I'm awful and you should run far away from me. Sound good?"

She smiled a bit more, then stuck her hand around my elbow and steered us toward the shop where we started. I took that as a good thing and walked with her, weaving between the mass of bodies in the area, back to Kau Kau and her friend.

CHAPTER THIRTEEN

*K*ylie...

"So," Remi said once we were on the train back to Capitol Hill.

"It was fun," I said, but I could feel the blush run up my cheeks.

"You like him," he said. It wasn't a question, so I didn't answer. "Think you'll see him again?" he asked.

I shrugged, pulling my backpack up further on my shoulder. We'd picked up enough groceries to last us through to the middle of the week. He and I had shared the cooking responsibilities and household chores well, each picking up where the other lacked, and splitting things mostly fifty-fifty.

I had to admit, though, that he was the better cook. I could make some things, but Remi was a bona fide chef in the kitchen, something I couldn't match if I tried. On the other hand, he couldn't keep track of a calendar or his schedule or anything like that. No, when it came to organization, he was a lost cause.

"I don't know," I said, replying to his question about seeing Cole again. "I mean, he seems nice, so I don't want to taint him with my whole life."

"You have to stop that," Remi said. "You are not that little girl anymore. You're a beautiful woman who is smart and capable and so worthy of everything good in this world. I love you so much it hurts, and I want nothing more than for you to be happy."

I shrugged. I mean, there really wasn't much I could say as a response to that. I wanted to be happy, too, but at what point did I stop thinking about my history and start building a future with someone? Logically, I knew that my father would never be able to physically hurt anyone again. But that fear from the initial shock, and everything that followed it, still weighed me down and made me feel like I really wasn't worthy of much of anything.

"I get the feeling this guy could handle damn near anything thrown his way," Remi said. "He certainly handles the pitchers on the field in fine form. Mighty fine form if you ask me."

"Everything with you is an innuendo, isn't it?" I asked.

"Might as well have fun when you can," he said. "You only get one life to live, so make the most of it."

"I guess," I said, but was still unsure whether I should pursue a relationship of any kind.

The thing was, I did like him. He had seen me in a state that most never did, and he hadn't shied away from the drama of it. In fact, he had jumped in and done a little bit of a rescue, getting me somewhere I could center myself. Maybe Remi was right in that I couldn't go on the way I had been. I had to get out there and actually live my life. Maybe this was the first step in that direction.

"There we go," Remi said, and I looked at him. "You just decided to jump right in, didn't you?"

I laughed a little at his enthusiasm for this relationship.

"What are you getting out of it?" I asked.

"You being happy," he said. "And maybe some free tickets to games. I mean, those seats we were in last night were awesome, but I bet that the players get even better ones. Can't wait to find out."

My phone buzzed in my hip pocket and I shifted my backpack around so I could slide it out.

Hey. It's Cole. Wondered if you wanted to come to the game tomorrow afternoon. I can put a couple of tickets aside for you and Remi if you want. Just let me know.

"That looks promising," Remi said, and I looked up at him.

"Wanna go to the game tomorrow?" I asked.

"You know I do," he said. "This time we'll dress in proper attire for a game, instead of what we wore last night."

"Good," I said. "I definitely don't want a repeat of the icky that happened."

The automated system had announced our stop, so we slid off the train and started the short walk to our apartment. It didn't take long, and soon we were climbing the two flights to our floor, Remi unlocking the door and leading me inside.

"Text him back," Remi said as we set our packs down.

"Let's put the groceries away, first," I suggested.

"Do eet," he said, emphasizing the last word with the quirky way he said it.

I rolled my eyes, but pulled my phone out and sent a response that we'd love to come. He sent back instructions on where to go in the stadium to get our passes almost right away, and I couldn't help but smile. I thanked him, then shoved the phone back into my pocket, picking up my bag and heading to our kitchen. The rest of the evening went pretty much the way most of our evenings went, with us finishing the things we tended to miss during the week like laundry and such, then making dinner, cleaning up, and getting ready for bed.

"We should watch the game," Remi said. "This way you can see your boy in action and maybe get a little more educated on the game itself."

"We can watch the game," I said. "But he's not my boy, nor am I going to push that on him or me. We'll see what happens. It may be that he hates everything I love, which would be a real downer."

"I don't see that happening," he said. "Now, go get in your jammies so we can be all comfy cozy watching the game. I'll make some popcorn for a snack, too."

"Okay," I said, heading into my room to get changed.

I was actually looking forward to going to the game, despite the knowledge that the crowd would likely be huge. Remi would be with me, so I'd feel safe. And Cole seemed to be a really nice guy, too, so that was a bonus as well.

CHAPTER FOURTEEN

*C*ole...

"You're here early," Hennings said as he stepped into the batting cages below the stadium.

I'd come straight to the stadium after lunch, figuring I could get some workouts in before the majority of the team showed up. I was heading out of the batting cage area when he walked in.

"Had lunch close by, so decided to get in extra work," I replied.

"With a certain someone you met last night?" he asked, the smile telling me he was sure it was.

"It was," I replied, not at all ashamed. "She's actually a really great person. Her friend seems a bit overly protective, but his heart is in the right place."

"You sure they're just friends?"

"I am," I said. "He likes me, so it's a good thing."

"Just be careful," he replied. "You never know what kind of crazy may attach itself to you."

"Speaking from experience?" I asked, laughing.

"You know it," he said, then flipped the switch to turn the pitching machine on.

I headed into the clubhouse, hoping to get a shower before the real practice started. I'd worked up quite a sweat in the cages, but I was starting to see some progress in my hitting. It hadn't been too bad, but there was always room for improvement, and that was just what I was working toward. There were only a handful of players in, it being still pretty early in the day, but Kors was there, and he was pitching that night.

"Hey," I said to him, knowing that anything more would be too much.

He gave a head nod in my direction, then went back to getting himself ready to warm up. Some pitchers needed time to themselves, and he was one of them. I hit the showers, toweled off, and got my gear on to get some stretching and running in before the actual batting practice started.

"Got a minute?" Coach Roof asked as I stepped out into the dugout.

"Sure," I said, climbing the few steps to the field.

"Wanted to run a few things over with you before the game," he said. "You're likely to see more running tonight, so thought we could get some drills in before we really get going."

"Sounds good," I said.

We walked toward the outfield and I dropped my gear on the ground. Knowing Coach, I wouldn't need it. Sure enough, he proceeded to work with me on my pop-up after a pitch, my throws, and handling balls in the dirt. I was the everyday catcher, which required the work. Ramirez showed up after a bit, and we both worked on our fielding and throws until Coach was sure we could handle damn near any situation. Ramirez was pretty green, him being a rookie, but with Franklin getting hurt during spring training, he stepped up and worked hard to make sure he wasn't a detriment to the team.

"Nice job," I said as we were walking back to the dugout.

"Thanks," he replied. "I'm just glad I'm getting the chance to play. I feel bad about Franklin, but I'm just gonna use this opportunity to show my worth."

"I get that," I said. "It's hard to see someone go down with an injury, but you have to take advantage of the chances you're given. I'm glad you're doing that. It will help you a ton in the future, whether it's with us or somewhere else."

"I hope I don't go anywhere else," he said. "I really like it here."

"I get that," I replied. "But trades happen. All you can do is do your best, work the game, and be a consummate professional. Then, there's nothing you can't do. If you get traded, you may get more playing time. It's a tradeoff sometimes, though, so just be ready for anything."

"Thanks," he said.

"Absolutely," I replied.

We'd made it to the dugout, and I'd stowed my gear on the back of the bench, picking up a bat to head out to get some swings off a live person. It was very different from hitting from a pitching machine. While you could ask them to throw something specific, humans were imperfect, and sometimes you had to try to hit a not-so-perfect pitch. If you could do that, you'd go far.

"COLE," JENN SAID AS I WAS STEPPING OFF THE FIELD AFTER THE WIN. "Tell us about what was going on tonight. You seemed to be better than I've seen this year at the plate."

"It's all about doing the work," I said. "Put in the work during practice and it will show up on the field."

"I noticed Kors was having some issues in the first inning," she said. "How were you able to get him to settle down and get into the groove? That first inning was brutal, but he came out like a new pitcher in the second."

"He's good," I said. "Sometimes you just have to remind him that he's the pro we all know. That his stuff is good and he should trust himself to throw the pitches and for the rest of us to back him up."

"Whatever it was, it seemed to help," she said.

"Always does," I replied. "He's got his head on straight, just needs to be refocused if he gets off track. Not a big deal, and it didn't hurt us in the long run."

"I'll let you get back to your team," she said. "Guys. Back to you."

The light on the top of the camera went off, and the reporter thanked me for taking time two days in a row to talk to her. By the time I made it into the clubhouse, most of the guys were in the showers. I took my time, getting my gear stowed away, then headed to the showers myself. After a long, hot one, I toweled off and got into my street clothes, grabbing my bag and phone to head home. Thankfully, by the time we were done with our after-game shit, the crowd was pretty much gone and our drives home weren't a struggle.

As I climbed into bed, I couldn't help but wonder whether Kylie had been watching the game tonight. I didn't normally care about who was out there watching, or what they might be seeing, but something about her made me want to be the best I could, show her that I was someone she might want to be around.

Hopefully I'd proved that today when she had a panic attack and I settled her. I was sure that everyone's reactions to those situations were very different, but the only thing I could do was do what I knew worked for my sister. It wasn't much, but she seemed to have taken it like it was the biggest thing anyone could have done for her. I was just glad I acted when I did, as I would have hated it if she'd suffered any more than she already did. The fact that Remi seemed impressed said more than anything. He seemed like a great guy, someone who really cared for Kylie, and there was no way I would want to kick him out of her life, so I was glad he had approved of me.

CHAPTER FIFTEEN

*K*ylie...

"Ready?" Remi asked.

"I think so," I replied. "Do we even know where we're sitting or how to get the tickets or anything?"

"I put the app on my phone," he said. "Then gave him my email address so he could send the tickets. We're all set."

"Okay," I said, but I was still worried. I guess that was just my way. Worry so much I get sick from it.

"Hey," he said, turning my attention to him. "We got this."

I nodded a little too fast, and he chuckled. He grabbed my hand and held onto me while we walked from the train up and around to the stadium. We passed the entrance we'd used the last time and kept walking around what seemed like the whole building. The crowd was pretty big, but it was the middle of the day and on a weekend, so that shouldn't have surprised me. It was like what it was anywhere in the city when the sun was out, or it wasn't raining heavily. Us Washingtonians just loved to get outside when the weather permitted. Honestly, we'd be outside even when the weather was bad, just more so when it was nice.

"How far do we have to go?" I asked when we'd gotten to the end of the stadium and passed at least three entrances.

"Special entrance for special guests," he said with a smile.

I trusted him. He was always good at making sure I was safe, so this was no different. Finally, after we went almost to the store that was in the building, he turned us into an entrance that seemed to be pretty posh for just anyone.

"Tickets," the man who was just inside the door said.

Remi pulled his phone out, unlocked it, pulled up the app, and let the guy scan it. He smiled and pointed us to the desk that was behind him.

"Can I see your tickets?" the woman behind the wraparound asked. Again, Remi showed the app on his phone. "Perfect," she said after scanning it. "Here are a couple of lanyards for you two. Keep these in sight. It will help to make sure you can get into the family areas in case you end up splitting up."

"Thanks," Remi said.

We walked past her to a double door in the wall and stepped into a whole new world I'd never been in before. The lighting was dim enough that it felt like a bar or something, but bright enough that it wasn't unsafe. There were shiny wooden tables set around with plush-looking chairs. The bar itself was a rich deep wood grain with brass fittings throughout. A bartender was behind it, and he had on a nice button-down shirt and tie, his sleeves rolled halfway up his forearm.

Last game I felt completely overdressed, but this time it was the opposite. We'd opted to go with jeans and team shirts instead of the club clothes we wore on Friday. In this area, though, everyone seemed to be dressed much nicer, with button-down shirts and slacks on the men and many of the women in very nice dresses.

"I feel out of place again," I said low, only for Remi's ears.

"You're perfect wherever you are," he said. "Drink?"

"No," I said.

It was still technically morning, what with this being an early game, and I didn't want to drink anything at this time of day. Many of the people around us had glasses or cans of beer, so I guess it wasn't that much of a big deal, but I just didn't want to chance me drinking too much too soon.

"We can eat," Remi suggested, but I shook my head. "Well, I'm gonna get something and you can nibble off my plate."

"Okay," I said.

I was still in awe of my surroundings, not really sure how we ended up being able to be in this place. It was probably gonna be a one and done kind of thing, though, because Cole probably wouldn't be interested in me at all. I mean, I wasn't exactly beautiful, and I was sure there were women who were way sexier that hit on him all the time. The fact that he got to see my horrible anxiety in full-blown meltdown was just another thing that would probably turn him off. Except, he'd invited us to the game after that, so maybe he wasn't as easily run off as most guys.

"Earth to Kylie," Remi said, and I looked at him, confused.

"What?" I asked.

"I've just been saying your name for like forever," he said. "Where were you just now?"

"Off in my brain somewhere," I said.

"Well, keep up," he replied. "We have food to eat and a boy to say hello to."

"He's not gonna—"

"He invited you," Remi said, cutting me off. "You are wonderful and he said he wanted to see you before the game. We're gonna quickly get something in your stomach so you don't pass out, and then we're gonna go say hello."

"You're really bossy," I said, and he laughed, then shoved a fry into my mouth.

We grabbed a table and ate the fries he'd gotten, me drinking from the water bottle he'd grabbed for me, and him sipping his beer. After what seemed like no time at all, he was tossing the tray for his fries into the recycling bin they had for those types of things and pulling me toward the seating area.

Stepping out into the sunshine, with the roof open over the rich green grass, we could see that the Cascades were the ones on the field warming up. There were so many of them on the field that I wasn't sure I would be able to pick Cole out. I shouldn't have worried, though, because Remi spotted him right away, standing behind the big cage thing they had where the batters stood when they were hitting. Remi had waved, and Cole had excused himself from whoever it was he was standing with and headed over to where we were.

"Hey," he said, smiling. "Glad you guys could make it."

"This is really nice," Remi said. "Thanks so much for getting us these seats. That club is one I won't forget."

I stood there, smiling, my heart pounding in my ears, as I waited for Cole to turn to me. When he did, he gave a brilliant smile, his dimples on full display, and my heart sped up that much faster.

"You doing okay?" he asked. I nodded, not trusting my voice. "Glad you could come."

Smiling like the dork I am, I stood mute, unable to utter a sound.

"She gets this way sometimes," Remi said. "It's not you, I promise."

"I figured," he said. "Anyway, I'm glad you guys could make it."

"You playing today?" Remi asked.

"Nah," Cole replied. "Ramirez is starting behind the plate today. It's nice to get a day off every once in a while."

"I bet," Remi said. "That's a lot of work. I never liked it when they put me at catcher in little league."

"You played?" he asked.

"Yeah," Remi replied. "Up until I was about fifteen. By then I was more interested in the players than the game, and they didn't seem to like that."

"Kids can be dicks," Cole said, and I laughed. He turned to me and smiled. "Figured I'd finally get something out of you."

"Sorry," I muttered.

"Hey, now," he said, stepping closer. "Nothing to be sorry about. You do you, cause you're just fine."

I shrugged and smiled, feeling the blush running up my face.

"You know you're even prettier when you blush, right?" he asked.

The only thing this accomplished was making me blush even harder, which of course made his smile even bigger.

"Tell you what," he said. "You promise to cheer really loud and I'll get you tickets for the next home stand. You wanna come to another game for me?"

I nodded, smiling like a fool, not saying a thing. God, I had to get over this. I mean, I wouldn't always have Remi around, and I needed to figure out how to be a more adultier adult if I was ever gonna do anything in this life.

"Perfect," he said. "I'll keep inviting you two until Kylie feels up to coming alone. Not that I won't still invite you," he said, looking at Remi. "I just want to make sure that I do at some point get some one-on-one time with this beautiful lady."

"I'll keep coming until I can hook up with my own player," Remi said. "Unless you wanna introduce me to a stud today."

Cole laughed and said, "I'm not sure who swings that way, but if I find someone who does, I'll definitely introduce you. Maybe we can double date some time."

"See," Remi said to me. "I knew he was gonna be good for a whole lot. Not just a pretty face to look at."

"Oh, no," Cole said. "I'm much more than just a pretty face. I tend to think that I have quite a bit to offer someone, especially someone as beautiful and kind as Kylie."

I was dumbfounded. There I was, standing in the poshest section of the stadium, and my roommate and this guy who was damn near everything I could ever want were making plans about me like I was someone who needed help with the most basic of things. I mean, it wasn't wrong. There were many times I didn't leave the apartment for days on end unless Remi made me go out with him. I liked my space, my privacy, and being alone. Honestly, though, I was beginning to feel lonely. Maybe this would be good for me, help me come out of my shell a bit more, and really get to enjoy this whole life thing.

CHAPTER SIXTEEN

*C*ole...

"Hey," I said as I stepped to the edge of the stands. "Did you have fun?"

"Yeah," she said.

"Sorry I wasn't playing," I said.

"That's okay," she replied.

"That Ramirez isn't half bad," Remi said. "Not as good as you, but not terrible."

"I'll make sure to tell him," I said.

Her friend was a good guy, I could tell. From the first time we talked, he was very much all about making sure she was taken care of. He'd said they'd known each other for a long time, and he considered her his sister, so that made a lot of sense.

"We're heading to Sacramento tonight," I said. "After that, we'll head down to LA and then over to Houston before we get back."

"That's a lot of travel," she said. "How do you do it?"

"It's all part of the job," I said. "I've gotten used to it, honestly, and it's probably not much more than you going into the office every day."

"Oh, I don't do that," she said.

I looked at her, completely confused, and asked, "Why not?"

"I don't have to," she said. "I work from home and only go in when I absolutely have to, which is almost never."

"That'd drive me nuts," I said. "Don't you miss hanging out with friends and stuff?"

She stared at me, blinking, like nothing I was saying made any sense.

"Yeah," Remi said after a bit. "She doesn't do social things. Stresses her out."

"Sorry," I said.

"Oh, no," she said, her worry clear in her voice.

"I get it," I replied. "I'm kind of the social butterfly of the team, and some of the guys just don't do social things. Like, the other night made a couple of them really uncomfortable. Not that I wasn't, except when I was with you. You made everyone else just fade away."

Her eyes got big, like I said something completely profound, and I was a bit mystified as to what I could have said that made her look at me like that.

"Decker," Bridge called, and I looked at him. He was already showered, which meant that I had been here longer than I should have.

"Shit," I said. "I gotta go. Can I call you?"

"Umm, sure," she said.

"Or is texting better?"

She nodded, smiling.

"Okay," I said. "I'll try to text you when I land in California. Hopefully my phone won't turn into a brick like Hennings' did last year. If I don't text, it's probably because it's late and I don't want to wake you up, or my phone is being dumb. It isn't because I don't want to, okay?"

"Okay," she said.

"I just wanted you to know that I wouldn't do that to you," I said. "I try to be considerate and feel like I want to make sure you know when I get there."

"Okay," she said.

"Come on, man," Bridge called again.

"Coming," I shouted over my shoulder. "Talk to you soon," I said to her, and was rewarded with a brilliant smile, which I had to answer with my own.

I squeezed her hand through the break in the netting, then backed away, finally turning once I got close to the dugout. It was this weird sixth sense thing that just had me knowing where things were without really looking, especially in this ballpark. I'd barely gotten to know her, and I was already missing her. This was not what I expected, but it was definitely something I could get used to.

"WHERE'S YOUR HEAD AT?" COACH SHOUTED AT ME.

We were in game two of this three game set with the Redwoods, and I'd missed at least three pitches in the dirt, something I never did before.

"Sorry, Coach," I said.

"Sorry, my ass," he barked. "You're done for the night. Hit the showers and pull your head out of your ass. This isn't like you. I don't know what's going on, but you need to figure your shit out and get your head in the game, otherwise you're gonna find yourself with a flat ass from riding pine."

Coach was right, my head had been somewhere other than between the lines, and it was messing with not just my job, but everyone else on my team. I just couldn't get Kylie off my mind. I'd texted her when we landed, told her that I missed her, and she'd been sweet, saying she missed me, too. Now, though, I couldn't do anything but think about her, and how absolutely adorable she was. I wanted to get to know her better, learn whatever it was that made her shy and reserved, and find a way to help her battle that demon.

I walked down the tunnel to the clubhouse and tossed my gear into the locker, stripping off my uniform and heading to the showers to try to drown whatever was fucking me up out of my head. Unfortunately, the only thing on my mind was the pretty girl who was more skittish than a trapped rabbit. Maybe she'd feel brave enough to tell me what was going on if I called her. If I could get her to open up to me, I might be able to help her get over whatever it was that was bugging her. But we were still new in this relationship, and asking those kinds of questions was for a later date.

"Fuck," I mumbled as I glared at my phone.

"What's up?" Bridge asked.

I whipped around, not realizing that anyone else was in the room with me.

"Nothing," I lied.

"Bullshit," he said. "I know you don't get into these kinds of funks, so what's going on?"

"You really are the dad of the team, aren't you?"

He laughed, then just waited.

"Fine," I grumbled. "There's this girl."

"There always is," he said, but it was definitely said in jest, not as an insult.

"She's adorable," I continued. "Sweet, shy, but absolutely great."

"How long have you known her?" he asked.

"Since Friday," I replied.

"And she's already got you in knots," he said.

"I don't think you understand," I said.

"Then enlighten me," he replied, sitting down at the locker next to me.

"The night we had that event thing after the game," I began. "Well, I saw her in the stands. She just popped right out like it was meant to be, as if there was some reason she was sitting right there behind the dugout. With the way she was dressed, I was sure she would be coming to the event, so as soon as I got there, I started to look for her. I got sidelined a couple of times by some cougar trying her hardest to lay claim on me, but finally I found her. I gave her my number and asked her to let me know if she wanted to go have some lunch or dinner some time."

"You're pulling plays out of Hennings' book," he said, but didn't seem too upset about it.

"I am, but not like he was," I said. "Never would I do what he'd done to some women. Besides, this girl just seemed to be way too nice. Like, she was super shy, but friendly at the same time if that makes sense."

He nodded but didn't say anything.

"Anyway, she texted me," I said. "Like, she must have just stepped out of the stadium and sent it to me. She said we should have lunch the next day, so we did. Went to the International District and met her at a Korean barbecue place, which it was delicious by the way. While we were there, she had a panic attack. I don't know what brought it on, but she had gone wide-eyed and terrified."

"You take care of her?" he asked.

"Of course I did," I said. "Threw some cash on the table, way more than enough to cover the food, and picked her up and took her outside. Her friend was close by, so he saw what happened, and between the two of us, we were able to get her settled. We stopped at another shop after that, but it wasn't nearly as long as I'd wanted to spend with her. Instead of just bailing on her, though, I made sure she was with her friend and then told them I'd give them tickets to Sunday's game."

"Very nice," he said. "So, why are you all screwed up in the head? What are you not telling me?"

"I don't know," I said. "Like, she's really nice, but I can kind of tell she has some deep, dark secret or something that is probably really bad. I don't know what it could be, though, because I see nothing wrong with her, no reason for her to be so…"

"So different?" he offered.

"Yeah," I agreed. "She's just super quiet."

"So, not at all your type of girl," he said.

"Except, I think she is," I said.

We all knew we could go to him with questions about damn near anything, from romance to parenting to figuring out how to find an apartment. Basically, anything adult-ish we needed to know; Jonathan Bridge was the guy to ask.

"So, what's wrong?" he asked.

"I don't know," I said. "I guess I just need to give it some time and eventually it'll figure itself out. Or it won't."

"It will," he said. "It always does."

He slapped his knees with his hands and stood up, making his way back out to the dugout. I guess he just came in to talk to me, not for any real reason, which was kind of nice.

CHAPTER SEVENTEEN

*K*ylie...

Remi and I had damn near every streaming service imaginable, and we'd never felt the need to have any kind of cable system, but we soon realized that we couldn't watch the games unless we set up yet another service or got cable. My best friend, of course, found a streaming service that was less than five bucks a month that had the channel we needed to watch the games, and I'd been doing that the last couple of nights.

While I was trying my best to learn the sport, I was woefully unknowledgeable about it. I knew some things, like when we were in the field, we were trying to stop the other team from going all the way around the bases. When we were up to bat, as Remi said it was called, we were trying to get our players all the way around, and as many as possible. I'd noticed that Cole had been having a hard time catching balls when they were thrown in to him, and because of this, players for the other team were getting around the bases faster than they should.

That night, after one of their players hit the ball, it was thrown in to him, but he missed the catch, then got plowed over by the player coming in to score. I was worried about him being hurt, but he seemed to be okay when he got up. After that, though, he didn't come back out to catch the ball from the pitcher again for that game, and that made me wonder if he got hurt. I sent him a text, just to see if he was all right. I didn't expect anything to come back soon, so I went ahead and shut the television off and headed to bed. It was already late, Remi was out with friends, and I had a pretty big project that needed serious work done the next day, so I climbed under the covers and crashed.

I'd apparently forgotten to set my alarm, and when Remi went to leave and didn't see me up, he came into my room to ask if I was okay.

"What time is it?" I asked.

"It's just about eight," he said.

"Oh no," I cried, sitting up fast, rushing to get out of bed.

"What's the matter?" he asked as he followed me to the bathroom.

"I'm late," I said.

"No you're not," he replied through the door. "I'm just getting ready to head into the office. You can't be late because you're working from home today."

"Except I'm not," I shouted, flushing the toilet, and pulling a brush through my hair. "Shit," I said, snagging a knot at the nape of my neck.

"Let me get some clothes out for you," he said, his voice pulling away as he obviously went into my closet to find something.

I pulled the bathroom door open and shouted at him, "Pants. I haven't shaved my legs."

"Got it," he said, rummaging around in my closet. "Here," he said, thrusting a deep blue pantsuit at me, along with a burgundy blouse.

It was one of my favorite pieces, and he always knew how to make me feel like I was dressed perfectly, even when I was wearing leggings and an oversized shirt. I pulled my tee shirt off, clasped on my bra, and pulled the blouse on, buttoning it up the front. Remi had found shoes to go with the outfit and had placed them on the floor next to my bed.

"Laptop," I said.

He went out of my room to the desk I used in the living room, unplugged the machine from its docking station and slid it, as well as my mouse and headset, into the backpack I had for transport when I was working in the office. Within five minutes, we were out the door and hustling to the train station to catch a ride into downtown.

"What would your boyfriend think of you changing in front of me?" he asked when we were finally on the train.

"He's not my boyfriend," I argued, but didn't answer the rest of the question.

"Have you heard from him?" he asked.

"When he first got down to California," I said. "But not since then."

"You should text him," he said. "Remind him of how gorgeous you are and that you miss him."

"It's not that kind of a relationship," I said. "Besides, I don't want to sound desperate."

"You're not desperate," he said. "You're just interested. Nothing wrong with that."

"But if I come on too strong…"

"Nonsense," he said, squeezing my shoulder. "You're a beautiful girl, he's a beautiful boy. You two were meant for each other. Now, text him."

"As soon as we get to the office," I promised.

"I'm gonna hold you to that," he said, giving my shoulder another squeeze just as the train pulled to a stop at our destination.

We walked off the train, tapped our cards on the way out, and headed to the office. My big project was nearly done. I just needed to add a few minor touches to it, and then I would be meeting with my immediate supervisor to go over it and what to expect when it was presented to upper-level management.

Remi left me when he stepped off the elevator, but not before reminding me to text Cole. I just smiled and nodded, waiting to head up to my floor where I would be meeting with Jim Carlson, my supervisor. I found a cubicle that was unoccupied and began to set myself up.

"Hold up there," Jim said as I pulled my laptop out. "We're gonna meet in my office. I want to see what you have before we let anyone else see it."

"Okay," I said, dropping my laptop back into the backpack.

I followed him to his office, and he closed the door behind me. The space was fairly bare, what with most of us working from home in this department, but he did have a picture of his family sitting on the desk. I went to sit on one of the chairs across from the desk, but he ushered me to his own.

"Might as well get used to it," he said. "It will be yours as soon as I retire."

"What are you talking about?" I asked, completely confused.

"They're giving me the option to pick my replacement," he explained. "Told me that as long as the person I picked was a good worker, company focused, willing to learn and lead by example, they didn't really care who it was."

"But what about—"

"Nothing," he said, cutting me off. "You are the best one to take over. The work you do is phenomenal. You have good people skills, even though you say you don't, and honestly, I want this for you. You've worked really hard here, and you deserve to get this position."

"I don't know what to say," I confessed.

"Thank you would be a good start," he said. "Now, let's get this show on the road."

I was dumbfounded, completely caught off guard by this, and simply couldn't imagine myself in my boss's shoes. Apparently, though, I was the only one who thought that.

CHAPTER EIGHTEEN

ole...

> Hope you weren't hurt. Let me know when
> you can that you're okay. Good luck.

Kylie's message was not what I expected. I knew she wasn't a regular watcher of games, at least that's the impression I'd gotten. This message, though, was kind, thoughtful, and really just so sweet. It had come in an hour earlier though, so I figured she wasn't up, but went ahead and responded.

> Nothing but my pride is hurt. Thanks for
> checking in.

When I got up the next morning, I hadn't received a response. Not that it was necessary, but it was a bit surprising. She was usually pretty good about getting back quickly. I put it out of my mind, though, instead focusing on practice and preparing to watch Ramirez take my place on the field. It wasn't unusual for him to take the day game after a night one, but not usually two in the span of four games. I was definitely feeling the emotional bruises, along with the couple that came from my collision at the plate during the game the night before.

Ramirez had some questions about what to expect from Tanner, our Aussie, so I walked him through how the pitcher liked to get himself ready for the game. He was very thankful that I would willingly give up the secrets, but it wasn't like that. It was obvious that he felt bad about being put in, but I reassured him it was all part of the game, and everyone had an off day and needed to get themselves squared away sometimes. This was just one of those times for me.

It was well into the fifth inning when Ramirez hit a high fly ball toward the left field fence. It didn't go over but bounced off the wall. He tried to stretch it into a double, but their left fielder had a rocket for an arm and the throw was right on the money. Jose slid into the bag but was tagged out. Unfortunately, the way he slid, something happened to his wrist, and he didn't get up right away. When their short stop waved for the trainer to come out and check on him, I knew I would be going in to catch in the bottom of the inning at the very least.

The way their team was looking, it did not bode well for Ramirez at all, and I wondered if it was worse than just a jammed finger or something of the like. When he finally stood up, cradling his left hand, I knew it was bad. His hand hung in a really awkward way, and he wasn't letting the training coach even touch it. Coach Johnson caught my eye as they neared the dugout and nodded to me. I'd already pulled my mitt on and headed down toward the tunnel that led to the clubhouse, snagging Bridge to help me get warmed up.

Since Ramirez was the second out in the inning, I knew I wouldn't have much time to get ready, so I pushed myself with Bridge and was feeling comfortable by the time the next out happened, just a few pitches later. I trotted out to the field with my gear on, pulling my helmet down over my face and squatted behind the plate, waiting for Tanner's warm-up pitches. Somehow, I felt like he was relieved that I was back there instead of Ramirez because his warm-up tosses were all cutters, diving hard each time.

Fortunately, my brain had kicked into work mode, and I seemed to have left everything that wasn't related to the right here, right now of the game in the clubhouse. It was actually enjoyable to be back on the field after the struggles of the last two games, and I was able to snag balls that were so far out they should have gone to the backstop. Whatever was troubling the rest of the team seemed to fade away as well, and we pushed four runs across in the top of the sixth, three more in the seventh, including my two-run homer, and another couple in the eighth. We went from failing to crushing it in half an inning, and it felt good to be part of that.

After the game, the sports announcer for our local Seattle station grabbed me for a post-game interview.

"Were you expecting to come in today?" she asked.

"The game was all for Ramirez," I said. "He's been showing some great skill, and we wanted to give him a better chance to catch some of the nastier pitchers we have in our pen, so I was glad to give him the shot."

"Do you know what happened to his arm?"

"Not really sure," I said. "Sliding headfirst always has a risk of injury. Most of the time it's quick and easy to shake off, but this seemed to be a little bit more than that. I have no idea what they've done, or any of the answers as to what happened. I was just happy to be able to pick him up."

"Let's talk about that," she said. "You two play really well together. There's no competition between the two of you for that spot?"

"There's twenty-five on our roster," I said. "We all have our parts to play. The only competition is in the other dugout, and that's the way we like to keep it. I know every single player would love to play every day, but we can't do that. We have to share the load, and I think Jose and I do that pretty well."

"You do seem to," she agreed. "I'll let you get back in there. I know you're heading out right after the game, so I don't want to hold you up too much."

"Thanks," I said.

"Back to you," she said, and the light on the top of the camera went out.

"You don't know what's up?" she asked.

"I haven't heard anyone say anything," I said. "Could be just a jam, could be something worse. Not my job to figure out what it is, or how to fix it. I leave that to the much smarter people in this business."

"It certainly didn't look good," she said.

"No, it didn't," I agreed.

"Thanks," she said, and I made my way back to the dugout to head down the tunnel.

She was right in that we were heading out right from the stadium, so I didn't really have extra time to lose. I was quick with my post-game shower and dressing before we all loaded up on the bus to take us to the airport. Next stop was LA, which would be nice. I'd given my parents a couple of tickets to the game, what with it being not too far from where I grew up. It would be good to see them again.

CHAPTER NINETEEN

*K*ylie...

The day was insane, what with me going over the project with Jim, adding the final touches to it, then presenting it to the higher-ups. It was just so much. Add to that the fact that Jim was working really hard to make sure that I knew everything I needed to know before his retirement and my move up, it was just crazy. By the time I had a minute to myself to even think of anything other than work, I reached into my purse only to discover that I had left my phone at home in my haste to get out on time. I guess my text to Cole would have to wait until I got back home. Not that it would matter, he had a day game that day. At least I thought he did.

When Remi wandered over to my cubicle in the early afternoon, I was confused by the concern on his face.

"What's up?" I asked.

"You haven't answered any of my texts," he said.

"I forgot my phone," I replied. "No texts received at the office. Sorry."

"Oh, thank God," he said. "I was worried you were mad at me or something."

"Why would I be mad at you?" I asked.

"No reason," he said, but I knew he was lying.

"What did you do?" I demanded.

"Nothing," he said, and again, it was obvious he was lying.

"Just tell me," I said. "If I'm gonna get mad, might as well be here instead of in the comfort of our home where I can yell at you for it."

"It's really nothing," he said, and I knew it was a lost cause trying to get out of him whatever it was that he did. Once he'd made his mind up, swaying him took the work of a god or goddess, and I had neither's powers.

"Fine, whatever," I said. "It's been super crazy here today, so I really haven't been able to think about anything other than work."

"I heard a little something," he said.

"Oh, yeah?" I asked.

"And I'm all for it," he said.

I looked at him, completely baffled, because I had no idea what he was talking about.

"Your promotion," he said, much louder than what I would have liked.

"Shh," I said, trying to get him to be quieter. "I don't know who all knows."

"Everyone knows," he said. "Not officially, but everyone really knows."

"How?"

"You don't think gossip runs through the office like wildfire?"

"I know, but…" I stopped, realizing that he was right.

That was one of the reasons I'd never talked about my past with anyone here except Remi. He knew because he was there for most of it, but he also knew how shitty people could be if they knew the truth. It was why he was happy for me when I changed my name and every-thing that had anything to do with finding a job had been done under the new name.

"Yeah," he said, knowing what I was thinking. "So, we gonna go celebrate tonight?"

"Probably won't have time," I said. "You should see all the things

Jim has to do. It's nuts. I'm gonna need someone to keep me organized or something because it's a complete nightmare."

"You never need anyone to keep you organized," he said. "You're the most organized person I know. You have color coding for damn near everything in the house, and a plan for when things need to be done. Like, you should start a business on being organized, you're so good at it."

"I don't have time for anything like that," I said.

"If you wanted to, you'd make time," he replied. "I have the feeling you could do damn near anything you set your mind to."

"I mean, I guess," I said.

"Fine," he said. "I'm cooking you something amazing for dinner tonight, then you're gonna call your man and have a nice long chat with him in the privacy of your own room. Feel free to get freaky, babe, you deserve it."

I was laughing by the time he finished what he was saying. Like, I'm not that kind of person at all. I don't do freaky things, don't do anything like what he does. I mean, I was still a virgin for fuck's sake. He expected me to do something intimate over the phone with a guy I've known for less than a week? Sometimes he didn't make any sense. He still made me laugh though, so I guess he was good for something.

"Gotta run," he said, giving me a hug. "Congrats, like big time."

"Thanks," I said and watched him walk to the elevator.

I sighed, then sat down and started to work on the project's final pieces so I could get it into the system. I did wonder what Cole was doing, though. He'd been on my mind much more than anyone ever had in the past, and I wasn't sure whether it was a good thing or not.

CHAPTER TWENTY

$\mathcal{C}$ole...

I hadn't heard back from Kylie since the text I sent Tuesday night, but I didn't think much of it. She was probably working and didn't have time to be chatting me up. Honestly, it was probably good I wasn't distracted, especially having to head into the game so suddenly after Jose's injury. Turns out he had a severe sprain on his wrist, so they listed him as day to day. That also meant we had to call up another catcher, which meant sending someone down to the minors, at least for a couple of days.

While going back to the minors wasn't that big of a deal, some guys saw it as a failure on their part. That usually wasn't the case, though. Roster moves were a normal part of the year, and I'd done the back-and-forth shuffle when I was first moving up, so knew the struggle. I always looked at it as a way to improve myself, to get better at my position to ensure I would stay with the team long term at some point.

The most important thing was we were winning pretty well, even though it was still early in the season. Flying down to LA was so quick, it wasn't worth really getting comfortable, and once we were on the ground and heading to the hotel, I pulled my phone out for another check to see if I'd heard from her. Since there were no messages, I decided to send one just to let her know we'd made it to LA and were heading for the hotel.

> Landed and at the hotel in LA. Hope your day was good.

Sweet and innocent, just like her. I didn't know what her schedule was, or whether she was a work all day and night kind of person but was glad to get a response fairly quickly.

> Sorry, forgot my phone at home. Worked in the office today and lots going on. Did you win today? Did you play?

I thought about texting back but decided to give her a call instead.

"Hello?" she answered.

"Hi, Kylie," I said. "It's Cole."

"Oh, hi," she said. "Can you hold on for a minute?"

"Sure," I said.

I could hear her saying something, but her hand must have been over the microphone because it was muffled. Then I heard her moving from where she was to somewhere else, but I didn't know what that meant. Finally, after a bit, she came back to the phone.

"Sorry," she said. "Remi has a friend over and I figured we could talk better if I was in my room instead of sitting next to them on the couch."

"Privacy is nice," I said. "So, how was your day?"

"I got a promotion," she said, and while she sounded excited, there was something on the edge that made me unsure.

"Congratulations," I said. "Unless it's a bad thing."

"It's fine," she said. "I mean, it's good. At least I think it's good. Oh, I don't know."

"Hey," I said, trying to have a calming sound to my voice. "Why wouldn't it be a good thing?"

"It's just so much responsibility," she said.

"They wouldn't give you the responsibility unless they thought you could handle it, right?"

"I guess not," she said, but she didn't sound convinced.

"What all does the new position require?" I asked.

"Basically, I'd be doing what I do now, but also working with other people on the team to make sure they're doing what they're supposed to be doing," she said, speaking in a rapid-fire way that all the words nearly ran together.

"Slow down," I said, drawing the words out. "You're going so fast I can barely understand you."

"Sorry," she said and I could almost hear the blush running up her cheeks.

"No need to be sorry," I said. "It sounds like you're excited."

"And terrified," she added. "It's just so much. I don't know if I can do it all."

"Of course you can," I said. "I think you could probably do anything you put your mind to."

"But I might have to be in the office more," she said. "I don't know if it's worth it."

"You don't like going into the office?"

"Not if I can help it," she said. "I'd much rather just do my work in the comfort of my own place and not have to deal with all the office politics."

"Can you do the new job from home?"

"I mean, Jim does," she said. "He's just in the office more than I am. I'm usually only in there once every couple of weeks, so I'm not sure what would have to change with that schedule."

"You could always decline the offer," I said.

"Yeah, right," she said.

"What?" I asked. "You could. There's no rule that says you have to accept a promotion at your job."

"Isn't that kind of a slap in the face of the company, though?" she asked.

"Depends on how you word it," I said. "Like, you could say that you appreciate the confidence they are showing in you, but you would be more comfortable staying at your current position for the time being."

"Still sounds ungrateful," she said, and sounded dejected.

"So, then, take the position," I said. "You'll do well, I'm sure."

"How do you know?" she asked. "You barely know me."

"If they're offering it to you, they believe you can do it," I said. "I don't have to know you to know that."

She sighed, deep and heavy, like she was pondering the entirety of the world's problems. Finally, though, she came back to me.

"I'm gonna do it," she said. "But I'm gonna ask that they make it a temporary position for a little while, just to make sure I can handle it."

"You sound like a supervisor to me," I said. "Already problem solving and finding solutions. Good job."

"I guess," she said.

"Well, I'm proud of you," I said.

"Thanks," she replied.

I waited, wondering what else I could talk to her about. I didn't want to just hang up because I liked to hear her voice. It's not like we had any kind of a relationship that we could discuss or anything, but it was still nice to listen to her talk. Honestly, she could talk about anything and I'd be happy to listen.

"Did you play today?" she asked, and it took me a bit by surprise.

"Oh, yeah," I said, finding my voice. "Jose slid into second and screwed up his wrist, so I had to go in to take over."

"Oh no," she said, concern clear in her voice. "Is he going to be okay?"

"Nothing a couple of days off won't cure," I said. "At least, that's the hope. We'll have to have someone fly down to finish out the next few days, but it shouldn't be a big deal."

"Wait," she said. "Do you have extra players around or something?"

"There are several levels of the team," I said. "I forget you don't watch it, so probably don't know all the things I do."

"Yeah, I don't know much of anything, honestly," she replied. "But I'm trying to learn. Remi has been a huge help with that, too."

"Gotta say, that means a lot to me," I said. "That you'd be willing to learn the game so you understand what I'm talking about."

"It's been really fun to learn," she said. "Like, I had no idea how many little things happened during a game that meant so much to the whole thing. I mean, who would have thought that the guy throwing the ball could do it at over a hundred miles an hour? That's kind of ridiculous."

"You should come out to the stadium one day and do some pitching," I said. "We can see how fast you can pitch the ball. Could also hit a batting cage some time, just to show you what it's like."

"I don't think so," she said, and it was almost as if it were a finality, like something she couldn't even fathom.

"Why not?" I asked.

"I am absolutely *not* athletic in any sense of the word," she said. "I would probably hurt someone, or myself, if I tried to do either of those things."

"Nah," I argued. "I'd be right there with you, making sure you did everything just right."

"I don't know," she hemmed, but I think she was actually thinking about it, which just made me happy.

"Tell you what," I said. "Let's plan on doing something when I get back to town. I'll get everything set up so you don't have to do anything, just meet me. That sound good?"

"Umm," she said, clearly trying to decide. "Okay," she finally said. "Let's do it."

"You want Remi to come with you?" I asked, not wanting her to feel like she had to do this all alone.

"Oh, no," she responded. "I think I can do it myself."

"Great," I said, very glad it would just be the two of us. "I'll set everything up and let you know. Any day or night that would be best?"

"I work during the week," she said. "But I'm usually off by around five or so. Of course, you probably work at night, so that might not be the best. I'm almost always available on the weekend, though."

"I'll look at our schedule tomorrow and figure out a day that will work," I said. "I think we have an off day in the next home stand, so can probably do something that day."

"Okay," she said. "That sounds fun."

She actually did sound excited, which I was glad for. I didn't want to push her to do anything she wasn't comfortable with, but I really did want to get to know her better, and in a more casual setting.

"I'll text you the details," I said. "I should probably go, though. Gotta get some sleep before tomorrow's game."

"Okay," she said. "Sleep well and good luck tomorrow. Oh, wait, am I not supposed to say good luck?"

"It's completely fine," I said. "Sleep well."

"Goodnight," she said, then disconnected the call.

I smiled and plugged my phone in. This was turning into something more than just my usual flirting, and I was here for it. I really did like Kylie, and it seemed the feeling was mutual.

CHAPTER TWENTY-ONE

*K*ylie...

"Goodnight," I said, then pushed the call end button on my cell.

I had no idea why I'd agreed to meet with him and do that baseball stuff he was talking about. He had no idea what trouble he was heading for with me. My coordination when it came to sports type things was beyond awful. And he wanted me to try to throw the ball and also to try to hit a ball? Yeah, this was probably going to go about as well as a fart in church.

Heading back to the main area of the apartment, Remi looked up from the couch, his arm around his friend who had fallen asleep on his shoulder.

"Was that Cole?" he asked in hushed tones.

"Yeah," I said. "He invited me to go and throw a ball and hit one, too. Said he wanted to see how fast I could throw it."

"Does he know you're about as coordinated as a baby giraffe?" he asked.

"I tried to tell him," I said. "He said it wasn't a problem, that he'd help me out with everything and be there to show me how to do it."

"You okay with it?"

"I think so," I said. "He asked if I wanted you to come with, but I said that I could do it on my own."

"That's my girl," he said. "You're growing up so fast."

I laughed, probably a little too loud, as his friend shot me a look that said I was clearly disrupting his sleep or whatever. Remi obviously saw my reaction and jostled his friend.

"Time for you to head home," he said, which was odd since I thought the guy was going to stay the night.

"Probably," he mumbled, clearly thinking the same thing. "Call me?" he asked, looking at Remi when he stood up.

"Sure," Remi said, but I heard the rest of the statement he didn't say.

He was so not going to call the guy back, and I couldn't blame him. The guy didn't really do much when they were together. He'd eat our food, drink our beer or wine coolers, and not bother to clean up after himself or bring some of his own to share. Remi was a patient guy and put up with a bit, but when it wasn't reciprocated, he was done.

The guy probably knew this as well, as he said goodbye several times before walking out the door, like he was waiting for Remi or me to tell him it was fine and he could stay. Once the door was shut, Remi let out a long sigh and shook his head.

"Should have ended this a long time ago," he said, getting up and going to the door to lock the deadbolt. "He's a user, and honestly, I'm over it."

"Know your limits," I said.

"Exactly," he replied.

That was a phrase he'd taught me when we were kids and first met. The kids at school would pick on me and tease me because of who my dad was, and that my mom died. They'd say absolutely horrible things to me, and about me, behind my back, and nearly every day I would end up crying by the time I got back home.

Thankfully, Remi was bigger than most of the kids, having had his growth spurt early on. He towered over almost everyone at fourteen, so everyone was afraid of him. Add in the fact that his parents were very open and willing to let him experiment with his identity that he had run out of fucks before we even met. His booming deep voice was another thing that freaked the kids out. He'd do this crazy thing where he talked from his throat instead of mouth and the way his words sounded were terrifying. He'd told me it was the devil in him, but honestly, I think he just liked to fuck with people, and found the most innocent way to do it and not get into trouble.

He'd put his arm around my shoulder and squeeze me to him, saying, "Know your limits." When I'd asked him what he meant, he said that we can only handle so much, and when we reached the limit, we were done. Didn't matter if someone else could handle more, or if it was less than we handled before. In that moment, we knew that we had reached the limit and could do no more.

"You wanna talk about the promotion?" he asked.

"Ugh," I said, flopping down on the couch. "I don't know what to do."

"Take it," he said.

"That's what Cole said," I replied. "He said I could do it. Said they wouldn't have offered it to me if they didn't think I could."

"He's right," he said. "You can do it, for sure. Jim will help you get everything set up and organized so that you will do amazing. Besides, it's not like you don't know what you're doing. It's the same stuff, right?"

"It is," I said. "But I have to tell people what to do."

"No," he countered. "You have to delegate to them what you need them to do to make sure that the project as a whole goes forward. You're all part of the same team. You just happen to now be the captain. Jim will make sure you know who is best at doing what, so don't worry about that."

"I guess," I said, although I didn't even sound enthused to my ears.

"Girl, look at me," he said, and the seriousness in his voice was something I hadn't heard before. "You are a brilliant woman who knows so much about so many things. You're just not confident in yourself, which has got to stop. I love you with all my heart, but it's time you started looking at yourself as a winner instead of the daughter of a loser. What your dad did was horrible in every single way possible. But his faults do not define you. He made his bed and is having to lie in it by himself."

"I know, but—"

"Nope," he said cutting me off. "There are no buts except your fabulous one and mine. He's trash, but you aren't. You're all your mama and grandparents. They raised you right, and that's the most important thing. I know you cut down on your visits with your therapist, but I think now would be a good time to set something up. Just to talk out what's going on right now and how it's effecting you."

"You're probably right," I said.

"So," he said, drawing the word out.

"I'll call and get something set up tomorrow," I said, knowing he was right.

"Good girl," he said. "Now, let's hit the sack so you can rock your new job starting first thing in the morning."

"Ugh, don't remind me," I said, but it didn't seem as daunting as it had just a few short minutes earlier.

CHAPTER TWENTY-TWO

*C*ole...

The games in LA were pretty awesome, as we won three of the four there. My parents were happy to see me as well, and we had lunch on Saturday before the game. It was nice to catch up with them and tell them about what had been going on in my life. They said Rachel was doing well and holding her own in her new job, which was really good to hear. Her struggles had been bad at one point, but the fact that I made enough to help pay for some medical stuff for her really was a good thing. I was happy to help out, especially since it seemed to be working, and she was getting her life back on track.

I told them about Jose's injury, and that I was working hard to keep my head in the game, especially now that we were down one catcher and had a rookie as my backup. It was nice to have a normal conversation and meal out with them without having people bugging me for photos and autographs. I didn't mind it sometimes, but people really needed to read the room. There was a time and a place for everything, and often they chose the wrong of both.

I'd been able to talk to Kylie before the game on Saturday, and she said she had been watching the games with Remi to learn everything she could from him. She said she was really starting to understand things, which was a really nice thing to hear. Flying to Houston was a nightmare because of a huge storm that had come through our path. I didn't usually have any issues with flights, but this one was really rocky. Some of the guys even ended up hurling in flight, which then created a domino effect through the plane. Thankfully, I was spared that unpleasantness, but it still wasn't great.

Games with Houston were always interesting, especially after the scandal from the previous season and all it revealed. The fans hated us because we were the ones who figured it out, and the players hated us for stealing their secret. It was just so much pressure, and we ended up losing two of the three games we played there. It wouldn't be the end of the world or anything, I just hated losing to that team in particular. Something about it just felt icky.

By the time we got home it was late and I didn't want to bother Kylie with my usual text saying I'd landed, so I just took my shit home and crashed. I woke up to a message that both warmed my heart and made me feel like a dick.

Let me know you made it home safe. You didn't text, so I wasn't sure.

I wanted to call her and apologize, but figured she was at work and I didn't want to mess with that, so I just sent a text.

We got back late and I didn't want to wake you. Sorry if you worried. I missed you.

I'd already sent it before I realized what I'd written at the end and couldn't take it back. It was the truth, though. I did miss her, but it shouldn't have been something I pushed onto her. She already had enough on her mind with her new promotion in the works, which it sounded like she was excelling at from our texts and calls while I was gone.

I headed to the bathroom to get things going for the day with, as my dad would say, "A shit, shower, and shave." He'd been in the military after high school but was already out when he met my mom. It was apparently a phrase he'd used during his time in, so who was I to argue? I mean, it was exactly what needed to happen, so there we were.

Once my ritual was done, I headed to the kitchen to grab some breakfast before heading into the stadium. I always tried to make sure there was at least something available the first day back from a trip, and I'd done that this time as well. Not quite everything I wanted, but definitely enough to get me through until I could grab some stuff.

After food and cleaning up, I grabbed my bag, my phone, and my keys and headed out to work. It was a quick drive, and I got to the stadium pretty timely. The nice thing about getting there early was that I could hit the batting cages and get my workout in before a lot of the guys got in, which was nice. Turned out I was the first one in, so I got it all done early. Ramirez had been taking some catches in Houston during warm-up, and was feeling pretty good about his wrist, so I figured he'd probably catch tonight, but wasn't positive.

"Hey," he said as he came in. "Can you work with me?"

"Sure," I said, knowing that it was likely going to be needed if he was going to start.

We headed to the field and began the game of catch, starting fairly close and moving further apart with each toss, just a step or two, until we were almost as far apart as the throw from home to second. He was accurate and fairly firm in his throws, so I figured he'd be ready to go in.

Then it happened. He threw the ball to me and winced. It was quick, just a flash across his face, but I held the ball and walked toward him.

"What's up?" he asked.

"I could ask you the same thing," I said. "What was that flinch?"

"Just a twinge," he said. "Nothing to worry about."

"You don't know that," I argued. "Think we better talk to Gryffin and see what he has to say."

"He'll pull me," he said.

"If you think he's gonna pull you, you should do the right thing," I said. "If you screw it up more, it'll just delay your return. Do you want to be out the rest of the year?"

"Fuck," he muttered.

"Better safe than sorry," I said.

"I guess," he said, walking with me back to the clubhouse.

We saw the trainer as we walked in and I made sure I told him exactly what I saw, which kind of pissed Jose off, but he would learn to live with it. No one wanted to have something screw you up, especially this early in the season. It was better to have a short stint on the injured list than end up out for the season with something that a little time could take care of.

By the time the game started, I was focused and ready to go. Would have been nice to see Kylie, but it just wasn't gonna work this time around. At least we had a day game on Wednesday and the day off on Thursday, so hopefully I could convince her to have dinner with me and see if we could get things going in the romance area of the relationship. I didn't want to push, but it was getting hard to hold out and just wait for things to progress slowly. I wouldn't rush, but also wanted to make sure she wanted the same things I did.

CHAPTER TWENTY-THREE

*K*ylie...

It had been over a week since I'd seen Cole in person. Even though I got to watch him play on television, it wasn't the same. When I woke up to a text on Wednesday morning asking if I was free for dinner, my heart did a little jump I didn't expect.

I'd been working hard ever since Jim told me he wanted me to take over for him, and I'd found that I really enjoyed mapping out a schedule and slotting people into the places they excelled in and letting them go. The transition would not be painless, of course, but the rest of the team seemed good with me being in charge.

While I was learning the new role, I'd spent time in-office more than at home, which was not as much fun as I liked, but it was a necessary evil I could endure. Luckily, though, I'd planned to work from home on Wednesday, so I would have plenty of time to figure out what I wanted to wear and get ready early enough to not look like a troll when I met him.

"You good?" Remi asked when he walked in at lunch.

"What are you doing here?" I asked.

"Working from home this afternoon," he said. "Didn't you get my text?"

"Obviously not," I replied.

"Have you eaten today?"

Remi was always taking care of me. I realized that I'd done nothing but drink coffee since I got up that morning, and by the time he'd come home, I was on my fourth or fifth cup. Holding the mug up, I watched him scowl and head to the kitchen, mumbling under his breath something about me being dead if he weren't around. He was probably right, though not for lack of food in my system. No, he'd been keeping me alive and away from trouble since the first day we met, and there was no one I'd rather have doing that than him.

Before I knew what was happening, he shoved a bowl of cottage cheese in front of me with a spoon, along with a cup of fruit we had cut up from earlier in the week.

"Eat," he said.

"Okay, I'm just gonna—"

"Eat," he barked with more authority. "This will wait."

I rolled my eyes so hard I saw my own brain, but set my coffee cup down and picked up the spoon. The first bite was much better than it should have been, and I realized that I should probably get on a schedule to get food into me on a regular basis without having to rely on Remi. He'd disappeared into his bedroom after fixing me lunch, and when he came back out, he was in his lounge pants and a tee shirt.

"You look comfy," I said around the bite of apple in my mouth.

"The office was stifling today," he said. "I needed to have my brain free from the constant comments from the nags in the office."

"I thought you got along with everyone there," I said.

"June," he said.

I looked at him, very confused, and waited for him to explain what he meant, but he just flopped down on the couch and turned on the television. Deciding that I would just let him do whatever he needed, I finished my food and set the bowls aside to dive back into my work.

When my phone started ringing later, I was thoroughly engrossed in my project and jumped at the sound. I picked it up and answered without even checking to see who was on the other end.

"Hey," Cole said.

"Oh, hi," I said, blinking.

"I thought we were meeting at six," he said.

"We are," I replied.

"It's almost seven," he said, and I looked at the clock on my laptop.

"Oh my God," I groaned. "I am so sorry. I completely got lost in work. I'm kind of a hot mess right now but can grab a shower and meet you if you still want."

"Why don't I come to you," he said.

"Umm," I hummed, looking around the apartment. "How long until you would be here?"

"Don't know where you live," he said.

"Oh yeah," I replied. I rattled off our address, then added, "Let me just make sure Remi's cool with it."

"Sure," he said. I pressed the mute button on the phone and hollered to my roommate.

"What?" he shouted from his room.

"You okay with Cole coming over?" I asked.

"Absolutely," he said. "You shower, I'll clean. It'll be fabulous."

"He said yes," I said into the phone. I could hear him saying something, so was confused, but then realized that I hadn't unmuted it, so I did that and repeated myself.

"Great," he said. "Should I bring something for all of us? Does he have anyone else there with you guys?"

"You don't need to do that," I said.

"I want to," he said. "What's the use of having money if you can't share it every now and then?"

"Umm, okay," I said. "It's just him and me, I think."

"I'll be gone," Remi said. "You need to have some alone time with him."

"I guess Remi has plans," I said, looking at him like I was gonna kill him, but he just smiled at me.

"Okay," Cole said. "I'll get something for the two of us. Any preference?"

"Whatever you want is fine with me," I said, because I honestly couldn't remember where we'd said we were gonna meet.

"Perfect," he said. "Is there parking near you?"

"I think there might be some street parking," I said. "I honestly don't know because I don't have a car."

"Don't worry about it," he said. "I'll figure it out. Be there in about half an hour if that's good."

"Sure," I said.

"Can't wait," he replied, then disconnected the phone.

"Go," Remi said when I looked at him. "Shower and get all sexy. I got this."

He was in the kitchen, washing up the leftover dishes from the day, which was really all there was to do as far as cleaning up went, so I headed into my bathroom to get a quick shower. When I came out of the bathroom, Remi had laid out a nice dress with some pretty sexy underwear. It probably should have been odd that he was picking these things out, but it wasn't for us. We were siblings for all intents and purposes, but the kind that were also best friends. He had done things like this before for me, although not quite this intensely.

I dressed in what he set out and stepped out of the bedroom to see a completely transformed shared space. Remi had tidied up my desk, put a tablecloth on the little dinette set we had, and set it with dishes, including wine glasses and candles.

"Let me look," he said from the kitchen.

I blinked and looked at him, then showed him the dress he'd picked for me.

"Stunning as always," he said. "I've got both a red and a white wine chilled and in the fridge. I didn't know what you were eating, so didn't want to assume. I'm heading over to Craig's for the night, so you have the whole place to yourselves. Do things I want to do with him but be safe."

"Remi," I chastised, turning what was likely the same shade of red as the wine he'd put into the fridge.

Just then there was a knock on the door. Remi went to it, picking up his backpack with what I assumed was his laptop and a change of clothes, and opened it up.

"Good to see you," he said. "I was just heading to a friend's house. Have a good night."

With those words, he was out the door and Cole was left standing stupefied in the portal.

"Come on in," I said, walking toward him.

"He's something," he said with a laugh.

"Yeah," I replied, closing the door after he'd come in. "Smells good."

"It does," he replied, then looked around. "I see you're all set up."

"Remi did that," I admitted. "He's kind of a hopeless romantic, but I love him."

"Where shall I set this?" he asked, holding up the bag with the food.

"Let's put it here," I said, leading the way to the kitchen. "Red or white?" I asked after opening the fridge.

"Not much of a wine drinker," he admitted. "Whatever you think is best."

"I'm not much of one, either," I said. "It's kind of Remi's thing, so I just go along."

"I'm good with whatever you want," he said, placing the bag of food on the counter.

He opened the bag, and the aroma wafted from it, setting my stomach to groaning.

"I guess it's a good thing I got here when I did," he said, laughing. "Sounds like you're starving."

I just stood there, blushing, not exactly sure what to say. I was embarrassed about my body being stupid, but also the fact that I was alone in my apartment with a very handsome man who made my body react in ways I wasn't used to. It was just too much and I could feel myself shutting down.

CHAPTER TWENTY-FOUR

*C*ole...

"I guess it's a good thing I got here when I did," I said with a laugh. "Sounds like you're starving."

She blushed standing there, but the way her eyes were, I wondered whether she was going into a panic attack.

"Hey," I said, reaching my hand out to her elbow. "You good?"

She startled at my touch, but then took a deep breath and nodded.

"Good," I said, smiling. "Shall we dish up in the kitchen or at the table?"

"Let me grab the plates," she said, moving to the table with its fine setting.

We dished our meals in silence. Watching her move in her own space, knowing where everything was, and being quite confident in it, was wonderful. She was absolutely beautiful, almost ethereal, in her movements, and I wanted to just stand and stare at her.

"What?" she asked when she caught me watching her.

"Just watching your confidence," I said. "It's amazing."

"Really?"

"Yeah," I replied. "When I first met you, you were shy and reserved. Even when we had lunch, you were on edge, as if something might jump out at any moment and snatch you away. The way you are here, though, is a wonder to behold."

Blinking, she just stared at me, like I'd said something completely unrealistic or something she'd never thought of before.

"I don't know what to say to that," she said, finally.

"Nothing needs to be said," I replied. "Shall we eat?"

"Oh yeah," she said, realizing we'd just been standing next to each other, our plates fully loaded.

She picked up her plate, and I did the same with mine, following her to the table that had been set very nicely with candles and everything.

"Do you want me to light the candles?" I asked.

"Umm, sure," she replied.

"Matches or a lighter?"

"Oh, yeah," she said.

Retracing her steps to the kitchen, she opened a drawer and pulled out one of those barbecue lighter things. The ones with the long black tube where the fire came out at the end. She handed it to me and I pushed the safety up and let the fire kiss the wicks of the candles, bringing them to life on the small table. The only light that was on in the room was the one over the sink in the kitchen, so it had been somewhat dim in the space. The candles brought a warmth to it, shining on her face with dancing shadows that just made me want to stare at her for hours.

She looked at me, one hand on the back of her chair, and the other on the edge of the table next to the lighter. I wasn't sure what she was waiting for, but also didn't want to disrupt whatever spell she seemed to be under. Without taking her eyes off me, she slid into the seat. I did the same and watched as she pulled her napkin from under her fork and set it on her lap. I mirrored her move, placing my napkin down below the table. Finally, after about a million years, she blinked and looked down at her plate, picking up her fork to begin the meal.

"I hope you like it," I said.

"Smells good," she whispered, not raising her eyes.

Instead of eating, though, she kind of just pushed the food around her plate. I reached over and placed my hand on hers. She jumped, her eyes wide, looking right at me. Pulling back, I tried to figure out what just happened.

"Sorry," she said, and tears welled up in her eyes.

"Oh, hey, no," I said, getting up, letting my napkin fall to the floor as I rounded the table to squat next to her. "Nothing to be sorry about. What can I do to help?"

Her eyes were wide, her breathing shallow, and she was just sitting there. I couldn't stand the fear I saw in her eyes. My body just did what it thought was best, which was to gather her into my arms and hold her. She kind of fell out of the chair onto me and we sort of fell to the ground, her on my lap, sort of, and my arms around her.

"I'm sorry," she stammered, trying to shift away.

"I've got you," I said, holding her still, while trying desperately to make sure she couldn't feel the reaction my body had to her being so close, especially in this awkward position.

"I'm sorry," she said again, then said it one more time, just repeating the phrase over and over again.

I rubbed her back, holding her still, and eventually she relaxed enough that she wasn't stiff in my arms.

"I've got you," I repeated several times, while her body sort of settled itself.

Eventually she started to laugh. It bubbled up from her swiftly, and she clamped her hand over her mouth to try to stifle it.

"Are you laughing at yourself or me?" I asked.

"I don't know," she said through the giggles.

"Honestly, I don't even care," I said. "I just really like that sound."

She was so close, her face just inches from mine, and I could see to the depths of her soul in her bright blue eyes. There was pain there, something that was so deep she tried to shield it, but it poked out somehow. I took my hand and brushed some of her dark hair from her eyes and she sucked in a breath. Without moving much else, I eased my lips closer to hers, giving her plenty of time and space to stop it if she wanted, but she didn't stop it. Instead, she moved toward me with an equal measure of hesitancy, as if we were both afraid we'd break something if our lips met.

Instead of breaking, though, we shared a sweet, simple, delicate, and chaste kiss, one I hadn't had with a girl in a long time. It was something that was both perfect, and not nearly enough. Her eyes had fluttered closed, her breath soft and sweet. When she pulled back, she took a minute before she regained herself and opened her eyes.

"Sorry," she said, her voice raspy with an emotion I couldn't quite name.

"I liked it," I replied.

"Oh," she said, obviously surprised. "I figured you'd had your fair share of women who actually knew how to kiss, and since mine was so awful, and it was so short, and I didn't even do it right, and..."

I stopped her rambling with another press of my lips to hers, showing her exactly how I felt about the sweetness of our first kiss. My guess was she wasn't very experienced in these things, although I could have been completely wrong on that assumption as well. Either way, it stopped her words. When I pulled back, her eyes were closed and her hand lifted to her lips, as if she could feel me there with it, holding the memory in for future reference or something.

Finally, she blinked her eyes open and stared at me. Whatever she was thinking of asking died on her lips as she smiled. I don't know what was showing on my face, but whatever it was must have made her feel confident or something, because she placed a hand on my cheek and leaned in one more time for a quick peck on the lips.

"I'm hungry," she said, shifting her hips against my lap.

The expression on her face when she felt my body's natural reaction to her closeness was both comical and adorable. Her eyes went big, and she turned to stare right into my eyes.

"Umm," she hummed, obviously unsure what to think.

"Sorry," I said. "Natural reaction. Not anything I can help."

I shifted myself under her, which only made things worse for me, but helped her to her feet. Standing up myself, I shifted my erection to hopefully make it less awkward and pulled her chair out for her to sit down once again.

"Thank you," she said when I pushed her in.

"You're more than welcome," I replied, picking up my napkin from where it had fallen just a few minutes before.

Holding her fork in her hand, she scooped up some of the pasta on her plate and went to take a bite. I stared, watching every movement of hers as she slipped the fork into her mouth. I couldn't help but let out a little groan as she closed her eyes to savor the flavor. Unfortunately, that caused her to open her eyes again and stare at me, confusion clear on her face.

"What?" she asked around the forkful of food in her mouth.

"Just appreciating the view," I said. "Sorry, that was rude. I just..."

Yeah, nothing I could think of would make what I just said any better, and I knew it was sort of creepy and cringe worthy, but it just kind of tumbled out. Instead of being embarrassed or angry, though, she laughed. Like full on, from her gut, laughed out loud. Smiling, I let myself relax and enjoy the meal we shared.

CHAPTER TWENTY-FIVE

*K*ylie...

"Just appreciating the view," he said. "Sorry, that was rude. I just..."

I damn near choked on my food as I laughed. I had no idea what he was talking about with a view, but it seemed somewhat, I don't know, erotic? No, maybe, I don't know. All of this couple type stuff was so far out of my league it wasn't even funny.

"Aren't you going to eat?" I asked after I'd swallowed, wanting desperately to get the attention off me and onto anything else.

"Oh, yeah, sorry," he replied, picking up his own fork.

Watching him eat, after what he'd said, and the kiss we'd shared – which was so sweet and not nearly enough – was fascinating. It was like I realized that mouths could do so much more than just speak and eat. They were meant for things other than those two simple actions. He smiled at me watching him eat, and I felt embarrassed, so I picked up my fork and continued eating my meal.

We ate our meal in silence for a little bit, which was nice and not awkward at all. It was what I'd feared would happen when I ran out of things to talk about or whatever. It was actually really comfortable to just share a meal without any ulterior motives pressing against us.

Like we could simply share the same space and not need to add words to it.

"How was your day?" he asked after a bit.

"Pretty busy," I admitted. "I'm really sorry I stood you up and you had to come all the way over here."

"It was no trouble at all," he said. "I was glad you felt comfortable enough to invite me."

"You kind of invited yourself," I said.

"But you let me come," he replied. "You didn't have to. You could have said you just weren't able to make it because of work, but you didn't. I appreciate that."

"Thanks," I said.

"Have you lived here long?" he asked.

"A few years," I replied.

I could see he was pretty much finished with his food, and I was definitely full enough to be done as well but had leftovers. How did that work in this kind of situation? Did I keep them for myself, or did I send them home with him? I mean, he paid for them, so technically they were his. But I ate from this dish, so my germs were kind of all up in it, too.

"You sure are thinking hard over there," he said with a smile.

"Sorry," I replied, looking down at my plate.

"Hey," he said, getting up from his chair. He placed his hand under my chin and raised my head so that I was looking at him. "You never have to apologize to me."

I nodded, unable to form words around the lump in my throat. He smiled at my nod, then bent low to lay another sweet kiss on my lips.

"Let's get these leftovers in the fridge," he said. "Unless you're not done."

"I'm done," I said, standing to take my plate.

Scraping the leftovers back into the box they came out of, I closed it up and set it in the fridge. He took the initiative to run water over the dishes, looking around the kitchen.

"No dishwasher?" he asked.

"We are the dishwasher," I replied.

"I'll wash and you can dry," he said, rolling the sleeves of his button-up shirt over his forearms.

"I can just wash them later," I said.

"No need to wait," he said. "I ate, so I can help clean up."

I didn't really have any time to argue because he turned the water on and grabbed the scrubber that sat on the edge of the sink, wetting it, and pressing the pump on the soap dispenser to add the cleaning suds. It took a minute for it to register, but I got to work, grabbing a cloth to dry the dishes as he handed them to me after rinsing them. In just a few minutes, we had the dishes washed, dried, and put away in our cupboards.

"See," he said, drying his hands on the towel. "Didn't take long at all. Now you don't have to worry about them later."

"Thanks," I said, dropping the towel on the edge of the sink.

We stood there, standing close, yet not touching. It was nice, but also awkward. I wasn't sure what was supposed to happen next. He raised his hand slowly, placing the palm against my cheek, his thumb tracing along my lips. It was a gesture I hadn't experienced before, but it was nice. Closing the space between us with one step, he lowered his head, ever so slowly, down to press his lips against mine. His hand pushed into my hair at the back of my head, holding me to him, but not so forcefully that I couldn't get away if I wanted. I didn't want to move anywhere, and honestly, I just kind of let my body do its own thing.

My hands slipped around his waist and held him to me as his other hand went to the small of my back. He pulled me closer, even though we were already touching, and I could feel his erection press into my stomach which made me gasp a little. He used that small movement of my lips to plunge his tongue into my mouth, not forcefully, but firmly.

I had absolutely no experience with intimacy of this nature, and I kind of froze, unsure what to do. He must have sensed my uneasiness and pulled back, looking into my eyes, concern creasing his brow.

"I'm sorry," he said, moving away from me.

I pulled him back with my arms around his waist and said, "I'm sorry. I don't know what I'm doing."

"We can wait," he said, though the bulge in his pants pressed into me begged to differ, as I felt it throb against me.

"I've just never…"

I let the sentence trail off, not sure how to broach the subject of my virginity in all things romance. His lips curved into a smile that made his dimples show, and that brought a smile to my lips.

"We can stop any time you want," he said. "No problem at all. I don't want you to be uncomfortable in the least, so if you want to stop, you just stop. Okay?"

I nodded, not trusting my voice at all. Again, slowly, he leaned down and pressed his lips to mine. Instead of thinking, I just let my body do whatever it wanted, which was to open to his kiss, allow him to invade my mouth in a way no one ever had before, and enjoy the feel of everything. My eyes had fluttered shut and my hips pressed against him, like I couldn't get close enough. Then I moaned. I had no idea I'd done it until I felt his lips turn up. He pulled away from me and smiled down at me with something like a sparkle in his eyes, which made no sense since we'd blown the candles out before coming into the kitchen.

"You want to sit on the couch?" he asked, and I nodded, still not sure I could voice any words that would make sense.

He guided me toward the couch without letting me go. It wasn't like he was hauling me over to it, more like gently persuading me in the direction he wanted me to go. He sat down first, right at the end of it, then pulled me down onto his lap. I went without question, still so unsure of how this whole thing worked between couples. The arms of the couch were high, so the way I was sitting had my back against the arm, my legs over his one leg that was up against it. His arm around my back was up on the top of the rest, his hand on my shoulder, the other on my knee, which was bare.

The warmth from his palm was an odd sensation against the shudder I felt in my body. I wasn't cold at all but felt like my body was just humming with an energy I couldn't place.

"You okay?" he asked.

"Yeah," I replied, surprised my voice didn't quiver.

"Good," he said, then pressed his hand on my shoulder to move me toward him.

I went with the motion, leaning down to press my lips against his, my hand coming up to rest on his chest just below his shoulder. The hand on my knee started flexing, his fingers sliding up and down, not moving anywhere, just kind of kneading my leg. Between that and the kiss, my mind kind of was trying to short circuit or something, unsure where its focus should be. Instead of trying to figure anything out, though, I just pressed myself more against him, my chest against his. He moved his arm to the back of my head, holding me somewhat in place where he just kept kissing me.

After hours or days or seconds, I couldn't tell which, he released me and shifted under my butt. Whether it was by design or an accident, it shifted me so that I nearly fell off his leg, leaning more onto him than off. The hand that was on my knee shifted to keep me from falling, but also managed to run right up under the skirt of my dress to my ass. That warm hand right there was something that I didn't know what to do with. It wasn't that I didn't like it, I just didn't know what to do.

My face must have shown my shock and confusion because he quickly made sure I was stable before pulling his hand away. Instead of letting it go, though, I reached down and stopped its movement, effectively pinning his hand on my hip. His eyes were wider than I remember them being and he smiled again, with those dimples that a girl could get lost in.

"You doing okay?" he asked. "Cause we can stop if you want."

"I don't want you to stop," I said, and the tone of my voice was raspy, which only made him smile deeper.

"You're sure?" he asked, which was really nice that he wasn't being forceful at all.

"I am," I said, pushing his hand back to where it had been just a moment before.

"You keep this up and things could get messy," he said.

"If you help me clean up, I think we'll be fine," I said.

Instead of staying the way we were, he kind of lifted me up to straddle his lap, shifting away from the arm of the couch enough that there was room for my leg to be beside him. Both of his hands found their way under my skirt, but stayed somewhat respectable and simply held my hips. In that moment, I realized that my panties were wet, which was not something I expected.

I mean, I knew about sex, it wasn't something I didn't have *any* knowledge of. I'd just never experienced it, or even anything close to it. Hell, I hadn't even ever masturbated, which, oh God, that was awkward to think about. My life from the time I was thirteen was more about keeping any mention of sex away from me because of my father. Now, though, I realized that I wanted to experience it, and Cole would be someone that would make sure it wasn't awful or awkward or anything like that. No, he would be kind and gentle with me, I was sure.

CHAPTER TWENTY-SIX

*C*ole...

    I could feel the warm wetness against my dick and I wasn't sure if she was aware of it. Judging by the look on her face, my guess was she either wasn't, or wasn't aware of what it meant.

"Have you ever..." I stopped. She'd said she'd never kissed anyone, so my guess was she hadn't had sex, either. She shook her head back and forth, her eyes kind of misting over, like she was embarrassed, but it wasn't just that. No, there was something else behind her eyes that made me take a moment to pause.

"I want you to be comfortable," I said. "I don't want to push you too fast or make you feel like you have to do something you're not ready for. You're in control, okay?"

She nodded, but it was almost too quick, like she had to say yes.

"Hey," I said, stroking my hand along her thigh. "We can stop if you want. We don't have to do anything at all. I'm fine if we just sit next to each other and cuddle and watch something on the tube."

I watched her face as what I said resonated with her, and she realized that I really was okay with slowing down or stopping. When the tears started to fall, I wasn't sure what they were from, so I pulled my hands out from under her skirt and wrapped them around her back, holding her close to me as she wept. There was no noise, but her body shook with sobs. My shoulder got wetter and wetter with her tears, but I didn't say anything. I didn't want to upset her more, but I also wanted her to know I was here for her.

Finally, after several minutes, she sniffed and pushed back, raising her head from my shoulder. The way we were sitting, her face was just barely above my own. She swiped under her eyes where her mascara had run from her tears.

"Just breathe," I said, smiling what I assume was a sad smile.

"I'm sorry," she began, sucking in a breath.

"No need to apologize," I replied. "Sometimes we get emotional and need to let it out. There's no reason why you shouldn't. Want to talk about it?"

She shook her head, her eyes wide. I knew it was something in her past, something that she must have had some experience that threw her, but I didn't know what it was, and didn't want to push. Hopefully, eventually, she'd trust me with her secrets. For now, I'd just let her be safe with me.

"You want to just cuddle?" I asked.

Nodding, she shifted, and I helped her to sit next to me on the couch. It wasn't what I wanted, but it was still nice.

"Wait, don't you have a game tonight?" she asked once we were snuggled up.

"Played today," I said. "Day games are sometimes great, but they can also suck."

"That seems like it wouldn't be very good for your sleep schedule," she said.

"It's not," I replied. "But they usually happen during the middle of the week, so we can get some good sleep the day after."

"At least there's that," she said.

She was warm against my side, tucked in like she fit there, and I was feeling some type of way about what that meant. My dick had, thankfully, toned it down, so I was comfortable that way. I waited to see if she was going to turn on the television or something, but she didn't. Instead, she just snuggled in closer, as if she couldn't quite get enough of the contact. I wasn't prepared for her to just doze off, but that's what she did. Her breathing deepened, and she relaxed more and more until I realized that she was so worn out that she just let go. It was nice to be that space she felt safe in, so I didn't want to move.

Unfortunately, my phone decided to go off, and I had it up kind of loud for some reason. She startled awake, sitting up and looking at me with sleep still in her eyes.

"It's nothing," I said, turning the volume on my phone down. "You can go back to sleep."

She looked at me with both confusion and embarrassment in her eyes.

"I'm sorry," she said, her voice cracking a bit with sleep.

"I'm just sorry I woke you," I replied. "You comfortable here, or you want to go to your room?"

Her eyes went big, and I realized that I probably said the wrong thing, so tried to fix it.

"I meant to sleep," I said. "I can get you tucked in and head back to my place if you want."

"Oh, no," she replied. "I don't want you to go, I just…"

She let the words trail off, but I had a sneaking suspicion that she wanted to make sure I wasn't going to try anything with her.

"I can lay on top of the blankets," I suggested. "That way nothing will happen. I'm fine with it, honestly."

Blinking, she ran through what I said in her sleepy head, then nodded. Standing up from the couch, she reached her hand down to me and I took it, holding it tight as I stood up myself. I trailed behind her as she made her way to her room.

"Bathroom's in there," she said, pointing to one of the doors on the side of the room. "I'm going to grab something to change into, then you can use it."

She'd let go of my hand and walked to her tall dresser, opening a drawer, and pulling out an oversized shirt and some shorts that looked entirely too small to do anything but fuel my imagination. While she took care of her own business, I pulled my shoes off and set them at the foot of the bed. I'd worn a white tee under my button-down, so felt fine with removing that bit of clothing and setting it on a chair that was in one corner of the room.

When she emerged from the bathroom, her hair was down and it looked like it had been brushed thoroughly.

"Your turn," she said, and her voice was still soft with the sleep she was bolted from.

"Thanks," I replied and went into the smaller room.

I thought about quickly relieving myself of the strain that was once again growing in my pants but thought better of it. When I heard her talking softly on the phone, I couldn't make out everything she said, but my guess was she was talking to Remi. I distinctly heard her say, "He's staying the night," and "It's not happening."

While I wanted "it" to happen, I didn't want to push, either. Nothing screws up a relationship of any kind more than one person being overbearing to the other when that isn't what they want in the relationship. Nothing wrong with that dynamic if it's already set up, but at the beginning of a relationship, things needed to move a bit slower.

Flushing the toilet, I washed up, ran my hands through my hair, pushing it off my face a bit, then turned the light out and stepped out the door. She'd turned on a bedside lamp and turned the overhead one off, which threw the room into a softer feel. She was on the side of the bed closer to the window and away from the door to the rest of the apartment. Since they lived on the third floor, the door was definitely a better escape route in case of fire, but something about the way her bed was positioned, and the things I hadn't really paid attention to on the nightstand that now stood out, made me realize that it was the defensive position in the room. Again I wondered what had happened to her that caused her to need to protect herself so much.

She'd pulled the covers down from the side of the bed she wasn't on and looked at me expectantly. I sat down, but before I could turn to get comfortable, she spoke.

"You can take your pants off," she said quietly, barely above a whisper.

I looked over my shoulder at her and asked, "You sure?"

"Yeah," she said. "As long as you have underwear or something on."

"I guess it's my lucky day," I said, since I was indeed wearing boxers.

Normally, there would be nothing under my slacks, but for some reason I put them on that morning. I undid my belt, then unbuttoned the pants, unzipping the fly and lowering them down. After sitting back on the edge of the bed, I pulled first one foot then the other out, and stripped my socks along with it. I got up and put them nicely on top of the shirt on the chair, tucking the socks inside the shoes. When I got back to the edge of the bed, she was staring at me. I couldn't tell if she was happy, amused, or terrified.

"You sure you're okay with this?" I asked.

She nodded, that too fast movement again, and I stopped.

"You know you can say no, right?"

"I know," she said, that soft voice barely above a whisper again.

"At any point you can say stop, get out, or whatever else falls into your head," I said as I sat on the edge of the bed.

"I know," she said, again with the soft voice.

Sliding my legs up under the covers, I pulled them over my torso, lying on my side facing her, my head on her pillow. It was a smaller bed than I was used to, but it wasn't overly small. I wasn't the biggest guy on the team by any stretch of the imagination, but being in this small of a bed with her, even though I was nearly falling off the edge, was still close quarters, and I didn't mind it a bit. She shifted, turning her upper body away from me as she clicked the bedside lamp off. I could feel her moving, and it didn't take long for her to snuggle against me, her back to my front.

"Can we scooch a bit your way?" I asked. "I'm afraid I'm gonna fall off the edge."

I felt more than heard her giggle as she moved slightly away from me. Instead of trying to figure anything else out, I moved away from the edge and right up against her. Her ass was warm and snug against my dick, which just made it come back alive again. I felt her intake of air as it throbbed, but then she settled again. Wrapping my arm around her middle, I tucked it under her side, just below her breasts, where it wouldn't necessarily be sexual, but was still fairly intimate. She sighed deeply, then drifted off. It was amazing that she felt so comfortable with me nearly naked behind her almost naked body. I must have given the right impression at some point, because the feel of her in my arms was exactly what I needed to drift off myself.

CHAPTER TWENTY-SEVEN

*K*ylie...

It was too hot, like unbearably warm, and I shifted, only to feel a body behind me and wrapped around me. I froze, unsure of what was going on, but I knew I couldn't stay where I was. Not only was I too hot, but I also had to pee like crazy. Pulling the arm that was around my middle away from me, I slipped out from under the covers and padded my way to the bathroom. I shut the door to do my business and turned on the small light that was where I kept my makeup. It wasn't too bright but would filter light into the bedroom so I could see who was in my bed.

Nothing felt off or odd as I emptied my bladder. My clothes were on the way they normally would be. I wasn't sore anywhere abnormal, and the only thing that I could smell, other than my own smell, was a cologne of some sort that was somewhat spicy, but rather nice. After I'd finished my business in the tiny room, I slowly cracked the door open, allowing the little bit of light to cast across my bed.

I gasped. It was Cole. He was in my bed. Oh God, this was not a good thing. Like, why was he in my bed? Did we do something that I didn't remember? Did he make me let him stay? Nothing made sense in that moment, and I just stood there in the space between the bathroom and bedroom, trying to figure out what exactly happened.

"Hey, beautiful," he mumbled, his voice gravely with sleep. "You okay?"

I couldn't move. I couldn't answer him. Nothing would work in my body at all.

"Oh, hey," he said, sitting up in the bed.

He tossed the blankets off himself and stood up, moving slowly toward me like I was some cornered rabbit that would bolt from the predator that was in my space. But I didn't bolt. No, I didn't get the flight or fight part of the automatic reaction. No, I got the freeze. The don't move, don't blink, don't breathe, and maybe he'll go away. He didn't go away, though. He kept coming toward me, ever so slowly. When he got to me, he stopped, just shy of touching me.

"You okay?" he asked, again, looking down at me expectantly.

I tried to breathe, tried to respond, tried to do anything, but my body just wouldn't cooperate.

"Okay," he said, slowly raising his one hand to lay it on my shoulder. "I've got you. You're safe. You're home. No one is going to hurt you here."

The words were deliberate and concise, like they were part of a deprogramming system used to undo whatever it was that ramped me up to well past ten on the fear scale. It only took a few more words from him before I crumbled. He caught me, though, not letting me fall to the floor and curl up like I wanted to. Instead, he picked me up and carried me back to the bed.

He didn't try to lay me down, though. He sat on the edge, holding me in his lap, and making a shushing sound with words of affirmation next to my ear. The low tone of his voice, the steady rhythm of his heartbeat against my body, and the even breaths he was taking, reminding me how to breathe again, eventually pulled me from wherever I'd gone and back to the here and now.

Finally, after I felt like I'd gotten myself under control, I sat up a bit away from his chest and looked into his eyes. He brought his hand up and tucked my hair behind my ear, caressing the edge of it ever so softly. I sucked in my breath. I couldn't help it. The touch from him was so kind, so gentle, so everything I needed that I was afraid I was going to fall head over heels for him only to find out he was a monster like my father.

"Hey," he said softly. "Everything is fine."

My last thought must have shown on my face because he'd been smiling up until then, but that look was replaced with concern. I nodded but couldn't really say anything.

"I'm here," he said. "I'm not going anywhere. You're safe with me."

Those last words broke me and I sobbed, so sure he was going to see that I was crazy and run away from me as fast as possible.

"I got you," he said low in my ear as he gathered me to him once again and held me tight as I lost myself.

~

THE ALARM ON MY PHONE WAS GOING CRAZY, SO I REACHED OVER AND shut it off, stretching in the bed, trying to wake up. Remi must have been making breakfast because I could smell bacon and coffee. God did I need both. Rolling out of bed, I hit the bathroom to get my morning mission complete, then padded to the door of the bedroom and swung it open.

"Good morning, beautiful," Cole said, and I stopped dead in my tracks.

Blinking, I ran through my memories to see if I could figure out how in the hell Cole ended up in my kitchen cooking breakfast. Staring at him, I realized that he was only wearing boxers and a tee shirt. That meant that at some point he'd taken his clothes off. In my apartment. Maybe even in my room. Oh, God, this was not happening.

"Feeling better?" he asked as he plated whatever was in the pan on the stove.

I nodded, not sure what he was talking about. Then it hit me. He'd come over for dinner, we'd kissed, like a lot, and then we ended up sleeping in my bed. Oh no, the terror I thought was a nightmare was real. I woke up and broke, but he caught me. And he stayed. And now he was cooking breakfast. This was all too much, and I didn't know what to do.

"I hope you don't mind I helped myself," he said. "I made enough for you, too."

He held up two plates, both piled high with eggs and toast and bacon.

"Thanks," I managed to squeak out, then went to the coffee pot and poured myself a cup, adding some milk from the fridge.

He'd set the plates on the table, back where we sat the night before, and pulled one of the chairs out to allow me to take my place. I grabbed the other mug that was on the counter and brought it with me to the table, setting it where he'd set his own plate, then sat in the chair that was offered to me.

It was all so domestic and normal that I wasn't sure exactly what was going on. It wasn't a bad thing, that's for sure. He'd found the peppers and cheese in the fridge and had sliced them up to add to the eggs, making a sort of Denver scramble type dish, with the bacon on the side. It looked amazing and smelled even better.

Picking up my fork, I shoveled some of the eggs into my mouth, and oh man was it delicious. I must have moaned because he laughed a little, causing me to look at him. His smile was bright, those dimples right there, and it all made me feel so warm and tingly that I couldn't help but return the smile.

"Thank you," I said after I'd swallowed.

"It's my pleasure," he replied. "Are you feeling better?"

I shrugged. I didn't remember what had happened the night before, other than that we'd had dinner and kissed. Oh, did he kiss well. I guess he must have been talking about my midnight freakout, but I couldn't be sure. Those moments were always scattered after the fact, so what I did remember didn't usually match what actually happened.

"If you ever need me, please let me know," he said. "I really like you."

The smile I had on my face must have gone up by a bunch, because his returned one was brilliant.

"Do you work from home today?" he asked, as if it were a normal morning and we were a normal couple.

I thought for a moment, but then nodded. I still didn't have a set schedule of any kind, other than to get my projects done. Working from home was definitely something I could still do. Once I moved up and took over Jim's duties, that would probably change. Not necessarily the no working from home bit, but that my schedule would likely be more structured. I thrived in a structured environment, though, so it would be worth it.

"Do you mind if I shower?" he asked, and I realized that I'd eaten nearly all the food that he'd put on my plate, which was way more than I usually did.

"Sure," I said almost automatically.

"You can join me if you want," he said, giving me a devilish smile that I had a hard time saying no to. "No pressure," he added. "But I wouldn't mind if you joined me."

My face must have been redder than the peppers in breakfast because his smile broadened, splitting his face open in an absolutely beautiful way. He stood up, took his plate to the sink, rinsing the remnants of breakfast from it before setting it down.

I'd followed him and mimicked his behavior, then watched as he walked into my bedroom, pulling his shirt over his head as he went. My whole body quivered, like an electrical current went through it, and I just followed him into my room. He'd dropped the shirt onto the bed and was already in the bathroom when I got through the door. I heard the water start up, the shower curtain run along the rod, then the change in the sound of water as it began to come out of the showerhead.

Instead of thinking, I just pulled my shirt over my head, dropping it next to his on the bed. Pushing my sleep shorts and panties down, I stepped out of them and tried to be brave. I stepped into the bathroom, moving the curtain just a little bit to slip in behind him. He glanced over his shoulder at me with a smile, but kept his eyes focused on mine. I'd been sure he'd let them roam over my whole body, do that leering thing that guys sometimes did, but he didn't, and that earned him some serious points.

Turning back around, he ducked his head under the spray to wet his hair, rubbing it with his hands. I watched the muscles in his back flex and move with his effort, and it was both fascinating and erotic. Squeezing my thighs together, I tried to stop the thrum reverberating through my body, but it was no use. Especially when he turned completely around to lather up his hair.

I really tried to stay focused on his face, but my eyes headed south on his body, down past the hair on his chest, past the abdomen that was tight with ridges from his muscles, to the… Oh, yeah, he had one, and it was hard and standing out and oh my God. I snapped my eyes back up to his so fast I nearly got whiplash, only to discover he was grinning at me. I couldn't help but kind of chuckle a little bit, slapping my hand over my mouth when the noise came out.

"First time you've seen one?" he asked.

I simply nodded, trying desperately to keep my eyes on his face, something safe, which was definitely not his giant erection down *there*. My thighs had a wetness between them, again, like what had happened the night before. Squeezing them together was not helping anything because I still could feel that energy running through me. I jumped, nearly slipping, when his hand rested on my shoulder.

"Breathe," he said, his face calm and concerned.

"What is happening?" I asked, unsure of whether it was a question about my body or his.

"Normal reaction," he said. "The first time you've seen something you don't personally own is sometimes a little jarring. It's okay, though. Nothing is going to happen unless you want it to."

I nodded, then shivered, which had nothing to do with the fact that there was a sprinkling of water coming off around him from the shower. No, I wasn't even cold. In fact, I was much warmer than I should have been, but I couldn't figure out what was going on.

He rinsed his hair after having shampooed it, then looked at me.

"Your turn," he said, shifting to the side and guiding me past his body to be under the water. I brushed against his, well, him, and it gave me a shudder I didn't understand. "Let me help," he said, turning me so my back was to the water and my front was to him.

He tipped my head back with a couple of fingers under my chin, and the water washed over my hair, his hands moving through it to get it all wet. Once that was done, he kind of rung it out and turned me to face away from him while he grabbed up the shampoo bottle. I heard the top pop and shortly after felt him massaging my scalp. I just relaxed to the touch. It was firm enough to feel but wasn't so firm it was uncomfortable. After his hands left my scalp, I felt them at my back as he continued to work the shampoo through the rest of my hair. It wasn't super long, not like when I was little, but it was well past the bra line on my back.

When he'd finished, he reached around me and rinsed his hands, then gently turned me back around to let me rinse my hair. The whole time we were doing this, his eyes never wandered from my face. I mean, I didn't know if he checked my ass out when my back was to him, but when I was facing him, he was looking into my eyes, watching me to make sure I wasn't getting freaked out or anything.

It didn't take long until my hair was rinsed and he picked up my little scrubber thing I had hanging on the side of the shower and reached around me again to get it wet. He picked up the bodywash I had in there, squeezing a small amount onto the scrubber then gently began rubbing it on my shoulder. Nothing about what he was doing was in any way sexual, but I just kept getting hotter and hotter. My legs kept squeezing together more and more. In a way that was the sweetest and yet so sexy, he washed my body, watching me, making sure I was still comfortable.

As he went lower and lower on my body, he crouched down, lifting one foot up so he could wash my thigh. I gripped his shoulders for support, because falling over in the shower was not how I wanted to die. He did the same with the other foot, lifting it up and washing me. Once he was done with that, he stood back up and turned me around and began the same thing along my back, down lower and lower, being very careful to not linger too long on my ass. I stood there, letting him wash me, and just soaked it all in, my eyes closed, enjoying his touch.

When he turned me back around to rinse my back, I could see that he still had his erection, and it was looking kind of painful. I was hesitant, but reached out and kind of just grabbed it. I had no idea what I was doing, but I just kind of held it for a second, then looked up at him. His eyes were closed and his teeth were gritted.

"Sorry," I said, making to pull my hand away.

"No," he said, probably firmer than he intended because he followed it up with, "No, it's fine. Just wasn't expecting it is all."

"I'm probably doing everything wrong," I said, still with my hand kind of just holding his dick.

"There aren't too many ways to do it wrong," he said. "Do you want me to show you?"

I nodded, unsure exactly what he was talking about. His one hand was on the wall of the shower, but the other came down and kind of covered mine. He worked my fingers so they were a little looser than what I originally had, then began moving them down toward his body and up toward the tip, back and forth in a slow, methodical motion.

It took some time, but I must have figured out his rhythm because he eventually pulled his hand off mine and let me do it myself. His breathing was stuttered, his chest kind of quivering, and he just kept smiling this little smile that barely made it past his lips. All of a sudden, he kind of stiffened in my hand and I looked down to see a thick whitish liquid coming out of him. I almost stopped what I was doing. He must have anticipated it because his hand was back over mine again, keeping the slow pace up until he finally stopped.

When his eyes opened and he looked at me, there was something there that I hadn't ever seen before. It was almost like he was proud of me or something. He shifted himself so that we were kind of side by side in the spray of the showerhead, and rinsed himself, as well as my hands off.

He kissed my forehead and said, "Thank you." I thought it was weird but wasn't sure how this was supposed to go.

When he pulled back, he must have seen the confusion on my face because he smiled about as big as I'd seen him smile so far.

"You didn't have to do that," he said. "I appreciate that you did."

I smiled because I couldn't help myself, then looked away from his face.

"I'm happy to return the favor any time you want," he said against my ear as he shut the water off.

Whisking the curtain back, he grabbed one of the towels that was on the shelf next to the tub and wrapped it around my shoulders, rubbing my skin dry with the terrycloth material. He'd shifted us so that we weren't so close and had more room to maneuver.

"Do you want a separate one for your hair?" he asked.

I nodded, so he grabbed another one, then wrapped my hair up in it at the top of my head. It was like he'd been doing it forever. I wondered whether he'd had girlfriends before, which led to me wondering whether he thought I was a simple girl for not knowing how to do whatever it was that I just did for him. He must have noticed the shift in my posture because he finished tucking the towel that he'd pulled for himself around his waist and pulled me to him, wrapping his arms around me and holding me close.

"Whatever you were thinking needs to stop," he said. "I don't know what it was, but I'm sure it was something that didn't make you feel good, and I don't want that for you."

God, this whole thing was a nightmare of me being too stupid to understand adult relationships because I'd shut myself away from the rest of the world for so long. Not that anyone would blame me if they knew about my history. But he was just being so kind and gentle and everything that it was hard not to think that it was some kind of pity thing he had going on, and I didn't want that. I didn't want to be with someone who was only with me because they pitied me. No, I couldn't have that.

CHAPTER TWENTY-EIGHT

*C*ole...

By the time I got her all dried off she was more settled than she'd been in the shower. Was she perfect? Absolutely not, but neither was I. She was so innocent she hadn't even known how to jack me off, which was kind of adorable and yet so sad. Whatever had happened in her past had really shut her down and sheltered her. I wanted to ask what it was, who had hurt her so badly, but it would have to wait.

She grabbed some clothes and headed back into the bathroom to dress while I put the clothes I'd worn the day before back on. I must not have heard the front door open because when her friend popped his head into her bedroom I jumped.

"Oh, sorry," he said, pulling his head back out the door.

I'd been mostly dressed, just needing to put my shoes on, so I did that, then walked out of the room.

"I didn't know you were still here," he said, his back to me so I couldn't really read him.

"No worries," I replied, having picked up that statement from Tanner over the last couple of months. "You work from home, too?"

"Sometimes," he said, turning toward me. "I wanted to check on Kylie. She okay?"

"I'm fine," she said, coming out of her room wearing a pair of leggings and an oversized sweater that hung nearly to her knees.

Her hair was up in a bun on top of her head, still wet from the shower, and her cheeks were pink, which I attributed to the hot shower and not any embarrassment, but I couldn't be sure.

"Coffee?" she asked me, walking to the kitchen.

"Unfortunately, I can't," I replied. "I gotta run home before heading to the stadium. You have plans for the weekend?"

She looked at Remi, who just shrugged.

"I can get some tickets for you guys if you want," I suggested. I'd walked over to where she was making coffee for herself and gave her a hug. "I know you don't do crowds on your own."

"I have something during the day on Saturday," Remi said. "But I'm free Sunday if you want me to go with you."

"Sure," Kylie said, pouring herself another cup of coffee from the pot.

"I'll send them to you," I said, looking at Remi. "See you then?" I asked Kylie.

She nodded but didn't answer. I wasn't sure what was going on in her head, but I knew that she probably wanted to talk to Remi without me there, so I kissed her on her forehead.

"Text me," I whispered in her ear. "Let me know if you're okay. I'm worried about you."

Once I'd said my peace, I headed to the door, nodding at Remi before opening it up and walking out. I walked down the stairs and out the door to my car that I'd left on the street. There hadn't really been anything indicating street parking needed to be paid, so I was thankful I didn't come back to a ticket.

I didn't go home, though, because I really didn't even want to. Fighting traffic to get to the stadium was bad enough. I didn't want to deal with it at all, so pulled into the stadium parking lot for employees and decided to hit the gym before anyone else showed up. By the time I'd worked up a good sweat, several other players had shown up.

"Early day," Bridge said as he sat on one of the machines next to me.

"Late night," I replied.

"Someone new?" he asked as he shifted the weights around on the machine he was using.

"Newish," I replied. "But not sure where it's going. I need to get to know her a bit better, still, but I definitely like her."

"Didn't think you were the type to stay the night, or even go home with a girl," he said, grunting as he pushed the bar up for the bench press machine.

"Nothing like Hennings," I said with a laugh.

"No one is like that boy," he replied on his next rest.

"You okay?" I asked. "You aren't usually in here this early."

"I got something going on," he said. "Nothing to worry about, but Coach wants me to do some strengthening."

"Don't screw yourself up," I said.

"I won't," he replied. "That's the last thing I want to do. Especially right now."

"Why right now?"

"Can you keep a secret?"

"Better than most," I replied, knowing that whatever he had to tell me was obviously important to him.

"I'm gonna pop the question to Lucy," he said, and I swear his eyes twinkled with the thought of it.

"That's great," I replied, patting him on the shoulder. "When?"

"Trying to figure that out," he said.

"How long have you two been together?" I asked, because I honestly couldn't remember.

"Almost two years," he said.

Just then, a couple of other players walked into the weight room, so I stopped my questions and let them do their thing.

"Catch you later," I said to Bridge before heading into the clubhouse to get my second shower of the day. It definitely would pale compared to the first one.

CHAPTER TWENTY-NINE

*K*ylie...

As soon as the door shut and Cole was out of the apartment, Remi came up to me, pulling me into a hug. It was like he could read my mind or something, because I really wanted to keep Cole there, but I didn't want to seem clingy or anything, which was totally all in my head, but still.

"You good?" Remi asked after we'd stood there for a couple of minutes.

I took a deep breath and nodded.

"He stayed the night," Remi said, pulling away from me, but keeping his hands on my shoulders.

Another nod of affirmation, but I couldn't quite look at him.

"Hey," he said, tipping my eyes up to his with one of his hands. "Did he force himself? Did he rape you? Are you okay?"

The questions were rapid fire, so I didn't get a chance to answer one before the next one was out.

"He stayed the night," I began. "We didn't have sex. Well, we did do something in the shower, but it wasn't actually sex. He didn't force anything, and he didn't rape me. I'm fine, just sort of confused a little bit and need to talk."

"Girl, I got you," Remi said, then pulled me into another hug. "But I do have some work stuff to do."

"Me, too," I said, shifting away from him to make my way to my desk.

We were so fortunate to have gotten the apartment we did when we did. It was one of those right place, right time kind of things. It was a two bedroom, each with our own bathroom. The main part of the space was large enough for each of us to have our own space for a desk and still have plenty of room for the couch and television. We'd set it up so that our desks were right next to our rooms with plenty of natural light from the windows, but we also had our own desk lamps.

I didn't have to set anything up because I'd just left it all ready the night before, so I was up and running before Remi had a chance to set his laptop up. While he was setting up, he looked at me and began the interrogation that I was sure would come at some point.

"I am going to need a play-by-play of the night, you know," he said. "From the time I walked out that door until the moment I walked back in. You have about twelve or thirteen hours to account for, missy."

The words were the same that my grandparents had used with me when I first started finding my wings. They weren't meant to be harsh, just to ensure that I knew someone cared about what happened to me and how I was doing. Unfortunately for me, I had never been doing anything worth being concerned over, so their line of questions often ended with me stating I'd been studying with Remi, or at the library, or some other boring activity.

"He helped me get dinner plated," I began. "He was really nice about it, too."

I proceeded to give him most of what happened since he'd left the apartment. There were a couple of points where he asked for more information, but other than that, he let me just dump my night on him. When I got to the point where Cole had headed into the shower, though, I kind of just stopped.

"You gotta tell me," Remi said. "He went into your room, pulling the shirt off his back on the way. Then what?"

Right at that moment, I got a notification on my laptop that I was scheduled to be in a meeting with Jim, so I just looked at Remi as I pulled on my headphones and clicked in.

"Hi, Jim," I said as a greeting.

"Hey there," he said. "I was thinking you were going to be in the office today."

"Sorry," I said. "I was kind of under the weather, and with working late last night, I just couldn't make it. That isn't a problem, is it?"

"Oh, no," he said with a smile. "We can go over things virtually, as long as you think you can come in tomorrow. I know it's Friday, and most people like to bail early that day, but it would be helpful for you to be in the office if at all possible."

"No problem," I said. "I can definitely make it in tomorrow."

"Good," he said. "I wanted to show you how I mapped projects in the spreadsheets, so I'll share my screen with you and we can talk it out."

With that, my brain went into learning mode and work mode and the rest of the world and all its issues fell to the wayside. It was something I'd figured out how to do when I was a teenager, to turn everything off but what needed to be done at the moment. It's how I got through the trial and the aftermath. How I was able to endure seeing my father for the few years that I was required to go.

I didn't realize we'd been working for so long until Jim sat back and gave a stretch.

"I need a breather and to grab some lunch," he said. "Let's meet up again in an hour or so. That should give you a break as well."

"Sounds good," I replied, then clicked out of the virtual meeting.

"Lunch is served," Remi said, and I turned to see that he'd pulled the leftovers from the night before out and set a plate up for me at the table.

"Thanks," I said. "Just have to go pee first."

I headed to my room and emptied my bladder before coming back out into the main room of our apartment.

"And you can finish your story," he said, sitting across from me at the table. "Was he hot? Well, I know he's hot. But did he have tattoos? Cause those are hot, too."

"Remi," I said. "Can you give me just a minute to un-work myself?"

"Sorry," he said. "I just wanna know all the things."

I laughed, because Remi was my best friend, and I didn't think even a girlfriend would ask all the questions and be interested in my guy as much as he was. Most girls would probably want to know whether they could have my guy, but Remi was just happy that I was happy. I took a deep breath, took a bite of my food, then continued the story I was telling him from earlier.

"He doesn't have any tattoos," I began, because that was one of the specific questions he'd asked. "But yeah, he's hot." I could feel my face flush, but it was just Remi and me, so it wasn't that big of a deal. "He pulled his shirt off on the way to the bedroom and dropped it onto the bed, then I guess took his boxers off and went to shower. It took a minute for me to get the courage up, but then I followed him. He was already in the shower when I got in there, so I just undressed and climbed in behind him."

"You little minx, you," Remi said. "Tell me more."

"Well," I said, after taking another bite of my lunch. "He washed his hair, which, you know, whatever. Then he turned around, and he was…" I stopped. I didn't know if I could even say what was going on, even though it was Remi.

"Hard?" Remi asked, obviously realizing that I was kind of floundering.

"Yeah," I replied, then took another bite of food.

"Was it big?"

"I don't know," I said, exasperated. "I don't know what's big or what's small or what's anything. You know this."

I was getting frustrated because Remi knew my aversion to all things sex related, so the fact that he was kind of pushing me was really upsetting me.

"I'm sorry," he said, and it was clear he was. "I just want what is best for you. I want you to be happy and to have someone you can love

149

and who can show you all the amazing things that a great sex life can offer."

"He probably thinks I'm childish or something," I said. "I'd be surprised if he never came back and never bothered to contact me again."

"You're being too hard on yourself," he said. "Does he know about your dad?"

"Oh, God, no," I said. "I never want him to find out about that."

"He's gonna figure it out eventually," Remi replied. "It would be better to tell him before the press comes after him."

"But my name was changed," I said.

"And that hasn't stopped him from sending you stuff," he replied. "What about that purse that you got a couple of years ago? That came from your dad, right?"

I stopped. Just stopped everything. I don't even think I breathed when the realization hit me that my dad was still, even after six years, trying to make me want to be around him.

"Hey," Remi said. "Don't go there. I just want to make sure that if he's gonna find out, it should be from you and not some reporter asking him about dating you and what he thinks of your dad."

"I didn't even think about that," I said. "What am I supposed to do?"

"Well," Remi said, picking up the plates. "I think a phone call at some point would be in order, if not a face-to-face meeting. If he comes here, you can tell him and then he can leave if he wants to. I'll be here for moral support."

"I'll text him and ask him to come over on Saturday," I said.

"I won't be here then," Remi replied. "I got that thing with that guy, remember?"

"A thing with a guy?" I asked.

"I'm not sure where it's going," he said. "I don't want to jinx it or anything, so I'm keeping it on the down low for now."

"So, I have to share my love life but you don't?"

"I'm not dating a baseball player," he replied. "Besides, once things are more settled with this guy, I'll be telling you all the gory details. Even how big he is."

"Remi," I shouted, slapping his arm as he went to hug me. "You're horrible."

"But you love me, anyway," he said with a laugh. "Now, get back to work. We'll finish this all up afterward with some wine to loosen you up a bit."

"Jerk," I said, but was laughing.

He really was the best friend anyone could ever ask for.

CHAPTER THIRTY

$\mathcal{C}$ole...

I'd gotten a couple of seats and sent the tickets to Remi's email address for Sunday's game, then got to work on getting ready for the game that night. Replaying the morning in my head, I smiled because it was just so sweet and innocent, but then I thought about what might have caused her to not have much knowledge about sex, and it started to make me uncomfortable. I mean, it's not like I can just ask her why she is the way she is, but then again, I probably could. She seemed like the kind of girl who would be willing to share that with me, as long as it wasn't too hard on her.

"Earth to Decker," I heard, and turned to see Hennings staring at me.

"What?" I barked.

"You were all kinds of lost there," he said. "What's going on?"

"Just some stuff that doesn't matter to you," I said.

The last thing I wanted to do was share information about Kylie with this dog. Sure, he'd mellowed out since he met Fi, but he was still somewhat the same, and Kylie didn't need to be in his head at all.

"If it's fucking you up on the field, it does matter," he said.

Which, in all honestly, if it was going to mess up my performance on the field, he was right that it was sort of his business. But it wasn't, at least not if I could help it.

"I've got this," I said. "No need for you to worry your pretty little head about it."

"If anyone understands the way off field shit can fuck with you, it's me," he said. "So, if you need to talk, I'm here. If you need a professional, check with the team. They've got good people to recommend."

"Will do," I replied.

We headed out to the field to get regular batting practice started, and I lost myself in the feel and rhythm of the game and all it entailed. I worked with Coach Rodriguez on some fielding issues I had been having, then took a good amount of hits in the cage before going out to the outfield to shag some balls and get warmed up a little more. By the time we got back to the clubhouse to change for the game, I was in a much better place mentally, and ready to catch for the night.

Berg warmed up easily, and we were ready to start the game on time. Indigo City had been playing great so far, so we were hoping to at least split the long weekend series and win at least two games. Unfortunately for us, their best starter was in, which meant we would have to work extra hard to get anything resembling an offense off him.

The first couple of innings were quick on both sides, each team only sending the minimum of three players up to bat. Bridge was in for Cote at second, and when the Anglers' short stop came up to bat, he hit it just out of the reach of our guy. He rounded first hard, and it was a race to see whether he would make it to second before the throw came in. Unfortunately, the throw was a bit high and when Bridge came down from grabbing it, he landed on top of their player awkwardly, falling off to the side.

We called time, and the umpire agreed to give us the moment to check on our injured player. The trainer came out with Coach Johnson and they checked our utility guy to see what was wrong. Being so far away from the play, I wasn't sure exactly what happened when he landed, other than to know it was definitely not right. Bridge was holding his right arm, and the wrist looked like it was at an odd angle. We gathered around enough to see what was going on, but to still be out of the way enough for the trainer and coach to do what they needed doing.

I peeked over to the dugout and saw Cote grabbing his gear. He popped out of the dugout and tossed a ball to Matsui to get warmed up quick to come in and take over at second while they took Bridge back to assess the damage. When Bridge stood up and began to walk off the field under his own power, even while cradling his damaged arm, the crowd did what they always do and gave him a standing ovation to show their love and support.

Cote was in and stretching while the rest of us settled back into our positions to take on the next hitter. I could see the pitcher struggling a bit, so I stood up and stepped in front of the plate, holding my hands out in front of me and pushing them down in a manner to indicate that he should just slow down. He'd stepped off the rubber and nodded at me, then took a walk around the mound.

I'd seen players hurt before. We all had. But Jonathon Bridge was a good guy that none of us wanted to see hurt. Whether this was a short time off the field or the end of his career, none of us knew. We just saw the injury, and that was it. We had to put it behind us, out of our mind, and continue on with the game. Eventually we'd know what it meant for him and our team, but for now, and for him, we had to keep on keeping on. And boy did we.

Berg struck out the next hitter and we were out of that inning. When we came up, I was hitting second, and it felt like we just had to hit every ball, which didn't exactly happen, but we came close. Nearly each of us that came up that inning got a hit, one after the next after the next. We just kept getting the ball into the field. It was the old adage of 'hit it where they ain't' mentality, and we were on it. By the time we got to the third out, which was unfortunately me, we had driven in six runs and were set to finish out the game without many issues.

When the top of the ninth started and the music came up for Strawberry to come in, the crowd was on their feet, the team was more than pumped, and it felt like this was game seven of the World Series and we were on the brink of winning it all instead of a mundane first game of a series in late May. The pitcher's no-nonsense approach and ability to ignore everything but the ball and my mitt was mastery, and he only needed seven pitches to get out of the inning and finish the game for us with a win.

We were all happy with the win, but it was cooled some when we found out that our friend and teammate had been taken right to Harborview for surgery on his wrist. Turned out he'd broken it, and pretty badly at that. It wasn't the news we wanted to hear, but injuries were part of the game. The manager wasn't sure what his recovery was going to look like, so they were sending word to the Shoremen in Tacoma to send up an infielder we could plug in as needed. The conservative guess was we may have him back by the first series after the All-Star Game. I was hopeful we would, but it was one of those things where you never knew.

As I drove home, I thought back over my day and realized that waking up with Kylie in my arms was one of the best things that had happened to me in a good long while, and I wanted to see if I could make it happen again. I shot a text to her when I had parked, hoping it wouldn't wake her up, letting her know I was thinking about her and that I wouldn't mind another dinner date, or even lunch on Saturday, what with my game that night.

By the time I got to my apartment, I was hard and needing relief. I thought about how Kylie had grabbed my dick in her hand, so firm and hard, to the point of pain. Then, with help and direction, she figured out the stroke to help me relieve my discomfort. It was always different when someone else took care of me than when I did it myself, but I would have to handle it on my own tonight and hope that at some point, we could move past the hand job phase and onto more intimate connections. Time would definitely tell, but I had a feeling she might just be the right one.

CHAPTER THIRTY-ONE

*K*ylie...

True to his word, once we'd finished working for the day, me much longer than him, he made dinner and opened one of the bottles of wine he'd put into the fridge the night before, pouring me a very full glass that would likely send me to bed much sooner than normal. After everything was settled, and we were sitting in front of the television waiting for the game to start he began asking questions.

"You never told me what happened in the shower," he said.

"Oh, God," I replied, covering my face with my hands.

"It can't be that bad," he replied and I could hear the smile in his voice.

"I don't know what it's called," I said. "But I kind of just helped him to…"

This was horrible. I didn't even know what terms to use for sex. Why had I decided that sex in any form was so off the table that I didn't even want to learn about it? How had what my dad done messed me up so badly that I didn't even know how anything related to relationships worked.

"With your hands?" Remi asked, and I nodded, not wanting to move my hands from my face. "That's called jerking off. At least that's what I call it. It's technically called masturbation when you do it to yourself, but since you helped, it's not called that."

"Okay," I replied through my hands. "But I probably didn't do it right."

"Did he come?" he asked, and I pulled my hands down and looked at him. "Did he ejaculate? Was there semen present?"

Again, I covered my face, only nodding a confirmation.

"Then you didn't do it wrong," he said. "Honestly, for your first sexual encounter, that doesn't sound all that bad."

"He had to help me so I knew what to do," I cried, pulling my hands away from my face and picking up my glass, taking a large sip from it. "Like, I didn't even know how to do the most basic thing. He'll never come back. I just know it."

"He'll be back," Remi argued. "He already sent me tickets for Sunday, so you'll see him then at the latest."

"How am I supposed to face him after that?" I asked. "I'll just embarrass myself and you know it."

"Not gonna happen," he replied. "I'll be with you to keep you level. Besides, I want you to enjoy this. You deserve someone who will make you happy and satisfy that burning desire that was likely awakened in your belly."

"About that," I said, the wine giving me some bravery. "I was kind of…"

I didn't know how to explain what had happened to my body, but I kind of just motioned to myself, down there, and looked to Remi to explain.

"Girl," he said with a shake of his head. "I have failed in my schooling if you don't even know how your body works. I think this calls for some special education. It's not gonna be hands on, mind you, but you need to know how things work. I'll be right back."

He got up and went to his bedroom and came out with his very old laptop. It was probably a good five or six years old at this point, but it still worked for some things. He opened it up after plugging it in and we waited for the endless process as it whirled to life, finally coming to the screen where he could log onto it.

"I'm gonna start you off with some basics," he said, pulling up a web browser and typing in a URL. When the screen came up, I could see nearly naked people in the images on the website he'd gone to and all I could do was stare. "Let's start with the first steps, which is, of course, masturbation. Do you want to start with guys or girls?"

It finally dawned on me that he'd pulled up some sort of porn site and I just sat there staring at him, mouth open, completely baffled. When I hadn't answered, he looked at me and smiled. It was the kind of smile that made people uncomfortable, but I knew him and knew that he would never do anything to hurt me intentionally.

"Guys it is," he said, clicking on an image. "This way you know what you did for Cole, and how he likely does the same to himself."

In abject horror, I watched as the video he'd selected came to life. It was a man lying in a bed, naked but covered with a sheet. Slowly, he began rubbing himself through the sheet and I watched, rapt with interest at what was happening on the screen. It didn't take long before the guy had moved the sheet and his dick was there, hard just like Cole's had been. This guy was a pulling on it, stroking it up and down with his hand, twisting his wrist at the end for some reason, so I made a mental note to try that next time I was with Cole.

Oh, wait, next time. What if he wanted something else next time? I didn't know how to do anything else, and yet, he had been kind when I was clearly out of my depth that morning. I continued to watch the video as the man kind of bucked on the bed as he was pulling on himself, until finally, he groaned and I saw the same type of goo come out of him that came out of Cole that morning.

"Ejaculation," Remi said, and I turned to him, having forgotten he was even there.

"Okay," I said. "I get that and see that this is what happened this morning."

"Good," he replied. "Now, was Cole this big? Or was he bigger or smaller?"

"I don't know," I said as I looked at him. "It's hard to tell."

"Understandable," he replied. "Do you want to watch another one, or shall we switch to girls?"

Oh, he was serious about this whole education thing. I thought he'd been kind of joking, but I guess that was an incorrect assumption.

"Remi," I started, then swallowed. "I can't sit here and watch porn with you. That would be like watching it with my brother, and I'm not at all okay with that."

"Fair enough," he said, turning the laptop back to him.

He clicked a couple of things, likely opening tabs or something, then unplugged the laptop and walked to my room.

"Where are you going?"

"I'm going to get it set up so you can see what is what," he replied over his shoulder. "When you're ready, all you have to do is log on and watch. You can see what happens for both guys and girls. It won't be with me, but you can explore it, and even try some of the things out."

"Oh. My. God," I said, emphasizing each word. "You really are serious, aren't you?"

"As a heart attack," he replied, then walked around the corner of my door toward my bed. It didn't take long before he was coming back out. "I made a note of the password to get into the computer so you have it for whenever you're ready. I'd suggest you watch a couple of the girls only that I have open. Also," he said, sitting down on the couch. "Don't just click on links. I've opened a bunch that I think are safe and tame enough for your first go at seeing how sex works. I don't want you to end up in some dungeon porn site where things are so not normal. Okay?"

I could only nod, because clearly there were things I needed to learn. I just wasn't sure that porn was the best way to go about it. But the thought of Remi trying to talk me through things, and the thought of Cole wanting to do more and me not having a clue what I was doing, made me realize that this might be the easiest way to go about it.

The announcers on the television were sharing the line ups for each of the teams, so I was thankfully unable to continue this line of conversation with my roommate. But he'd given me a lot to think about, and honestly, I really wanted to know.

"Before you watch more," Remi said, interrupting my thoughts. "I want to warn you that porn is not real. Are the acts something that could happen? Maybe, in that guys and girls can get it on in the ways they describe. But they are actors, performing for the camera. Not all sex is awesome, and not all sex is good. You know that, already, but I don't want you to be disappointed if you see something and real life doesn't live up to it."

"Okay," I said, trying not to look at him. "Can we please stop talking about it now, though?"

"Sure thing," he said, and that was that.

We watched the game for a little while, but with the odd night before, the long day I'd had, the very large glass of wine I'd drunk, and my curiosity piqued, I headed to bed much earlier than normal. I'm sure that Remi knew I wanted to see more of what to expect, but he was good enough to not say anything when I went to my room and closed the door.

CHAPTER THIRTY-TWO

*C*ole...

My alarm started yelling at me entirely too early, but I knew I had shit to get done today, so I only snoozed it a couple of times before turning it off and getting up. We were heading out of town in just a couple of days, so I needed to get laundry done and get my bag packed and ready to go. It took most of the morning to get everything done, and by the time I was ready to head into the stadium, I was already a bit tired.

Most of the guys were already there, so I walked into the clubhouse feeling a bit self-conscious about being late. I checked my phone to make sure I hadn't missed an email or text, but nothing was there. Fortunately, most of the guys were still stowing their bags and gear, so it wasn't noticeable that I was late.

"Guys," Coach Johnson said as the clubhouse quieted down. "I've got some bad news."

All the players kind of looked at each other, but we were all suspecting what he said next.

"Jonathan's gonna have to have surgery," he continued, which we already knew. "Unfortunately, it looks like it's gonna be the end of his career."

I looked around the locker room and realized that he wasn't there. The rest of the team was having the same realization.

"What does that mean for this year?" Mitch asked.

"We have a new kid coming up from Tacoma to take over his spot on the roster," Coach said. "He won't replace him in our hearts, but he will fill the slot. He's been showing good signs down there, and I think he'll make a good fit. Please be kind and don't haze him too much. He'll probably deal with some performance anxiety coming into the clubhouse to replace the established player. No need to screw with his head any further."

There were murmurs of agreement, but when I looked at Hennings and Huffman, I could see them conspiring something. Leave it to those two to be assholes to the new guy. As long as they didn't pull Adams or Swift into the mix it would likely be mild.

Instead of trying to figure out what they were up to, I pulled my phone out and shot a text to Bridge to let him know I was thinking about him, and that if he needed anything to let me know. Then I shut my phone off, stuffed it into my bag, changed, and headed to the batting cage to begin my warm-up.

The rest of the day went as I expected, with batting practice, a few words from Coach Roof about the plan of attack for today against the Anglers, and getting in some fielding. We'd done well the night before, especially after the injury to Bridge, but tonight was a different game. That was one of the best things about baseball. If you screwed up one night, you just forgot about it the next and started with a clean slate. Of course, over the course of a season, bad days adding up tended to reduce your playing time, but the good games could give you the boost you needed to right the ship.

By the time the game started, we were all settled into our places, doing what we were good at, and playing exceptional baseball. Kors was on fire, and their pitcher seemed to be a rookie, as none of us remember him from the previous year. With the fact that we hadn't seen him before, he was able to pitch to us with an upper hand, knowing what we liked and didn't like, and it showed in the early innings. Unfortunately for him, though, we caught a couple of his tells and figured out what he was throwing at certain times and took advantage of it by hitting a couple over the fence.

At the end of the game, we were up two games to none in this small series and would at least get a split of it by the time Sunday rolled around. Heading into the clubhouse, I watched as Huffman did his after-game interview. It was his least favorite thing to do, but Coach had instructed him to be polite and at least say a few words when asked. The reporters knew he wasn't a fan, so didn't ask him to comment unless he was one of the few players who did well that game. Considering he hit two home runs, that qualified.

After my shower, I pulled my phone out to see a text from Bridge thanking me for thinking of him and asking how the team took the news. I replied that we were sad that this may be the end of his time on the roster, but we hoped for a full recovery. Then I sent a text to Kylie inviting her to have lunch with me the next day. She likely wouldn't see it until the morning, but it was what I could do. I was surprised to feel my phone buzz as I walked to my car, so once I was inside, I tapped to open it up.

> I would love to do lunch. Do you mind
> coming to my place?

There was no way I would say no to going to her place. Maybe she was feeling bold, or maybe it was because her roommate was going to be occupied that day. Either way, I confirmed and asked her for the best time.

> I'm usually up by nine on the weekends, but
> any time would work.

I laughed at the thought of showing up at her place at nine. While that would give us lots of time to talk and do whatever else she had in mind, I knew I wouldn't be able to be functional then. Instead, I offered a later time, and she agreed. I was entirely too excited about this prospect and wondered whether I'd get any sleep that night. Starting my car, I put it in gear and headed out of the stadium parking lot for players and made my way home.

CHAPTER THIRTY-THREE

*K*ylie...

It was good that I'd gone to bed early on Thursday, especially since it was an in-office day for me on Friday. By the time Remi and I were back home, though, I was itching to look at the videos that he'd set up for me to watch. Whether I was able to do anything about the itch I was feeling in my belly, however, was something I'd have to wait on. If what he was saying was true, though, I might just find something to help.

"I picked something up for you at lunch today," Remi said as we were climbing the stairs to our apartment.

"Should I be worried?" I asked.

"Absolutely not," he replied.

I opened our door when we reached it and walked to my desk to drop my laptop off before turning to him.

"Sit," he said, pointing to the couch. "You don't want to be standing up when you open this."

"Now I'm scared," I said with a laugh.

He handed me a black shopping bag that had some weight to it, then sat and watched me expectantly. I kind of just looked down into the bag, unsure exactly what to expect.

"If you don't open it, I'm gonna be mad," he said. "Besides, it's not gonna hurt you."

That comment simply made me more nervous, but I pushed it aside and reached into the bag. I pulled out the box and kind of just stared at it. The picture on the front was this very odd, purple... thing. Like, I wasn't even sure what it was. It was sort of longish, with this thing that stuck out of the middle of it that had two little... rabbit ears or something, and I had no idea exactly what it was or what it was for. I looked at Remi and he was barely holding in his laughter.

"What the fuck is this?" I asked.

"Oh my God, your face," he said, laughing. "You look like what I would assume a deer in headlights looks like."

"Because I feel like that," I retorted. "What even is this thing?"

"It's called a vibrator," he said after finally containing some of his laughter. "I asked at the shop and they assured me that this would be a good first toy for you to try."

"Toy?"

"Yeah," he said, as if it should be obvious what he was talking about. "You use it to help you get off."

"Get off what?"

"Oh, honey," he said, and the condescension was there and I damn near shut down. "Oh, no you don't," he continued when I started to shove the thing back in the bag. "You take that out, pull the bottle of cleaner that's in there out, and take them to the shower. I want you to go in there and watch that video I had cued up for you to watch next. When you're done, you're gonna go in and shower with this and see if it works for you. If it doesn't, we're gonna do some more exploration and find out what does. I don't want you going back into that cave you lived in before you experienced anything sexual. You need to know the beauty of what sex can do for you."

I stared. I mean, what else could I do? He was so pushy sometimes, but he always had my best interest in mind, even if I didn't like it when he pushed me outside my comfort zone. He'd been right about Cole, and he was probably right about sex. I just had to get over my hang up about it and figure out how I could think of it as something other than what it was for my dad.

Shoving the box back into the bag, I got up and walked to my room, slamming my door for effect, but then slumped onto my bed and pulled over his laptop. This was going to be an interesting night.

While the laptop was warming up and getting itself going, I pulled the box back out of the bag and opened it up. There it was, this giant purple thing, along with a cord that had a USB on one end, while the other had a small output like a headphones jack. The bottom of the contraption had a hole where it could be plugged in. I took the vibrator into the bathroom with the cleaner that was also in the bag and gave it a good washing. If this was gonna go where I thought it was gonna go, then I wanted to make sure that it was *very* clean, because infections were the worst.

I dried it off and took it back to the bed, plugging it into the cord and plugging the USB into the charging deck on my nightstand. A little blue light lit up at the end of the device, so I knew it was plugged in and charging at least. I might not use it, but at least it would be ready if I wanted to. I put in the code Remi had given me for his laptop and the images came up once again. I selected the tab that said *Woman Pleasures Herself* and waited for it to come up.

Looking at the woman on the screen in the thumbnail, I wondered why anyone would want to have that kind of look on their face, and also what would cause it. She looked like she might be in agony or something, but instead of just closing the laptop, I clicked the play button.

The image changed to the woman lying on the bed, blankets over most of her, but her arms and legs were out in the open. She was running her hands up and down her body, from her crotch to her boobs and back again, over, and over. I didn't have the volume on because I didn't want to hear that. Instead, I just watched as she began to squeeze her boobs with both hands. Her head went back some as she pinched them over the covers. My guess was she was pinching her nipples, but I wasn't sure.

Next, she moved her hands down, and the sheets came some with them, exposing one of her boobs, but leaving the other covered. The one that was covered she was still squeezing, so that was probably why the sheet stayed where it was. Her other hand went down to her crotch, and she began rubbing over the sheet, up and down along the crack in herself, her head going back some more as she was obviously moaning in enjoyment. She rubbed slowly at first, back and forth with her whole hand, then she started shoving her fingers into the space there, with the sheet between her body and finger.

After what was probably only a few minutes, but felt like an hour, she moved the sheet away and I could see her pelvic area, which had much less hair than I did. *Oh God, he probably thinks I'm a child because I have so much hair down there.* She just had a strip of hair that barely showed and was bare around the rest. Instead of worrying about what Cole might think of me, I decided to ignore that obvious difference and just watch to see what she would do. I don't know that I was prepared for it, but she slipped her middle finger inside her, lifting her hips off the bed as she stroked in and out of herself.

My thighs involuntarily clenched together as that wetness grew between my legs. Instead of being completely grossed out by what I was seeing, though, it was kind of making my stomach feel sort of warm and bubbly. I continued to watch as she stroked in and out of herself with first the one finger, but then adding another to the mix. All the while, she kept squeezing her boob and pinching it. Eventually, she removed the sheet altogether and I could see that my initial assumption was true, in that she was pinching her nipple.

Watching what she was doing, my hand went to my breast and I could feel the padding of my bra, which was kind of frustrating. I paused the video and decided it was now or never, so I pulled my shirt over my head, stripped off my bra from under my tank top, and toed off my shoes, shoving my jeans down and stripping them off with my feet, my socks coming with them. I was now just in my tank and panties, so I scooted up to the headboard of my bed and pulled the laptop over to where I could see it. My nipples were hard, poking out against the fabric of my tank, and my panties were wet, which was probably normal, but I didn't know what normal was.

I had sex education in school, but there were more questions than answers from that, and even my parents didn't really want to talk about it with me. Remi had been the only one to even discuss sex with me, but he knew he was gay from the beginning of time, or at least as long as I'd known him, which went all the way back to when we were like seven or something. After my dad was arrested, no one wanted to talk about sex, and when I found out the details of his crimes, I didn't want to talk about it, either. Now, here I sat, watching porn my best friend picked out for me, on my bed, my body reacting in a way that was probably totally normal, and I was all awkward about it.

Stop thinking about it and just do it, I scolded myself inside my head.

Following my own instructions, I pushed the play button once again on the video, then backed it up a bit so I could see exactly what she had been doing. Following her hand movements, I rubbed and squeezed my boobs, but it kind of just hurt, so I moved on from that and tried to figure out exactly what she had been doing with her hand. I rubbed myself over my panties, feeling the friction the fabric caused against my delicate skin. It was one of those things where it was weird, but still felt good.

When she got to where she moved the sheet and pushed her finger inside her, I paused it again, sliding my hand up to the top of my panties before slipping it inside. My fingers slid through the liquid that was there easily, so I slid it back and forth the same way she had and had to admit that it was a nice sensation. I separated my lips and slid my finger inside myself and damn near knocked myself out when my head went back from the feeling. I didn't move, not my finger, not my body, hell, I didn't even breathe. I just kind of sat there, my finger inside me, waiting to see what would happen next. When I felt like I could move again without killing myself, I pulled my hand out and shoved the panties off my hips and onto the floor.

My nipples were throbbing for some reason, so I moved one hand up to rub them, which only caused my stomach to clench and my head to go back once again. God, this was probably going to kill me. And Remi wanted me to do something like this in the shower? There was no way I was going to stand in a slippery tub while my body reacted this way to being touched.

Closing my eyes, I let my fingers move on their own, just kind of letting them go where I thought might feel good. One hand stayed on my boob and the other dipped between my legs. I began to rub myself *down there* and feel the fluid continue to build up. My other hand was doing that squeezing thing on my boob, which I had figured out needed to not be so firm, but more of a gentle touch. Turning toward the laptop, I used the dry hand to turn the video back on so I could watch to see what might happen next.

Her fingers were sliding in and out of her and her other hand was pinching her nipple. I followed suit, pinching my nipple and shoving my finger in and out of me the same pace she was, and my God it was an unexpected feeling that kind of built up in my belly. It was like I couldn't get enough of what I was doing, and yet I wanted more than just those two things. Watching her hand, she started rubbing her thumb at the front of her pussy, around and around while her fingers were going in and out of her. It looked awkward, and she did eventually move the hand that was on her boob down to do that part. The camera angle had switched a few times throughout the video, but this switch showed her very clearly, and I could see she was doing circles with the fingers at the front, while her others were going in and out.

Copying what she was doing, I realized that whatever was right there, at the front of me, was the button that turned everything up. My head flew back into my pillows and I damn near exploded, clenching my legs together, my hips bucking up from the bed in quick movements, and stars burst behind my eyes. After a year or an hour or a few seconds, my body found itself again, and I pulled my hands free. There was a knock at the door and I about died.

"You okay in there?" Remi asked through the closed door.

"Just fine," I replied, though it came out shrill and breathy.

"Just checking," he replied.

I heard him laugh on the other side, but at least he didn't come in to see what was going on. That would have been completely embarrassing. Instead, I dried my hand off on the quilt on my bed and pushed the pause button on the video. I got up, though it took a few tries, and was steady enough on my feet to make it to the bathroom. After washing my hands, I sat on the toilet and thought about all that I'd been missing. If this was what sex was supposed to do, I was down. The only issue I had was I hadn't ever done anything with anyone else, except for what Cole and I did the day before.

Feeling a little steadier, I stood up from the toilet and went back to my bed, pulling my tank top off in the process. This was going to take time, and I was going to be a willing student. I got back on the bed, this time pulling the blankets and top sheet down so I was at least in a position that I could cover myself if Remi decided I was too much and he had to come rescue me. I clicked the play button to watch the woman have the same reaction I had and saw the moment the thumbnail was snapped and realized that she was in the throes of ecstasy and not in pain. I understood the look on her face.

When she'd finished that, they went back to a full body shot, and she pulled out a toy similar to what Remi had bought for me. She clicked the button, and it began to move. I couldn't hear it because the volume was still down, but I could see the shift in it as she pressed it against her boob. She rubbed it across her nipple, back and forth on first one, then the other. The way she was reacting told me that it must have felt good, so I paused it and pulled my own over. I tried to turn it on, but it didn't seem to want to work. Unplugging it, I pressed the button again, and it jumped to life. I must have let out a squeak because I heard Remi laugh again from the other room.

I did what she had done, rubbing it along my nipple, and ho boy did it do things to me. It was enough of a sensation that my pussy throbbed, and I was thrown off by it because how are those two things connected? I continued to rub it against my nipples, back and forth between the two of them, and the sensation just kept getting stronger between my legs. Not sure what prompted me to do it, but I took my unoccupied hand and moved it down to my pussy, rubbing on the top where I had done so before, and that connection kind of just made me get all tingly.

My legs squeezed together, my pussy was pulsing, and I must have been making noise because there was a banging on the wall behind my head that just kind of shook me. Stopping what I was doing, I listened but didn't hear anything else, so decided to stop for now with my own thing and just watch what the woman in the video did. I kinda wanted to pound on the wall myself, just to annoy the neighbors, but I liked most of the people who were around us, so didn't do that.

The woman had moved the vibrator off her boobs and was running it along her pussy, back and forth. They switched cameras again and were showing her rubbing the vibrator up and down herself. After a bit, she shifted and pushed it inside her, twisting it so the little nub things that stuck out of the middle were right up against the top of her, that spot that had a bundle of nerves that had sent me off to space the first time I'd touched it. She slid the vibrator in and out of her a few times before pushing it in as far as it would go while still having the little ears outside and against her.

She pushed another button on the vibrator and it must have increased the speed or something because it was doing what it was supposed to if one could tell by her facial expressions. I looked at my vibrator and thought I might like to try it, but not on my bed. No, this was something I didn't want to get interrupted doing. I hit pause on the video and grabbed the box for my toy, checking to see if it was something that could be put in water. Sure enough, the instructions said it was fully immersible, so I decided that now was a good time to take a bath.

I got up, toy in hand, and headed to the bathroom where I got the water running to warm up. That was one of the things that was great about this apartment, the water was almost always warm. I think it had something to do with individual instant hot water tanks or something. Remi explained it to me when we first moved in a few years earlier, but I never paid it any attention.

Deciding that since I was going to indulge, I might as well get use of some of the multitude of bath products I'd accumulated over the last few months and grabbed a bath bomb from my basket. I pulled the plug on the tub and waited for the water to begin to fill up. While I was waiting, I turned my toy back on and began to rub it along my pussy lips. I ended up having to stop because I damn near fell over from the sensation of it. With the water level rising, I unwrapped the bath bomb and dropped it into the tub, watching as it fizzed and swirled around, turning the water a nice shade of purple. The smells coming from it were relaxing, which was what I was hoping for. Lavender did that to me, so I figured I'd get some experience with this new thing and get myself ready to have a good long sleep.

Stepping over the edge of the tub, I reached out and grabbed the bar on the side of the shower, keeping myself steady before pulling the other foot in. I turned the water off, then sank into the warm liquid, easing myself into it slowly. Once I was down, I pulled the toy under the water and turned it on again. The water moved with the motion of the toy and I was half tempted to just turn it off and soak, but I really wanted to see what else it would do, so I slid it down between my legs and pressed it against my opening.

The sensation of just the pressure of it against me made me moan, so I just laid my head back and let myself feel. I didn't move it, just let it sit there and pulse against me. Finally, I began to move it around, just a little bit, from the opening. I slid it up toward the front and it hit that nerve bundle and I slid down further into the water, my mouth under the top so that I could let my noise out, hopefully without letting Remi hear me. I mean, I'd heard him enough that I knew how thin the walls were, but I didn't need him hearing me. Stupid, I know, but still, sex had been a hang up for me for forever.

With what Dad did, then living with Granny and Grandpop, it wasn't something I knew much about. That's why Remi always made sure to instruct me on the dos and don'ts of it all, not that he'd needed to do much. My romantic life was nonexistent, so he didn't have to do much except make sure I knew how to keep myself safe. Now, though, he was opening a whole new world to me, and it was something I wouldn't ever be able to thank him for.

Somehow, in all my musings, I'd slid the toy back down and had pressed it into myself, just a little bit. It was a foreign feeling, not something I had ever experienced before, and I'm not sure what I had expected, but it was an amazing sensation. It was bigger than my finger, so there was more there. Instead of stopping and just experiencing it, I pressed it further in. Just a little bit at a time, so that I could get used to it invading my most intimate parts. Stroking it in and out of me, there was some friction because of the water.

I was becoming more frustrated with it, so I set it on the side of the tub and just decided to give up, at least for now. I was tired and knew that I wanted to watch at least part of the game, so I pulled the plug and let the water drain out, standing and pulling a towel around me to dry me off. Once I was dry, I washed the toy again, just to make sure it was clean, then grabbed some pajamas and got ready to watch the game.

"Well?" Remi asked when I came out of my room.

"We are not talking about this," I replied, feeling the blush rush up my face.

"I assume you enjoyed at least something," he said. "I did hear that much."

"I'm not talking about it," I replied, walking past him to sit on the other end of the couch. The television was on, but he had something else playing. "Are you going to put the game on?"

"I wasn't sure you would be watching anything out here," he said. "I mean, you seemed to have enjoyed at least something in there."

I sighed, deep and long, then turned to him.

"I enjoyed some things," I admitted. "I'm not going to tell you what, but just know that I am now open to more than just this life I've been living. I want to explore more, but that is all I'm going to tell you. Can we watch the game, now?" .

He watched me, reading something on my face, and shut whatever he was watching down and switched it to the baseball game.

"Thank you," I said as I heard the announcer begin talking about what was going on.

When I looked at the screen, I could see that the game was more than halfway over. I looked at my phone and realized that I'd spent a good three or so hours in my room. The only thing that did was make me blush even more, realizing that I must have been enjoying myself more than I thought. This could be a bad thing, but then again… how could something that's bad feel so good? Not anything I needed to figure out at that moment, thankfully, so I enjoyed watching the game with my roommate.

CHAPTER THIRTY-FOUR

ole...

> I hope you like tacos. It's what I'm making for lunch.

I heard my phone buzz with the incoming message, so I rolled over to look. Honestly, there was nothing better than waking up to someone thinking about you, except when you got to wake up next to that person, and Kylie was quickly becoming someone I wanted to wake up next to. I typed a quick response that tacos would be perfect, then looked at the time. It was just after ten, so not too early.

After a good stretch, I tossed the covers off and slid out of bed, padding my way to the bathroom to shower and get my day going. Hopefully Kylie would be in the mood to do more of what we started the other morning. Maybe I could return the favor for her. The thought of it made me hard, so I decided to get that out of my system now and not worry about being frustrated later.

I thought about how sweet she was, how innocent she was, and wondered exactly what it was in her past that had shut her out of sex. I mean, she'd never kissed anyone for crying out loud. How was that even possible? But she seemed to figure things out pretty quick, so she had to have some knowledge. Either that, or she was a really quick learner, with, being that her job seemed to be in computers, and she had just gotten a promotion at her age, seemed like that was likely the case.

Closing my eyes, I thought about how it had felt to have her hand on me, even at first when she grabbed my dick like it was something she had to hold on to for dear life. It had taken a minute for me to catch my breath at first, then to help her loosen her grip, but finally, after a few strokes, she had the rhythm down and was pulling exactly how I liked. I tried to mimic that rhythm, that feel of her hand, but I just couldn't. When that wasn't working, I just thought about her face. The way her eyes lit up when she smiled. How her cheeks grew red when she said or did something that was even remotely embarrassing. The softness of her lips when I'd first kissed her, how they melded with mine once she realized I wasn't going to hurt her. How she had been enthusiastic in returning my kiss, and how wet she got when we were sitting together on the couch.

All the little things that made her who she was were what got me over the edge and exploding in my hand under the spray of the shower. I had to hold on to the wall to keep from falling with the power. Usually, I had to envision actual sex to get off, but it wasn't like that with her. She brought out the best parts of me, and I couldn't wait to share everything I was with her. I finished my shower and got dressed to head out to her place. Today would be a great day, I just knew it.

I knew Remi wasn't going to be there, since he'd said he had something he was doing and couldn't come to the game. Maybe we'd get to more than just a little kissing today. I knew I'd have to leave shortly after lunch, so wanted to get there with enough time for more 'getting to know you' kind of things before lunch started. I just wondered whether I should ask more questions, or just let her talk without any guidance.

Driving to the stadium, I wondered whether I should have asked to bring something extra for lunch but opted to just bring myself instead. I'd have asked her, but I was out of the condo and on my way before it even occurred to me. I hated going to someone's place empty handed, so I made a stop along the way to pick up some flowers from one of the markets. At least that was something.

I parked at the stadium, knowing it would be easier to get to and from her place on the light-rail, then walked the few blocks to the station.

For some reason, I was nervous walking up the two flights of stairs to her apartment, and by the time I got to her door my hands were sweaty. I dried them on my pants, then knocked and waited.

"Hey," she said as she opened the door. "Those are pretty."

"Pretty flowers for a pretty girl," I said, realizing how cheesy it sounded, but saying it just the same.

"Come on in," she said, opening the door more. "I'll go find a vase for those."

I followed her into the apartment and to the left as she began to rummage under the sink. It was stupid to assume she had a vase, and I should have grabbed one of those as well, but it never crossed my mind. I know I didn't have one, but she was a girl, so maybe she would.

"It's not very big," she said, pulling one out. "But I think we can make it work."

I handed her the flowers, and she pulled the little packet of food or whatever that was on the rubber band around the stems. She cut it open with the scissors in her block of knives on the counter, then poured it into the glass vase. Turning the water on, she waited for it to warm up, which I thought was weird, and said as much.

"You actually want to put flowers in room temperature water," she explained. "Most people put them in cold, which is why they don't last as long."

After she'd gotten some water into the vase, she put a stopper into the sink and cut the rubber band from the stems, pulling the cellophane from around them as well, then set them into the water. Picking up a few pieces from the bouquet, she trimmed the stems under the water, then stuck them into the vase. It didn't take more than a few minutes before she had it all done and the arrangement looked even better than when I'd picked it out.

"You're really good at that," I said.

"Granny and Grandpop had an amazing garden at their house," she said. "We would make arrangements each week to take to friends and stuff, and it was my job to arrange them. Sometimes it was easy, but other times the pickings were slim and I had to improvise. I learned a lot about that growing up."

"Well, you're amazing at it," I said as she set the flowers onto the little table we'd shared dinner at just a few nights before.

"We've got a couple of hours before lunch, so what do you want to do?" she asked.

"That's a loaded question," I said and smiled. "Just talking or whatever you want is fine with me, though."

She blushed, and I wondered whether she had thoughts that were as naughty as mine, but I didn't have to wait long, because she simply reached out and grabbed my hand, leading me to her room. Following her there, she smiled at me and sat on the edge of the bed. She was dressed in leggings and an oversized sweater which hung off her shoulder. I could see that she wasn't wearing a bra, unless it was one of those ones that didn't have straps.

I sat down beside her and looked around her room. It was a good-sized space for an apartment in Seattle. She'd made her bed up, but the top was pulled down, as if she anticipated coming in here, which made my heart do a little flip. There was a laptop on the nightstand near the door that hadn't been there before, so I wondered if she'd been working in bed. The thought of her sitting there, her hair up in a messy bun like it was now, her legs crossed and her working hard on some project made me want to see that every day.

Turning my head, I saw her smiling at me taking in her space. She reached out and grabbed my hand, pulling it behind her to be around her back. Scooting closer to me, she shifted so she was facing me more, then put the arm between us up over my shoulder, the other rested on my knee. Her eyes were bright with a bit of mischief in them, and I couldn't help but smile.

"You're in an exceptionally good mood today," I murmured.

"I knew you were coming over," she said. "That makes everything better."

It was my turn to blush a bit, even though I didn't do those kinds of things. Slowly, I lowered my head to hers, our lips meeting gently at first, but then her arm went around my neck and she pulled me closer. Following her lead, I wrapped my free hand around her waist and pulled her onto my lap, kissing her deeply in the process. She came willingly, settling herself over me, body pressed against mine. I'm sure she could feel my erection, as the morning release didn't last very long.

Instead of just sitting there, though, she ground herself on me, shifting her weight forward and back, as if she was trying to find the right movement that would help her with her impending needs building up inside her. I pushed one hand up into the back of her hair, getting my fingers tangled in the mess of hair back there. The other hand dipped down to ride along the edge of her ass, just above the top of her leggings, but under the sweater she was wearing.

She shivered when my hand met her skin, and it only made me want her more. Sliding my hand up along her back, I let it slide over her soft skin, up and down her spine in a slow, methodical motion. Moaning, she arched herself more into me, and I had to come up for air, breathing hard with both the need for oxygen and a desire that was building inside me.

When she leaned back a bit, she reached her hands down and grabbed the edge of her sweater, pulling it up and over her head in one fluid motion, dropping it on the floor beside the bed, giving me my first real glance at her breasts. I did see them the other morning, but it was a peripheral view, rather than now where they were out for my viewing pleasure. I looked at her eyes and they were bright, a smirk on her face I hadn't seen before.

"This is new," I said.

"I've been learning a few things," she replied, then blushed deep, both up to the roots of her hair and down her chest, giving her breasts a pink hue.

"Have you, now?" I asked.

"You know I don't know much about this kind of thing, right?"

"That's what you said," I replied.

"Well," she began, but paused, as if she was trying to figure out what she should say.

"I'd love to let you practice what you've learned," I said.

"Remi's been teaching me things," she said.

"Remi?"

"Oh, no, no, not that," she stuttered flushing a deeper shade of red. "He's totally not into girls, and besides, he's like my brother from another mother, so that's just, *ew*."

"I wasn't sure," I replied, thankful that he wasn't the hands-on kind of teacher.

"No, he gave me some very specific videos to watch," she said. "Thus the laptop that is older than time."

"I didn't realize," I said.

"Yeah, well, my life has been…" she stopped, searching for the word. "Sheltered, let's say. My upbringing was very much not conventional, so I never really learned much about sex and stuff."

She shrugged, having folded her arms over her breasts.

"I want you to be comfortable," I said. "You don't have to do anything you don't want to do. You say stop and we stop, no questions asked, no pressure at all from me. Okay?"

I was rubbing up and down her back, keeping my hands low so as not to push anything.

"I want to try," she said. "At least some things, if you're willing."

"I'm willing to do whatever you want, baby," I said. "You're driving this ship, so steer us the direction you want to go."

With only a moment of hesitation, she opened her arms up and wrapped them around my neck, pulling me to her as she dropped her mouth on mine. Whatever Remi had shown her must have flipped a switch in her or something, because she was ravenous with my mouth, and I just wrapped her up and held her to me, devouring her in a kiss like none I'd had before. It was more than just the lips and tongues, but a whole-body experience.

She was mewling like a kitten, rubbing herself on my cock that was harder than it should be, what with me already having rubbed one out today. One of my hands was at the back of her head, the other slid down to the top of her leggings, pressing her onto me so she could feel what she was doing to me. Breaking the kiss, her eyes were shining with some unknown emotion, and she looked amazing.

"I want to feel your skin on my skin," she said, her voice raspy with lust.

Not one to argue, I sat back and worked to unbutton my shirt, but she must have been frustrated with me because she slapped my hands away and did it herself, much faster than I could have. Shoving it off my shoulders, she pushed the material down my arms, and I had to work fast to get them off completely or I'd have been trapped there. When I was free from the top, she pressed my shoulders down on the bed, following me with her own body, laying atop me and pressing her breasts into me, her eyes looking deep into my own.

"You doing okay?" I asked.

"Yeah," she said. "I like this."

"Me, too," I replied, running my hand up and down her back.

"I've never done it," she said, and just the terminology she used gave me a clear indication that she was, indeed, a virgin, and I would have to go slow with her.

"That's okay," I said. "I'll take it slow, let you lead, and answer any questions you have. You good with that?"

She nodded, a color flushing on her cheeks that may have had more to do with the arousal that I could smell from her than embarrassment.

"What do we do first?" she asked, a smile on her lips.

"Well," I said, shifting myself under her. "I think we've already got a good start. What do you want to do next?"

"I don't know," she said. "I feel like I need something, but I'm not sure what."

Her words were punctuated with the movement of her hips that was nearly my undoing.

"You keep that up and there won't be much I'll be able to do," I said with a laugh, which caused her to immediately stop all movement.

"Oh, hey now," I continued. "No need to freeze up. Just know that certain things tend to make it hard for a guy to last very long."

"Oh," she said, kind of sitting up a bit. "What do you want me to do?"

"How about you lay back," I said. "I'll help you get these leggings off and we can go from there."

She was blinking but shifted off me and scooched up toward the headboard of her bed. Shifting her hips, she shoved her leggings and underwear down toward her knees. I grabbed them and helped to pull them the rest of the way off, dropping them next to her sweater.

"You want me to close the door?" I asked, unsure how long we had the place to ourselves.

She nodded, which made me think that her roommate was going to be back sooner than later, so I did as she asked and closed the door firmly into the frame. Turning back, I looked at her laying there naked as the day she came into this world, and wondered whether she had any kind of knowledge as to what I wanted to do with her.

"You're so beautiful," I said. I couldn't help it, she really was.

Slipping my shoes off, I shoved my pants down and pulled them off, along with my socks. I'd worn boxer briefs today under my pants, just in case we wanted to take things slow. That, and they'd catch any precum that might escape if we didn't get very far.

"You tell me if you want me to stop," I said. "I don't want to do anything you don't want to do, so you're in charge. You say stop, we stop."

"Okay," she squeaked out.

"You sure about this?" I asked, and she nodded.

I'd sat on the edge of the bed, but shifted so that I was closer to her, lying next to her so that I could reach her, but also gauge her reaction to be able to stop if that's what she wanted. Sliding one hand up her leg, I let it linger a bit at the top of the thigh but was purposeful in not dipping it between her legs. She had them somewhat clenched together, my guess to stave off the reaction happening there. Instead of diving right down into her sex, I let my fingers slide up and across her stomach, slowly making its way to her breast. When my fingers grazed across her nipple, she sucked in a breath.

I'd been watching her face, but she'd been watching my hand, and it was interesting to watch her react as I got closer. Her breathing had sped up, her mouth opened a bit into that 'O' shape, and her eyes got bigger the closer I got to anything other than ordinary body parts that were available outside a swimsuit. She'd done the same thing when I got close to the top of her thigh, which was why I'd let that go and moved on. I must have chuckled or made some noise, because her eyes snapped to mine, wide with wonder and pleasure in equal measures.

"You still good?" I asked, my voice lower than normal.

She nodded, a bit too fast again, so I stopped and looked at her, willing her to talk to me.

"I'm good," she said. "It's just all so new."

"I'm gonna need you to tell me what's going on in your head," I said. "I can't read your mind, so if something bothers you, or you're uncomfortable, you have to let me know, okay?"

"Okay," she said, her eyes not leaving mine.

"Good," I said, resuming my hands travel, swirling around her nipple. "You like that?"

She nodded, so I stopped.

"Yeah," she said.

"Good girl," I replied. "Keep telling me what you like, okay?"

"Okay," she said, just a whisper.

Taking her agreement to heart, I resumed my swirling of her nipple, watching it peak with pleasure. I slid my thumb and forefinger around it, squeezing it gently as she arched into my hand.

"That feel good?" I asked.

"Mmhmm," she replied, her eyes fluttering closed.

"Good," I said, continuing to squeeze gently.

When I felt that I'd given enough attention to the first breast, I moved over to the other one, giving it the same attention, I had the first. Swirling around the areola a few times before moving to the peaked bud begging for my fingers to take it. While I was working on the far breast, I let my head lower to take the first one into my mouth, and the gasp she let out let me know she felt me. I stopped, peeking up to look at her face as she stared down at me, a mix of confusion and something else on her face.

"Is this okay?" I asked.

She looked a bit confused, but then nodded.

"I can stop if you…"

"Don't stop," she said, her voice strong, almost desperate. "I like it."

"Yes, ma'am," I replied, then dropped my mouth back around her nipple, swirling my tongue around the raised peak while pinching the other gently.

Her head dropped back a bit and her thighs rubbed together, sure signs that she was enjoying what I was doing. I didn't want to push her too far, this being the first time for her, so I stayed with the breasts for a bit, getting her worked up.

When she moaned and reached her hand down between her legs, I let her, shifting so she could do so without my blocking her way. I kept my eyes on her face, watching as she felt everything. Her legs shifted apart, I could feel it, and then I heard the wetness when her fingers began to rub. I glanced that direction just to see, and sure enough, she was fingering herself, stroking that bundle of nerves at the top of her sex.

Her moans deepened, and I turned back to her face to see her eyes closed, her bottom lip between her teeth. I applied more pressure to her nipple with my fingers and closed my teeth just a bit onto the one in my mouth, and her eyes squeezed shut further, her face becoming a mask of that pain and pleasure mix. Then she let out a long and drawn-out groan, deep in her throat as her legs shifted again, this time clenching together.

"Oh, oh, oh," she repeated, still from deep within her throat.

I loosened my grip on her nipples, releasing that blood rush and her eyes popped open, staring at me, blinking rapidly as she came back to herself.

"You like that?" I asked.

Instead of speaking, she just nodded, then her eyes kind of glossed over and tears started running down the sides of her face.

"Oh, hey, now," I said, shifting myself up to pull her to me.

"I'm sorry," she cried.

"No, no," I said, stroking her back as she wept on my shoulder. "Nothing to be sorry about. You did good. You did real good."

She sniffed a bit, gaining some composure, then looked up at me, her eyes still filled with tears.

"You're okay," I said, running one hand along the side of her face, my thumb catching the tears on her cheek. "You feel good?"

Nodding, she shifted a bit, and I realized she was going to wipe her hand on the sheets. Before she could get there, though, I grabbed her wrist, pulling her fingers to me, and sticking them in my mouth, licking her essence off them, and it was so sweet. She watched as I did this, her mouth dropping open a bit.

"You taste delicious," I said and her eyes widened even further.

I couldn't help but chuckle at her face, which only made her look at me even more confused.

"Didn't get that far in your education?" I asked, and she shook her head. "Don't worry," I added. "I'm happy to teach you anything you want to know."

CHAPTER THIRTY-FIVE

*K*ylie...

"You taste delicious," he said.

I looked at him like he'd grown another appendage or something.

"Didn't get that far in your education?" he asked, and I shook my head. "Don't worry. I'm happy to teach you anything you want to know."

I stared at him, confused, until it dawned on me what he was saying. He was willing to teach me anything I wanted to know about sex.

"Are you sure?" I asked, surprised my voice didn't waver.

"Babe," he said, brushing the strands of hair that had escaped my bun back behind my ear. "You seem like a very willing student, and I would be honored to show you anything you wanted to know. Just say the word and we will do whatever you want."

I couldn't help myself; I threw my arms around his neck and held him close to me, our chests pressed against each other. Shifting my weight, I moved to straddle him, and could feel that his erection had gone down some. With me sitting there, though, it started to harden up. I kind of wiggled my hips, trying to get him to be where he was sort of right along my privates, and it became even harder.

"You keep doing that and I won't get to show you much else for a bit," he said in my ear. When I froze, he added, "But I do like it."

I leaned back and looked at him, his smile pulling even further, adding those dimples in his cheeks. I returned the smile and shifted again, feeling him pulse beneath me.

"I don't suppose you have condoms," he said, and I shook my head. "I do have one with me, so we either keep to hands and mouths or we only get one shot. Unless you want me to run to the store."

"I *am* on birth control," I said. "It's because I have horrible periods, but it is supposed to keep me from getting pregnant. Never thought I'd need it for that, but here we are."

"That's not one hundred percent," he said. "Even with a condom, you could still get pregnant."

Realizing he was serious, I pondered again what the ramifications would be if we actually had sex. I mean, yeah, it might be nice, even great, but I could end up pregnant. The only thing that did to me was douse the heat that'd been running through me, and I shivered.

"Shall we stop for now?" he asked. "We can always pick it back up after lunch."

I was naked, he was in his boxers, and I was on his lap. I didn't want to stop, but I didn't want to really go, either. Sliding off his lap, I sat on the edge of the bed next to him. Instead of just getting up and putting his own clothes on, he reached down and grabbed my leggings, which were inside out, my panties stuck on them. He pulled them off, then helped me get into them, turning my leggings right side out while I pulled my panties up over my ass.

After my leggings were righted, he helped me step into them, then picked up my sweater and handed it to me to pull on. As I was doing that, he went to grab his pants and pull them on as well, sliding his arms through the sleeves of his shirt when he'd finished. It was all so anticlimactic that I was a little sad.

"Hey," he said, cupping my face. "You okay?"

"Yeah," I said.

"You seem upset," he said. "Want to talk about it?"

"Maybe," I replied, but I wasn't sure.

"Let's get lunch started," he said. "We can talk while we cook."

"Okay," I replied and grabbed the hand he held out to me, following him out of the bedroom.

We went to the kitchen, and I pulled the inner chamber of my pressure cooker that was already set up to go, and pulled the plastic wrap off the top. I dropped it into the machine on the counter and tightened the lid, making sure the release valve was closed. Then I hit the power button and set it to go for twenty minutes. The recipe I'd been given said fifteen minutes, but I'd never had the chicken cook in that amount of time, so always did it for a few more minutes.

"That was fast," he said, watching me go through my motions.

"Set it up this morning when I was making breakfast," I replied. "It's an easy recipe I found in a book I read one time. We actually make it all the time, now. I always make extra so we have leftovers for lunches during the week, too."

"That's smart," he said.

"Now we wait," I said, then looked at him.

He was watching me, and I wasn't sure whether it was out of curiosity or something else. Instead of waiting to give him all the gory details, I decided to start with the basics.

"My mom's dead, my dad's in prison, and I don't talk about it," I said.

"That's..." he paused, and I was sure he was just going to walk out, but he swallowed and continued, "That's a lot. Do you want to tell me the details? You don't have to if you don't want to, though."

"You're not running away," I said, a little sarcasm in my voice.

"Why would I?"

"I guess we should sit down," I replied. "This isn't a conversation to have standing up."

I walked over to the couch and sat on the far end. He followed and sat next to me, which was not what I'd expected. No, I thought he'd sit at the other end, as far away from me as possible.

"Whenever you're ready," he said, folding his hands in his lap.

The way he was sitting, turned toward me, was both a comfort and a confusion. I'd just laid out some pretty heavy stuff, and he'd opted to get as close to me as possible. He reached out his hand, offering it up for me to hold, and I took it.

I took a deep breath, then told him a very abbreviated version of my life. How my grandparents had taken me in when my parents were gone, and that they'd worked hard to get me away from my father, but it took a couple of years. Finally, after child protective services got involved, and my many therapists pushed for it, my father was out of my life, and I had a protection order against him that lasted until I turned eighteen.

At that point, I had made the decision to change my name, and the protection order continued with the new identity. I hadn't known he knew my new name until he sent me something from prison. When my grandparents died, I thought I could cut all contact with him, and I hadn't heard from him in several years.

The grants and scholarships I received from both my hard work and the victim's relief funds available from the state made it so I was able to attend college and get my degree. The only bright spot in my life through those dark times was the fact that Remi never asked about any of it. He was just there, letting me cry on his shoulder, vowing to take care of me forever, and being the absolute best friend that anyone could ask for.

Everything I told Cole was the truth. I just left some things out, so I didn't have to relive it all. Therapy was expensive, but a necessity in my life, so I had gotten good at giving enough information out without going overboard. When I'd finished, the pressure cooker beeped, and I got up to check the chicken.

I was surprised when Cole wrapped his arms around me after I closed the pot up to cook a little longer. His warmth at my back was everything I needed in that moment, and I leaned into it, holding his hands where they were on my stomach. We stood there for a few minutes, his head resting on the top of mine. I felt him take a big breath in, then let it out slowly. Turning in his arms, I looked at his face, unsure what I'd find there. Tears were not what I expected, and I reached up to wipe them away with my thumb.

"I'm so sorry you had a horrible life," he said.

"It's not all bad," I replied. "I have an amazing friend, a really good job, and a pretty hot friend who's promised to teach me everything I want to know about sex."

I'm not sure what he thought I was going to say, but I obviously surprised him because he laughed. Not a little chuckle or anything, but a full-on laugh, mouth open, eyes closed, totally and completely full of life. It was contagious, too, because I joined him, letting the tension out of myself with the laugh we shared.

"You're good at changing the subject," he said when he'd finally got control. "I really like that about you."

"Thanks," I replied. "Years of trauma will show you how to avoid things. Not the best way to learn it, but it is what it is."

"Thank you for sharing with me," he said seriously. "You can trust me with your pain and your troubles. I'm willing to help you share the load."

"Well, the first trouble I'd like you to help me with is lunch," I replied, then stepped over to the pressure cooker and flipped the release valve again after shutting the machine down.

"Tell me what you need," he said with a smile. "I'm at your disposal. At least until about three. Then I have to run away. Not that I want to, but I have to."

"I understand," I replied, then pointed to the cabinet where our plates were.

We got lunch ready together, then ate quietly while talking about things that were nowhere near as heavy as we'd shared before. All in all, I feel like it was a good day.

CHAPTER THIRTY-SIX

*C*ole...

"I'll see you tomorrow at the game," I said after kissing her soundly.

"See you then," she said, then watched as I walked away.

I turned around just before going down the stairs and she was still there, watching me. I waved, then dipped down the steps two at a time to head out to the stadium. Even though I didn't get more than to watch her get off, it was still a win in my book. Seeing how much she'd changed in just the few days we'd been apart, the fact that she was aware of her body, bold in her actions, and knew what she wanted, it was absolutely amazing.

Her life story was rough, for sure, but she'd kept things from me. I understood that she didn't know me well, so that made sense, but hopefully she'd trust me enough to share everything. I'd debated doing a search of her name, but I only knew her first name so far. She knew my name, but not the other way around. Going to the website for the company she worked for might yield me results, but I opted to just wait her out and let her decide what I knew, and when.

I stepped onto the train just as it arrived, which was perfect timing. It was extremely convenient to be able to park at the stadium and ride the light-rail over to Kylie's place, but I knew that eventually I'd have to figure out parking around there, especially after the season was over. It didn't take long at all to get down to the stadium station, and the walk up and over the railroad tracks after crossing Fourth was as uneventful as ever.

"Where'd you come from?" Hennings asked when I walked into the parking area.

"Visiting a friend," I replied.

"It's that girl, isn't it?"

"She's a girl," I confirmed.

"Good thing Bridge isn't here to yell at you," he said. "You know how he is when it comes to messing with the fans."

"I'm nothing like you," I said, remembering the first year he'd been with the team. "I don't screw everything in a skirt."

"Hey," he said, but he was smiling.

"Just calling it like I see it," I replied.

We walked into the stadium after showing our passes, then made our way through the tunnels to the clubhouse. The crowd was likely to be wild tonight, what with the giveaway they'd planned.

"You get one?" I asked him as we stepped into the clubhouse.

"They're supposed to put one in my locker," he replied. "I hope I don't look like a fucking idiot."

"It's a bobblehead," I replied. "Of course, you're going to look like a fucking idiot. That's the whole point of it."

"Fi's supposed to get one when she gets here," he said. "That means I'll have two. What the fuck am I supposed to do with it?"

"How the fuck do I know," I replied. "I've never had a bobble head made of me, so don't ask me those kinds of questions."

"You're useless," he said.

"Except when it comes to throwing to your short ass," I replied. "If it were any other catcher, they'd throw it over your head every damn time."

"Shut up," he said, but he was laughing.

It was the way of the world when it came to teammate banter. We could talk shit to each other, but no one else was allowed. My phone vibrated just as I was getting ready to stuff it in the locker.

> Play well. I'll be cheering you on from my couch.

She was just so damn sweet. I sent a quick text back to her.

> I'll imagine you like you were this morning. Naked and experiencing an amazing orgasm at my hands and yours. Maybe next time I'll be able to do it all for you.

Those three little dots came up, so I knew she was going to respond, but then they went away. Oh well, I sent another text really quick, just so she knew I wasn't ignoring her when I didn't answer.

> Heading to the field, so no phones until after the game.

Shutting the phone off, I stuffed it into the cubby they had for our personal items that were worth more than just our clothes. A few years earlier, at another stadium, some fan figured out how to get into the clubhouse during a game. He'd ransacked everyone's locker and stolen phones, car keys, and at least seven wallets before he was caught. The MLBPA determined that the players required their own locking box that would house important items during the game. It was a stupid prank, and he was caught before he left the stadium, but it was still a huge issue. Now, every stadium had mini safes in each locker for players to put valuables. It wasn't ideal, but it was what it was.

Once I'd changed, I headed out to the field to get a little batting practice in before some fielding work with the pitching coach. Tanner was pitching again today, so I knew we'd work through some things that were specific to his style of game. We'd worked well together since he'd come over, through spring training and the early few weeks of the season. It was nice knowing what to expect at any given moment, even when everything was expected to be unexpected.

Some folks said that the game was rigged, that everything was planned, but it was obvious they'd never actually played the game. If they had, they'd know how hard it is to hit a round ball with a round bat and make it go where no one was on the field. They'd also know the battle we faced with balls not going where we wanted them to on offense, and not being able to catch them well on defense. There was a reason that there'd only been one .400 hitter in the entire history of the game, and that it had been almost a hundred years since it had happened. The fact that a hitter could fail seventy percent of the time and still be considered at the top of his game should tell anyone how hard it was to play.

Fortunately for me, I'd been one of the few who had figured it all out. Not to say I was some prodigy or something, or that I was the best of the best, but I had figured out how to do the things that made it so I could play this game, earn a great living, and do a whole hell of a lot of traveling, all at my employer's expense. Add to that the fact that I was playing with some of the best guys in the game, and considered many of them friends, and I really did have the best life. The only thing that had been missing in my life was someone to share it with, and meeting Kylie was as if it were ordained by God himself.

CHAPTER THIRTY-SEVEN

$\mathcal{K}$ylie...

"How was your day?" Remi asked when he breezed in halfway through the game.

"Fantastic," I replied, watching Cole throw someone out at second base when they tried to steal. "How about you?" I asked, not taking my eyes off the television.

"Do you even care?" he asked, and I turned to him.

"Oh, hey," I said, seeing his face and the hurt in his eyes. "Come here and let me hug you."

He did, sitting next to me on the couch and dropping his head in my lap. I stroked his hair back from his face, combing through it with my fingers, scratching his scalp as he slowly settled.

"He's an asshole," he said, and I was a bit confused until I realized he was talking about the guy he'd been seeing. "He fucking hit on every damn person we saw today. We were supposed to be together, doing fun things out in the city, but he was more interested in trying to get every guy and girl's number along the way. I fucking hate him."

His venom was palpable, hatred spewing from him with each word. I hadn't met the guy he'd been seeing because he wanted to make sure it was going somewhere, but now that he was here and spitting mad, my guess was I'd never meet him.

"What is wrong with me?" he asked. "Why won't anyone just love me for me?"

"I love you for you," I replied.

"You have to," he said, rolling his head so he could stare up at me. "It's like a requirement or something because we're siblings."

"We're not actually," I replied. "But I get it. Even if we weren't absolute best friends, I'd still love you. You're one of the most amazing humans I know. You're smart, funny, a damn good dresser and cook, and you know how to get me out of my funks. Besides, you set me up with Cole and taught me all about sex, so you can't be all that bad."

"Ooh, speaking of sex," he said, sitting up and piercing me with his eyes. "Did you?"

"I don't think you're supposed to ask that," I said with a laugh.

"Except I can with you," he replied, a smile cracking his face.

"Fine," I said with a sigh. "But only because you're depressed and sad."

"Oh, no," he said. "I'm not depressed, I'm pissed. There is a distinct difference. Now, spill. Was it good? Did you do things you saw in the videos? Did he blow your mind?"

"Dude," I said, stopping the freight train he'd started with his questions. "We didn't actually do 'it'," I said, using air quotes. "But we did fool around."

"Spill," he said. "No, wait. I need wine. You want some?"

"No thanks," I replied. "But you go ahead. You look like you could use it."

"No," he replied, getting up from the couch. "I deserve it like the queen I am."

With that, he did a little flip turn and headed to the kitchen to pull something out of the fridge. Once he'd gotten his beverage of choice, he came back and plopped down on the couch right next to me.

"Okay, go," he replied and took a drink from the pink liquid in his glass.

"Ugh," I said, burying my face in my hands. "I didn't realize I was going to have to give you a play-by-play."

"Girl, you should have," he replied, taking another sip. "It's what girlfriends do, so spill. I ain't going nowhere till you give me all the gory details."

"I took him to my bedroom," I began, and he smiled like he was proud of me. "We sat down on the bed and he started kissing me."

"Is he good?" he asked.

"How do I know?" I retorted. "He's the first guy I've kissed."

"Did you at least like it?" he asked, softening his tone.

"I really did," I replied with a smile. "It's like he knows what to do to get me all tingly inside."

"Then I'd say he was good," he replied.

"I pulled my shirt off," I said, looking away from him. I knew I was blushing because I could feel the heat rushing to my face. "He was really nice about not just staring at my stupid tiny boobs, too. He never said anything bad about them."

"Not all guys want big boobs," he said. "And I'm not just saying that because I like guys."

"You're not making this easy with your constant interruptions," I said.

"Sorry," he replied, then faked that he was locking his lips, thought better of it and 'unlocked' them and took a drink before doing the gesture again.

"When I had my shirt off, we continued to kiss," I said, resuming my description of what happened. "After we were kissing a while, I wanted to feel his skin on mine, so I told him and he tried to take his shirt off, but it wasn't fast enough for me, so I did it myself, pushing it off his arms. It was really nice feeling his skin against mine. Like, I didn't know that was a thing, but I liked it.

"I could tell he was hard or whatever," I continued. "I could feel it against me, and I kept shifting to get it in the right spot, but I just couldn't do it for some reason. He finally helped me to get my leggings and panties off, and I was really uncomfortable until he took his own pants off."

"Boxers or briefs?" he asked, then slapped his hand over his mouth.

"Boxers," I replied, and he smiled. "Anyway," I continued, drawing the word out. "He had me lie down and started kissing up my leg. Each movement of him was amazing and frustrating because I didn't know what all he was going to do, and yet I knew he wasn't doing what I wanted or needed him to do to get me to get to that place where everything explodes."

"Did you tell him?" he asked.

"No," I replied. "He just kept moving higher and higher. He paused right by my…"

"Your pussy?" Remi asked, using the word I'd heard used for that most intimate of places on my body.

"Yeah," I replied, blushing harder. "Anyway, he paused for a moment before moving up my tummy and making it all the way to my boobs. Then, he took my boob in his mouth and was sucking on it. I knew that rubbing them and pinching them felt good because I had tried it when I was watching that video, but what he was doing was just that much more.

"He obviously knew I liked it because he kept at it for some time," I continued. "Then his hand rubbed up on the other one and started pinching my nipple, and man oh man did that do some things to me that I didn't know were a thing. Like, I was getting all wet and uncomfortable down there."

"Did you do anything else?" he asked after I took a pause to check the game.

"Well," I said, not wanting to look at him.

"Kylie Marie Harper," he barked, and I flashed my eyes at him. "You don't need to be embarrassed by any of this," he said, his tone softer. "It's all natural and normal. Just because your dad's messed up doesn't mean that all sex is bad. Besides, Cole's hot, so anything you tell me will just help me get over old jerkface even faster."

"Oh! My! God!" I said, emphasizing each word. "You are the *worst*."

"I'm the best friend you could ever want," he replied. "Besides, how else would you end up hooking up with a sexy baseball player?"

"I am *not* hooking up with him," I said.

"Are you sure?" he asked.

"Remi," I said. "This is about the most awkward conversation I've ever had. And I've had some really awkward conversations."

"I'm sorry," he said. "I know this is hard for you, but I really want to make sure you're being treated right. That if he's gonna do something with you, then he's considerate and kind and not at all pushy."

"He's not," I replied. "He was really nice and thoughtful. He even stopped when I freaked out about getting pregnant."

"Hold up," he said. "He wants you to get pregnant?"

"That's the thing," I said. "He asked if I had any condoms, and when I didn't, because why would I…"

"I do," he said.

"Remi," I said.

"I know," he said, took a drink of his wine, then did the locking the lips thing again.

"Anyway," I said, emphasizing the word. "I told him I was on the pill and he said it wasn't a guarantee. Even condoms aren't, so he said we would have to stick to hands and mouths, but it kind of killed the mood for me, so we stopped."

"Wait," Remi said. "The talk of hands and mouths killed the mood?"

"No," I replied. "The thought of getting pregnant killed the mood."

"That makes sense," he said, taking another sip. "So, no actual sex, but you at least got off, right?"

"If you mean, did I have an orgasm? Then yes," I said, looking back at the television.

"Did he?" he asked, and I looked at him, shaking my head. "And he seemed okay with that?"

"He actually suggested we stop," I said. "It was like he knew I was uncomfortable with it all, so he suggested that we make lunch and talk."

"Can we clone him and make him gay?" he asked, and I laughed. "What did you talk about? Did he tell you everything there was to know about him?"

"I actually told him about me," I said.

"You did?"

"Yeah," I replied. "I said my dad was in jail, my mom was dead, and I didn't want to talk about it."

"He let you get away with that?"

"What do you mean?" I asked.

"That's a big bomb," he said. "I want to know if he made you give him all the details."

"He didn't," I replied, looking at him. I reached out and took his wine glass, taking a sip before giving it back and continuing. "He said it was fine, but that he hoped I'd feel safe with him at some point to tell him everything."

"That's it?"

"Yup," I said, then heard the unmistakable sound of a hard hit and looked at the television. "Oh man, he just hit a home run."

I watched as Cole ran around the bases, giving a high five to the guy near third, then getting hugs at home base. They were all jumping up and down and I looked at the little score thing at the bottom of the screen to see that he had won the game with the hit.

"You should tell him before he finds out himself," Remi said, and I looked at him.

He was right, of course, but I didn't want to mess anything up. I mean, this was the first time I'd let myself do anything like this, and I wanted to keep Cole in the dark about my horrible family history for just a little while longer.

CHAPTER THIRTY-EIGHT

*C*ole...

It was one of those games where, no matter what you tried, nothing seemed to be working. At least it was that way for both teams, though. Tanner was killing it on the mound, and the guys behind him were doing phenomenal. Unfortunately, they had their ace on the mound, and we couldn't figure out how to make contact. We had three hits scattered throughout the first eight innings, but no one got past first base. One of their guys tried to steal on me in the sixth, but I gunned him down, which made me feel pretty damn good about myself.

Now, it was the bottom of the ninth and there were two outs and it was up to me to get us going or we'd be playing extras. I never liked being in this position, having to be the last man standing, but at least it wasn't a hit or go home situation, so I just had to try to make contact.

Walking up to the plate, I gave a few practice swings, then stepped into the box, tapped my bat on the plate once, and swung it through the zone. Their pitcher came set, nodded at the sign, then went through his wind up and threw the ball. It was well outside, but the catcher caught it.

"Ball," the umpire said, and I stepped one foot out of the box to give a couple more swings.

Stepping back in, I waited, wondering what he was going to throw. Again, with the nod, the wind up, and he tossed it, but it was inside this time, and I had to back out of the box to avoid being hit.

"That's two," the umpire said, then held up his hands to indicate the two balls, no strikes count.

Step out, give a swing, step back in, and wait. The third base coach had given me a green light if I liked what I saw, but also was fine to sit and wait for him to throw a pitch. Unsure what I was going to see, I stepped out, asking for time, and the umpire granted it. Sometimes you just had to adjust the rhythm and could find a good pitch to hit. I was hopeful that my adjustment would do just that.

When I stepped back in, the catcher tapped his mitt on the plate, which was an obvious sign for the pitcher to keep the ball down. Now I knew what to look for, something low in the zone, which just so happened to be my sweet spot.

The throw came in and it was as if it had been telegraphed to me. It was slow enough that I didn't have to worry about catching up to it, but it was fast enough that I could get good wood on it and give it a drive. I was a little fast, so it was going down the right field line. I leaned toward the field of play, willing the ball to stay fair, and by some miracle it did.

"Yes," I shouted, tossing my bat toward the first base dugout, and pumping my fists in the air.

The team was spilling out onto the field as I rounded first. Making sure I hit each bag, I went around as fast as I could, but not wanting to overdo it by sprinting. When I rounded third, the coach gave me a high five, and I continued on home.

About fifteen feet from home, I tossed my helmet up and barged through to the bag. The team was there, gathered around the base, with the umpire right there to make sure I hit it before backing out of the crowd around the base.

There were slaps on my back, pulling of my jersey, and someone had grabbed the Gatorade container to douse me with the sticky liquid that was left inside. All of it was absolutely perfect. The only thing missing was Kylie, and I would have loved to hug her with my wet jersey and sticky arms, but she was watching at home, so hopefully she saw it all.

By the time the celebration was complete and the team was heading back to the dugout and further to the clubhouse, I made my way toward the reporter for the local sports station that aired our games.

"What a finish," she said.

"Great way to finish a game," I agreed.

"Babcock was pitching really well tonight," she continued. "How did you finally guess right on that last pitch?"

"I don't want to give away secrets," I said, smiling. "Sometimes you just get a feeling, a sixth sense or something, and you kind of have to know that you know…"

Just then, I was doused again, this time with a cooler full of water. The reporter had backed away just in time to keep from getting wet herself, but I just turned around and smiled at the guys.

"I almost got it," she said when she came back to me.

"Yeah, sorry about that," I said. "The guys have been playing extra good now that Bridge is out for a bit. We all kind of want to make it through to get him back and be in a position to push to the playoffs."

"Speaking of Bridge," she said. "What have you heard?"

"We know he's gonna have surgery," I said. "After that, it's all about his rehab and what the doctors think. We're all pulling for him, though, and know he's strong and durable and one of the best players in the game. Not to mention, one of the nicest guys in this industry."

"Harley-James has been pitching well this season," she said, changing the subject with ease.

"He really has," I agreed. "It's always an odd thing to come to a new system and try to fit in, but Tanner has been putting in the work and doing everything he can to make the team better. Tonight's just the tip of the iceberg, I think."

"I'll let you go enjoy with your team," she said. "Back to you guys."

The light at the top of the camera went off, and she turned to me.

"Thanks," she said. "Seriously, though. What do you know about J?"

"Just what I said," I replied. "They don't usually tell us too much."

"Good to know," she replied.

"See ya," I said, then turned to the dugout to grab my gear and head in.

When I walked into the clubhouse, Coach stopped me and said, "They want you in the post-game."

"I got time to shower?" I asked.

"Better if you don't," he replied.

I dropped my gear in the locker and headed to the press room. It was a small room just off the clubhouse that had a back entrance for the players and coaches. A table was set up with microphones in the middle and chairs behind it. I sat in the middle chair right behind the microphone and our press person sat off to the side a bit, out of the camera's view, but still there to help if they asked things that were not something I would be answering.

We'd all learned last season how to handle questions outside our scope of information after the incident in Indigo City with Beckett. It was something they discussed in spring training, but it didn't hit us until that week. At that time, we didn't really know much of anything anyway, so it wasn't hard to not answer the questions.

"Cole," one reporter said once I'd sat down. "How have you been handling the pitching staff so well this season? Especially with all the changes in the rotation."

"It's always a learning curve at the beginning of each season," I replied. "You just have to get to know the guys and what their preferences are. Then it's just a matter of working together. I feel like we've been doing well this year, though, as evidenced by the low ERA our pitchers have."

"Was Babcock tipping pitches?" anther reporter asked.

"Not that I could tell," I replied. I didn't want to let the other team know that the pitch I hit out was tipped by the catcher, not the pitcher. "Sometimes you just guess right, which is what happened on that last pitch."

"How have the fans shown their acceptance of Harley-James since his coming over from the Dragons?"

"Off season is a funny thing," I said. "Players go from one team to another, shift up or down in the system, or leave the game altogether. This was no different."

"Some of the players who were traded from Houston have been getting booed when they come in," yet another reporter said. "We haven't seen that here in Seattle. Why do you think that is?"

"Seattle has some of the best fans in the game," I said. "Most understand that a few bad apples don't make up the whole team. From what I understand, it was out of the hands of the pitchers, which is why our guy has been accepted with open arms."

"What do you think of the pitch com now that it's in use in the regular season?"

"It's been great," I said. "It cuts down on the time between pitches, makes sure that everyone on our team knows what the call is, and ensures that we are all on the same page. Besides that, I don't have to paint my fingernails anymore."

There was scattered laughter through the room at that last remark.

"I think that's all," the press guy said.

I stood up and thanked the reporters before heading back to the clubhouse to shower. It was late when I finally got done and turned my phone on.

Your home run was awesome.

It was great to get that from Kylie. I didn't know whether it came in right after the hit or later because my phone didn't always keep the time correct if it was off. Either way, I figured she was already in bed, what with the game having been over for more than half an hour already. Not wanting to wake her, I opted to not respond and just head home.

CHAPTER THIRTY-NINE

*K*ylie…

With as late as Remi and I stayed up talking, I was surprised I was actually awake when the alarm went off at eight. They would let us in the stadium earlier than everyone else because we had the special passes Cole got us, but it was still going to be awhile before we would be heading out, so I had time to take a long shower and get myself in the mood to be around a stupid number of people.

I didn't really need to get up as early as I did, but I wanted to take extra care in dressing up for Cole. He'd been more than kind, and I really liked him and wanted to see where this could go, so I wanted to do everything I could to make sure that I was living up to the role of someone worthy of spending time with a professional athlete.

Drying off, I heard Remi coming out of his room, so I finished up and threw on my oversized shirt to greet him.

"Why am I up this early?" he asked.

"Because you love me," I replied. "Besides, you're the one with the tickets, so it's not like I can go without you."

"You could," he said. "But I wouldn't do that to you. I'm gonna need coffee, though. There's no way I am going to be able to function without it."

"You need help?"

"Nah," he said. "Go get pretty for your man."

I smiled and turned on my heel, heading back to my room to finish getting dressed. We'd already picked out my outfit, so it was just a matter of putting it on and finishing up with my hair. I wanted to wear it down, but knew that it would be better up, so I dried it out enough that it wouldn't stay wet all day, then threw it up in a clip at the back of my head.

Jeans and my team shirt that we'd picked up a week or so earlier were what I was wearing, along with an oversized cardigan to keep the still chilly late spring air off my skin. Pulling on my boots, I tucked my jeans inside, then headed to the kitchen to grab a quick something before we headed out.

"We need more coffee," Remi said. "There was only enough for one cup. Do you want it?"

"You need it," I said. "We can grab something at the stadium if I feel the need."

Opening the fridge, I pulled out the bowl of cut up fruit that was a staple in our kitchen and scooped some out into a smaller bowl. I held it up to Remi, but he shook his head, taking a sip of the coffee he'd doctored and sitting at the table. I covered the rest of the fruit and put it back, then joined him at the table.

"It's a good thing I love you," he said. "Anyone else would end up with me canceling and staying in bed."

"Getting out will be good for you," I said. "Besides, it'll give you a chance to look at some pretty sexy men on that field."

"If only they'd look at me the way Cole looks at you," he replied. "That would make my day."

"I can ask Cole if he can hook you up," I offered.

"I do not want to be hooked up," he said with a glare. "I like my relationships to be organic before they're orgasmic."

"Remi," I said, trying to look shocked, but failing with my laughter.

"It'll happen when it happens," he said.

"I just want you to be happy," I said, reaching out to hold his hand.

"Back at you, sister," he said.

I finished my fruit, then took the bowl to the sink and rinsed it out. Remi followed with his mug, doing the same, and I went and grabbed my purse down from the stand by the door. We walked out of the apartment and headed for the train, tapping our transit card on the kiosk at the entrance before stepping to where it would stop to pick up passengers. It was pretty sparse at our station, but we figured we'd run into some crowds the closer we got to the stadium.

It only took ten or so minutes before the train stopped at the stadium station and we were walking with more fans down the road from the station to the stadiums. Honestly, it took longer to walk to the stadium than it did on the train, which was an odd thing, but it was what it was. We had to wait to cross Fourth, but once we were across, we did the big wind around up and over the tracks, then down the stairs to street level where we would have to walk around most of the building to reach the entrance we used for our special tickets.

The crowd was really big, so I stayed as close as I could to Remi, my arm through his as he led the way through the throngs of people lined up to get into the stadium.

"What's with the crowd?" I asked once we'd made it through most of them.

"Dunno," he replied. "Hey," he said to someone walking by us. "They got a giveaway or something?"

"Yeah," the guy said. "It's bobble head night for the short stop."

"Ah," Remi said, keeping me close to him as we continued on.

"Bobble head night?" I asked.

"They make them up for players," he replied. "I think they do a bunch each year, but I don't know who the guy is."

"Oh," I replied.

We continued on down the street, weaving a bit through the other fans that were walking along the sidewalk. A few cars were coming up the street to park in the garage for the other stadium. When we finally made it to the end of the building, we turned the corner and walked past another group of fans that were lined up to get into the stadium at the entrance on the corner. We kind of had to go way around the lines and barriers that were set up there, and I wasn't sure we'd be able to get through to the place where we needed to get in.

"This is the shortest line," one woman said as we passed her.

"We're meeting someone," Remi replied as we walked past.

I just kept my head down and clung to his arm as he pulled us through the people. Finally, though, we broke free of the larger crowd and managed to find the entrance we needed.

"Tickets," the security man at the door said.

Remi pulled his phone out, brought up the app the tickets were in, and the guy scanned the bar codes for each, then let us through the door. We did the same thing when we got to the desk in the area before heading through the double doors that led into the posh bar under the seats.

Just like the first time we came through here, I felt a bit underdressed, but not quite as bad. At least I knew what to expect and planned for it. As we walked in, there was someone in a Cascades jersey with a big box next to her.

"You guys want bobble heads?" she asked.

"Thanks," I said, holding my hand out.

She handed one to me and another to Remi, and then we walked to the bar and ordered a beer for himself and a water for me. Once we had our drinks, we headed through the big doors to the stadium to find our seats.

It was still early, just past ten, when we made it into the seating area. I looked at the players on the field, trying to spot Cole, while I followed Remi to our seats.

"There he is," he said, pointing to the big cage that was around the home base place on the field.

I looked out to see him standing inside it and swinging his bat a bit before the guy on the bump threw a ball in. Cole swung and hit it really hard, but it went straight up and hit the cage that was around him, bouncing back down really fast to land and jump from the dirt at his feet. He tapped it out of the area with his bat and didn't seem at all phased that it nearly bashed him when it came back down. Instead, he just got back in there and waited for the other guy to throw another ball.

The next one he threw, Cole swung at and hit right back at the guy, the ball bouncing off the screen that was in front of him and off to the side of the field.

"This looks almost more dangerous," I said as we settled into our seats.

"I'm sure they do it to keep everyone safe," Remi suggested.

"But he almost knocked himself out with that first one," I argued. "Then, he almost hit that guy out there that's throwing the ball to him."

Remi just kind of chuckled, taking a sip of his beer. Cole took a couple more throws, hitting both of them out past the other fences that were scattered around the inner part of the field, then walked out of the cage and started talking to someone there.

"That must be the hitting coach," Remi said, pointing.

"Okay," I replied because I had no idea what any of that meant.

Cole turned to look toward us and smiled. He said something to the coach he was talking to, then trotted over to the edge of the field, waving for us to come down. I got up and headed in that direction, Remi following me, beer in hand. We walked up to the netting that was set up between the field and the stands right at the edge.

"Hey," he said, reaching his hand through the netting. "Glad you guys got here early."

"Thanks again for the seats," Remi said. "They're amazing."

"Glad you could come," he said, shaking Remi's hand.

When he dropped Remi's hand, he reached out to hold mine, and I was a little self-conscious, but took it.

"I should get your picture," Remi said, pulling out his phone.

"I don't like pictures," I said, turning a bit away from him. "You know that."

"Still," he said, giving me the 'do as I say' look he liked to give me.

I finally relented and turned so he could see both of us.

"Hang on," Cole said, shifting a bit to the side and shoving the netting apart where there was a seam I hadn't known was there. "This way there isn't the mesh in it."

"Good plan," Remi said, shifting himself as well.

I stood sort of still and stiff until Cole pulled me a bit next to him. It really was kind of awkward, but there was just enough space in the seam that I could be next to him and Remi could get a picture of us.

"Girl," he said, giving me another look. "You like him, so look like it."

"Remi," I barked, blushing to high heaven.

"Come here," Cole said, pulling me even closer and wrapping his arm around my waist.

He kissed my temple, and I closed my eyes, letting the rest of the world fade away until it was just the two of us.

"There we go," Remi said, and I opened my eyes and saw him smiling.

"I'm glad you're here," Cole said into my ear.

"Me, too," I replied with a smile.

"I gotta go get ready," he said, kissing my temple again. "See you after the game?"

"Sure," I said, my voice so low that only he could hear me.

He smiled, those dimples coming out the way they did, and then he kissed me quick on the lips before letting me go to head back to his coach.

"Come on," Remi said. "Let's get settled in to watch the game."

I followed Remi back up the steps to our seats. Hopefully we'd see them win today. It was kind of boring watching the warm-up stuff they were doing, so I jumped on my phone to check out some social media accounts I followed. All of my socials are locked down so tight that it's hard to even see anything if you aren't actually connected to me. It was something I did way back when everything happened with my dad. I just hadn't wanted anyone to see anything about me. I only had a couple of social media accounts anyway, so it wasn't like I had a lot of stuff out there.

"Can I post this pic?" Remi asked, showing me his phone.

I was amazed at what he'd captured in the photo. It was Cole and I, but we were both looking at each other, completely oblivious to the rest of the world, and the look on both our faces was clearly transmitted through the still image. It wasn't necessarily love, but it was definitely more than just two people hanging out.

"Don't tag me," I said, and he looked sad, but did what I had asked and posted it without connecting it to my account.

We watched the Cascades players move off the field and the other team come out with their dark blue warm-up outfits. They did the same thing that our team did, in that there were a few who went out to the outer area of the field while others stood near the cage to hit the ball. It was fascinating to see the different players as they went into the cage. Obviously, some hit from one side of the base and others from the other, but there were a couple who did both sides.

"Why are they doing both sides?" I asked Remi.

"They're switch hitters," he said as if that explained everything. When he looked at me, he could see I was confused. "Most players hit from their dominant side," he offered. "Some hit from the other side, though, and then there are those who hit from both. If they hit from both, they're called a switch hitter, meaning they can switch which side of the plate they hit from."

"What does Cole do?" I asked, having realized I had no idea.

"He bats right-handed," he said. "That's on that side of the plate."

He pointed to the guy who was in the cage at that moment and he was on the left side of the plate from where we were sitting.

"Okay," I said, still not understanding it all.

"I think a trip to the batting cages with Cole is in order for the next time you to get together," he said. "He can show you how it works, and you may just get him to show you really close, if you know what I mean."

He wiggled his eyebrows up and down and I just stared at him, completely confused.

"He will wrap himself around you," he said. "Hold your hands on the bat in front of you and swing with you. Your back will be up against his front. You'll get a good feel of his whole body."

"Oh," I said, drawing the word out, finally understanding what he meant.

Then I thought about it and could feel the blush running up my face.

"Now you get it," he said with a laugh.

I had a hard time concentrating on much of anything after that. All I could imagine was Cole wrapped around me, his hard body pressed against my back, similar to what it was when he slept over. Honestly, I really wanted him to do that again, but I wasn't sure exactly how to ask him.

My phone pinged, and I looked at the lock screen to see there was a group text from Remi. It was the picture he'd posted sent to me, and also to Cole. How he'd gotten Cole's number, I wasn't sure, but I didn't mind. Cole responded to the group text thanking Remi for capturing the moment. I had to agree that the moment was perfect, and I was glad it was captured in this way. Finally, after forever, with the crowd slowly filling up the seats around us, they started to pull the cages and stuff down, doing their before the game ritual of fixing the field and wetting it down and whatever else needed done.

It came time for the ceremonies before the game and we watched as an older woman came out to throw out the ceremonial first pitch. The player who caught the ball wasn't Cole. His jersey said Cameron on it. He had his baseball hat on backward, but his dreadlocks hung underneath, poking out from under the brim at the back of his head. The throw was a little bit wide, but she made it all the way to the player, which was something I was sure I wouldn't be able to do. The player snagged it out of the air before it hit the ground, then trotted out to where she was standing right in front of the hill in the middle of the field. They turned around and had pictures taken, then he signed the ball and gave it to her.

After that was all done, the announcer was talking about the starting lineups, announcing the other team first. Each player was named with their position, but it wasn't in any kind of order that made sense to me. After they were announced, he started with the Seattle team.

"And now," his voice boomed through the stadium. "Let's introduce the starting lineup for your Seattle Cascades."

The crowd shouted loudly as they all watched the giant screen up above the benches in the back of the stadium from where we were.

"Leading off," he continued, and a picture came up of one of the players. "Playing short stop, Beckett Hennings."

Again, the crowd shouted loudly.

"Isn't that the guy you were talking about earlier?" I asked Remi.

"Oh yeah," he replied, but was busy watching as the picture changed to the same man who had caught the ball from the woman for the first throw.

"Batting second," the announcer boomed. "Playing third base, Mitch Cameron."

Again, the crowd cheered, though not quite as much as they did with the first guy. The announcer continued, going through the entire list of people who were playing, but I only cared when they said Cole's name, cheering as loud as I could. Finally, after he had said everyone's name who was playing, as well as the coach, or I guess he's called the manager, he asked everyone to make noise and the players all came out onto the field, going to their places to begin the warm-up for the first inning.

I watched as Cole squatted behind the home base, catching the throws from the pitcher then tossing them back. Over and over, he did this, until the catcher did some kind of signal and he threw the ball one last time before Cole threw it down to the guy at the middle base, second base, and he did a sweep with his glove over the base, then tossed it to the short guy who tossed it over to the guy at the first base who threw it to the pitcher.

It was all so choreographed and perfect that I realized it was something they did each time. I noticed that the mascot was on the opponent's side of the field with a kid and a microphone and I was a bit confused. I mean, they'd already done the national anthem, done the ceremonial first pitch, as they called it, and the players were on the field, so what was this kid doing.

"And now," the announcer's voice boomed. "Let's hear those two famous words to get this show going."

"Play ball," the kid said, and the crowd cheered.

It was actually a really cute thing because the kid had a jersey on, along with a hat, and was beaming from what I could see on the big screen across the stadium. Then, the people who did the field stuff before the game helped to get the kid back into the stands, the microphone off the field, and the carpet he'd walked out on rolled up before the player from the other team came up to home base. The umpire pointed out to the pitcher and the other guy stepped into the little white box that was next to the base, scratching his foot back and forth, I guess to get the dirt right for him to stand there.

There were just so many little things that went into getting the game started that I was mesmerized by everything. Then, the pitcher threw the first pitch and Cole caught it and the umpire shouted something, but I couldn't make out what it was, except he threw his hand out and pointed away from the guy that was hitting. The crowd cheered, so my guess was it was a good thing.

"That's a strike," Remi said, and I nodded, as if that cleared everything up.

I'd watched the game a little bit when we were kids, but honestly, I was just there to cheer for Remi and didn't really understand the game at all. Now, though, I was picking up some of the things, but was still a long way off in my education when it came to the game.

"If he gets three, he's out," Remi explained, obviously realizing I didn't know what he was talking about.

"Thanks," I said, still focused on Cole.

The next pitch came in, and the hitter swung his bat, but missed the ball. Cole caught it and the umpire did the same thing with his hand, punching the air away from the hitter. That was two strikes, so one more and he would be out. I knew that they had to get three outs to be done being on the field and get the chance to come up to hit the ball, so obviously I had learned a few things.

Another pitch, and this time the hitter swung and kind of nicked the ball and it came sailing back toward us. I ducked and threw my hands up and Remi laughed at me.

"What?" I asked.

"That's what the net is for," he said.

"Still freaked me out," I replied. "Is he out now?"

"No," Remi said. "That's a foul ball, so he gets to try again."

"I thought if they didn't hit it in three tries, they were out," I said.

"Foul balls don't count," he said. "Unless it was a bunt."

"What's a bunt?" I asked.

"Don't worry about it," he said. "They don't normally do those. If they do, I'll explain it."

"Okay," I replied.

The rest of the game went like that. Me asking questions about what was going on that I hadn't learned yet, and Remi explaining them to me. I actually really enjoyed myself, even with the mass of people who were around us. The nice thing about the seats that Cole gave us was that most of those around us were family or friends of the players, so they were a little less wild than the rest of the stadium. The ushers were super nice as well, always asking if there was anything they could get for us.

The game went quick, but unfortunately, our team lost. The other team's really big guy hit a home run near the end of the game, and our guys just couldn't get anyone to come all the way around the bases. I knew the players weren't gonna be happy about losing, but I hoped Cole would still come see me after the game.

As the crowd was filing out, Remi and I stayed in our seats, gathering up what we had, which was really just our bobble head things we got when we came in. I knew that Cole had things he had to do, but I was hopeful that he'd at least come out and see me. Finally, after waiting for what felt like forever, he stepped out of the place where they sit and started walking over near where we were.

He took my breath away just watching him walk across the field. When he turned his face up to look at us, his smile melted my heart. Yeah, I was totally and completely gone for this guy, and he's the first guy I ever even sort of dated. Maybe those fairy tales were true and everyone had their prince charming out there. I'm just glad I found mine.

CHAPTER FORTY

*C*ole...

The game was brutal. We were fine on defense. Our pitching and fielding were absolutely outstanding. Our problem was we couldn't get a hit to save our life. Everyone was struggling on offense, and none of us could figure out what the issue was. A couple of the guys got hits, but they were few and far between and didn't add up to anything more than a few extra at bats down the line.

We only had one bad pitch, and it ended up in the bullpen. That one hit was what won the game for the Anglers and sent us on the road with a loss. At least we were going to get another chance to play them this season. Maybe we could take a game or two in their stadium later this summer. Only time would tell.

I made my way out of the clubhouse, up the steps of the dugout, and over toward where Kylie and Remi were sitting. If there was anything that might get me out of the foul mood I'd ended up in, it was her smiling face. I looked up to see her standing close to the field and I couldn't help but smile. She was like a ray of sunshine after a dark and stormy night. The absolute perfect respite from the turmoil my mind had found itself in.

"Hey," I said when I got close.

"Hey yourself," she replied.

"Sorry about the loss," Remi said. "That pitcher was wicked."

"Oh yeah," I replied. "He's one of the best in the league."

"Our guy was good, though," Kylie said.

"Phil's great," I said. "Not quite our ace, but he's still good. I don't have much time," I continued, squeezing her hand. "We're heading straight to the airport to take off."

"Oh," she said. "I didn't know you were leaving."

"Sorry," I said. "If I could, I'd stay."

"No, no," she said. "You have to go. It's your job."

"That it is," I said. "Best job in the world if you ask me."

"I'm gonna let you two have a minute," Remi said, reaching out a hand. "Thanks for taking care of her."

"Absolutely," I replied, shaking his offered hand. I watched as he walked up the steps a ways to sit in one of the chairs. Looking back at Kylie I smiled. "Don't cry," I said, running a thumb across her cheek where a tear had fallen.

"Can't help it," she said, her voice cracking. "I'm gonna miss you."

"We will have to talk by phone," I suggested. "Can even video call or something."

"How long will you be gone?"

"Unfortunately, this is our longest road trip of the season," I said, and I really was upset about that. "Flying to Miami tonight, then after there, it's Atlanta, DC, Philly, Boston, and Denver before we get home."

"Oh man," she said. "How long?"

"Almost three weeks," I said, pulling her to me. "I wish I could take you with me, though."

"They won't let you, though, will they?"

"It's complicated," I said. "You wouldn't be able to fly with me, but if you flew separate, we could still be together."

"I don't want to fly by myself," she said, and I heard the fear in her voice.

"Won't ask you to," I replied. "Just know that if I could, I'd take you with me the whole time and never let you out of my sight."

"Will you call me when you land?" she asked.

"Of course," I replied. "Every single time if you want. You'll be so sick of me you'll stop answering my calls."

"Never," she said with a laugh, but it was broken. "I really will miss you. I didn't think it would be a big deal, but it is."

"Yeah," I replied. "I kinda like having you around. Spending time with you when I'm not on the field is the best thing."

Her smile was sad, and the tears were welling up more. God, she was beautiful when she cried, but I hated it at the same time. Instinctively, I pulled her to me and kissed her. She let go herself and kissed me back with such passion I could barely stand. When we finally came up for air her tears were still there, but there was a light in her eyes as well.

"Keep watching those videos Remi found for you," I said. "I can't wait to see what you've learned by the time I get back."

Her mouth dropped open at my statement, then she burst out laughing, the sound echoing around the nearly empty ballpark.

"I have to go," I said, kissing her one more time. "I'll call you."

"Okay," she said and let me go.

It was so hard to walk away from her when all I wanted to do was take her with me everywhere I went. This was going to be the longest road trip of the season, but not just because of the time away from home. No, it was because I would be away from her, and that killed me.

"See ya," Remi called when he stood up.

"Thanks for being her best friend," I called back.

"It's been my job for a long time," he replied. "I'll be glad when you get to take on this role. Not that I won't be around, but because it'll make me less worried when I can't be."

"Well," I said. "I feel better knowing you're here when I'm not."

"Cole," Huffman shouted from the dugout. "Get your ass in gear."

"Bye," Kylie said, squeezing my hand one last time before letting go.

"I'll call you," I replied, then trotted over to the dugout to drop down the stairs.

"The fuck was that?" he asked when we got into the tunnel.

"That would be my girlfriend," I said, and couldn't help the smile that broke across my face.

"That's new," he said. "Should I be worried?"

"I'm not Hennings," I said with a laugh.

"I'm glad," he replied, his stoic nature still unbreakable.

We walked into the clubhouse and I gathered up my gear, tossing everything into the bag I had, then headed out to where the team bus was waiting to take us to the airport. No, this definitely would be the longest road trip of the season, and I could already feel the missing pieces of myself as I got further and further away from Kylie. Maybe it was too fast, but something about her and I just felt right. Like she was the yin to my yang, my missing piece. I was definitely gonna miss her.

CHAPTER FORTY-ONE

*K*ylie…

We walked down the steps and through the bar to the little lobby where we first entered the building. There were still lots of people out on the sidewalks outside the stadium, so as we walked out into the dimming sunlight, we had to get through the crowd. Remi was good about tucking my arm into his so we wouldn't lose each other as we walked to the train, but it was still uncomfortable.

At least by the time we got to the train, it wasn't nearly as crowded as I anticipated, and we got to actually sit down during the short ride north. By the time we made it to our apartment, though, I was more than a little exhausted.

"Go change," Remi said as he keyed the way in. "I'll make something quick for dinner and we can chill for the rest of the night."

"Okay," I said, walking to my room and grabbing my oversized shirt.

When I got back out to the main area of the apartment, Remi had a couple of salads dished out, dressing options on the table, and a big glass of water for each of us.

"Thanks," I said as I sat in my usual place.

I poured some dressing onto my greens and took a bite, enjoying the flavors as they mixed together. We ate in companionable silence, which was how it usually was for us. Like, we had lived together for a long time and had figured out our cohabitation rhythm without much fuss.

"You going in tomorrow?" he asked.

"No," I replied. "It was a scheduled work from home day, so I don't have to worry about it, which is nice. I'm exhausted."

"You looked tired," he said. "Go ahead and head to bed. I'll clean up."

"I can help," I offered, but he just shook his head. "Thanks," I said as he took my plate.

I went to refill my glass from the dispenser in the fridge, then headed to bed. Honestly, I would probably be asleep before Cole landed, so I decided to send a text to let him know.

> Heading to bed. Text me when you land.
> Miss you.

My phone buzzed almost immediately.

> Miss you, too, and I haven't even left. I'll text when I land. Sleep well.

It was really sweet that he sent that, so I plugged the phone in, set my water on the nightstand, and slipped between the sheets, drifting off quickly.

"KYLIE," REMI SAID, COMING INTO MY ROOM.

I had no idea what time it was or anything, but it was still dark outside, and I didn't feel like I'd been asleep very long at all.

"What's the matter?" I asked, rubbing my eyes.

"You're all over social media," he said.

"What?" I asked, grabbing my phone.

"Here," he said, thrusting his phone in my hands instead. "I've pulled up most of them, but it's all over."

I looked at the headline on the click bait he'd opened and my jaw dropped.

'Seattle Cascades' Backstop has New Girl' it read. I scrolled through the article to see exactly what it was saying and almost dropped Remi's phone when I found that they actually named me.

"Why would they do this?" I cried. "Do they not understand personal and private information?"

"Keep going," he said, and the grim nature of his voice terrified me.

As I went down the article, I saw the picture that Remi had posted, along with the caption he'd put on it. Then, further down, there was a picture that was taken as we were kissing right before I left the stadium. It was grainy and you could tell it was one of those that were taken from a phone a long way away, after zooming in, then had been zoomed in further to get as close as possible to us.

"What am I supposed to do?" I begged, tears running down my face.

"I already sent a text with a link to Cole," he said. "Hopefully he can do something about it. Otherwise, I think you better get ready for some backlash."

"Oh God," I said, barely above a whisper.

All of a sudden, everything that I'd eaten that day decided it would be a good time to come back up for a second helping, and I had to throw my blankets off and rush to the bathroom, throwing up and dry heaving for what felt like hours. Remi came in at some point, likely following right behind me, and was holding my hair out of the way.

This couldn't be happening. This was a nightmare, and I was going to wake up and laugh about the stupid dream I'd had. I knew that was what was going to happen. It had to.

Finally, when my body decided that there really was nothing left in my stomach, it let me have a reprieve and sit on the floor in front of the toilet. Remi let my hair down and flushed before handing me a glass of cool water.

"Swish and spit, baby," he said, and I followed his instructions, getting the last remnants of food from my mouth. "Toothbrush?"

I shook my head, not too much, though, because it hurt and made me dizzy.

"What do I do?" I asked, hoping he'd have an answer.

I heard his phone chirp in the bedroom and he headed that way, picking it up from where I'd dropped it on my bed. He thrust it into my hands after he'd opened the message.

Is she okay? What do I need to do?

It was from Cole, which meant it was later than I thought, or earlier, and that he had already landed wherever it was he was going.

"Can I call him?" I asked and Remi nodded, helping me to my feet.

"Better to do it from your phone," he said as he helped me to my bed. "I'll give you privacy if you want."

"Stay," I said, holding his hand.

He sat on the edge of my bed and handed me my phone. I opened it to see the text from Cole saying he had landed, but it was from a couple of hours earlier. I went to the phone and pressed his contact, selecting the call feature and waiting for it to connect.

"Hey," he said on the other end. "What can I do?"

"I don't know," I cried, then kind of just lost it.

My sobs were awful, clawing out of my chest in heaves. Remi took the phone from me and spoke to him softly. I have no idea what they said because I honestly couldn't hear anything other than my raging terror.

"I can handle her," Remi said, then he looked at me. "Do you want him to come home?"

I shook my head and managed to get the word, "Work," out, but that was all I could do. He must have relayed my message, understanding what I was saying without me actually saying anything. Before much more happened, though, I felt another wave of nausea hit me and I ran back to the bathroom, heaving once again from my empty stomach, bile rising into my throat and burning it as I continued to strain.

Remi came in some time after that, pulling my hair back into a ponytail to keep it out of my face, a wet cloth in one hand, and a cup in the other. I took the cloth, wiping it over my eyes and nose and mouth and oh, God, I was a hot mess. Tears and snot and bile and spit and everything was all over my face. Honestly, it was probably good that Cole wasn't seeing me like this. He'd never want to see me again afterward.

"Come on," Remi said once I'd wiped myself off. "Let's get you tucked back in."

I went with him, following him to my bed. He'd put my phone back on the nightstand and plugged it in, had the covers turned down, and my water bottle was full of ice and everything. Sitting on the edge of the bed, I swung my legs up under the covers and slid down. Remi pulled the blankets over me as I placed my head on my pillow.

"Want me to stay?" he asked.

"No," I replied, and my voice was harsh.

"I can if you need me to," he said.

"I'm fine," I lied, but at least it let him know I was okay enough for him to go across the main space of our apartment and to his own bed.

"If you need me, call," he said, kissing my head.

It was always like that with us. We were absolute best friends and siblings in everything but blood and we took care of each other. Mostly, though it had been him taking care of me. The only time the roles were reversed were when he was heartbroken and I held him as he cried and told him the guy was a douche canoe anyway. It was our way, our love language, and I don't think I would have gotten through the last ten years without him.

CHAPTER FORTY-TWO

*C*ole...

"Hey," I said when Remi called me back.

"She's going to sleep now," he said, but I heard the worry in his voice.

"Are you sure I shouldn't come home?" I asked again.

I'd never heard her so troubled. I mean, she had the panic attacks, but those were easy to help her through. This was something completely different and I didn't know how to help her.

"I think she would be mortified if you did," he said. "She doesn't ever want to be a burden on anyone, especially you."

"She knows she's not a burden, right?" I asked. "That I would drop everything for her if she needed me."

"I think she's afraid to scare you away with all her trauma," he said and I wondered, not for the first time, what had closed her off to the whole world. "It's not my story to tell," he continued. "But, if you get approached by media, just deny everything until you talk to her. Will you do that for me?"

"Absolutely," I said. "Can you give me a hint?"

"Nope," he said. "Not my story, not my circus, not my monkeys. She'll tell you when she trusts you. Until then, please try to downplay everything with her. Don't even acknowledge a relationship. When are you supposed to be back?"

"That's the thing," I said. "This is a super long road trip. I'm in Miami now, then one, two, three, four, five more cities," I added, counting the stops we had off in my head. "I don't think I'll be back until the middle of June. I just don't know the dates for sure, but it seems right."

"Wow," he said, and I heard the weight in the word.

"That's why I'm asking if I should come back," I added. "I don't want her to go through this alone. I know you're there, and I really do appreciate you, but I feel like it's my fault somehow."

"Not your fault," he said. "It's whoever the fuck figured out who she is and took that other picture. I didn't even tag her, or you, in the one I posted, so I have no fucking idea how they figured it out. Just know that more shit is going to come out if they figure out who she really is. I can't say more because it's not my place but know that it could get really awkward and awful."

"We have a whole team of PR people for the league," I said. "They will work with me to get this shut down, but I may need more information. Do you think she will talk to me tomorrow? Would she tell me what her secret is?"

"Not on the phone," he said. "I mean, I'm surprised she hasn't told you yet, but she has her reasons, I'm sure."

"I wish I knew so I could help her," I said. "I really don't want her to be all alone during this. Can she work from home?"

"She was already planning for tomorrow," he said.

"Good," I replied.

"I'll make sure she's taken care of," he said. "I know it's late there, but if there's anything you can do to shut this down, I would really appreciate it."

"I'll do my best," I said. "But without all the details, it might be tough."

"Just try," he said. "Let me know what you can do."

"I will," I replied. "And thank you for being there."

"Wouldn't want to be anywhere else," he said, but I heard the stress in his voice.

Yeah, this was definitely something I'd have to deal with pretty soon, especially if I wanted to keep Kylie around, and I really did. We disconnected the call and I sent a text to the manager asking if I could talk to him before the game the next day. He said that was fine and asked about the press he was sent. I told him that's what I wanted to talk about, so he agreed to meet me for breakfast before we headed out to the stadium.

With that figured out, I climbed into bed, hoping against hope that I'd be able to actually shut my brain off and get to sleep. Unfortunately, the only thing that kept creeping into my thoughts was Kylie and the horrible sounds I heard her making when she tried to talk to me. It nearly tore me apart hearing her anguish in her tears, her sobs. I was really glad Remi was there and that she wasn't alone. I don't know what I would have done if this all had come out and she was all by herself.

When sleep finally came, it was filled with horrible dreams, and I woke up more than once, fearing for Kylie's safety. Finally, after hardly any sleep, and feeling miserable, I got up and jumped into the shower. Sure, I'd have to do it again after the game, but I needed something to get me out of my head with everything going on. I turned the water on hot, hotter than I normally have it, and I ducked my head under the stream, letting it pound away at my brain as I tried to get myself together. Thinking about Kylie, I just kind of let go, giving a guttural scream into the void, likely waking whoever was in the room next to me, but I didn't care. All I wanted to do was run home to her and hold her and tell her everything would be okay.

Except, I wasn't sure that was true. I mean, if she freaked out this much just for showing up in the press, then how was she going to handle being my girlfriend? I mean, the press kind of follows players around, and with how well we'd been playing this year, it was only going to get worse.

"Fuck," I shouted, then heard a pounding on the wall opposite me.

I shut the tap off, pulled the curtain back, nearly pulling it off the rings that held it up, and snatched a towel from the rack. I dried off as quick as possible, then went to throw some clothes on. I sent a text to the coach to let him know I would meet him in the coffee shop in the lobby, then sent another one to Jonathan. It was still early at home, but he might be up with his kids. He was someone I could ask all the questions running through my head. He might even go by her place to check in on her for me if I asked.

I grabbed my key card, threw a sweatshirt over my tee shirt, pulled the hood up, and headed out the door to make my way to the lobby.

"The fuck is your problem?" Hennings asked, poking his head out of his door.

"Sorry, man," I said. "Shit's going sideways."

"Need to talk?" he asked. "Because if anyone knows how to handle shit going sideways, it's me."

"Thanks," I said. "Meeting Coach in a minute."

"Okay," he said. "If you need me, though, tag me in."

"Thanks," I said again, then continued on to the elevator, punching the button for the down arrow.

I felt my phone buzz just as the doors opened, but I got in and figured I'd check when I made it to the lobby. As it bounced at the bottom, I looked to see a text from Coach saying he was there and waiting.

"Hey," I said as I walked past him. "Just gonna grab a cup."

"Sure thing," he replied, a worried look on his face.

I ordered my drink, paid, and waited while the barista made it. She handed it to me and I went and sat with my coach.

"What's going on?" he asked.

I pulled out my phone, pulled up the link Remi had sent me, then turned it over to him. He looked at it, then looked closer and swore under his breath.

"What the fuck do they think they're doing?" he asked.

"That's what I'd like to know," I replied, even though it was mostly a rhetorical question. "Can we do anything?"

"Let me make some phone calls," he said, pulling out his own phone. He punched the screen, then held it to his ear. "Yeah," he said when whoever was on the other end answered. "We have a situation that needs your help."

I watched and waited, hoping like hell we could shut this shit show down before it got a mind of its own and ran roughshod over Kylie's life. Coach put a finger up to me, then stepped away from me and walked toward the front lobby of the hotel. I nursed my coffee as I waited for him to come back with any kind of news that might be helpful. Today had already gone to hell in a handbasket and it was barely light out. Finally, Coach came back in and sat down again.

"I'm afraid there's not much we can do," he said. "But there's more than just that one story."

"Yeah," I said. "Her friend said it was kind of blowing up."

"That's not what I'm talking about," he said, and the look on his face made me more than just a little uncomfortable. "How well do you know this girl?"

"I've only known her a few weeks," I said. "Really, not even that long. Met her the night that company had their after party. But, honestly, she's really a good girl. Like, no questions at all about her character."

"You good to avoid the press today?" he asked.

"That bad?" I asked.

"Worse," he replied. "I can send you home. Call it bereavement or something. Family emergency."

"Maybe I should," I replied.

"I'll get it set up," he said. "Go pack and wear your sunglasses and a hat. You don't want to deal with this until you talk to her."

"You have me worried," I said. "But I know her. She's absolutely amazing. I can't believe anything bad could be associated with her."

"Go," he urged. "I'll take care of everything. They'll have a ticket ready and will email you the confirmation within the hour."

"Okay," I said, standing. "You're sure?"

"I am," he said, and the cryptic way he said it was ominous as fuck.

CHAPTER FORTY-THREE

*K*ylie…

My head was pounding, and I felt like I'd swallowed an entire bag of cotton balls that had been soaked in some sort of acid. I shifted under my blankets and saw the light coming through my curtains.

"Shit," I said, pulling my phone over to see that it was almost eleven. "Shit, shit, shit."

I threw the blankets back and sat up, only to have my head spin and my stomach try to climb up my esophagus. That's when it hit me, everything that had happened in the middle of the night.

"Remi," I shouted, getting out of bed, and heading out of my room.

"Just a second," he said to the headset he had on, then clicked something on the laptop. "Hey, how are you feeling?" he asked me.

"Pissed," I said. "Why didn't you wake me up?"

"You needed sleep," he explained. "I already talked to Jim and he's cool with it. I told him there were some issues you had with a family member and that you were probably gonna need to take the whole day off."

"I have a project due," I said. "I can't take the day off."

"Yes, you can," he said. "Besides, you needed that sleep."

"Gah," I groaned, then headed to my bathroom, my bladder screaming at me.

After I'd taken care of that obnoxious need, I pulled my toothbrush out and squirted some paste on it, running it under the water. I had to get this foul taste out of my mouth, so I scrubbed with as much gusto as I could manage this early in the morning. After rinsing and spitting the remnants out, I put it away and went back to my room.

My leggings were on the end of the bed, so I pulled them on, grabbed my phone, and headed to my desk. No way any of this was going to stop me from doing my job.

"Kylie," Remi barked from the other side of the room. "You're not working. That's final."

"You're not the boss of me," I retorted, sticking my tongue out for good measure.

Remi got up and was stalking over to me when a knock rattled the door.

"No," I whispered, dread filling every inch of my body.

Remi went to the door and looked through the peep hole.

"Who are you and what do you want?" he asked through the closed portal.

"My name's Jonathan," the man on the other side said. "Cole and I play together on the Cascades and he asked me to come by and check on Kylie."

I sunk to my chair, dumbfounded.

"If she's doing okay, I can go," he continued. "I just wanted to check on her. I promise I'm not here for anything other than a wellness check."

Remi looked at me, asking without asking whether I wanted to let him in. I shrugged, figuring it couldn't get any worse than it already was. He unlocked the deadbolt and flipped the little bar we had at the top as an extra safety precaution, then opened the door. The man on the other side was older than Cole, but not by a ton. He looked like he was in good shape, but his arm was in a cast hanging to his side.

"You were the guy who just got hurt," I said.

"Yeah," he said. "I can come back if this isn't a good time."

"It's fine," Remi said, stepping back to let him in.

He held his hand out to Remi, who took it.

"Cole said she had a friend who lived with her," Jonathan said. "I'm guessing that's you."

"Best friend all our lives," he replied. "Want anything?"

"Oh, no," he said, turning to look at me. "Are you sure you're all right?"

"I'm absolutely not all right," I said. "But it isn't anyone's fault."

"I'm sure there's someone to blame," he said, coming closer to me. "Is there anything I can do for you? Get you anything?"

"No, thanks," I said. "I think I just need to take a day to get my head on, then I'll be fine."

The lie was one I'd told over and over again, every time someone asked if I was okay after my dad went away. I hadn't been all right since that point, that first moment. And I wasn't all right now, either.

"Let me leave you my number," he said. "I'm home for the foreseeable future, so I'm around and can help navigate things with you if you need me to. I live over in West Seattle and have a car you can use if you need it."

"Thanks," Remi said.

I just sat there, completely confused as to why this man was here at all.

"The team is family for most of us," he said, obviously reading my thoughts. "We help each other out whenever and however we can. Cole sent me a text asking that I check on you. I think he's coming home."

"No," I said, finally finding my voice. "Why is he coming home?"

"He's worried about you," the other player said. "He knows you're dealing with all the backlash from that stupid article, which the team is working to shut down, but you know how the internet is."

"Yeah," Remi said. "Once it's out there, it's out there forever."

"Exactly," he replied. "Hopefully we can get it quashed down at least some, but it will always and forever be out there. I'm so sorry this is happening to you."

"Thanks," I said. "I just don't know why he's coming home. He doesn't need to do that."

"Kylie," Remi chided. "He loves you and wants to protect you. Can't you see that?"

I looked at my friend. Was he right? Did Cole really love me? No, that couldn't be. It was too soon. We had only known each other for a few weeks, at the most six.

"I see those wheels turning," Remi said.

"I'm gonna let you guys go," Jonathan said. "Here's my number, and my fiancée, Lucy's number as well. Her husband, who passed away, was in cyber security of some sort and she might be able to help you out with some things if you feel like you need it."

I looked at the piece of paper he'd set on the table and wondered exactly how I'd ended up with such an amazing set of people who were worried about me. Why was I so special that they were all willing to do these things to help me? I heard the door click shut, then the bolt got thrown before Remi finally came over to me and pressed a bottle of water into my hands.

"Drink," he said. "Then take your sorry ass back to bed. You need more sleep."

I took the bottle, drank a sip, then screwed the top back on. Doing as I was told, I headed into my room and climbed into bed, setting my phone back on the night stand next to the water.

Honestly, I wasn't sure I was going to be able to sleep, but at least I'd try. I really was tired, so sleep was probably a good thing.

CHAPTER FORTY-FOUR

$\mathcal{C}$ole...

"Your ID," the TSA agent asked as he looked at my flight information on his computer.

I handed it over to him and he stuck it into his machine, verifying that I was who I said I was, and that I was indeed flying back to Seattle.

"Glasses," he said, and I pushed my sunglasses up on my head so he could see the real me. "That way," he said, pointing to a line of other people who were there to head to whatever was awaiting them at the other end of their flight.

Walking through the line, I dropped my backpack into one of the trays, slipped my jacket, hat, and glasses into another one, and my shoes into a third, along with my keys and phone. I didn't really want to take the hat and glasses off, but it was a necessity when it came to security, so I just hoped that there weren't any baseball fans around, and if there were, that they didn't know who I was.

It was fortunate that I wore a mask throughout most of the game, so my face was hidden, but with my luck, especially with the shit that had shown up already online, someone would recognize me and start asking questions. That was something I didn't want to deal with. When I got to the front of the line, I stepped into the little machine, put my feet on the markers on the ground, and held my hands up over my head as it did its thing to verify that I was a safe person to let through to the planes.

They hadn't given me much time to get to my plane, but the fact that I had no luggage and the airport was so close, it worked out. I walked to my gate right as they were starting to load the passengers. At least the team got me a first-class ticket, so I was able to get onto the plane right away, heading to my window seat in the second row and tugging my hat down over my eyes, my glasses firmly in place on my face.

"Anything to drink?" the flight attendant asked me.

"No thanks," I said, not raising my head much.

More passengers were filing onto the plane, and it filled up pretty fast. The guy who sat next to me had a business suit on and shoved his briefcase beneath the seat in front of him after stowing his carry on in the cabinet above.

"Mornin'," he said.

I kind of just ignored him, scrolling through my phone as if it were the most important thing I could be doing. Unfortunately, everywhere I looked I saw the story about me and Kylie. It was more than just a little frustrating that the team hadn't killed this before it started, but I guess some news outlets had no morals.

After a while, I just shut the phone off and stuffed it into my bag, scrunching down into the seat to try to sleep the whole way home. If I could sleep, it would make the flight more bearable, but to be honest, I was exhausted. All I wanted to do was hold Kylie and tell her I'd protect her from all the monsters in the world.

Seven hours stuck in this tube just to get to the woman I loved was not the way I wanted to start my day.

The woman I love.

Wow, I wondered when that realization came to me. A few weeks should not make that happen. But then again, my dad and mom met and were married within three months, and they've been together almost thirty years. It's not unheard of, but still seems quick, even for me.

"I saw him in line," someone said as they walked past our area.

"You're sure?" another voice asked.

"Yeah," the first said. "It's for sure him."

Fuck, I thought, but kept my head down. No need to engage or encourage them at all. Maybe, if I ignored it, they'd all go away.

Unfortunately, the opposite seemed to have been the case. I kept hearing whispers from the passengers that were coming onto the plane, then the people behind me started talking. They weren't even trying to keep it secret, which did nothing for my mental state.

Finally, the last of the passengers were on the plane and the flight attendants started their safety talks as the plane was moved to get ready to take off. With the number of flights that I'd been on, I could prob-ably have done the talk myself. Instead, I kept my head down, pretending to be asleep, hoping that it would become a reality and I could leave this space in my mind for a little while.

"They right?" the guy asked me, bumping my elbow on the armrest between us.

"What?" I asked, my tone clearly indicating that I was not at all interested in whatever it was he wanted to say.

"You're the player that showed up all over the sports news," he said. "That's you, right?"

I glared at him, trying my best to keep from screaming.

"Don't believe everything you hear," I said, hoping to dispel what-ever it was he was thinking.

"Whatever," he said just as the plane began its surge down the runway to take off.

There were a couple of bumps as it lifted from the ground, then when the wheels were tucked up inside, and we were climbing above the clouds. Too bad we couldn't climb out of this reality. I just hoped that Kylie would see me.

∽

I MUST HAVE FALLEN ASLEEP AT SOME POINT BECAUSE IT FELT LIKE NO time had passed since we took off, and suddenly we were descending into SeaTac airport. Soon, very soon, I could hop into a ride share and head over to Kylie's place and see for myself how she was doing. It was obvious that I'd slept at an awkward angle because I had a terrible crick in my neck that, no matter which way I twisted it, it gave me fits.

"Please put your seat up and tray away," the flight attendant said to the man next to me as she walked by.

"You must have been tired," he said once she'd passed as he packed up his laptop and stowed the table in the arm rest. "Slept damn near the whole flight."

I ignored him, shifting to sit up more, and pulled out my phone. We weren't on the ground yet, so when I turned it back on, it was still in airplane mode. I'd learned that turning it off saved the battery better than just leaving it in the right mode the whole flight, especially on these long ones. Once we landed, though, I would shut that off and see if I could reach Remi to let him know I was on my way over.

Apparently, ignoring my seatmate was not sufficient enough of a clue to let him know that I wasn't interested in talking to him because he asked the question he'd asked before I went to sleep again.

"So," he began as the plane started to shift and turn so it could land properly. "You are that guy on the news, right? The one who is dating the serial killer's daughter?"

The last question threw me off and it took everything in me to keep from punching this dude. Not gonna lie, it was close. My fist balled up next to me, my other hand clenching my phone tight. When I turned to look at the guy, he paled, so whatever look I had on my face was obviously more severe than I intended, but did exactly what I wanted it to, which was to shut him up. He quickly turned his head down and busied himself with packing the laptop away properly.

Serial killer? What the fuck? The statement kept running through my head, over and over on repeat, and I wondered whether this was the secret she had. No, that couldn't be right. I mean, she'd said her mom was dead. Maybe it was just domestic violence gone bad. I mean, that explains a lot. The fear, the panic attacks, all of it. I mean, I'd be

239

fucked up, too, if I'd grown up with someone who had killed my mom, but a serial killer? No...

If it wasn't for the fact that I literally couldn't call her, I would have dialed her up and demanded she tell me. Although, I probably wouldn't have done that. No, this was definitely a face-to-face conversation type of situation. Remi had said that, but obviously I had brushed it off as him being protective. Now, though, everything that had happened in the last couple of weeks made sense. Well, except for her naivete when it came to sex.

Did her father kill her during sex? Was that why she was so unknowing about it? That was actually a plausible concept, one which I hoped wasn't true. I couldn't imagine what she had seen or been exposed to if this were the case. My decision to come home was more important than I thought. If I could only will the plane to land sooner and allow me to get to her, then everything, hopefully, would be out in the open and we could work through whatever it was that was keeping her at a distance.

CHAPTER FORTY-FIVE

*K*ylie...
 Someone was pounding on the door, but I had no clue who it was. I was tucked into my bed and had been sound asleep before it started. Then I heard his voice, and I sat up.

"Kylie," he said as he came through the door. "You awake?"

"Yeah," I said, but had to swallow because my voice sounded like I'd swallowed a frog.

"Can I come in?" he asked, which was super sweet.

"Sure," I replied, clicking on the light next to the bed.

He was a sight for sore eyes if ever I'd seen one. His hair was a bit tousled, his shirt kind of wrinkled, and the look on his face was more than just a little bit of worry. It was as if he were terrified of what he might find. Sitting on the edge of the bed, he reached a hand out to me and I took it, squeezing it for a moment before letting it set there. He held on tight, as if I were what was keeping him anchored to this spot.

"Are you okay?" he asked.

I wanted to answer, to tell him that everything was fine, and we'd figure out whatever it was that was going on, but I couldn't do that. No, nothing would be fine again, and it was all my fault. I shouldn't have kissed him at the stadium, shouldn't have even been there. No, I belonged holed up in my little space, avoiding the rest of the world as a whole.

"Hey," he said, pulling me closer to him.

When I didn't budge, he shifted and settled next to me on the bed, keeping his shoes off the top, but still close enough that I could smell his distinct scent, feel the warmth that radiated from him.

"Talk to me, baby," he said, his voice low so it didn't carry.

That right there was what sent me over the edge and the dam broke, my tears flowing down my face. I didn't make noise when I cried. I'd learned that shortly after my dad went away. If Mom could hear me, she'd get upset as well, so I just learned how to do it without making a sound. My whole body shook, but no noise came out. He reached out and pulled me to him, cradling me in his arms, pressing my head to his shoulder and wrapping me up in his warmth and strength. Even though I didn't make any noise, I still let go, letting all the pent-up fear and unease go, giving me that solid thing to hold on to in the storm that raged through me. Everything came pouring out. I have no idea how long I cried, how long he held me, but I did know that when I finally came up for air, he was still there, still that strong presence that I needed in that moment.

"There you go," he said, shifting so I was kind of lying on him. "Just let it all out."

I pushed up off him and looked at him, his shirt a mess of snot and tears, but his face was wrapped in concern that I didn't understand.

"You good?" he asked, and I nodded. "Feel like talking?"

I took a deep, shuddering breath, then let it out slowly.

"No," I said, honestly. "But you deserve to know."

"You don't have to…"

"But I do," I interrupted. "If I want to be with someone, they need to know all my dirty little secrets. Just promise me you'll wait until I've finished before you judge me."

"Of course," he said.

With another breath, I began the tale of the horrors of my childhood.

"Dad was always working on something," I said. "Puttering around in the garage and out back in his shed. He worked long hours, too, so we didn't see him much. When he was around, he was very strict. Everything in the house had a place, and if it wasn't in its place, hell would come.

"When I was thirteen, the police showed up at our door," I continued. "I'd been home from school for maybe half an hour or so when they got there. Mom didn't work, so she answered the door. They asked if they could come in, and my mom asked why. It was almost surreal to hear them tell her that my father had been arrested. She invited them in, sat them at the table, and began to make coffee for them. Always the homemaker, always proper, that's the way she was. It was as if she were on autopilot or something."

I took another breath, taking a moment to center myself the way my therapist had taught me. Once I was there, I continued my story.

"Dad had been caught at an old, abandoned building near where he worked," I said, not looking at Cole. Not wanting him to look at me. "He had a boy about the same age as me tied up…"

I choked, almost losing my nerve as well as the contents of my stomach. He rubbed my back and made soothing noises in my ear, helping me to find that place where I was void of emotions.

"He was tied up to some sort of homemade torture contraption," I continued. "I don't know what it was, and I don't want to know, either. I'm sure there are pictures of it, but I've never wanted to see what it was. The boy had been bound to it, was naked, and had welts on his body. He was gagged with some sort of… I don't know."

Again, I had to take a minute. I hadn't told this story to anyone in years, but it was still just as hard as the first time I'd said anything to anyone.

"We can stop…"

"No," I said, my voice firm. "No, I need to get it all out or I won't want to."

"Okay," he said, still rubbing my back.

"They said he'd been raped and tortured for hours," I said, my voice flat even to my own ears. "All those hours that Dad had said he was working late, he had been at one abandoned building or another, torturing boys for his own pleasure. There were so many that had gone missing in the few years leading up to it, but no one knew what was happening to them.

"When they caught him in the act, he confessed," I said. "He said that he was only responsible for seven, maybe eight. That there were others who were doing the same thing, and he was brought into it by someone else. He never said who that other person was, or who else was part of this group of people. I don't believe anyone else was part of it. I think he was just a sick man who took advantage of people who couldn't fight back."

I paused, not wanting to continue, but knowing I needed to get everything out.

"After they caught him, he told them he would tell them where to find the bodies, but only if he didn't get the death penalty," I said. "They asked him exactly where, and he drew them a map. He said everyone he'd killed was in that location. They found more than he said he'd killed, but they figured they had everyone when they'd finished. He made a deal that gave him life in prison."

I stopped talking then, not sure what else I needed to say.

"You said your mom died," he said. "Did your dad kill her, too?"

"No," I said. "Well, not exactly. When he was arrested, Mom started the process to divorce him. She wanted to make sure that I didn't have to see him ever again, but he fought against that. It didn't take long until Mom died from a heart attack. The doctor said she was so stressed that her heart just gave out."

"I'm so sorry," he said. "To lose your mom like that after all that happened with your dad. That must have been really hard on you."

"It really was," I said. "When they told me I had to go and see him every week, I cried. I didn't want to see him. He was a monster. Mom didn't want me to see him, either, which was what she was fighting for. When she died, though, he became my only guardian. He wanted his little girl to see him every week."

"Wasn't there anyone who advocated for you?"

"My therapist did," I said. "She said that each time I saw him, I was re-victimized by him. Every visit was causing more and more mental strain, and she said she was afraid I would suffer the same fate my mother had if the visits weren't stopped."

"Did they stop?"

"Finally," I said. "Of course, the fact that once he was officially sentenced, he was moved to Walla Walla, that made visits really hard to accommodate. My grandparents couldn't take me every week, and they weren't gonna bring him back over the mountains from Walla Walla all the time, so I guess the system kind of fixed it for me without having to do too much more fighting."

"Kylie," he said, shifting to make me look at him. "Thank you for telling me. I know this was hard, and I would have understood if you didn't want to do it. But I feel honored that you trusted me enough to share."

"It was a lot," I said, seeing the love in his eyes. "Thank you for not judging me."

"Of course," he said.

"You'd be amazed at how people respond to this kind of thing," I said.

"How can I help?" he asked, and I wasn't completely sure what he meant. "With the whole press thing," he added. "Should I make a statement? Ignore the press? What?"

"I have no idea," I replied, almost surprised by the questions. "I usually just ignore them, but it's not like I've had much contact with them in the last few years."

"I'll check with the team," he said. "They may tell me what I can and can't say. That might be the easiest."

"Probably," I replied, feeling exhausted once again, but this time I knew it was the emotions racing through me.

There was a knock on my bedroom door, so I pushed up again to see Remi standing there, barely lit by my bedside lamp, especially with the full light coming from the rest of the apartment.

"You doing good?" he asked.

"Yeah," I replied.

"Jim wanted to know if you could call him," he said.

"Great," I said, feeling like my whole life was going to be taken away from me once again, and all because of my stupid father.

I sat up proper and shifted, moving to get off the bed. Cole had kicked his shoes off and was fully on the bed, which was odd because I hadn't heard them fall to the ground.

"You want me to come with you?" he asked, sitting up himself.

"Not really much you can do," I replied.

"Moral support?" he suggested, and I smiled.

Maybe he wouldn't run away. Maybe, just this one time, I would get to keep something good in my life and not have it stolen by the monster that was my biological father. When I was standing, I reached out my hand and Cole took it, standing up himself and following me out to the main area of the apartment.

"I told him you'd ping him when you were up and running," Remi said from his desk on the other side of the room.

"Thanks," I said as I pulled my chair out and opened my laptop to boot it up.

Cole pulled one of the kitchen chairs over to sit next to me, squeezing my thigh for reassurance. I got things running, and when my login was complete, I instantly saw that I had several messages on the communication system we used. They would all have to wait, though, as my boss wanted to talk, so that was the priority. I sent a note to him and almost instantly I had a request for a video conference.

Logging in, my stomach fell, farther and farther down, until I was sure it was sitting under my feet and not in the middle of my chest where it belonged. The system popped up, and I was looking at my boss, who looked just about as bad as I was feeling.

"Are you okay?" was the first thing he asked.

"I am," I replied, trying to look positive, but likely failing miserably.

"Good," he said. "I wanted to reach out to you as soon as I saw some of the stories starting to pop up, but knew you weren't feeling well."

"I appreciate that," I said. "It's been a bit overwhelming to say the least."

"I'm sure it has," he said. "I just want you to know that everyone at Pinaceae Tech is here for you if you need us."

"Thanks," I replied.

"With respect to your working," he continued. "Mr. Roberts has said that he is fine with you working from home for the foreseeable future. We know how much you prefer that, so we're good with you continuing on this way until things settle down."

"I don't want to be a burden for the company," I said and felt Cole squeeze my thigh. "I just didn't anticipate anything like this happening."

"Your private life should remain private," he said. "I understand it's none of my business, but are you sure you want to be connected to someone with such a high profile?"

I looked at Cole and smiled.

"I don't think I could have gone through this without him," I said. "He's actually been really supportive, even from afar."

"Well, it's your life," Jim said. "But know that some people are going to assume a lot of things about you just by who you are connected with."

"I know," I said, and that was the God's honest truth.

"As long as you're sure," he said.

"I am," I replied, smiling as Cole's hand rubbed my leg in slow circles.

"I'll let you get back to whatever it was you were doing," he said. "Will you be online tomorrow?"

"I should be," I replied. "I just kind of had a bad night last night and didn't really sleep well, so didn't want to have to redo any work that I messed up today."

"That's a perfectly fine answer," he said. "See you tomorrow, online that is."

"See you then," I replied, then left the video chat.

I logged everything off on my computer and shut it down, closing the lid once it was done.

"He seems like a good boss," Cole said.

"He really is," I replied. "They were really good about letting me work from home almost from the beginning. Since I do so much better when I'm home, it made sense to them for that arrangement to happen. Now, I'm just glad it's an option."

"Is that all you have to do today?" he asked.

"That's it," I replied.

My stomach growled just then, and I looked at Cole, my eyes wide.

"Have you eaten today?" he asked. I shook my head, and he pulled out his phone. "What do you want? I'm buying. You, too, Remi," he said over his shoulder. "Whatever you guys want, we'll order and have it delivered."

"You don't have to—"

"I want to," he said, cutting me off. "I'm the reason this is all happening. Now don't try to argue," he said, shutting down what I was going to say. "Your dad didn't make it any better, for sure, but I have that stupid celebrity status going because of what I do. If it weren't for me, your face wouldn't be splattered all over everything and no one would know who you were, which is what it seems like you'd prefer."

"You know you don't have to take the blame," I said.

"I'm not taking blame for the pictures," he replied. "That's all on whoever took it and then posted it everywhere. It would have been a non-story at best. Please," he said, taking my hands in his. "Let me do this for you. Let me help to ease something for you because of the turmoil I've caused."

The look on his face and the way he practically begged me to let him do this melted my heart. All he wanted to do was fix this situation, but there was no fixing it. Letting him do this one thing for me was something I could do for him. How had I gotten so lucky as to not only meet such an amazing man, but for that meeting to turn into what we had?

"Okay," I said. "I'm fine with most anything, so whatever you want will be fine."

He looked over his shoulder at Remi, who was staring at us with a look I hadn't seen before.

"Whatever," he said, though it sounded like he was kind of choked up.

"Okay," Cole said, flipping through the delivery app on his phone to find something.

He found something we all liked and placed the order before taking my hands in his again. The way he looked at me, as if he were seeing more than just my outward appearance, was something I hadn't experienced before. It was like I was connecting with him on a level deeper than anyone else.

"You guys go to Kylie's room," Remi said. "I'll let you know when the food is here."

Cole looked over at him and smiled, then pulled me to my feet once he'd stood. Hand in hand, we walked the short distance to my room, him closing the door behind him. As soon as it was shut, he pulled me to him, wrapping his arms around me, leaning down to kiss me. It was slow at first, but then he deepened it, teasing the seam of my lips with his tongue until I opened for him and he plunged inside. My arms were around his neck, and his hands split, with one going to the back of my head and the other to my ass. Pressing me against him, I felt he was hard and ready for whatever we decided to do, and honestly, it was probably the best distraction I could have asked for.

He walked me backward toward my bed, never stopping the kiss, and when I felt the mattress at the back of my knees, I sat down, pulling my lips from his. He looked down at me and his eyes were hooded, closed just enough to not be fully open. Kneeling in front of me, he grabbed the hem of my oversized shirt, watching me to see if I was okay with what he was doing. I nodded, as if he needed my permission, and he raised it up and over my head, my arms going up to let him pull it completely off.

Dropping it beside him on the floor, he leaned forward, taking one of my nipples into his mouth. The scratch from his whiskers was rough, but the way his lips and tongue felt on me was enough to just shut everything else out. I leaned back on my hands just a little bit, and he popped off my breast, shifting to give the other one the same attention.

"I want you," I said, and I have no idea where it came from, but it was the truth. "I want you to show me everything there is to having sex."

He looked at me, leaning back a bit.

"You're sure?" he asked, and the fact that he even bothered instead of shoving me down and having his way showed that the trust I was placing in him was well deserved.

"I am," I said, shoving myself further onto the bed.

He stood up, unbuttoning his shirt as quick as he could, shoving it off his arms and to the ground. When he unbuttoned his pants and slid them down, I realized he wasn't wearing any boxers or anything, so he was just right there in front of me. Stepping from his pants, he walked his feet back a bit to pull his socks off as well, then climbed up onto the bed next to me.

His hands were soft as he stroked my side, running his fingers up and down the side opposite him. Never did he take his eyes off me the whole time. It was as if he were waiting for me to tell him to stop, but I wasn't going to. As long as he was gentle and told me what he was doing, I was going to let him teach me everything he knew about this thing that had been shut out of my life for nearly... I stopped, realizing that I had been put off sex for almost half my life.

"You okay?" he asked, and I realized that something must have shown on my face.

"Just thinking about everything I missed," I said. "You're gonna have to catch me up."

The way he laughed, just a full-on belly laugh, was better than anything I could have imagined. Once he'd settled down a bit, he kissed me.

"It will be my pleasure to teach you more than you could imagine," he said, and the seriousness in his eyes was beautiful. "First, I'm going to teach you how to enjoy yourself. I want you to let go and just enjoy the feelings you get. Can you do that for me?"

I nodded and smiled. Yeah, I would probably do most anything for him.

CHAPTER FORTY-SIX

*C*ole...

"It will be my pleasure to teach you more than you could imagine," I said. "First, I'm going to teach you how to enjoy yourself. I want you to let go and just enjoy the feelings you get. Can you do that for me?"

The way she nodded was as if she were going to be an eager student. I knew I would have to take this slow, be very direct in what I said to her, and ensure that she was on board for everything before I started. Reaching my hand down, I slid it inside her panties, which was all she was wearing now. I pushed on the one side and she lifted her hips to allow me to work them off. Once she was completely naked, I took her in, and she was absolutely perfect.

I kissed her deeply, then moved slowly down to her jawline, shifting her head away from me a bit so I could find that spot behind her ear. When I pulled her earlobe into my mouth, she shuddered with an intake of air and I couldn't help but smile. She was so pliable, so willing, and so expressive with her pleasure, that it was going to be hard to keep things slow, but I was determined to do just that.

Ever so slowly, I paraded kisses down her body. Her shoulder, that little spot at the bottom of her neck where it went in at the clavicle, between the breasts that I had already enjoyed. Down and further down I went, past her navel and the top of the hair at the apex of her thighs. She was watching me, her eyes rapt on my descent. I shifted and pressed an arm between her legs to try to get her to open to me, but she was steadfast in keeping them together. I didn't want to push her, so I just reached to the other side to hold myself up.

The dark curls that hid the secret and sacred place on her were soft, and I couldn't help but plant a kiss right in the middle of them. Her sharp intake of air told me she was surprised, so I looked up over her body to see her watching me, her eyes wide in wonder.

"You like that?" I asked, and she nodded. "Open for me?"

My question confused her, so I shifted back so I could put my hand on her knee, pressing it away from the other. It took a moment, but she moved it away from the other one. I placed my elbow between her legs, then raised up, moving my body between them, pressing the other knee away a little more.

She was wet, I could smell it, and it just made me want to lap her up, but I didn't want to push, and I wanted to make sure she was okay with what I was doing.

"I want to taste you," I said and her eyes went even wider. "Will you let me?"

It took a moment before she nodded, although I could tell she wasn't sure.

"If you want me to stop, just tell me," I said. "I won't do anything you don't want me to do."

"I don't know what I want," she said, so soft I barely caught it.

"Do you trust me?"

"Yes," she said in a rush.

Leaning forward, I let my tongue touch the tip of her sex, the spot where the bundle of nerves was that would send most women sky high. I kept my eyes on her, watching as she shuddered, her eyes glossing over a bit. I licked again, this time starting a little lower, running my rough tongue up along her lips all the way up to her clit. Again, she shuddered, but this time her eyes slid closed and she let her head fall back some. I considered it progress, the fact that she wasn't watching anymore, just experiencing it.

Continuing slowly, I slid my tongue up her over and over again as her breath quickened and she slipped down off her elbows to lay flat on the bed. It didn't take long before her legs tried to close on me, but with my body between them she wasn't able to. Her hands clenched and unclenched the blankets to either side, her breath coming faster and faster.

I hummed against her clit, giving just a little bit of vibration to go along with my movements and she sucked in sharply, squeezing her legs against my body, her hands in knots in the blankets. Sucking her into me, I held her tight while shifting just enough to move my hand into position to press a finger inside her. I wanted her to know that I would stop any time, so once she settled a bit more, I released her from my mouth and watched her.

"You doing okay?" I asked and her eyes opened just enough to peer down her body at me. She nodded so I asked, "Should I keep going?"

Again, she nodded, this time a little quicker than before. I pressed my tongue against her, then pressed my finger against her opening. I didn't push it in too far, just enough that she could feel I was there. Waiting to see how she would react, she did as I hoped and arched her back some, pressing herself against my mouth and finger. Taking the signs to mean she was ready for more, I pushed my finger in further, slowly inching my way in and out of her with smooth strokes, each time going further into her wetness.

She was tight, even around my finger, and I worried that if we did more than just finger play, I would hurt her. I wasn't exactly huge by any stretch of the imagination, but there was more to me than just a finger. Continuing to push into her, I kept watch as to her reactions to my ministrations, and she did not disappoint at all. Her breathing increased, so much so that I wondered whether she would hyperventilate, but she seemed to be enjoying herself. I added a second finger to the first, slowly increasing the width she was taking.

"Oh," she moaned out, and I had to smile.

"That's it, baby," I hummed against her. "Let go. Just let go and come for me."

Whether it was my words, the vibrations of my voice, or the combination of stimulants, she tumbled over the edge, squeezing me tightly between her thighs as her fists pulled on the blankets. I kept my pace even, slow, and steady, letting her fly up and up and further still until she reached the stratosphere and exploded at my hands. When she finally settled down, I pulled my fingers out, licking them off before pushing up to crawl to her. She continued to shudder a bit but was definitely coming to that post high place of relaxation.

Pulling her to me, I wrapped her up in my arms, holding her tight as she settled down, coming back to earth in small increments. Doing my best to care for her as she exited her bliss, I just spoke in low tones, telling her she did well, and that I was proud of her. Finally, once she was about back to her own self, she looked up to me and smiled.

"That was amazing," she said and I couldn't help but laugh. "Seriously," she continued. "Why haven't I known about this my whole life?"

"No idea," I said. "But I'm happy to help you make up time on what you've missed."

She smiled at that, obviously still in that post bliss state.

"Hey," Remi said through the door, keeping it closed. "Dinner's here if you guys are done and hungry."

"I'm starving," Kylie said.

I laughed and said, "Sex will do that to you."

She tried to sit up but must have still been a bit wobbly from our little fun, so I helped her sit, then grabbed her panties and helped her put them on.

"Oh no," she said.

"What?" I asked.

"What about you?"

"I can wait," I replied. "I'm hungry, too."

She leaned in and kissed me, slow and sweet, then slid off the bed and picked up her shirt, pulling it over her head. She picked up my pants and handed them to me with a smile. Taking them, I pulled them on, standing to get them up over my ass.

"Do you think Remi will mind if I don't wear my shirt?" I asked.

"Remi has no problem with half-naked men in the apartment," she said.

"Oh really?"

"Not like it happens very often," she said. "Mostly just guys that are here overnight with him or something."

"He's not in a relationship?" I asked.

"No," she said. "And he's kinda not happy about it right now, so don't say anything if you can help it."

"Duly noted," I replied, zipping my pants up.

She opened the door, and I followed her out. Remi had everything dished up and sitting on the little table they had. He'd pulled his computer chair over so that everyone could sit together.

"Thanks for getting this all put together," I said.

"Absolutely," he replied. "Although, if you're gonna be here like this, we might need to get another actual chair."

"Probably," Kylie said. "I mean, I don't mind sitting on the couch, either."

"Not for dinners," Remi said. "We eat at the table like civilized humans."

"Okay," she replied, and the way she said it, they had had this conversation more than once.

"I'll have to have you guys over to my place," I said as I helped Kylie into her seat. "Not to brag, but I actually have six chairs."

Remi had just taken a sip of his wine and it came out his nose, which only made him laugh more. Kylie was also laughing at his reaction, and I joined in. It was honestly one of the nicest nights I'd had in a long time.

CHAPTER FORTY-SEVEN

*K*ylie...

I couldn't believe that Cole had come home. There really wasn't a need for him to do that, but I was glad he was here. He was going to take the next couple of days off with me, then meet his team in Atlanta, which was their next stop on this super long road trip. The fact that he had blown my mind when he first arrived was a giant bonus, for sure.

Now that dinner was done and we were watching the game, things had settled down some. None of us had been on our phones because we didn't really want to see all the chaos that was going around. It was hard enough to deal with the normal amount of insanity that was my life, but to add the national attention to it was not what I wanted.

Sitting next to Cole, cuddled to his side, with Remi on the other end of the couch, was the perfect evening in my opinion. Remi headed to bed when the game was getting close to being over. We were winning, and the catcher who was filling in for Cole was doing pretty good.

"You worried he'll take your spot?" I asked during a commercial break.

"Nah," he replied, kissing the top of my head. "He's good, and he's getting better. This will be a good test for him to handle a few pitchers, and a few games in a row, to get him built up to take on the full-time role when he's ready."

"Will that mean you'll be out of a job?" I asked.

"Probably not," he said. "He'll just go to another team, or we'll share more of the main role. It'll all be good. We all want the same thing, and whatever gets us to the championship is what we want. If that means I watch more and play less, I'm good with that."

"You guys really are a family," I said, remembering what the player who stopped by earlier said.

"We are," he replied. I yawned, and he asked, "You tired?"

"Kinda," I said. "But I don't really wanna get up."

"I could carry you," he said, shifting beside me.

Pushing myself up, I smiled and looked at him and smiled, then stood up and held out my hand. He took it and rose, pulling me into his arms and kissing me soundly before stepping back and scooping me up to carry me to my room. My arms naturally went around his neck, and while I wasn't exactly huge, I wasn't tiny by any stretch of the imagination, either. Except he acted as if I didn't weigh much as he strode across the living room and stepped through my door, shutting it with his foot.

He set me down on the edge of the bed and began to undo his pants, watching me the whole time. I did the same, watching him as he undressed in front of me. I was mesmerized and couldn't take my eyes off him, watching the muscles in his arms flex and bend with the process. It was like he knew I was watching because he was very deliberate in his actions, slowly pushing the button from the hole, pulling the space open to unzip in an agonizingly slow motion, until finally he was finished and began to push the pants down and he sprung free.

As if I were drawn in, I reached out my hand and grasped him, remembering the interaction in the shower a few days ago, I was gentle with my grip, simply holding him in my palm. He was warm and his skin was soft even though he was firm and solid. I stroked him from the tip back to press my hand against his body. He'd let his pants fall and stood back up, allowing me to do whatever I wanted, which was such a power trip to me. I was in control of this, and he was letting me take charge.

I looked up at his face and saw him smiling as he watched me. Not knowing anything about sex other than what we'd done, but knowing that mouths were a thing, I leaned forward. He rested his hand on my shoulder, stopping me and I looked back to him.

"Only if you want to," he said, and I knew he knew what I was about to do. "And not for very long because I won't last."

"I don't know what I'm supposed to do," I confessed.

"Lips and tongue, only," he said. "I prefer no teeth."

I laughed because I couldn't help it.

"Who uses teeth?"

"Some guys like that," he said.

Instead of continuing to talk, and trying to avoid losing my nerve, I leaned closer and took the tip of him into my mouth. He sucked in air, so obviously I did whatever it was I was doing right. Pressing closer, he slid across my tongue and further into my mouth, and it was an odd yet satisfying feeling to have him there. I pulled back, keeping my lips closed as I came to the tip of him, then pushed forward again, the tip coming to the back of my mouth. Even though I had him all the way into my mouth, he still had more of him left, and I wanted to try to get everything into me, so I pulled back again and relaxed my jaw, closed my eyes, and just went forward.

He hit the back of my throat and I backed off quickly, trying to not cough while I had him inside me.

"Slow down," he said, putting his hand on my shoulder. "No need to push past your comfort zone. Just slow strokes are fine. You're doing good, baby."

The confidence he placed in me, the approval he showed, made me want to take him all the way in even more, so I pulled back again, almost all the way off of him, then leaned in again, this time, relaxing my throat to let him graze the back. I only held him there for a moment, but it was such a satisfying feeling to be able to accomplish this that I almost let him go and cheered. Instead, I worked to do it again, then again one more time before he held me away from him, my lips coming off him with a pop.

"You gotta stop," he said. "I'm not gonna last if you keep doing that."

I looked up at him and asked, "Don't you like it?"

"I like it too much," he said, his eyes heavy, his hand still on my shoulder, keeping me away from him.

"You want me to stop," I said.

It was a statement, and I couldn't keep the disappointment from my voice.

"Hey," he said, tipping my chin up so he could look me in the eyes. "You are doing everything right. I just really like this feeling and will lose control if we don't stop. I don't want to just do this. I want to make you come again, several times, in fact. I can do that, but I'd love to be inside you when you go, if you don't mind."

Pulling in a deep breath, I thought about what he'd said. I was doing good with what I was doing, but he wanted to actually have sex with me. *Oh,* I thought. Yeah, that was what he was saying.

"So," I began, swallowing. "If we keep doing this, you can't have sex with me?"

"I can," he said. "It'll just take a while for me to be ready again if you keep this up. I'm happy to do both, but I don't want to push you too much."

I smiled and pressed forward, and his hand slid from my shoulder to the back of my head, holding my hair out of my face, but not forcing me to do anything I didn't want to do. It was firm, but there was no pressure, nothing that indicated he was forcing me, just helping me. With new confidence, I pulled him into my mouth again, sliding his hard length along my tongue and all the way back to the back of my mouth. I didn't hit my throat the first couple of times, but as I continued, it became more and more arousing to have his most intimate part within my control.

As I was sliding him in and out, his hips shifted a couple of times, as if he were having a hard time keeping still, until I began to taste a salty flavor. I assumed it was natural, so kept on going. His hand on my head was guiding me, not firmly, but steadily, and I continued to go in and out on him, bumping the back of my throat each time, until his hand stilled me and his hips took over. He wasn't thrusting deep, but the pace was more erratic, and I was at his temp, going faster and faster until he pulled himself out and grabbed himself, stroking until he exploded in his hand.

"Oh," I said, watching as the jet comes out of him in spurts.

"He let go of my head and was trying in vain to keep it all from spilling on the floor and everything around. Without thinking, I pulled my shirt over my head to catch the overflow, letting it puddle into the material as he finished. Taking the shirt from me, he used it to wipe up what he could, then looked at me and smiled.

"Sorry," he said. "I kind of couldn't stop."

"I don't mind," I replied. "Here," I continued, standing up. "Let me toss that in the hamper."

Taking the shirt from him, I saw there was still some left on him, so I wiped it off with the edge of the shirt and he shuddered. Walking to the closet where my hamper is, I toss the shirt in. Considering I was going to be doing laundry anyway, I didn't worry about it being in there and getting nasty.

"Wanna shower?" he asked in my ear, low and almost like a growl, which caused me to shudder myself.

"Sure," I said.

"Gonna need to lose these," he said, pushing my leggings down, my panties going with them.

His hands were warm, soft, and so sensual as he undressed me. Stepping out of my clothing, he steadied me, ensuring I didn't fall. We walked into the bathroom, his front to my back, and I could still feel some wetness when he pressed against me. I reach to turn on the light, but he takes my hand, keeping it from the switch.

"Let's keep it dark," he said, his mouth right next to my ear.

"How will we…"

"Trust me," he said.

"Okay," I replied, knowing I did trust him.

Probably more than I should, but there it was. He reached around me and turned the tap on, letting the water flow until it got to a decent temperature before pulling the lever to switch the flow to the shower-head. Once he felt the water was right, he stepped into the tub from behind me, then held his hand out to steady me as I stepped in.

He turned me so that my front was to his and walked me back under the spray of water, allowing it to cascade down my hair and back, wetting everything in its warm flow. His hands never left my hips as he dipped his head down and captured my lips in a sweet kiss, shorter than I wanted, before raising his arms and massaging my hair, allowing the moisture to get all the way to my scalp. It was such an intimate thing, showering together, him doing this for me, that I kind of just zoned out and let myself feel whatever it was I was feeling.

The day had started like shit with everything hitting the news, but now that it was just Cole and I, it was absolutely perfect. Just the two of us, in the dark, connecting physically, without any interruption, was the best way to end the day. Once I was solidly wet from the water, he held me to him, his strong arms around me, keeping me in the space I felt safe from everything. It was becoming a place I longed to be.

"You okay?" he asked.

I nodded, my head resting on his shoulder. He stepped away, reaching out to grab the shampoo, and poured some into his palm before beginning to rub it into my hair. It was slow, methodical, and perfect, and I relaxed more and more with each stroke of his hands through my locks. When he felt it was good and clean, he stepped me back again and under the shower's spray, rinsing the suds from my hair. I held him at his hips to keep myself steady and languished in his touch.

When he was done rinsing, he pressed against me once again and turned so that he was under the spray. He grabbed the shower gel and went to pour some into his palm, but I placed mine on top, capturing the fragrant gel in my hand, wanting to give him what he had given me, someone to care for him in this moment. I rubbed my hands together and began with his chest, massaging the soap into his skin and hair, rubbing it firmly as he stood still under the spray.

As I dipped lower and lower on his body, I felt him shiver under my touch, and I looked up to see his eyes closed, a smile playing across his face. Dipping down, past his stomach to his waist and further down, he sucked in just a bit as I rubbed along his length. I'd held it when it was firm, but not as it was now, which was soft, but still not tiny. I stroked it in my palm and felt it begin to firm up.

"Keep that up and we're gonna have to do something about it," he said, his voice low and barely above the sound of the spray.

Not one to shy away from a challenge, I continued to hold and stroke him as he continued to grow more and more firm with each stroke. Finally, after not nearly enough time, he stilled my hands.

"Let me rinse off," he said. "Then we can start again."

I nodded, and he turned his back to me, allowing the water to cascade over him. I held my hands on his back, using the water that was coming down to rinse them off as he rinsed his front. He shut the water off and pulled the curtain back to pull a towel off the shelf next to the tub. Turning to wrap me up, he started with my hair, drying it some with the towel before shifting to my shoulders.

The tender way he dried me was something I hadn't expected but was totally something he would do. He cared about me, it was obvious, but that extended to more than just the intimate times we'd shared. No, he flew all the way across the country to come and check on me when the world decided to shatter my privacy in such a cruel way. He felt the guilt of having caused it when it wasn't his fault, and that was more than anyone had ever done for me.

When the top half of my body was dry, he wrapped the towel around me and helped me from the tub. Pulling another towel down, he quickly dried himself off, then squatted to finish drying my legs. It was sweet and kind and all the things that Cole had been to me since we first met, and I could tell that when he decided that I was too much trouble, it would probably kill me when he left.

"Hey," he said, pulling me from my mind. "I don't know what you were just thinking but stop. Nothing is this bad. I've got you, okay?"

I nodded, not able to voice my thoughts. He kissed me on my forehead, then hung the towels on the shower rod, turning me toward the door and holding me as he walked me to bed. I tried to stop at my dresser to pull out some panties, but he kept me going, not stopping at all.

"I want to feel all of you next to me," he said in my ear. "Is that okay?"

Nodding, I moved with him to the edge of the bed and slid between the sheets. He followed me, sliding next to me, his body warm against mine, a nice clash for the coolness of the covers. Switching off the bedside lamp, he pulled me to him. I went, snuggling up against his side, my head on his chest, his arm around my back holding me to him.

The steady cadence of his heart under my ear, and the smooth and even breaths he was taking, lulled me to sleep quickly.

CHAPTER FORTY-EIGHT

*C*ole...

The gentle chimes were soothing yet distracting at the same time. She shifted beside me, then reached across to turn the alarm off.

"Mornin'," I said, my voice scratchy.

"Sorry," she replied. "I didn't mean to wake you up."

"It's okay," I said, holding her to me. "You gotta work?"

"Yeah," she said, although she did snuggle back against me. "I don't wanna get up, though."

"I know the feeling," I replied. "I would lay here all day with you in my arms."

"Awe," she cooed. "That's super sweet. Not to break this romantic moment, but I gotta pee."

I laughed as she slipped over me and onto the floor. Watching her walk to the bathroom in the early morning light streaming around her curtains was something I could get used to. As she closed the door she was smiling, and I wondered what she was thinking about. I stretched out, my arms above my head, and then settled in to watch as she walked back out of the bathroom. Definitely wasn't disappointed in that view, either.

"You're gorgeous," I said, and she stopped and looked at me. "What?"

"I don't know if you're just saying that or what," she said.

"When have I ever lied to you?"

"Never," she admitted. "I just…"

She stopped, and it wasn't the first time she hesitated to tell me something.

"You just what?"

"I'm just not used to this," she said, her eyes cast down as she stood stock still next to her dresser.

"Well, you better get used to it," I replied. "Cause I'm never gonna stop telling you that."

She looked up then and smiled, and all it did was make her more beautiful. I'd sat up in the bed already, and I slid from beneath the sheets to walk over to her, naked myself, with a morning wood that was standing proud. When I got to her, her eyes were glued to my dick, and it did wonders for my self-esteem.

"Eyes are up here, baby," I said, and she popped her head up as if caught watching something she shouldn't.

"Sorry," she mumbled.

"Never have to be sorry," I said. "I was just teasing. You good?"

"Yeah," she said. "Just a little tired."

"I get it," I said. "You got time, or do you have to get to work?"

"Hang on," she said, slipping past me to her phone and checking the time. "I have about an hour or so."

"Give me a minute," I said, then stepped into the bathroom. "Be right back. Don't change."

I shut the door and took care of my morning business, then washed up my hands and dick and headed back out. She was still standing next to her bed watching me and I just felt so blessed to be in her presence.

"Shit," I said, realizing that the last thirty-six hours or so hadn't been kind to me. "No condoms, so no sex."

"On the pill," she said, confident in her response.

"I don't want to pressure you," I said, then she stopped me with a hand and said, "Hang on."

She threw on another one of her oversized shirts and walked out the bedroom door, leaving it open. I watched as she went to Remi's room and knocked, then opened the door. She stepped in, disappearing into the darkness beyond, then came back with something in her hand.

"Problem solved," she said, shutting the door behind her as she came in.

I looked down, and she was holding a box of condoms. It was unopened and there appeared to be plenty for several rounds.

"Let's start with just one," I suggested, and she smiled.

"Remi said he'll pick more up for himself if he needs them," she said, then set the box on her nightstand and pulled the shirt over her head, letting it fall to the floor.

I blinked for just a moment to let my brain catch up, then stepped to her, pulling her against me and kissing her hard, pushing my tongue into her mouth, claiming her as mine. She responded like she always had, arms twining around my neck, body pushing into me, getting as close as possible without me being inside her. Taking the step or two needed, I pressed her down onto her bed, laying on top of her, my one arm holding my weight from being too much.

When I came up for air, she shifted up further, laying her head on her pillow, her dark hair a mess around her head making her absolutely irresistible. I pressed my lips to her thigh, then continued kissing all along her body, simple little pecks until I reached her breasts. Pulling her nipple into my mouth, I sucked it to a point, then pressed my teeth together just enough to apply pressure, but not pain. She arched under me, pushing herself further into my mouth, and I obliged her desire, taking more of her in. When I felt she was primed enough, I moved to her other breast, giving it the same attention that I did the first, getting the same reaction, revving her higher and higher. When I released it, I moved to her collarbone, pressing my lips against the sharp protrusion before moving up her neck and along her jaw to her earlobe.

I let my body press her down into the mattress, just enough that she could feel me, but not enough to smother her. She sighed out with the weight, and it was a contented sound.

"I want you so bad," I growled in her ear, pushing my pelvis against hers so she could feel my desire. "Do you want me?"

She nodded; I could feel it.

"Tell me you want me," I said, putting some force into my voice.

"I want you," she whispered, as if she were afraid to say the words.

"That's my good girl," I said, shifting so I could see her face.

Her eyes were nearly closed, a smile on her lips as if she were in another dimension already. I reached over and grabbed the box of condoms, ripping it open one handed, and pulling the foil packets out. Once I'd gotten them out, I tried to tear one from the strip, but was struggling hard.

"Let me," she said, grabbing it with one hand and reaching her other around my neck, effectively pulling me against her again, and separated one from the pack, dropping the extras next to her on the edge of the bed.

I took the packages and shifted, laying on my side just off her so I could open it and begin to slide it on. Her eyes were open now, fascinated with what I was doing, and she watched as I pulled the rubber disk from the package and lowered it to my cock, squeezing the tip to give myself room before unrolling it down my length.

"I didn't know if it would fit," she said, her voice full of awe.

"Most are fine," I said, shifting again to drop the wrapper off the edge of the bed. "Pretty standard size that fits most guys."

"Okay," she said, looking back at my face. "Now what?"

"Now," I said, lowering my lips to her to kiss her deeply before continuing. "Now, I get you ready."

I slid my hand across her thigh, and she opened almost instantly, trusting me in a way that was wonderful. Sliding my hand to her center, I stroked her along her lips, paying attention to her clit to hopefully get her aroused enough that I wouldn't hurt her when I entered her. Her eyes fluttered closed, and I felt the moisture increase as I continued to stroke her. After a short time, I slid my middle finger into her and she sucked a breath in, then relaxed as I continued to slide it in and out, using my thumb to rub her clit and bring her closer to climax. Slow and steady, in and out, round, and round, until she was clenching the blankets at her side, the hand that was around my back pressing me to her.

As she moved beneath my hands, I slowly shifted over her, placing myself between her legs, but keeping my hand moving, keeping her steadily climbing that uptick she was feeling, getting ever closer to the top where she would tumble over the edge. I slid my finger out of her and pressed the head of my dick against her opening. I didn't want to just shove in, so slid it up and down along her lips as her breathing quickened until I finally found purchase and slipped in, just the tip, and her eyes popped open.

"You good?" I asked, having stopped my motions. She nodded, rather quickly. "Gonna need you to tell me if you're good," I said.

"I'm good," she said. "Don't stop."

"Whatever you say, baby," I said, taking her at her word. I slid back, not exiting her, but it was close, then slid forward again.

Inch by inch I moved, gaining ground with each movement, until I felt a pop and she gasped. Stopping, I held firm, watching her face.

"What was that?" she asked.

"Your hymen," I said, and she looked confused. "First time you have sex it pops."

"Oh," she said, though she was still looking uncomfortable.

"You want me to stop?" I asked, and was hoping beyond hope that she would say no.

"Can you hold it for a minute?" she asked.

"Whatever you need, baby," I said, thanking whatever deity there was that she hadn't wanted to end.

With a couple of deep breaths, she shifted her hips, and I twitched inside her. She snapped her eyes to me, wide with wonder.

"That's what you do to me," I said.

Instead of saying anything, she shifted again, sliding her hips up toward me, causing me to press further into her.

"You like that?" I asked, and she nodded. "You want to be in control?"

Again, she nodded, so I slowly pulled myself back, leaving her warm intimate embrace and sliding over to lie on my back next to her. She watched me, confusion on her face.

"Straddle me," I instructed. "I'll help you. This way you are in control and can do what makes you feel good."

Shifting on the bed, she pushed up to a sitting position, then swung a leg across mine, sliding herself up along my length, back and forth against me as my dick was pressed between us, not in her, but still giving her pleasure.

"That's it, baby," I encouraged. "Do what makes you feel good."

As she was sliding up and down, she leaned forward and pressed a hand to my chest. She opened her eyes and looked into mine.

"Help me put you in," she said and then lifted her hips some.

I pressed an arm around her back, leaning her forward even more as I reached between us and shifted my cock so it was angled to enter her. Sliding it along her lips, I found purchase, and she knew it as well, as she slid her hips back and down, pulling me into her warmth.

"Mmm," she hummed, her eyes slipping closed.

Watching as she shifted, raising, and lowering her hips, feeling everything there was to feel, getting more and more animated with each movement.

"That's it," I said. "You are so beautiful."

My hands were on her hips, but I slid one off and between us, sliding my thumb against her clit and began pressing and stroking her there as well.

"Oh," she hushed, the word coming out in a breath. "Oh, yeah."

Her gentle words and sweet tones showed that she was still learning, but enjoying her discoveries, and I was more than happy to let her experience everything with me. I would do almost anything to keep her in this blissful state and as far away from the drama the last several hours had thrust upon her. If I could keep her with me, cocooned in my arms and away from it, I would.

CHAPTER FORTY-NINE

*K*ylie...

He was pressing his thumb against the top of my sex, moving it in circles as he pressed inside me, and it was almost too much. The first push was uncomfortable, but only a little pain, and once I got over that, the pleasure shut it out of my mind completely. Now, though, he was letting me do whatever I wanted, to use his body for my own pleasure, and it was exhilarating. Pressing my hands to his chest, I sat up higher, giving his thumb more access to me as he stroked along those nerves and wound me up tighter and tighter.

When his other hand slid up my side and to my breast, rubbing along my nipple, then pinching it between his fingers, I fell over the edge and tumbled into the stars, floating on a breeze that was all in my mind. My pussy clenched and unclenched as I squeezed him, and I leaned forward, nearly falling onto his chest as he caught me and held me as I quivered in his arms.

After a lifetime, I came back to myself in small pieces until I was fully restored and wrapped in his embrace.

"Hey," he said, shifting me and sliding his thumb under my eye. "Don't cry."

I hadn't realized I was crying until he said it, and then I realized that I had tears streaming from my eyes.

"I'm here," he whispered in my ear. "I've got you. You're safe."

His words of encouragement were exactly what I needed, and I pressed myself further into his embrace where I was safe. When all my emotions had been spent, I sat up a bit, shifting with him still inside me, and it was a strange and foreign and wonderful feeling.

"How can I help you?" I asked.

"Mind if I drive?" he asked.

"Tell me what to do," I said, and he smiled.

"How about you slide off and let me get on top," he said.

Doing as he asked, I slid off, pulling up first so he slid out of me, and that was another sensation I hadn't been prepared for.

"On your stomach," he said, and I looked at him, confused. "Trust me?"

I nodded, then pressed my stomach to my bed, my ass hanging out for everyone to see. He sat up, running a hand down my body from my shoulder, down my back, and then over my ass, giving it a squeeze.

"That is one fine ass," he said and I couldn't help but let out a little giggle.

He leaned down then, pressing his lips to my butt cheek, the stubble scratching it a bit, and I sucked in, surprised by the sensation. Shifting up, he pressed a knee between my legs and I opened them for him. Once he had the other between my legs, he pulled one of the pillows from the head of the bed and slid his arm under my belly, pulling me up a bit and sliding the cushion underneath me.

"There we go," he said. "God, you're beautiful."

I looked over my shoulder to see him looking at me, naked and open to him. He bent down and kissed my ass again, then pressed his face into my crack and licked me from front to my pussy, and I shuddered.

"So sweet," he said. "So delicious."

He licked me again, and I felt the reverberations from his hum run through me, making me pulse from within, and I wanted to feel him inside me once again, the way he was when I was on top of him.

"I don't think I could ever get enough of you," he said, sitting up more and sliding his hands up my legs to my hips. "I want to eat you all over again."

My breathing increased, and I was nearly panting with want, something I'd never experienced before, and it was glorious. I felt alive. So alive and free.

"Mmm," he hummed, holding my hips where they were on top of the pillow.

He moved closer, lining himself up at my entrance, and used his hand to guide him right to where I was open for him. He slid his dick up and down before pressing it into me, and I sighed as he did, feeling like I was full and exactly where I wanted to be.

"You feel so good," he said, looking at me. "I want to stay right here forever."

Instead of staying, though, he began to move, rocking his hips back and forth, sliding in and out of me, slowly at first, then picking up speed. It was a very different sensation than when I was on top of him, but it was wonderful all the same. He continued to move, in and out, over, and over, keeping a steady rhythm, holding my hips in place as he pressed all the way into me, then pulling nearly all the way out. In and out, in and out, and oh, it rubbed on just the right places inside me.

My eyes fluttered shut, and I felt him moving in me, holding me in place, keeping me safe as he took his pleasure and gave me mine. His breath had been slow and steady, but it ramped up, coming faster and harsher as he increased his speed. Everything he was doing was what I needed, and I let go of all my inhibitions and let the pleasure roll over and through me, falling again into that blissful place where stars burst behind my eyelids and my entire being turned to liquid.

"Oh yeah," he gritted out. "You feel so good, so good, so very good."

He punctuated each word with a thrust into me until finally he pressed hard against me and tensed up, gripping my hips so hard I worried I'd have bruises. A few more movements and he collapsed on me, not pinning me, but completely surrounding me with his whole being.

I sighed out at the feel of his chest against my back, even with the sweat that slid between us. I was truly spent and felt like nothing in the world could break me, as long as I had Cole beside me, behind me, and inside of me.

With a deep sigh, he pressed a kiss to my temple, then sat up, his hand going to the space between us as he pulled out, the movement rubbing my already raw nerves in a way that just made me feel even better.

"I'm gonna grab a cloth," he said, pressing his lips to my ass again. "Don't move. I'll be right back."

It wasn't as if I could do anything but lay there in my post coital state. No, I was on such a high that nothing short of a miracle would get me to be able to move. I heard the water turn on, then off again, and soon he was back, warm wetness was being pressed against my sex, gently running up from the front to the back along my crack. It was both pleasurable and painful, and I wasn't sure where one sensation began or the other ended.

"You doing okay?" he asked as he lay next to me.

"Mmhmm," I hummed, not wanting to do anything but enjoy the afterglow.

"I hate to do this to you, but it's getting late," he said, and I slid over, looking at him. "Don't you have to work?"

I blinked a minute, then realization dawned on me.

"Oh, shit," I said, trying to get myself up.

"Easy," he said, helping me right myself. "Let me help."

He was good as his word, untangling the panties and leggings that were on the floor from the night before to help me into them, then going to my dresser at my direction and finding a shirt for me to put on. I grabbed the sweater that was at the foot of my bed on the cedar chest I'd inherited from my grandmother and pulled it over my head as I headed to the door.

"Morning, sunshine," Remi said as I stepped out. "Coffee's ready if you want some. I started your computer, so you can log on anytime you're ready."

I headed toward the kitchen when Cole slid his arm around my middle.

"I'll get your coffee," he said in my ear. "You get to work."

He kissed my temple, then let me go, guiding me toward my desk and heading into the kitchen himself. I heard the cups come down from the cupboard, then the sound of the carafe being pulled from the maker. All of this while I was logging into my laptop and getting into the programs that I needed open for my day's work.

"Remi?" I heard Cole ask and turned to see my roommate hold his cup up and shake his head. "Here you go," he said, setting a cup next to me on my desk.

"Thanks," I replied.

He pressed a kiss to the back of my neck and I kind of just turned to goo, closing my eyes, and enjoying the feel of him at my back, his lips on me. My computer pinged, and I jolted, opening my eyes to see a request for a video chat with Jim.

"Gotta take this," I said.

"I'll be in your room," he replied, kissing me one more time on my temple. "I can order breakfast if you want, or lunch, or whatever."

"No thanks," I said, distracted by why my boss requested this meeting as soon as I signed into the system. I pulled up the video chat, slipped my headphones on, and clicked into the meeting.

"Kylie," Jim said, and his face was flushed. "Are you okay?"

"Yeah, why?" I asked.

"You must not have seen the news today," he said.

"I literally just woke up," I replied. "But now that you say that, I don't wanna know."

"They've pulled your info from the website," he said and my eyes widened.

"Am I being fired?" I asked, terrified that this was what was going to happen.

"Not at all," he replied. "They're trying to protect you."

"What happened?" My voice didn't shake or sound any way other than normal, and I was surprised, what with all the fear running through my veins.

"Your dad's back in the news," he said, and I paled. I could feel all the blood rush from my face, my heart started beating, and I wasn't sure what I should do. "Are you okay?"

"I'm fine," I said, but how the words came out, I have no idea. "I have to go."

Before he could say anything, I disconnected the video call. The room was spinning, going around and around and I couldn't see anything as the tears welled up and fell.

Oh, God, I thought. *Not again.*

CHAPTER FIFTY

*C*ole...

I heard her say she was fine, but there was something off about the words. I stepped from her room and saw her sitting there, just staring into space. When the tears began, I went to her, kneeling next to her. I checked the computer and the video chat system seemed to be shut down, so I just put my arms around her waist, holding her where she was. She turned and looked at me, and I about died to see the sheer terror on her face.

"Come here," I said, sliding to my ass and pulling her down.

She came willingly, nearly collapsing onto me, clutching at me as she sobbed. The first time she did this, it was silent. Not this time. No, now she was openly breaking apart. Her body was racked with sobs and sucking in of breath, wailing sounds coming from her as she completely fell apart. I had no idea what just happened, but I was glad I was there to catch her.

Remi came over, I saw him in my peripheral vision, and he looked worried. Instead of just letting me take care of her, though, he knelt next to us and wrapped his arms around her from behind, effectively making her the meat in our sandwich. Both of us were using reassuring words, mine in one ear and his in the other, as we held her together.

After a while, when her sobs slowed, her roommate leaned back a bit, looking more worried than I'd seen him before. Every other time we'd interacted, he was confident, smooth, and all put together. Now, though, he was also crying, and I squeezed his arm as he pulled away, mouthing thanks to him. Instead of going anywhere, though, he kind of just sat opposite me, his legs next to mine, with Kylie in my lap.

Pushing back from me, she wiped her face with her sleeve, though it was less than effective, what with the tears and snot that were happening there.

"Sorry," she mumbled.

"No need to apologize," I replied. "You fall apart any time you need to. I'll be here to hold you together until you're ready to do it on your own."

"Oh, no," she said, trying desperately to get up.

Helping her, I shoved her ass to get her standing, and she took off to her room before I heard the bathroom door slam and the sound of her throwing up echoed through the door.

"She's a stress vomiter," Remi said as a way of explanation.

"What happened?" I asked, and he just shook his head. "She needs to tell me?"

"She'll have to," he said. "I have no idea what's going on."

I got up, and went to her room, opening the door to the bathroom to see her squatting in front of the toilet, her hair a matted mess, retching over the bowl. I went to her, gathering her hair from around her head so that it could hopefully be spared the splatter from her sickness. When she finally seemed done with it, she turned her face away from me.

"Oh, hey," I said, grabbing a towel from the counter. "Let me help you."

"I don't want you to see me like this," she said, her voice harsh from the incident.

"Please let me help you," I begged, trying to turn her toward me.

Finally, she turned a bit and snatched the towel from my hand, rubbing it over her face, I'm sure to get most of the ick off. I let her hair down, turning the tap on to fill the glass next to it with some cold water. I went back to her, handing her the glass, and she took it, having tossed her towel into the tub. Taking a sip, she swished it around, then spit it into the toilet, doing it one more time.

"You want your toothbrush?" I asked, but she shook her head. "What can I do?"

She looked at me, her eyes red from the crying, cheeks spotted with red blotches and pinpricks from broken blood vessels, and I could honestly say I had never seen anyone look so terrible and beautiful all at the same time.

"Hold me," she said, reaching her arms out.

I took the glass from her hand and set it on the counter, then knelt and scooped her up, holding her as if she were a little child. She was helpless, but not in the way most thought. No, she was as strong as any warrior, and braver than anyone I knew. She just had this one weakness that crippled her. Like Achille's with his heel, she had one point of entry, and that was straight through her heart.

Turning, I walked through the door and into her bedroom, the one we'd christened just a short time earlier, and lay her on the bed, shifting the sheets and blankets so she could be under the covers.

"I'll be right back," I said, standing up and walking out her door.

"She okay?" Remi asked, concern etched on his face.

He'd stopped crying, but there were lingering tears in his eyes. Honestly, I don't know whether I had a friend in my life that would be there for me the way he was for her, and I was a bit disappointed that I didn't.

"I think she'll live," I replied. "Do you have any sports drinks or something that will help increase her electrolytes?"

"I think we have something stuffed in the back of the fridge," he said. "Let me look."

With purpose, he marched to the aforementioned appliance and nearly ripped the door off when he opened it. Shoving things around, he grabbed something and pulled it out.

"Not sure if it's expired," he said. "Not sure if this shit even does expire."

"I'm sure it's fine," I said. "As long as there are no floaters in it, we should be good."

He shook the bottle of blue liquid, then handed it to me.

"Can you take care of her computer and stuff?" I asked.

"I got it," he said. "I just wish I knew what happened."

"You and me, both," I replied. "I'm gonna try to get her to sleep. If she'll tell me, I'll let her, but I'm not gonna push."

"She doesn't respond well to pushy people," he said. "As reserved as she is, she does know how to stand on her own two feet and fight for what she wants. Just depends on the situation."

"I get it," I said.

"I'm glad you're here," he said.

"That makes two of us," I replied.

I took the bottle with me into the room and Kylie was still where I'd left her, though her eyes were closed now. I didn't want to wake her, but she needed to get something in her, so I set the bottle on the bedside table and touched her shoulder. She flinched and her eyes flew open, terror etched across her beautiful face.

"Shh," I whispered. "It's just me. Can you drink something for me?"

She shook her head, but reached one arm out, beckoning me to join her. I slid my pants off and scooted under the covers next to her and she wrapped herself around me tighter than she ever had before, clutching me to her and holding me as if she were afraid to let me go. My arm was around her back, and I pulled her to my side, taking the other arm to lay on her thigh across my stomach. There were a couple of shuddered breaths, then she seemed to even out her breathing. Any time I shifted, even if it was just my hand on her leg, she tightened her grip.

After a bit, I must have dozed off, because I woke with a start when she slid up on top of me, straddling me. She'd taken her shirt off, as well as her panties, because I could feel her wet warmth rubbing up and down my cock, which hardened on its own. Watching her move above me, sliding up and down my length, I wondered whether this was her way of freeing herself from the terrors she'd experienced, or trying to forget everything.

She leaned forward and snatched a foil packet from her bedside table, tearing it open with her teeth. Sliding back, she stroked me, ensuring I was fully erect before sliding the slippery disk down my cock. Once she had it in place, she shifted up, rising above me, using her hands to guide me into her opening. It was a slow, tedious process, but she worked to get me fully seated inside her, a smile crossing her lips when she settled down against my body.

The slow and methodical movements she made, forward and back, up, and down, trying to find the best way to get the fireworks going, was beautiful. This innocent girl had learned the wonderful side of sex, the way it could get you out of your own head and make everything else disappear for just a little while. I let my hands slide up her thighs, up her stomach, and over her breasts, massaging them, softly at first, until the buds of her nipples hardened and I could squeeze them, rolling them between thumb and forefinger.

Her head dropped back, the tangle of curls falling over her shoulders and down her back as she writhed atop me, taking the pleasure she needed to alleviate her mind, to get rid of the horror that had been plaguing her. Higher and higher she floated, crawling up the side of that mountain until she finally reached the top and tumbled over, falling apart in a completely different way than she had earlier. Hearing my name on her lips as she fell was better than any sound I could imagine, and I just reveled in her pleasure.

Finally, when her flame simmered and slowed, she lowered herself to me, my hands moving from her breasts to her back, holding her to me as she slowly shuddered, reclaiming her body from the atmosphere she'd experienced. Her breathing slowed and she nodded off, my cock still hard inside her. I didn't want to move her, but I knew this wasn't going to work for me. I wasn't going to be able to relax or hold her the way I wanted. Instead of trying to wake her, though, I just sort of rolled to the side, slipping out of her as I did. She shifted with me, her one leg still around me, falling to the small of my back as we shifted.

It was obvious that she was sleeping when I went to take the condom off, not wanting it to get stuck on anything, and just releasing the uncomfortable feel of it all. They were fine in the moment, but awkward feeling if I wasn't using it for its intended purpose. After I was back to myself, I held her to me, and we both slept.

CHAPTER FIFTY-ONE

*K*ylie...

I was safe here. Protected. Treasured. Nothing bad could happen to me when I was wrapped in Cole's arms. The demons that had plagued me my entire life were held at bay. The monsters who terrorized my nightmares were quieted. Absolutely nothing could hurt me here in this safe space.

There was a tap on the door, then I heard the latch click and saw the light from the main part of the apartment seep through the sliver of space.

"Kylie," Remi said. "There are a couple of police detectives here. They want to talk to you."

Cole hadn't moved, but I knew he was awake. I really didn't want to do this, but it was what had to be done.

"Give me a minute to get dressed," I said.

"Okay," he replied, then shut the door.

The arms around me tightened just a bit, holding me steady as I geared myself up to face yet another beast. I sighed deeply then pushed away, just a bit.

"I've got you," he said.

Those few words, the handful of letters strung together in such a way as to comfort me, were exactly what I needed. Another sigh and I was sitting up, sliding over the top of him and onto the other side. The side that was closer to the horror that was my father and all the havoc he'd released on the world.

I reached down and pulled Cole's pants up onto the bed next to me. Rummaging around in the near dark I couldn't find my panties or anything else I'd had on earlier. Frustrated, I got up and walked naked to my dresser, pulling out a pair of panties from the top drawer. Holding the piece of furniture, I steadied myself and slipped first one, then the other foot through the holes, pulling them up over my ass. Next came a pair of leggings, which proved to be harder to do one handed.

Cole was there, steadying me and helping me pull them on. Never would I tire of having him there to be my rock, my steady and constant force to keep me sane in this insane world. I grabbed a tank top and pulled it on, then pulled a sweater over my head. My hair was chaos around my head, but instead of dealing with it, I went to the bathroom to grab a hair tie and pull it up. Later, after the world fell apart, I would deal with the tangles that were likely there.

"You ready?" Cole asked, standing in the doorway wearing his slacks and button-up shirt, looking so much more put together than I was.

"Might as well," I said.

"Hey," he said as I went to go past him.

I looked up at him, unsure what he was going to say or do. He lowered his head and kissed me, soft and sweet, just for a moment.

"You are stronger than anyone I know," he whispered. "Whatever this is, you can handle it. And if you can't," he added, pulling me back to look me in the eye. "I will be right there with you, making sure you're safe and protected until you can stand on your own two feet."

It was as if he knew what I was thinking, reading my mind, and knowing exactly what I needed to hear in that moment. I squeezed his hand, then pulled him behind me as we went to face reality.

The two men were standing near the door, dressed in suits that reminded me of the old police shows my granddad watched when I was a kid. They weren't fancy, but they were functional, and it suited the role they were playing in my life at the moment.

"Ms. Harper?" the taller one asked.

"I'm Kylie Harper," I said, walking toward them. "Do you want to sit down?"

"We're fine," the shorter one said.

Both men were taller than me and looked as if it had been a while since they had been to a gym of any kind. Not that they were out of shape, per se, but more like they had let themselves go.

"I'm Detective Guttierez," the taller one said, holding a business card out to me. "We're here because of your father."

"I suspected," I said, taking the card and laying it on the counter. "What's he done?"

"He sent us a message," the other detective said. "Gave us coordinates out near Maple Valley."

"Okay," I said, waiting for the rest of the bomb to explode.

"Maybe we should sit down," Cole said, pulling me to him and away from the men.

He led me to the chair in our living area, sitting down and pulling me onto his lap. The detectives followed, each taking a seat on the edge of the couch. Remi stood behind Cole and me, one hand on each of our shoulders.

"Well," I prompted when the silence became too heavy.

"Preliminary results indicate that it is another body," the shorter detective said. "Nothing concrete, yet, but ground penetrating radar is showing that there is definitely something down there."

"If this proves to be true," Detective Guttierez added. "This will be the first one found in almost a decade."

"What does that have to do with Kylie?" Cole asked.

"He's made a request," Guttierez said and I could feel my blood run cold.

"He wants to see me," I said.

It wasn't a question. I knew that was what he would want. He had forced it of me from the beginning, and there was nothing I could do about it then. I was a minor and he was my father, but only in title. No, he stopped being my father a long time before he went to jail.

"He does," the other detective said.

"There is every indication that this is one of many victims that weren't known," Guttierez said. "But he's only going to give us this one until he gets a chance to talk to you."

"Kylie," Remi said, his hand holding me firm.

"I know," I said.

We'd always suspected there were more victims. My father was a master of saying just what the authorities wanted to hear, only giving them the bare minimum. The search of our house right after he was arrested indicated that there were so many more out there, but he wouldn't say anything. They had him on seven, but there was just so many more trophies that it was clear they hadn't found them all.

"We wanted you to know so you had time to think about it," Guttierez said. "He's made the request, and we're going to move him back over here from Walla Walla this week. Until we can confirm the identity of this victim, we won't be giving much more to him other than the move. You're free to say no, but the families of the remaining missing deserve some sort of closure."

"I know," I said.

I was dead inside. Just like I had been when we first found out, when he was taken away so many years ago. Everything changed so quickly back then, and now that I had things going my way. Now that my life was moving in a wonderful direction, he was back to rip me apart. Take everything I loved away from me. My security, my life, it was all going away because when daddy dearest spoke, the whole fucking world paid attention.

CHAPTER FIFTY-TWO

*C*ole...

"We'll be in touch," the detective said as he left.

I couldn't help but be amazed at the way Kylie held up under the pressure. Once the door closed, though. That was a different story. She sagged in my arms, losing every ounce of stability she'd been holding onto. Catching her, I lifted her up and walked with her to the chair I'd just moved from, pulling her onto my lap once again as she shattered to pieces.

"Why does he have to do this to me?" she cried.

"You don't have to go," I said. "It's not your responsibility to do this."

Remi looked at me and I knew exactly what he was thinking. She would do this. She would sacrifice herself in order to give others the peace they deserved. In the short time I'd known her, she had shown me that she was as selfless as they came, always putting everyone else's comfort over her own. Once she'd helped them, she'd fall apart. Whether she could put herself together afterward was never her concern.

"Do you want me to stay?" I asked, knowing that I would do whatever I needed to do to make this work if that was what she wanted.

"It could be weeks," she said, and she sounded normal. "You have a job you have to get back to. I'll be fine."

Her demeanor was off somehow, and I was concerned with the switch she'd flipped.

"You could come with me," I offered. "Maybe a change of scenery would be just what you needed. How about it?"

"No, seriously," she said, shifting to stand. "I'm fine. It's all fine. I can do this."

She walked away from me to her room and shut the door. I looked at Remi and he seemed as confused as I was.

"What just happened?" he asked.

"I think she broke," I said. "That's not her."

"It's not," he agreed. "She can shut down if she has to, but she's never been this cold, this..."

"Missing?" I asked.

"Yeah," he said. "She's just gone blank inside or something."

"I don't feel like I should leave," I said. "Coach said I could meet them in Atlanta on Thursday, or even Friday morning. I'm just not sure she's okay, though."

"You know she's gonna insist you go," he said.

"She can insist all she wants," I argued. "I'm my own person, and if she needs me, I'm staying."

"Cole," she called from her room.

I got up, gave one last look at Remi, then walked to the door and opened it. She was naked, sitting on the edge of the bed, her clothes neatly folded at the foot on top of her cedar chest. The bedside lamp was on and there was a vibrator sitting on the nightstand.

"Come here," she demanded.

Shutting the door behind me I walked to her. She scooted up on the bed a bit and reached over, grabbing the toy and unplugging it.

"I want you to use this on me," she said.

"I don't know what you mean," I replied.

"You need to use this," she insisted, holding it out to me. "I need to forget. I need to get lost in bliss. I need you to make the whole world go away. Will you do that for me?"

"Can we just…"

"No," she barked, her voice giving no room for argument. "You're going to have to go away and I need to know what this thing can do so I can use it to forget when everything goes to shit. You have to teach me."

Her eyes were glossed over, not like tears were trying to escape, but like she was gone somewhere else. I unbuttoned my shirt and set it on top of her clothes, then slid my pants down and set them there as well. She'd shoved the blankets nearly all the way down to the foot of the bed and was lying back, several pillows bunched behind her.

Taking the toy from her hand I looked it over, trying to get an idea of what it might do. It seemed like an ordinary vibrator with some protrusions on one side. I assumed they were there to stimulate the clit, which was a brilliant design. Sitting near her feet, I looked at her. There was fear in her eyes, but a determination behind that as well.

"Okay," I said, determined to help her figure out a way to find peace in the chaos she'd just been thrust into.

I kissed her knee that was up in the air, then pressed the inside of it out so it lay on the bed. Doing the same with the other one, her legs were like butterfly wings, fluttering out to the side, opening her up to me and allowing me to see the most intimate parts of her. I set the toy to the side and began with my fingers, sliding them up and down her slit, working to get the juices flowing, so to speak.

She watched with rapt attention, her own hands sliding up to her breasts to massage them. Kylie might have been an innocent young woman, but she was a sponge when it came to learning about her body and what made it tick.

"That's it, baby," I encouraged, sliding one finger inside her as her head fell back.

She was wet, but not overly so. Completely understandable considering what she had just been through. My goal was to get her to forget, even for a moment, that she was living in a nightmare. Continuing to slide my finger in and out, I pressed my thumb to her clit, rubbing it in circles, applying pressure in what I hoped was a magical combination to send her out of herself and into the atmosphere, away from the chaos surrounding her.

"Oh," she moaned, straight from her throat.

I added another finger going in and out of her, trying to push just the right combination of buttons to set her off. I wanted her to come before I started with the toy. Watching her tease her tits, twisting the nubs in her fingers as her back arched, pressing her pussy into my hand was absolutely everything.

Her breath was coming faster, her hands pulling her nipples from her chest, and she was getting wetter and wetter, until finally she called out my name, her legs coming up from the mattress to press against my body between her legs.

"That's it," I encouraged. "Let it all go and come for me."

She shook under me, her hands coming from her nipples to pull at the sheet on either side of her. I slowed my rhythm as she settled, her eyes opening to look down her body at me. I couldn't help but smile at the absolute wonder on her face.

"You want a break?" I asked. "Or should I start with the toy?"

CHAPTER FIFTY-THREE

*K*ylie...

Cole kept at it, between the toy, his mouth, and his dick, he kept me in an almost constant state of bliss. We slept off and on throughout the day, and I knew my time with him was growing short. He wouldn't want to leave me, but I had to make him go. As much as I wanted him to be next to me, by my side the entire time I dealt with this new serving of horror, I didn't want to mess up his career.

As Wednesday dawned, I got up before he woke up and went to the bathroom to get my morning started. I was as quiet as I could be, coming out and grabbing clothes to throw on. My body was sore, but it was a good kind of feeling. It made me feel alive. More alive than I'd ever felt in my life.

"Hey," Remi said as he saw me.

"Hi," I replied.

"You good?"

"Yeah," I said, making my way to the kitchen to grab some coffee.

My computer was on by the time I went to my desk and I looked over to see Remi settling back in his seat.

"Thanks," I said.

Moving the mouse, I got myself into work mode, just wanting to dive into something that I could control. The complexity that came with programming, with making the ones and zeros jump at my command, was where I had been able to find freedom when I was a kid and all of this started. Back then I didn't know all the complexities of who my father was, what he had done. All I knew was that he was bad, someone who wasn't who I thought he was.

I had no idea how long I'd been working when I felt him kiss my head. Turning to look up at him, I smiled.

"You were up early," he said.

"Gotta work," I replied.

He kissed me again, this time a little longer, then went to the kitchen to find his own morning beverage. He pulled a kitchen chair over next to mine and sat down.

"I'm gonna have to head out tomorrow," he said.

"I know," I replied, not looking at him.

"You gonna be okay when I'm gone?"

"I'll be fine."

Nothing would be fine for me, but he didn't need to know that. No, I needed to present to him a façade that said that he could leave me for a while and I would survive. I didn't want to be a burden. I'd been that for so many people in the past and I couldn't do that to him. He'd proven that he would be there to catch me. Now, I needed to prove to him that I could stand on my own.

"If you're sure," he said, placing a finger under my chin to turn me to look at him.

"I'm sure," I said, forcing myself to smile.

"Okay," he said. "I'll make arrangements to fly out tonight."

"Okay," I said, turning back to my computer screens and the code that was sliding across it.

We had lunch shortly after, and then he was heading to the airport. I kissed him a long time, knowing that he wouldn't be back for almost two weeks. I would miss him, but I had to get used to that if I was going to be with him.

The next morning, I woke to an email from the detective who had been by the other day saying that they would be scheduling a time for me to come in and speak to my father. I made it clear that I had some stipulations I wanted before I agreed to anything. Remi and I watched the game that night, and I was glad to see that Cole was playing and seemed to be doing well. At least I hadn't screwed up that for him.

CHAPTER FIFTY-FOUR

*C*ole...

I landed in Atlanta long before the team was scheduled to, so took the shuttle to the hotel where we were staying. They let me check in, even though the rest of the team wasn't there, yet, and I found my way to my room to unload my suitcase. In a way, it would be good to get back to the normal, the ordinary, the things I'd been doing for years.

But I missed Kylie. Not just the sex, but spending time holding her, talking to her, learning about her life and what she had to deal with growing up. How she managed to get through her teen years, attend and succeed at college, find an amazing job that she excelled at, and do it all while having the dark cloud of her father's crimes hanging over her, was beyond me. Any of the blows she took would have likely crippled me. Not my Kylie, though. No, she had simply soldiered on, plowing through every obstacle without missing a beat.

As I lay in the bed, waiting to hear the rest of my teammates coming down the hall, I pondered what life would look like with Kylie at my side. She was definitely better than me, stronger, and more secure in who she was. Even with her panic attacks, her falling apart when her father was brought up, and her desire to stay away from the press, she still made me a better man.

Even with the short amount of time we'd known each other, it felt like she was the other half of me. The missing piece that I'd been searching for my whole life. This separation would be a test as to how we would handle my work's impact on our lives, but somehow, I knew she would have no trouble with it. No, she'd just figure out how to make it work within the life she was living. My phone buzzed, and I looked to see the text she'd sent.

I miss you.

It was a simple text, something that I would expect, yet it was more. There was something she wasn't telling me. Instead of texting back, I called her.

"Hello?" she answered.

"Hey, baby," I said.

"Cole," she replied, and just the way she said my name made my heart do flips.

"I miss you," I said, echoing the text she'd sent to me.

"My bed is cold," she replied.

"Any news?" I asked. I didn't have to tell her what I was asking about, she knew.

"I got an email from Detective Guttierez," she replied, and I heard the heaviness of it. "He said they have to wait for confirmation before they bring him over. Maybe in a week, maybe less, he wasn't sure."

"If you want me there…"

"No," she said, her voice firm as she cut me off. "I don't want to cause you any more issues with the team. You stay with them and do your work. I'll be fine."

There it was. The strength she had been forced to build up.

"It's no problem," I said.

"I'll be fine," she said, and I knew she would.

"I know," I replied, voicing my confidence in her. "But I will come if you need me. Just tell me, and I'll be there."

"Thank you," she said.

We were quiet, each of us in our own thoughts.

"Do you play tomorrow?" she asked, and the change of subject was nice.

We discussed the Atlanta team and what I expected from the games here. Then, I told her the rest of our itinerary for the road trip, about the way we would play each team, approach their players, the best places to eat in each of the cities we would be visiting. It was honestly one of the best conversations we'd had that didn't involve her past life and the trials she'd been through.

Before long, I heard the guys in the hallway, and I knew I would have to go to sleep in order to play up to my potential the next day, so I bid farewell to Kylie before sticking my head out into the hall.

"Hey, Decker," Beckett said. "When did you get here?"

"Earlier," I replied.

"Duh," he said, but it was light. "Oh, hey, is it true?"

"Is what true?" I asked.

"About you and that girl," he said. "And about who her dad is."

"Yeah," I said. "Kylie's dad's a monster, but she's sweeter than anyone I've ever met."

"He's locked up, right?"

"Oh yeah," I replied. "Has been for a good long while, too."

"Good," he said.

"Why you asking?" I asked.

"Personal issues," he said. "I'm working through them, though."

"Okay," I said as he continued on down the hall.

It was one of the oddest interactions I'd had with him in my life, but then again, he was an odd guy, so it shouldn't have surprised me. I shut my door and thought about Kylie as I climbed into bed. As much as I worried about her, she was showing that she was stronger than I had previously thought. Even still, I'd be damned if I let anything or anyone hurt her.

～

"WELCOME BACK," COACH SAID AS I CLIMBED ON THE BUS.

"Thanks," I said, taking a seat.

"You get everything figured out?"

"As much as I could," I replied.

"Good," he said from his own seat. "We need you in there. Ramirez is good, but you can control the pitchers better than him. The Miami series was rough, even though we took two."

"I'm here now," I said. "And I'm ready to dive back in."

"Bet your ass you are," Ramirez said as he sat beside me.

"You don't like the starting position?" I asked.

"For a minute," he said. "But not for the long haul. How the f-heck do you do it day in and day out?"

The way he censored himself was comical. Coach didn't mind us swearing, just as long as we kept it away from any kids or the press. On the bus, in the clubhouse, hell, even on the field, we were allowed to express ourselves colorfully, which was probably a good thing since several of the players were known to use swear words like punctuation.

Once we arrived at the stadium, though, my mind went into work mode and I just did what I had been doing for years. Gear up, warm up, then head to the bullpen to work with the starting pitcher. It was nice to have this routine to fall into when my head was still kind of stuck in Seattle. If the meeting had been set to happen while I was there, or even any day this week, I would have stayed with Kylie, just to be there for her. She was insistent, though, that I had a job to do and she could handle it.

I was beyond proud of her for how well she held it together while the detectives were at her apartment, but when she fell apart, I was also glad I was there to catch her. I would always catch her. It was in my job description and I took my job very seriously.

"Ready?" Hennings asked from where we were sitting on the bench.

"I've missed this," I replied. "But I wouldn't change going back for anything in the world. It was the right call. I needed to be there for her."

"And you don't now?" he asked.

"I do," I replied. "But she wants me here, wants to stand on her own two feet. I'm trusting her to tell me when things go south. For now, she's holding her own. Besides, she's got Remi there for immediate help if needed."

"He's not fucking her, though," my teammate said, and I had to look at him for a minute before he cracked a big ass smile and laughed.

"No," I replied once I'd gotten my laughter under control. "She's not exactly his type."

"Of course, she isn't," he said, still settling from his laughter. "But it may be what she needs when shit goes down. How's she gonna handle that?"

"We've already talked about that," I said. "She's got other options."

"Other guys?"

"Nope," I said, not at all wanting to discuss Kylie's sex life, especially with him.

"Good," was all he replied.

The game was a good change of pace, and everything we were doing on the field was getting us noticed even more. Hennings and Huffman were on a tear, hitting anything and everything thrown at them. Our infielders were like damn vacuum cleaners if anything was hit toward them, sucking the ball up and pitching it over to get the runner out. In the outfield, every single guy was running faster, jumping higher, and laying it all out on the line when going for the ball.

Then there was the pitching staff. I have no idea what they'd been eating, but it must have been fueled with some sort of turbo charged energy because they were hitting their pitches, throwing everything I called, and playing like their lives depended on that next pitch. As if every time they took the mound their career depended on perfection. We weren't perfect, because we were human. But we were much better than anything I'd seen from the team in a good long time.

We left Atlanta with four losses and took our happy asses on up to the nation's capital to see if we could keep up with our streak and hand the Senators their ass before changing direction and going over to Philly. If we could keep this pace up, or even stay close to it, we may just end up in first place and looking at championship rings by the time fall rolled around.

Every night was filled with a call to Kylie. She'd tell me what her day was like, compliment me on my play, and fill me in on the fact that the detectives were still waiting for confirmation before beginning the transport and visit with her sperm donor. I told her I was proud of her for holding herself together, and that if she needed me to just call and I'd drop everything and come running. Whenever I told her that, she'd laugh and tell me to not be so dramatic, but it was the truth. I would do whatever it took to keep her safe and protected, especially from the monster who called himself her father. It wasn't until we were leaving Philly and heading over to Boston that she told me she had an appointment scheduled.

She was fortunate that her insurance allowed for mental health treatment at no cost because she had been using that benefit at regular intervals long before any of this started. Now that that man was back in her life, she had increased her visits, and was working to get through the face-to-face with him without completely breaking down. I'd told her I would come home and go with her, but she was insistent that it wasn't that big of a deal.

I'd texted her when we landed that I was there if she needed me. Even if the game had started, one of the coaches would have my phone to answer any call she needed to make. I needed her to know I was here, no matter what. The waiting, after the scheduled time of the meeting, was the hardest part, and Coach Johnson told me that Ramirez would be catching that day so I could be ready to run at the drop of a hat. Hell, he'd even had me bring my suitcase with me to the stadium just in case. Honestly, everyone on the team was working hard to keep me sane while my heart was on the other side of the country and in danger.

CHAPTER FIFTY-FIVE

*K*ylie...

"Can I help you?" the woman at the desk asked.

It had been over a week since I'd gotten the email telling me they were setting up a meeting. While I was anxious the entire time waiting, it was as if spending time with Cole, having him love me, had made it easier to deal with the wait without losing my marbles and going cata-tonic. The fact that we had talked every night since he left had kept me sane as well. When I got up and was getting ready to head out, he'd sent a text saying that he was available, no matter what. I wasn't sure why I deserved him, but he was there, and I was glad for it.

"I'm here to see Detective Guttierez," I said.

"Your name?" she asked.

"Kylie Harper," I said and her eyes flashed up to mine.

"Oh," she said. "Just a minute."

She picked up the phone and pressed a button.

"She's here," she said into the receiver. "Absolutely," she added after a pause. "He'll be right out," she said once she'd set the receiver back in its cradle.

True to what she said, the door next to her opened and the detective who had come to my apartment the week before stepped out.

"Ms. Harper," he said. "Thank you for coming."

"Not like I had much of a choice," I replied dryly.

"You did," he said. "But I'm glad all the same. Come with me."

He stepped back through the door, holding it open so I could walk through it before letting it shut behind me. He led me down a small hallway to an area that had doors on either side of the room. Unfortunately, Remi had a meeting that couldn't be postponed or moved, otherwise he'd have been with me when I went. I'd told him it was fine, that I had my phone and would call him if something happened that I needed him. Really, though, I wanted to do this by myself. Wanted to prove that I was capable of handling my shit when everything went wrong.

"It'll be just a minute," he said. "They have to bring him in. You can wait here, and I'll come get you when we're ready."

Sitting on one of the industrial chairs in the space he'd left me, I bounced my knee, something my father said was a sign of a weak mind. I used to believe everything he told me back then, but now – now I knew better. Everything he'd said was a way to get what he wanted. It wasn't a weak mind that caused my leg to bounce, it was nerves. A nervous energy that needed an escape, and since screaming would cause too much turmoil, a bouncing knee would have to do.

After some time, how long I couldn't say, the detective came back and said they were ready for me.

"I don't want him to touch me," I said.

"He'll be on the other side of the table," the detective assured me. "He'll have shackles on both his wrists and ankles, and those will be bolted into the table and floor. There will also be two officers in the room with you at all times. I will also be in there, so if you need me to help with anything, just nod to me and I'll get you out."

I took a deep breath, let it out slowly, then stood up.

"Let's go," I said, pulling my shoulders back and straightening my spine.

The walk was short, just a few feet down another hallway. When the door opened, I was shocked. Instead of the monster I remembered, he sat there, small and unimpressive. It had been years since

I'd seen him, but I hadn't thought he'd change so drastically in that time.

"My little Kylie," he cooed, his voice making me want to throw up.

"I don't belong to you," I said with a force I didn't know I possessed.

"You'll always be my little girl," he tried, the desperation coming off him in waves.

I stepped into the room and sat in the chair on the opposite side of the table from him. I knew I was far enough away simply by the fact that the table was a good three feet wide. Still, it was ominous to sit this close to a man who had taken so many lives.

"Why did you want me to come here?" I asked.

"I wanted to see you," he said in what I assumed was him trying to sound fatherly. "I've missed you. Missed all the things you've done. Look at you. You look just like your mother when she was your age."

"They said you were going to tell them where more bodies were," I replied, not giving in to his desires to get under my skin. "I'm here, so talk."

"Kylie," he said.

"Jeffrey," I replied.

"Call me Dad," he insisted.

"You stopped being my dad a long time ago," I replied, letting the chill I felt inside seep through my words. "Honestly, you probably never were a dad to me. You just pretended."

"Kylie Marie Somerton," he barked.

"That's not my name anymore," I shouted.

He rose up some, but the chains kept him where he was.

"I named you," he spit. "I gave you that beautiful, wonderful name. You better thank me for it, and right now."

"You saw me," I shouted, standing, and letting the chair I was in topple over. "Now that you've seen me, give them the names. Tell them where the rest of those boys you brutalized and killed are. Be a real man and own up to your mistakes. Or are you too much of a pussy to even do that?"

I was pissed. This man who donated sperm to make me exist was never a father. He was just a ghost who pretended to be. It felt good to get those words out, honestly, and the look on his face when he realized that I wouldn't just sit down and shut up and listen to him was better than anything I could ever have expected.

"You don't get to tell me what to do," he sneered, his teeth showing like the feral animal he was. "You're just a little girl, too scared of her own shadow to do anything against me."

"That's where you're wrong," I said, standing up taller. "I'm the one that's free while you're just the caged animal you always were. At least now you don't get to do what you want. I'm surprised you can sit down. Don't they rape child molesters in prison? Or do the real men not know you like little boys? Maybe I should figure out who's around you and write them a letter. Tell them everything you did to those kids who trusted you. Maybe then you'd get the justice you so richly deserve."

"You little cunt," he spat. "You're just like your mom, nothing better than a warm, wet hole to stick a dick in. I bet you're the life of the party, aren't you? Opening those legs for any man who comes along? Giving it away for free? You certainly did snag a good one with that baseball player."

"You shut up," I shouted. "You could never be half the man he is. He was there when I needed him, unlike you. No, you were always too busy with your 'projects.' I'm just mad I didn't realize how horrible you were before. Maybe I could have saved those boys."

"Those boys died happy," he said, smiling a sick smile I hadn't seen in almost half my life. "They loved everything I did to them. The way they moved under my hands when I forced them down on their knees..."

I bolted through the door. I couldn't listen to any more of this. Running down the hall, I turned into the bathroom, losing the little bit of food I'd put into my stomach that morning in the toilet, retching into the metal bowl. I heard the door open.

"Ms. Harper," Guttierez called.

Using my sleeve, I wiped my mouth, flushing the waste down the drain, then stepped from the stall to walk to the sink.

"Sorry," I said, splashing cold water onto my face.

"No," he said. "I'm the one who should be apologizing to you. I never should have put you in that position."

"He won't tell you anything," I said after I'd rinsed my mouth. "It's partly my fault, but I don't think he would have, even if I had been the little girl he remembered."

"Don't hold this burden on your shoulders," he said. "He's a monster, and I'm sorry I put you in that close a proximity to him."

"I just wanted to help the families of the ones they never found," I said, looking at my reflection in the mirror above the sink. "They deserve to know where their loved ones are. Deserve to give them a proper burial. The chance to say farewell and lay them to rest in peace."

A sob broke free, and I crumpled, dropping to the dirty floor of the bathroom, pulling my knees to my chest. When the detective's arms wrapped around me, I let go. It didn't last long, but it felt good to let it out.

"I'm okay," I said, pushing back from him.

"You sure?" he asked.

He'd squatted down next to me and held me but didn't get fully on the ground. It was something I noticed but would never fault him for. It wasn't his job to do that. If Cole had been there, he'd have been sitting on the floor, completely ignoring the grime that was around us. It was something that dawned on me in that moment. Cole was exactly who I needed him to be, and I was thankful he'd be coming home soon.

"I'm fine," I reiterated. "Help me up?"

The detective held his hand out and I used it to leverage myself to my feet. Once I was up, I washed my hands, not wanting whatever was on the floor to get anywhere near an opening in me. God only knows what germs were writhing around on this floor. When I'd finished, I turned and followed the detective out into the hall. I looked toward the room I'd run from and saw them pulling the monster from the room by his shackles.

"You can't make me go back there," he was whining.

I laughed. I couldn't help it. He was trying so hard to be relevant, important, strong, when all he would ever be was the terrifying monster who was caught. Maybe I would write a letter to some of the inmates in the state prison. Let them know that he was available for their pleasuring, and to not go easy on him.

When he heard me laughing, he turned, and it did nothing to dispel my amusement. It was as if he were a mouse, caught in a live trap, squealing out nonsense that his captors didn't care about. No, a mouse wouldn't have deserved being caged. That man, that filth that I was biologically related to, he deserved everything he got, and then some. Maybe they would be able to get him to talk. Maybe he'd try to find a way to make his life better by giving things up. I knew it wouldn't be because he wanted to do the right thing. That had never been a goal of his.

CHAPTER FIFTY-SIX

*C*ole…

"Hey," I said when she called.

"Are you playing?" she asked.

"No," I replied. "Game's over and I'm at the hotel."

We'd won the game, but I hadn't paid much attention to it at all. Instead, I was watching my phone, willing it to ring and let me know that Kylie had made it through the meeting.

"Did you go?" I asked.

"Yeah," she said. "It was awful, but I did it."

"I'm proud of you," I said. "Do you want to tell me what happened?"

"No," she said, and it was so low I almost missed it.

"Okay," I replied. "If you change your mind, I'm here."

"Thank you," she said.

We were quiet for a bit, each of us in our own minds, but my thoughts were on her. I needed to know she was okay, that she would get through the next couple of days before we headed home. Instead of my usual conversation topics, I tried a different tactic.

"You in your room?" I asked.

"I am," she said. "Why?"

"Let me see you," I said.

"What?"

"We can change to a video call so I can see you," I suggested.

"I'm a mess," she complained.

"I don't care," I replied. "I want to see you. And I want you to see me."

I heard her suck in a breath, hold it, then let it out slowly before my phone gave me the indication that the call was switching to video.

"Hi," she said when I switched.

She was beautiful, as usual, except she was very unkempt. Her hair was kind of slopped into a bun at the top of her head, wispy tendrils floating around her face. She had blotchy cheeks, and her eyes looked tired, but her lips were full and begging to be kissed. If only technology had advanced so that I could bring her here with me in an instant.

"What are you thinking about?" she asked.

"How beautiful you are," I replied. "And how I wish I could pull you through the phone and hold you."

"I wish you were here," she said.

"Soon," I replied. "In the meantime, what can I do to cheer you up?"

Her eyes flitted to the side, then back to the camera. She looked at her nightstand, which meant she looked at her toy. Lying naked in bed, my cock hardened just at the thought of her wanting to use it.

"You wanna play?" I asked, dropping my voice lower.

She nodded, a sly smile coming to her lips, and I did my best not to groan.

"I think you're a bit overdressed," I said, noting she was still wearing her oversized sweater. "Is there somewhere you can set your phone so I can watch you undress?"

Again, she looked to her nightstand, then reached over, past the camera on her phone to shift something around. I was disoriented as she moved the phone into the little rack-thing she had there for all her devices. Once it was placed, she moved it again so that it was facing the rest of her room.

"How's that?" she asked, stepping in front of the phone.

"I can see you," I said. "But you've still got too many clothes on."

"Okay," she said, then grabbed the hem of her sweater and pulled it over her head, tossing it onto the cedar chest at the foot of her bed.

"Better?"

"We're getting there," I said, smiling and stroking myself.

Doing a little shimmy, she slid her leggings down, keeping her panties on. Once they were to the floor, she walked out of them, her socks going with the material.

"Keep going," I said, still stroking myself.

I swear, just watching her undress was doing it for me. I needed to remember this for future road trips. Reaching down again, she pulled her tank top over her head, letting it fall to the floor. She was there, just in panties and a bra, and it was one of the sexiest things I'd ever seen.

"My turn," she said, moving closer to the phone and picking it up, her face filling the screen.

"I'm way ahead of you, baby," I said, tipping the phone down so she could see me holding my cock in my hand, the tip glistening.

"Oh," she said, and I could almost see her face, even though the camera was tilted away from me.

"I wanna watch you watch me," I said. "Hang on."

I fiddled with the phone, getting the camera turned so that I could watch her face while the phone watched my dick.

"There we go," I said, smiling.

"You're ready," she said, and it was kind of an awestruck statement.

"Any time I think about you, I'm ready," I replied, stroking up and down.

"I can't wait until you get home," she said, her eyes focused on the screen.

"When I get there," I said. "We can do this in person. I want to hear you call my name while I'm inside you."

She licked her lips, but her eyes never wavered. I stroked slow and steady, watching as she bit her bottom lip, opened them up with awe, and licked them. Each movement of her lips proved to be stimulation for me, and it didn't take long for me to climax. I had to shift the phone because I almost hit it, and she laughed at that.

"My turn to watch," I said, flipping the camera back around so I could she could see my face.

Putting the phone back into the rack, she turned it so that she could see me and I could watch her.

"This isn't as easy," she said, trying to get it so she could see me and still show what she was doing.

"Sorry," I said. "Do you want to quit?"

"No," she replied, her eyes getting big. "I need this. I just need to figure out how to do it and watch you."

"Would it be better on the computer?" I asked.

"I am not doing that," she replied. "Too easy to hack. Phones are bad enough. I might just not get to watch you watch me. Not that it would matter. I usually end up with my eyes closed anyway."

"I'm not closing my eyes," I said. "I want to watch you come."

She didn't say anything to that, just slid the phone in such a way that I could see down her body. It was a beautiful sight to see, her simple bra and panties still on her, but there was something sensuous about the view.

"What should I do?" she asked.

"You want me to tell you?" I asked.

"Yeah," she said. "I mean, I have done a couple of things, but I'm not very good at it."

"I'm sure you're amazing," I said. "But, if you want direction, I'm happy to do that for you."

"I do," she said, and I heard the excitement in her voice.

I took a deep breath and thought about her, about what she'd been through in her life, and what she likely had gone through earlier that day. Instead of being firm and mean, I wanted to let her guide me, even if I was telling her what to do.

"How do you feel?" I asked.

"Dumb," she said.

"No," I said. "How does your body feel? Run your hands from your shoulders down your body. Will you do that for me?"

"Okay," she said, her voice quiet.

She took her hands and ran them over her body in a pretty quick motion.

"Slow down, baby," I said. "I want you to enjoy this."

Once again, she brought her hands up to her shoulders and slowly moved them down, purposefully avoiding her breasts.

"Bring them back to your breasts," I said when she got to her waist. "Run your hands over the material of your bra. Can you feel your nipples getting hard?"

"Mmhmm," she hummed, and I could tell she was finally warming up to this.

"That's my good girl," I said, and she sucked in a breath. "Is it okay that I say that?"

"Yeah," she said, but something was off.

"Kylie," I said and waited for her to shift the phone and look in it. "If my saying that causes you to be uncomfortable, I'll stop. Do you want me to stop?"

She shook her head, but her eyes went low.

"Hey," I said. "Baby, look at me." She did then, tilting her eyes to look at the camera. "I don't want to do anything that makes you uncomfortable, so I need you to talk to me. Do you want me to stop saying that?"

"I don't know," she said, and I could hear tears in her voice.

"You don't know if you want me to stop?"

Again, she shook her head.

"How about I stop for now and we can come back to that at another time," I suggested, and she looked right at me.

"I don't..."

"It's okay," I said. "I don't want to do anything that you don't like. You have a voice in this. You're in charge of what happens with your body. I can want everything under the sun, but if it doesn't work for you, or it makes you not feel good, then we don't do that. Okay?"

She nodded, the smile coming back to her lips.

"Okay," I said. "No more talk like that. Maybe later, but not tonight."

"Okay," she said.

"Kylie," I said as she shifted to move the phone. "I miss you."

"I miss you, too," she said.

"Do you want to keep going?"

"Uh, yeah," she said, drawing the last word out.

"I'm glad," I replied. "Now, where were we?"

She moved the phone back to the place it was being held and settled down, running her hands from her shoulders down to her breasts, moving purposefully over the material that stood between them and the soft flesh underneath. Moaning as she did this, she then pushed one of the cups away, so that her skin was exposed. Even though I'd just come, I was growing hard again, so began stroking myself as I enjoyed watching her pleasure herself.

Reaching her hand behind her, she unhooked the bra, pulling it from her arms and dropping it to the floor. Both hands began moving, one on her breast, pinching the nipple which had peaked under her touch. The other hand moved lower, down, and down, sliding under the waistband of her panties.

"Oh, yeah, baby," I said. "Tease yourself, just like that."

I could hear the little moans she was letting out, what with the phone being right next to her head. It was erotic and turning me on even more with every sound she made.

"Will you pull your panties off?" I asked, and watched as the hand that was massaging her breast left it and she lifted her hips to shove the material down. "That's it," I encouraged. "I want to watch every part of you."

She let the material fall from her foot off the edge of the bed, then returned her hands to where they had been previously. It didn't take long for her to be writhing again. The hand that had been on her breast reached up and blocked my view for a moment, but then I saw the toy she'd had come into view.

"Oh, yeah, baby," I said, still stroking my now much harder dick. "I want to watch you fuck yourself with that."

As soon as the words left my mouth, I realized I'd fucked up. She stopped everything and pulled the phone over to look into it.

"I'm sorry," I said. "I was just kind of in the moment."

She closed her eyes and took a deep breath.

"As much as I want this distraction, I can't seem to get really in the mood," she said. "I know you want this, and I kinda do, too, but it's just all of a sudden feeling weird. I'm sorry."

"Oh no," I said. "You don't need to apologize. I messed up with my words. I know today's been a mess, and I thought this might help."

"So did I," she said. "But I think I need to be done."

"Okay," I said, not able to keep the disappointment from my voice.

"When do you come home?" she asked.

"I have a couple more games here, then I'll be home," I replied. "If you want, though, I can come early."

"No," she said, nearly shouting the word. "No. You don't need to do that."

"Hey," I said, trying to get her to look at me better. "I will come home if you want me to. Coach has already said I can, and the team will survive a couple of games. So let me know…"

"I said no," she said, looking right in my eyes.

"Okay," I said, a little put off by her tone.

"Sorry," she said, and I saw her shiver a bit. "It's just something he said."

"Do you want to talk about it?" I asked, willing to do whatever I could to stay on the phone with her.

"I have an appointment with my therapist tomorrow," she said. "I'll talk to her."

"Can you tell me what I said that you didn't like?"

"I'm not sure," she said. "I just know that I always had to do what he said when I was growing up. No questions asked. If I dared to say no, he'd ground me, so I kind of hate it when someone pushes me like that. Since I started therapy, though, I've been able to realize that I have the right to say no to anyone for anything. Honestly, it was a really good lesson to learn."

"I'm proud of you," I said, and meant it. "I'm sorry I pushed, but I didn't want you to feel like it would be a burden for me to come home. I think we both need to work on how we talk about things."

"Everyone can use therapy," she said. "Even people who are normal."

"Don't be calling me normal," I said with a laugh, and she lightened her mood and joined me.

"I need to go," she said once we'd settled a bit. "I'm really tired."

"Okay," I replied. "I kinda need to clean up anyway. I'll see you Wednesday."

"See you then," she said.

"Good night," I said, then watched as she turned her phone off before mine went black.

I got up and took my sticky self to the shower. I just wish I'd not fucked things up. Hopefully, though, my homecoming would be better received.

CHAPTER FIFTY-SEVEN

*K*ylie...

The next couple of days were slow and tedious, but I managed to get a couple of projects moved to the final stages, which was really nice. I hadn't been out of the apartment since I heard about the body being found, save the one trip to the King County Jail to meet with him. I was getting a bit of cabin fever but was terrified that a reporter would be standing just outside my building waiting to pounce on me if I dared go out.

Even when I went to the station, I was worried someone would be there. I'd worn a hat, sunglasses, and an oversized coat to try to disguise myself, but no one was there. I wasn't sure whether to be relieved or upset, but I leaned to the former and was happy I didn't have to deal with any of it.

"Hey, girl," Remi said when he came home. "Isn't Cole coming home today?"

"He is," I said, smiling.

"Then you should be getting a shower and finding something sexy to wear," he said. "Don't want to miss an opportunity like this."

"You're horrible," I said, but was laughing. "Besides, it's just barely after five. He probably won't get here until at least seven or eight."

"You sure?"

"I assume," I said.

"And we all know what happens when you assume," he said, looking at me pointedly.

"Yeah, yeah," I replied.

He was right, though. I didn't know for sure when Cole would be getting home, or if he was coming straight over before going home or what. I had a few more things I had to finish with work, so dove into those to try to get a little ahead for the next day, which I knew was gonna drag. When I heard a knock at the door, I looked over my shoulder as Remi went to open it.

"Well, hello," Remi said, pulling the door wide for Cole to come in.

My breath caught as I saw him. He was even more beautiful than when he'd left, and I was just so happy to see him. I jumped up and ran over to him, nearly tackling him as I leaped into his arms.

"I missed you, too," he said against my ear, having dropped his suitcase and grabbed me mid-flight.

I held him as tight as possible, trying to get as close to him as I could. I inhaled his unique scent of wood and grass and all things base-ball. He moved us into the apartment, setting me down on the back of the couch.

"You are a sight for sore eyes," he said. "I have truly missed you."

"I'll let you two have the room," Remi said. "I know you want to get freaky, so feel free."

I laughed. I couldn't help it. Cole was blushing a bit, but he also laughed, then kissed me. It took me off guard for a moment before I returned the kiss with enthusiasm. As if I were dying in the desert and he was a fresh spring, I devoured the kiss, his hands sliding up and down my back, just lighting my fuse.

The ping from my computer jolted both of us.

"Do you need to get that?" he asked.

"I should probably look," I said.

Moving off the back of the couch, I slid down his body and felt his very hard erection against me and I shivered with delight. Not wanting to stop touching him, I held his hand and brought him with me to my desk. When I sat in my chair, he stood next to me, his hand on my shoulder.

"Shit," I said, mousing over the message I just got from my boss. "I have to do this thing, and it's gonna take a bit."

"It has to be done now?" he asked.

"Unfortunately, yeah," I said.

"Kiss me one more time, then I'll go take a shower," he said, leaning down.

I turned my face up to him and presented my lips, which he took with his and opened me up to plunge his tongue into my mouth, sliding it along my own, arousing me and making me wish I didn't have this stupid project looming. When he pulled back, his lips were plump, and I assumed mine were as well.

"I'll be ready when you are," he said, walking over to pick up his suitcase before heading into my room.

"Gah," I groaned, but dove into the work that needed to be done.

I had no idea how long I'd been working, but when he opened the door, standing there in just his boxers, holding my toy in his hand, I kind of realized it must have been a while. Looking at the clock on my laptop, I realized that two hours had passed, and that just wasn't fair. I sent a quick message to Jim to let him know that I had finished what I could, but that I needed to rest and get fresh eyes on it in the morning, the proceeded to shut everything down. Spinning my chair to face Cole, I went to get up, but he'd come over to me and knelt in front of me.

"I sent a text to Remi to stay in his room," he said. "I don't want you to only think of this chair for work. When you sit in it tomorrow, I want you to think about me. Are you okay with that?"

I nodded, unsure exactly what he was going to do, but intrigued nonetheless. He reached up and placed the toy on my desk, its bright purple color looming in front of my work stuff. I double-checked that the laptop was indeed off but folded the screen down onto the keyboard just to be sure. No need for the camera to accidentally catch any of this. That would be one of the worst things I could ever experience.

When I turned back to Cole, he reached up and grabbed the hem of my shirt, sliding it up my body so slowly I wanted to scream. Everything he did was deliberate, and I decided to just let him do what he wanted and enjoy the experience.

"Arms up, please," he said, and I obliged, raising my arms above my head as he slid my shirt up and off me, dropping it to the floor next to him.

I hadn't worn a bra today because, well, why? I was at home, no one was coming in, and it wasn't like I really needed to wear one.

"You are so beautiful," he said, leaning forward and taking one of my nipples into his mouth.

Arching my back, I pressed it further in, wanting to feel his warm mouth on the soft skin. His suckling shot a bolt to my pussy, and I really wanted to reach down and start to rub it but wasn't sure if he would be upset.

"You taste wonderful," he said, moving to the other breast.

My hands clinched on the arms of my chair, my knuckles turning white with the pressure. His hands were resting on my hips, squeezing them some, but mostly just holding himself up. I must have made some noise, because he pulled back and looked up at me.

"What do you want?" he asked.

"More," I said, somewhat embarrassed about my needs.

"Show me," he said with a little lilt at the end, almost making it a question.

I took one hand off the armrest and slid it down into my leggings, sliding it between the folds at my most intimate point, and the relief I felt just having a little pressure there was enough to make me moan.

"Oh yeah," he said, his hands sliding into my leggings. "Let's give you more room."

He helped me stand, then pulled the fabric down my legs before inclining his head so I could sit on my chair. I'd never sat in it naked, but the feel of leather against my bare ass was a different experience, something that I might have to replicate if things went well. When he pulled the pants and panties off my legs, my socks came with them, and he set those aside.

"Let me see you," he said, looking to me for permission.

I nodded, and he slid his hands to my knees, pushing them apart ever so slowly, exposing my most private part to him. He smiled as he did so, sliding a hand up along my thigh to graze against the top of my pussy, the spot that had all the nerves, the place that was dying to be touched.

A shiver went through me, and it had nothing to do with the temperature of the room. His other hand had followed the same path on the other side, sliding up and grazing those nerves, just not enough for my pleasure. Leaning forward, he took a swipe with his tongue, sliding from my opening to the top, sucking in the lips that were there, holding them in his mouth.

My head went back, and a moan escaped my mouth before I had a chance to stop it. I slapped my hand across it, trying to hold the sound in, but he reached up and grabbed my wrist, pulling it away.

"There is nothing to be ashamed of," he said. "Let the world know you're enjoying yourself. Shout to the world that you are a beautiful woman who is having a wonderful time."

"But Remi…"

"He won't care," he said. "How many times have you heard him?"

The comment made me stop and think, and he was right. Remi never toned anything down just to save my sensitive ears. He'd always said he just couldn't help himself, and I'd never understood that until I met Cole.

"There we go," he said, smiling. "Now, shall I continue?"

"Yes," I said, the word tumbling out before he'd even finished the question.

He chuckled, then leaned in and ran his tongue along my slit and driving me mad. I was gripping the armrests again, just experiencing him having his way with me, eyes closed and at his mercy. When he slid a finger in me, I tensed, but then relaxed as he began sliding it in and out, in and out, a slow and easy pace that was just right.

My breath quickened to a near pant as he slowly massaged me with his tongue and finger, and when he pulled the finger out, I couldn't help but whimper until I heard the buzz of the toy and felt it against my opening. The vibrations moving along my slit, sliding in my wetness, was something I was learning to love, and when he found purchase and pressed it inside, I slid down, forcing it in faster than he intended.

"In a hurry?" he asked.

"Oh, yeah," I said, the words a whisper of my desire.

I felt him moving but didn't want to open my eyes for fear of losing the feeling going on. His warm mouth wrapped around my nipple again, his sucking pulling me taut in his mouth, at the same time as he was sliding the vibrator in and out of me at a maddeningly slow pace. My hips bucked a bit off the chair, urging him to speed up, but he would not oblige.

Pulling my hand from the armrest, I slid it between us, grabbing hold of the machine and trying desperately to work it in and out of me faster, but his grip was strong, and he chuckled against my breast.

"Let me love you," he said, and my eyes popped open, unsure that I'd heard what he said. "I want to give you pleasure. Will you let me do that?"

The way he said it, and the warmth in his eyes, made me realize that I was fighting against what was best for me. Everything Cole had done with me, for me, and to me, had been eye opening, and more wonderful than anything I had ever experienced before. My heart melted all over again, and I let go. Letting him be in charge of getting me going and over the top was what he had wanted me to do, so I did just that.

His hand that wasn't holding the vibrator reached up and pushed back on the back of my chair, moving it into a more reclined position. It was a good idea, but the springs in this thing were strong, so instead of completely letting him do things, I reached under the chair and pushed on the lever that allowed it to stay back. He smiled at me, then kissed me before returning to my breast, which was just one of those things that got me over the top.

His hands moved against my skin, his mouth sucking my breast, and the vibrator sliding in and out of me, all collided together to make me explode into a billion pieces, falling apart in the most beautiful way.

As I came down and returned to myself, I felt him lift me, holding me to him, the vibrator lying on my stomach. When we got to my room, he'd already pulled the sheets down and turned the bedside lamp on. There was a box of condoms on the nightstand, and it was a much larger box than the one we'd borrowed from Remi the first time we had actually had sex.

When he laid me down on the bed, he slid his boxers off, then climbed in next to me, scooting me against him, my back to his front, and I could feel him hard against my ass.

"I want to love you until the end of time," he said in my ear, his voice full of emotion. "Once time runs out, I want to keep loving you."

I tried to turn around, tried to look at him, but his strong arms around my waist held me fast. One arm was under my head, coming down to massage my breast, the other dipped down to slide among the fluid that had built up on my pussy.

Everything this man did had a purpose, and he slid his fingers in and out of me at the awkward angle for a minute before shifting me forward just a little ways, my legs sliding apart. His hand pulled back and slid against my ass cheeks, massaging the globes firmly. Then, he picked up the toy that had fallen onto the bed in front of me and slid it along my ass crack, not actually into the crack, just along the edge of it. With it on and vibrating, it was a different sensation, but I wasn't sure what all he was going to do.

When he moved it more toward my front and was sliding it through my wetness, I had a bit of relief and relaxed. Again, he slid it inside me, this time making sure that the little nubs at the front were placed on my clit, and it was such a wonderful feeling. He slid the vibrator in and out of me, but not too much, so as to keep the nubs connected.

I felt him scoot down along my body, pulling his arm from under my head. Shifting, I sort of turned onto my stomach, opening my legs more to allow him better access. He must have pulled the pillow down with him because he worked it up under my tummy, effectively putting my ass up in the air and on display.

Pulling my legs a bit more apart, he hummed as he looked at me, and it was more than anything I'd ever wanted.

"You are so fucking gorgeous," he said, and I looked over my shoulder at him and smiled. "I want you to come one more time before I open that box. Think you can do that for me?"

I nodded, and he gave me a look that said he wanted to hear me say it.

"Yes," I said.

"Good," he replied, working the vibrator in and out of me once again, his finger finding its way to the top of my sex to work the nerves there.

He was so amazing at making my body wind up and fall that I didn't doubt it when he said he wanted me to come, he would do whatever it took to get me there. His hands were like magic, moving against my skin, sliding in and out of me, and squeezing just the right places to make me fly. And fly I did, catapulted to the stratosphere, falling among the stars, galaxies away, and riding on a slipstream of consciousness that didn't exist. It was the most peaceful place I'd ever been, and I never wanted to leave.

EPILOGUE

Kylie…

"They look so happy," I said, Cole's arms wrapped around my middle.

"That's because they are," he said, kissing the shell of my ear.

It had been eight months since I'd met Cole, almost six since I'd faced the monster that was my father, and each and every day was more wonderful than the last. He'd taught me so much about myself, and encouraged me to learn about him, answering every question I asked. Baseball was another thing I was learning more and more about, and I felt confident that I could figure out exactly what was going on during any game.

During the all-star break, which was the middle of July, he took me to Southern California and I got to meet his parents. His sister didn't want to come. She told their parents that she wasn't in a place to see a happy relationship yet. Cole had explained that her ex, the one who had gotten her into drugs, had also abused her. It was the most vulnerable I'd ever seen him. He'd even cried when he talked about how messed up she had been when she'd called him out of the blue to come rescue her. She'd refused to call her parents and made him promise he wouldn't let them know what had gone down.

The other thing he had done for me was to bring me into his base-ball family, the men he worked with day in and day out. They traveled together, played together, worked together, and shared a special bond that was more than just friends. When he'd gotten the invitation to his teammate's wedding, he had asked if I wanted to go with him. I was hesitant, not sure how I would be with all those people around, but he'd promised he'd be right beside me, and if I felt like I needed a break, he'd walk me out of the space and help me settle myself.

I'd never been to a wedding before, and it was actually amazing. The bride was beautiful in her peach dress, holding tulips as she walked down the aisle. Each of the players were dressed in their finest, and the groom, who was the man who had come to check on me that day so long ago, was without the cast, and looked nearly as handsome as my date.

"Shall we dance?" he asked, and I turned to look at him.

"I don't know how," I confessed.

"Just hold on to me," he said. "I'll make sure you do everything right."

It was a wonderful experience, and when it was time for the couple to head off to their honeymoon, each of the players held up a bat, making a tunnel for them to go through, until they got to the end, when the last two guys crossed their bats in front of them and everyone cheered as they kissed once again.

An amazing evening, followed by an amazing night where Cole showed me just how much he loved me, by making love to me over and over again. I didn't think it could get any better than this. My life had started in chaos, but finding Cole, my anchor, my steadfast rock, helped me to become the best person I could be, and I would forever be grateful for that.

NOTE FROM AUTHOR

Images and Blurbs available upon request.
I would ask that you obtain high quality headshots and cover art images directly through me, rather than taking them from either my website or Amazon, however, blurbs are readily available through both places.

ABOUT THE AUTHOR

Born and raised in the Pacific Northwest, CM Kane was fed a steady diet of sports, particularly baseball. Having this love of the game instilled in her at an early age, she found that nothing was better than getting lost in the game. Storytelling was another gift that was encouraged in her youth, and she's taking to the written word to explore a new aspect to the game she loves.

Social Media and Website Links:

Website:
https://www.authorcmkane.com

Facebook:
https://www.facebook.com/AuthorCMKane

Instagram:
https://www.instagram.com/authorcmkane/

Amazon:
https://www.amazon.com/author/cmkane

BlueSky:
https://bsky.app/profile/authorcmkane.bsky.social

ALSO BY C.M. KANE

Neon Lights & Country Nights (Coming June 1, 2025)

Stand Alone Titles

A Switch in Time